Futuristic Romance

Love in another time, another place.

LADY'S KNIGHT

Deana arched up, clutching his bare shoulders. "Please, Lorgin, don't." Her pleas came out a wispy rasp as the feel of his mouth through the material combined with the feel of smooth, rippling male flesh under her hands. She gasped for breath, overwhelmed by the potent force that was this man.

He paused to look down at her, eyes now bright with iridescent pink sparks. He rested his lower body fully against her as his hands cupped the back of her head, his bent elbows raising her face to him.

"Give me your mouth." His tone was implacable and raw, all earlier traces of humor gone.

Deana gazed upon his beautiful countenance, so masculine and alive with passion. She knew in that moment, no matter what she said or did, he would not stop. He meant to have her.

"Give me your mouth," he repeated, his glance falling to her full, soft lips. When she did not respond to his words, he pressed his lower body tight against her, his hips rocking seductively in the cradle of her. She shivered at the intimate feel of him. Raising his eyes from her lips, he captured her with his brilliant, heated stare. His ragged breath caressed her face.

"Kiss me," he whispered hoarsely. "Kiss me, my Adeeann."

Knight of a Trillion Stars

DARA JOY

LOVE SPELL NEW YORK CITY

*For Percy Charles, who could talk a circle
and make it meet. I remember, my friend*

LOVE SPELL®

Published by
Dorchester Publishing Co., Inc.
276 Fifth Avenue
New York, NY 10001

Cover Art by John Ennis

The name "Love Spell" and its logo are trademarks of Dorchester
Publishing Co., Inc.

Printed in the United States of America.

"The beginnings of all things are small."
—Cicero

Prologue

Planet Aviara, Star System Tau Hydra, 5186 m.u.

Lorgin ta'al Krue gazed sadly at his old friend and mentor, Yaniff. No one really knew Yaniff's age, but the elder mystic had always seemed timeless. For the first time in Lorgin's memory, Yaniff, the ancient one, showed signs of his vast years. His shoulders were stooped; his face was etched in lines of worry that had not been there the previous day. Bojo, Yaniff's winged companion, perched silently on his right shoulder.

In a comforting gesture, Lorgin placed a hand on the old man's arm. "So, there can be no doubt? You've rechecked the alignments?"

Yaniff sighed deeply. "Yes, it is certain. This is most disturbing . . . most disturbing." He shook his head, his long silver locks flowing about him.

"Can nothing be done, then?" Lorgin asked.

"Not by me. My knowledge cannot extend to this area."

"Then it is hopeless. If you, the wisest among us, are powerless . . ." Lorgin's words trailed off.

Yaniff's eyes, darker than the darkest night, pierced Lorgin. "I did not say that."

Lorgin's head snapped up. He knew his old teacher well; Yaniff in his convoluted way was getting to something. Lorgin crossed his arms over his massive chest and leaned against the balustrade. "What exactly did you say?"

Yaniff closed his eyes. He was pleased with this Lorgin ta'al Krue, his favorite of all his students, if truth be told. "I said I could do nothing. I did not say that *you* could do nothing."

Now it comes, Lorgin thought, smiling to himself. Yaniff unfolds as slowly as the tazmin flower in the sun. "What may I do, Master?"

The ancient words of service were spoken.

Lorgin had given his life and measure to Yaniff to command as he saw fit. *Again.* Many a campaign had he waged on behalf of Aviara and the Astral Alliance. He awaited Yaniff's words.

"You must go on a quest, Lorgin. Find out what is causing these rifts in space and time. You know the disturbances on the rim must be stopped."

"You wish me to go to the far sector?" This surprised him. It was a difficult journey. Few survived it. The risk of death did not concern him so much as the enormity of the task. It was an impossible mission.

The ancient mystic read his thoughts. "Perhaps for most, Lorgin. Maybe not for you."

Lorgin wished he had Yaniff's certainty; he himself had doubts.

"It is good to have some doubts, Lorgin. They will serve

you well when you need them. Thus I have trained you."

"Yes, it is so."

"Come, my young friend, we will go to the Hall of Tunnels. Your journey is to begin." He took Lorgin by the arm and together they traveled through the city.

Lorgin faced the first tunnel. It spiraled away from him in a myriad of brilliant lights, pulsing in time. Before he entered, he turned to bid his mentor and friend goodbye, then stepped through the portal.

"Safe journey, my friend," Yaniff softly said as Lorgin dissolved into the swirling mists.

How long Lorgin had been traveling he knew not. What he did know was that his journey was far from over when he was suddenly and powerfully yanked out of the space/time continuum . . .

Chapter One

It had been a horrible day.

Horrible.

First, she had been fired from her job. Excuse me, laid off. Amounted to the same thing. Strange how being overqualified hurts you when you're applying for work, but doesn't help you when you're given the sack.

It was just the beginning of a day that would live in infamy.

On the train, leaving the city, she thought herself lucky to spot a seat, an occurrence that came around with the frequency of Halley's Comet. Naturally she dived right for it—into a seat of something *wet*. It was not pleasant and it smelled.

She stood quickly enough, but the damage had been done. At least she had been wearing her raincoat, not that it had had the decency to rain, yet. Thankfully, her person was relatively dry, though the coat wasn't—it stunk. People were giving her strange looks, putting as much space as possible between her and themselves.

In Deana's present mood, this suited her just fine.

When she got off the train, the last stop, *of course*, she removed the offensive coat and impulsively threw it in a trash receptacle. She was just in that frame of mind.

Her troubles were only beginning.

Just as she reached her car, she had the good fortune to see two cars back into each other in the parking lot. Their bumpers crunched and unbelievably locked together. Both drivers, being courteous and polite Boston commuters, exited their cars like wild bulls at a rodeo, snorting and stamping while circling their automobiles.

Deana didn't have to guess whose car they were blocking in the lot.

When the police finally came, she was informed she would have to wait for the tow trucks to clear the space. At rush hour, they estimated a good 45 minutes.

As she looked around for a place, any place, to escape to, her eyes lit on a small, decrepit-looking resale shop across the street.

She headed for it like a person who has just discovered they had hit the lottery, and that was where they had to collect.

As she entered the store, a bell tinkled over the door. Observing the seedy interior, Deana revised her original evaluation and demoted it from resale to *junk* shop. Cartons were piled haphazardly everywhere. Books, old furniture, glassware, broken toys—they haunted the room like the ghosts of consumers past. At least it was blessedly quiet in here.

As she was viewing this white-elephant graveyard, a curtain in a doorway parted and an old geezer wearing a Red Sox baseball cap sauntered out.

"Got caught in the commuter blitz, did you?" His eyes crinkled at the corners as he smiled. He seemed like a nice old guy.

"How did you guess?"

"Happens all the time. Keeps me in business. Do you want to look around?" This was said in a hopeful voice.

"Sure, why not?" Deana turned and, walking toward the rear of the long, narrow store, started looking through what could only be called trash.

She thought of her now defunct job. *Here I am, Deana Jones, twenty-six-year-old soon-to-be bag lady.* Better get used to this, she lamented.

After about a half hour, she did find an interesting necklace, sort of. It was under about five cartons of junk, but Deana had had a feeling there might be something good under there.

She held the necklace up to the dim light.

It was tarnished and dirty. Made of metal, it was a collar type necklace which reminded her of a torque from the days of King Arthur. In the center of the band was a dark, rough-shaped stone which seemed to be black, although it was hard to tell in the poor lighting.

She scrutinized it more carefully.

Yes, it might polish up quite nicely, although she doubted it was silver and couldn't find any stamping on it.

She brought it to the front of the store and placed it on the scruffy countertop.

"How much for this?" she asked the proprietor.

The old man picked up the necklace and eyed it with distaste. "You want to buy this?" As if no one in their right mind would.

Deana immediately defended it. "It's not that bad." He looked at her incredulously. "Okay, so it is that bad. How much?"

He shook his head, the enormity of the task of trying to put a price on it overwhelming him. Finally he said tentatively, "Fifty cents?"

"Sold." Deana slapped two quarters down.

While the old man was putting the necklace in a bag for her, she looked out the front windows, noticing that the tow trucks had arrived and were clearing the cars out. Thanking the man, Deana grabbed the bag and left the shop, already tasting the strong, hot cup of coffee she was going to make as soon as she got home.

She was exhausted. Thank God she had already packed for her trip tomorrow—the trip she had paid for well in advance, could not cancel, and therefore didn't have to feel too guilty about taking in her present economic circumstances. Nice of them to fire her the day before her vacation was to start.

Deana peered warily at the low black clouds coalescing above her. *Perhaps if I hurry, I just might make it.*

Thunder sounded briefly before the sky opened and rain pelted the ground in torrents. She ran pell-mell across the tarmac of the lot. Without her raincoat, by the time she made it to her car, she was soaked to the skin.

What did I do to deserve this day?

Due to the rain, the traffic was horrendous on the way home. What should have been a twenty-minute drive turned into an hour. When she finally pulled into the private drive that led to the cottage, Deana almost sobbed in gratitude.

Until she got out of the car to check the mailbox at the end of the drive. Three rejections from two editors.

She stood in the driveway letting the rain pelt down on her. Resignedly, she got back in her car and drove the quarter mile up to the cottage.

Gazing tiredly up at the little three-room house, Deana blessed her grandfather, her last remaining relative, for leaving it to her in his will. At least she would always have a roof over her head. *As long as I pay the taxes,* she amended.

Once inside, she closed the door and quickly threw the

deadbolt, locking the rest of the world out of her private domain. Groaning in relief to be back in her nice, warm home, she headed straight for a hot shower, removing her soggy clothes on the way to the bathroom.

Never had a shower felt so wonderful. Feeling almost human, she braided her waist-length hair and stepped into a comfortable pair of well-worn jeans. Even though it was the beginning of September, the damp air was chilly, so she donned a sweatshirt before padding into the kitchen to make that long-awaited and well-deserved cup of java.

While she was waiting for Mr. Coffee to do his number, Deana retrieved the necklace from the bag and stared at it. What had possessed her? It looked even worse, removed from the other junk that had surrounded it. *Perhaps if I clean it up . . .*

She headed to the utility closet, returning with a polishing cloth and some jewelry cleaner. As soon as she started to remove the tarnish from the band, Deana felt a lot better about her purchase.

The necklace gleamed silver under the kitchen light, although Deana doubted it was sterling. It almost looked like platinum, but that would mean this piece was very valuable, and even though the old geezer in the store seemed eccentric, he didn't seem to be anybody's fool. Besides, she didn't think platinum tarnished. *It must be some alloy.*

Whatever it was, it attracted the light like crazy.

Examining the stone under the bright kitchen light, she noted it wasn't black, as she had originally thought, but a deep, dark green. Well! This had turned out very nice. The only ray in a bleak day, she mourned. Deciding to take it with her on her trip, she went back to the bedroom to toss it in her suitcase.

It was time to forget this awful day and remember that she

was taking her long-awaited trip tomorrow to San Francisco. She was going to the Worldcon! Once a year, science fiction aficionados from all over the world met in some predetermined location for the worldwide science fiction convention. This year it was the City by the Bay.

Deana could hardly wait to see all her old friends from around the globe, thoroughly enjoy herself, and forget all of her troubles for one week. The prospect of the trip lessened the rejection of her science fiction stories immeasurably. Besides, she'd probably see The Editors there, and perhaps could chase them around until she got some input on her writing.

She chuckled as she envisioned herself clutching a stack of dog-eared pages to her breast as she bore relentlessly down on some hapless editor who was screaming and running through a hotel corridor, the Twilight Zone theme music playing in the background.

Returning to the kitchen, Deana poured herself a mug of coffee and turned to go into the family room.

A man was sitting on her couch, staring at her intently.

Deana blinked twice, but the strange vision didn't disappear.

The mug slipped out of her hands and crashed on the tile floor of the kitchen. Thoughts raced across her brain in rapid succession.

Oh, God, how did he get in here?

Some sane part of her mind distinctly recalled deadbolting the door when she came in. An even more disturbing thought followed: that he had already been in the house when she had come home. But it was not possible; she had been in every room. Her forehead briefly furrowed in confusion. What did he want?

Don't be an idiot, Deana, what do you think he wants, a cup of coffee?

A sweat broke out across her forehead. She had never been so terrified in her life. Somehow, she found her voice.

"Pl-please, d-don't hurt me. I'll do whatever you want. Do you want money? Take whatever you want, just please don't hurt me."

He said nothing, but continued looking at her with a puzzled expression. His eyes seemed strange somehow, but she was too far away from him to see their color, and was not about to get any closer to him. A tiny crystal point dangled from a small gold hoop in his left ear, catching the light and refracting it.

Could she get to the phone next to the Lazy-Boy? No, he was sitting too close to it. Besides, she would never have the time to dial. Her gaze flew to the front door. It was bolted. So how had he gotten in? More important, how long would it take her to unbolt the door and get out? She glanced over at him speculatively.

He was a big man, even seated; she could see that. She assessed his height at around six four. The cottage was isolated. A man that size could probably overtake her before she even reached the porch.

It didn't seem wise to try it. At present he seemed to be studying her with a peculiar thoroughness. Deana stood stock still; she didn't want to give him any reason to move.

Thinking quickly, she decided that her best option at the moment was to use this opportunity to study him as carefully as he was studying her. If she made it out of this, at least she would be able to identify him. Not that she would forget anyone who looked like *him*. She examined his face carefully, noting the strong forehead, beautifully shaped eyes, straight nose, perfectly chiseled lips, and strong chin with a slight cleft.

He was devastatingly handsome for a maniac.

The man seemed to be in his early thirties. His hair was straight, thick, and long; it hung to the middle of his back; a true golden color, it had no yellow in it. The golden hair complemented his skin tone which was a warm golden tan.

Next, she noted the strange outfit he was wearing.

His black pants appeared to be made of a soft leather, hugging his muscular thighs like a second skin. He wore high black pirate boots that cuffed above his knee. His shirt, a white silky material, laced up the front ending in a low vee neck. A great velvety cape, black as night with strange golden symbols, was draped across his broad shoulders. He was quite a sight to behold, that was for sure.

They continued to stare at each other in silence.

Something isn't right here, Deana thought. His clothes were too attention-getting for an intruder.

But not for a science fiction fan.

The thought hit her like a bolt of lightning. It was all clear now. She smiled suddenly at him, causing him to narrow his eyes.

"All right, who put you up to this? Was it Loraine? She always did love a practical joke." He looked blankly at her.

"No, no, don't tell me; I'll figure it out." She snapped her fingers. "Jimmy! It had to be Jimmy." No response.

"Well, don't worry about it, I'll get it soon enough."

Relieved, she walked over to the couch and sat down next to him. Jeez, he was *big*. He looked down, watching her through veiled eyes.

"So, are you going to the convention? I can hardly wait. The program looks awesome and—"

She stopped in mid sentence because now she was close enough to see that there was definitely something strange about his eyes. Framed in a thick, beautiful fringe of black lashes, *they were lavender*. Not violet, not blue. No, more like the color of French lilacs in spring . . .

She swallowed. No human ever had eyes like that.

No human . . .

She shook her head. This was stupid. He was obviously wearing contacts. She peeked up at him. They didn't look like contacts. Of course they were. What was she thinking, that he was an *alien* for God's sake!

"What flight are you taking? I'm—"

He turned to her, abruptly placing a long, beautifully tapered finger against her lips. She froze, eyes wide at this gesture. What was he doing?

He leaned close to her; using his other hand, he placed two fingers against her temple. She felt warmth and a slight tingling sensation. Now that he was close enough, she could discern the scent of . . . sandalwood incense? Mmm, very nice . . .

She closed her eyes for a moment.

Lorgin ta'al Krue looked down at the woman. He hadn't been able to understand her strange words, but he would correct that now. He gazed upon her face as the decoding process took place. Her beauty radiated out from her like a light from within. She more than intrigued him.

A smooth, deeply compelling voice penetrated Deana's senses. "By what name are you called?"

Her eyes flew open. "Deana . . . Deana Jones."

He touched his forehead briefly. "A-dee-ann?"

So what was with this guy? A weird form of dyslexia? "Deana," she repeated slowly for him.

"Adeeann." He confirmed. "What do you call this place?"

"Home." She looked at him strangely. "What do you call it?"

"Forgive me. My neural translator is slow to adjust to this language."

Neural translator? What is he talking about?

Lorgin tried to rephrase his question. "What planet is this?"

She looked at him and burst out laughing. "What planet is this? How many others have you been on?" She smirked at him. *Typical science fiction fan!*

He looked at her stone-faced. "Countless others. I ask you again, what planet is this?"

Okay, she'd play along. "It's called Disneyworld." This she managed with a straight face.

To her surprise, he didn't react in any way to this bit of information, other than to absorb it. He nodded at her. "I have not heard of this Disney World. What star system are we in?"

She looked at him strangely. "Sol, Milky Way galaxy, Virgo supercluster. Does that help you?" *Cripes, get a life, pal!*

He blinked for a moment. "I have not heard these names— something is amiss here."

He seemed so serious, she was becoming slightly concerned for him. *Maybe he's losing his reality base?* "Please, be straight with me. Who sent you here? Jimmy?"

"No one sent me here. I was pulled out of the space/time line of continuum on my way—"

"Whoa!" She put her hands up. "What are you talking about? Who are you?"

"I am called Lorgin ta'al Krue of the planet Aviara, star system Tau Hydra. As you can see, I am a Knight of the Charl and on a quest the nature of which need not concern you."

"*Get real!* Quit the role playing and give me some honest answers here."

His eyebrows slanted over his eyes. "I have just given you

21

the answers you seek, woman! Why do you persist in . . .'' He stopped and reached inside his cape, pulling out something from a hidden pocket. He opened his palm in front of her face. ''Does this look familiar to you?''

Deana's face blanched. Floating above his palm was a perfect hologram image of a star system. Needless to say, she didn't recognize it. Her eyes flew to his face. ''Wh-what is that thing?''

''It is . . .'' He thought better of what he was about to say. ''That is not important. It is obvious to me you know not this place.'' He returned the strange image to his cloak.

Deana discreetly moved a few feet away from him on the couch. Whatever that thing was, it hadn't come from *Earth,* and her uninvited visitor was an honest-to-God extraterrestrial!

She closed her eyes and groaned.

Her thoughts tumbled around in her head. *Why me? How do I get into these things? I can't believe that of all the gin joints in the world, he pops into my living room! It's the day! This unbelievable awful day! Cripes, a real alien . . . What do I do with an alien?*

Lorgin noted her distress. ''You are disturbed by me?''

Deana felt a fingertip touch her cheek. She opened her eyes and gazed at him, sighing. That would be an understatement. Even if he hadn't been from another planet, she would be disturbed by him, and so would any other female who was breathing. She had never seen *anyone* who looked like him. He was . . . he was what her friend Kristen would leeringly call a ''man of consequence.''

She gathered her wayward thoughts. After all, as a representative of her planet, it wouldn't do to drool all over him. She would just have to ignore his incredible face. Her eyes covertly skimmed the length of his body. His incredible physique. *Those eyes . . .* Stop it!

She blinked in an effort to clear her thoughts and was surprised to see him sitting cross-legged on the floor, eyes closed, palms up on his knees, in a classic lotus position. She tentatively knelt in front of him.

"Are you meditating?" she whispered. *Cripes, an alien!*

"Trying to get a spatial fix. A moment . . ." His light amethyst eyes abruptly opened. "I have not just jumped the space/time continuum. It appears there has also been a dimensional phasing as well."

"You mean you're from another dimension?" She sat back on her haunches. "This is too weird."

"Another dimension, another space, and another time. Three shifts—I have never heard of this happening before." Stunned, he stood up and went back to the couch. Sitting down and leaning forward, he rested his arms on his knees while running his hands distractedly through his long hair. "I must try and ascertain the significance of this."

"Lorg-in?" She pronounced his name the way he did. He looked over at her. She joined him on the couch, placing a hand lightly on his arm. Forget the dimension thing, she needed to know when he could vacate the premises. *An alien.*

"You can get back to where you came from, can't you?"

Lorgin stared at her, amazed that she would ask him such foolishness. Why would the woman think he would leave this place before he found out why he had been brought here and the significance of it? Such knowledge would surely dictate his next step. He stated firmly, "I cannot go back."

Deana groaned at his response, entirely missing his implacable expression. Now this was a bombshell! He couldn't go back to wherever he came from! That was sad for him, but what was she going to do with him? Should she turn him over to the FBI? No, she'd seen too many xenophobic movies where horrible things always happened to the poor dolt of an alien whose only mistake was landing on this planet. The men in suits would probably dissect him, or mate him to a gorilla.

She couldn't do that to him.

Although, on the other hand, it didn't seem right to keep such a momentous discovery to herself. What she needed to do was bide her time here, think about her options. In the meantime, it wouldn't hurt to subtly pump him for information. She had to admit her curiosity was boundless.

Deana darted a look at him. He was deep in thought, his gold hair hanging over his shoulders as his head dropped forward on his hands. She took a deep breath, then exhaled slowly. My God. *He's too gorgeous for words* . . .

No, wait a minute. Maybe he's too gorgeous to be *real*. A brilliant notion seized her. Perhaps he's an android! *Or a Terminator.* She swallowed convulsively.

"Are you human?" she blurted out.

He turned to her. "What is *human*?"

Good question; certainly her ex-boss wouldn't fit into that category. "Can you reproduce?"

His eyebrows shot up. Strange little pink sparks appeared in his luminous eyes. Without warning, he leaned toward her on the couch, his strong arms coming around her like a steel vise. Alarmed, she pushed her hands against his solid chest, feeling the silk of his shirt slide against her palms. Her action was about as effective as a gnat pushing a lion away. Why had he reacted . . .

She instantly knew exactly what he thought she had asked him.

"No! I don't *want* to reproduce! I just want to know if you can."

"Why?" Obviously, there were still translation problems. He did not release her.

"Why? Because—I do!"

"Then let me show you, so you will *know*." He started to lower her down onto the couch. She shoved him. He didn't release her, but he stopped his downward slide. She tried again.

"Are you a machine?"

He grinned rather sexily at her, revealing perfect white teeth. "Some have said."

She blushed, realizing what he thought she meant now. This was getting worse every time she opened her mouth. "I'm not asking about your prowess. Are you . . ." How do you ask this? "How were you made?"

The meaning sunk in. He released her immediately. "Ah! I am like you—human. I was not made; I was"—he hesitated for the right word—*"conceived."*

So, he was humanoid, after all. Let's see what else she could find out. "You mentioned a quest. I gather coming here was an unscheduled pit stop." He looked totally confused now. She rephrased the question. "You didn't mean to come here, did you?"

"No. Yet here I am."

"Yes, here you are. I was thinking . . . perhaps if you told me more about this quest—"

"This is not for you to know." His lips lifted slightly at the corners, in almost, but not quite, a smile. He blinked slowly, his innocent expression not really masking the knowledge evident in his eyes.

He knows that I'm pumping him for information. Drat! So much for subtlety.

"Okay. Why don't you tell me about your world. Are there others—"

He sliced his hand through the air. "This is not for you to know either."

She folded her arms across her chest. How aggravating! "Why not?"

"None of this is relevant to you. Such information could prove dangerous in certain circumstances. The only thing of import is why I have been brought here."

She expelled a breath. He wasn't going to answer her questions. Apparently he was too smart for that, or else he had seen the movies she had been thinking of earlier.

"All right. Let's try to figure it out. Maybe you were brought to the house?" This was an idea. Had Gramps been hiding more than his Jack Daniel's in the cellar?

Lorgin shook his head. "Not house . . . *lifeforce.*" He leveled his gaze at her. *"Yours."*

"*Me*? No way! You must be mistaken."

He regarded her thoughtfully for a moment, tuning out all other disturbances. "Yes . . . I am Chi'in t'se Leau. I cannot leave your side."

What did he mean by that? "What is this chin something?"

He smiled at her attempt at his language. "Chi'in t'se Leau. How to translate . . . guardian, protector, one who walks beside . . ."

"I don't need protecting!"

He shrugged as if to dismiss that nonsense.

Realizing she wouldn't get far arguing with him about it, she tried another track. "How do you know this stuff anyway? I don't understand how—"

"I know. You do not need to understand. I was brought here; I will stay by you. It is a *sacred* trust. This cannot be broken."

What in the hell was he talking about? Some nonsense about a sacred trust—was he mad?

"Look, I think you've made a grave error here." He snorted at the very notion. "Really. It has to be something else."

He smiled at her indulgently. "I think not. But even if you were right, which you are not, I would still protect you."

She gritted her teeth. "I've already told you, I don't need protecting!" He didn't bother responding.

So, he was going to stick by her side was he? Protect her? She'd like to see his expression tomorrow when some guy dressed as the Blob approached her at the convention . . . At the convention!

"There's something you should know. Tomorrow I'm going to a convention in San Francisco for a week. You'll just have to stay here and wait for me—"

He interrupted her. "No. I will go to this sanfrancisco with you."

"You can't!" She gasped. He folded his arms across his chest and narrowed his eyes at her. The effect was rather formidable. Nonetheless, she had to make him see reason. There was *no way* she was taking an alien with her to the convention. No way.

"I mean it. You cannot go with me." She spaced her words firmly, letting him know she meant it.

He raised an eyebrow, but did not respond.

"Look, I don't care if you're an alien or the reincarnation of Albert Einstein. I'm not canceling this trip." She added the words that strike terror into every traveler's heart. *"It's non-refundable."*

He still said nothing, but his eyes had definitely narrowed some more.

She was getting exasperated now. "Do you understand? I can't take you!"

The slow smile he gave her chilled her to her bones.

He's going to follow me. I just know it. Damn!

She exhaled noisily. "You think you're going, don't you?"

The look he gave her was implacable and faintly amused. "I *am* going."

27

The man was serious. Double damn! She took a moment to size up her adversary, and silently admitted defeat. He didn't look the malleable type.

She supposed she'd have to buy him a plane ticket and everything. She groaned. If an alien had to "fall" on her doorstep, why couldn't he at least have a gold card? Thank God she had plastic.

She paused a minute, wondering if she was losing her mind.

An alien was in her house and she was lamenting the fact he didn't have a credit card! Shock. It must be shock. She peered at him. He still regarded her with a piercingly intent expression.

"Oh, all right! Let me call the airline and see if I can get you a ticket."

Grudgingly, she went to the phone to call the airline, hoping there wouldn't be any seats left. The ticket agent cheerfully informed her she got the last seat available in coach. It figures, the way this day has been going. She slammed down the phone.

"I don't suppose you have a change of clothes either, do you?" she snarled at him.

He grinned at her, revealing an engaging dimple in his left cheek. "No, Adeeann; I do not." He didn't bother to add that clothes of his quality were always purchased with a self-cleaning spell put on by the Weaver's Guild wizard. And it was so stated on the label.

She threw her arms up in the air. "I don't believe this!" she fumed. "What do you think this is, an intergalactic mission house?"

He regarded her strangely, having no idea what she was talking about.

"We'll just have to go to the mall later and get you some

clothes. You can't go walking about dressed like that.''

That got his dander up. ''I will have you know these garments are of the finest—''

''Yeah, yeah, can it. I'm starved. I'll go see what I can find for us to eat in the kitchen.''

Lorgin watched her stomp off, his thoughts returning to his appearance on this planet and the nature of his quest. Were they somehow linked?

Deana stormed into the kitchen, opening cabinets and slamming doors, looking at the choices. Popcorn and popcorn. *I guess it's popcorn.* Three minutes, ten seconds; she punched the timer on the microwave and hit start. Deana figured she might as well clean up the spilt coffee on the floor, and was about to do so when the popping started.

With a grace and speed she wouldn't have thought possible in a man his size, he bounded off the couch, leapt over the coffee table, cape flying, and ran into the kitchen. In an instant he spotted the source of the popping and whipped out a rod-like object from his waistband, flipping it over agilely in his hand and causing a four-foot beam of blue light to appear.

As she watched gape-mouthed, he swung the light saber in an arc over his head, then through the microwave, which seemed to hiccup once, let out a belch of black smoke, and die. It was cleanly sliced in two.

Of course, the Berserker was smiling as if he had just slain Loki himself. He retracted the light blade and returned it to his waistbelt.

Her microwave! Her sweet inoffensive microwave!

Which she hadn't finished making the payments on yet.

Shock was rapidly being replaced with anger. It was the last straw! No one should have a day like this. No one! She had reached her limit.

''That's it! You are out of here, pal!'' She stormed over to the kitchen door, flung it open, and pointed in the general direction of the backyard. "Out!"

He stood silently leaning against her refrigerator, arms crossed over his chest, staring at her. A gust of wind blew up and slammed the door shut.

Damn it, nothing was going right today. Nothing! Nothing! Nothing! She swung the door open again.

"I said out!"

Another gust of wind blew up and slammed the door closed. Only this time she realized that the wind had come from *inside* the kitchen.

"I think not," he stated firmly.

"You—did you do that?" He quirked his eyebrow. She sat down on the kitchen floor. "Oh, my."

He came down on one knee beside her, his cape floating around him. "Something has upset you, Adeeann?"

Her gray eyes were huge as they focused on him. "Lorgin, you have supernatural . . . *powers?*" she squeaked.

He put his warm hand on her shoulder. "Powers of the Four, yes. Do not concern yourself with this, Adeeann. I am beginning to accept that this is an unenlightened world and as such—"

"What do you mean, 'powers of the four'? Like, can you read my mind?" Her expression turned horrified at the thought. Especially concerning her earlier thoughts of him.

He laughed outright at the expression on her face. "No, Little Fire, I cannot."

Little Fire? Her hand went unconsciously to her red hair. He noticed her action and seemed amused by it. She supposed that at five foot five, she appeared to him as nothing more than that gnat she had compared herself to earlier. *Little Fire, indeed!*

"Powers of the Four," he broke into her thoughts, "over

earth, wind, water, and''—he looked at her hair pointedly and grinned—"*fire.*"

Don't count on it, buddy, she mused. It seemed as though her alien had a streak of arrogance in him about as wide as the San Diego Freeway. "Are you saying you have pyscho-kinetic ability over the elements?"

"I believe that is how you would phrase it." He looked at her and his pastel eyes twinkled. "Only a seventh-level mystic could read your mind, Adeeann. I have several incarnations to go before I achieve this state. Besides, this state can only be acquired after the harmonic—"

"Please, you're giving me a headache. I have no idea what you're talking about." She put a hand to her forehead.

He stood, offering her a hand up. "Perhaps it is this hunger you mentioned earlier." She placed her small hand in his large one, choosing to ignore the strange frisson that traveled up her arm at his touch.

"Yes," she replied, standing. "We might as well pick up a hamburger on the way to the mall."

It had begun as soon as they had left her house.

Lorgin seemed very uncomfortable in her car, almost turning green when she got onto the highway. This from a man who traveled space, time, and dimensions. Of course, Boston drivers could make anybody sick, she supposed, reluctantly giving him his due.

As soon as she spotted the yellow arches, Deana swung the car in, drove through the drive-thru, and ordered them some burgers and fries. He was suitably impressed with the speed with which the food was delivered to them.

Swinging into a parking space, she handed him a bag of food, saying, "Wait until you taste this! I bet they don't have good greaseburgers where you're from."

With this endorsement, Lorgin eagerly took the bag and dug in. The horrified expression on his face said it all. Forcing himself to swallow, he looked at her aghast. His voice bellowed in the confines of the closed automobile.

"Are you trying to poison me, woman!"

Deana winced, supposing that with an undiscriminating palate, anything was possible. "Would you like me to get you something else? How about a frozen yogurt?" she offered placatingly.

He looked wary. "What is that?"

"Soured milk from an animal, chilled—" She stopped when he visibly shuddered.

"Never mind. I am not hungry. Your driving has taken care of it."

Cross the universe and men were all the same! Blaming all of life's misfortunes on women. "Okay. Have it your way." She chuckled at her pun to which he was totally oblivious.

Of course, she finished her meal, being careful to exclaim over the delights and nuances of the combined flavors to him. Lorgin did not seem to appreciate the critique.

The mall was another story. Here, he was entranced, turning in a 360-degree circle, enraptured by the three tiers of consumer paradise.

"Surely, it is like a city!" He marveled, gawking. By no coincidence, people were gawking at him. Taking him by the cape, she led him to the nearest department store.

Lorgin, stopping at almost every counter, was amazed at the sheer number of choices of apparel, the materials and color combinations. Perhaps they'd be out of here by midnight, she silently fumed. Thankfully, the men's department was fairly close to the door.

After a long and tortuous argument, Deana managed to get him into a pair of Levi's 501's, button fly. Button fly, because the man turned that same shade of green he had in the car when she demonstrated zipper action to him.

There was a sticky moment or two when he walked out of the dressing room with a jeweled dagger stuck in the waistband of the jeans. Deana thought the salesclerk was going to faint. She rushed over to Lorgin.

"Where did you get that dagger?" she hissed.

"It has been in my family for sixteen generations." As if that answered her question!

"Why didn't you leave it in the dressing room?" He looked at her as if she had a gear loose. She gave up and walked away, praying the salesman wouldn't call security.

They ended up with three pairs of assorted jeans, three long-sleeved shirts, and various sundries. Her credit card was not happy. He looked over her shoulder while she was paying the bill.

"What is your token of exchange?" he curiously asked.

"Hmm? Oh . . . plastic," she answered distractedly while signing the receipt. She happened to look down at his feet and, noticing his piratical boots, felt another expense coming on. Deana sighed resignedly, knowing she was going to have to spring for some shoes as well.

She brought him to the shoe department, intent on getting him a pair of Nikes. He had other ideas. He headed straight to the boots, picking up an expensive pair of brown Tony Lamas.

"I will have these."

"No, you won't either," she firmly responded.

"Do you not think these go well with these Leave-eyes I am wearing?"

"Yes, they're dynamite, but—"

The salesgirl walked over, interrupting her. "Can I help you?"

Lorgin turned to her. "We will take these. She has plastic." The salesgirl looked at her.

"Wrap 'em," she mumbled, feeling like a gigolo's favorite patroness.

When they finally got back home, Deana flopped down on the sofa, exhausted beyond words. She was beat. Really beat. What a day! She had gotten fired, sat in God-knows-what, got rained on, got caught in a traffic jam, been rejected *three* times, and, as if that weren't enough, sponged on by a mooch of an alien knight who claimed he was protecting her from household appliances. She'd laugh if she wasn't afraid she'd burst into tears.

She supposed she had to drag herself off the couch to get him some bedding. It was an effort to go to the linen closet and get blankets and a pillow. Half asleep, she made up a bed for him on the couch. Saying good night, she marched straightaway to her bedroom.

Deana didn't realize he was following her until she entered her room. She would have to remember that about him: despite his size, he was an amazingly quiet stalker. She turned abruptly, and Lorgin almost walked into her.

"Where do you think you're going?" she challenged him.

"I will sleep where you sleep."

She snorted. "You will not."

"I have a sacred—"

She pointed in the general vicinity of the couch. "Go!"

He studied her a moment, noting her sincerity. His right arm crossed his chest, placing his hand on his heart. "*By your desire.*" He turned and proudly strutted out of the room.

She firmly closed the bedroom door.

Chapter Two

The alarm went off at six a.m.

It was still raining; the air felt raw and chill. Deana groaned, shut the alarm off, and rolled over in bed.

When next she opened her eyes, the clock read half past six. She peered at the traitorous clock in disbelief. 6:30!

She bounded out of bed almost tripping over her long flannel nightgown. The plane left at nine! Knowing the vagaries of Boston traffic to Logan Airport, she prayed she would make it in time.

Running to the bedroom door, she hurled it open, and immediately tripped over a large body curled up on her door frame. The alien!

Two strong arms shot out and grabbed her before she could hit the floor. She fell back onto Lorgin's lap, her hair flying around her in disarray.

"Where are you going in such a hurry, Little Fire?" he murmured sleepily. His eyes, a strange light in them, gazed

35

on her loose hair. His hand slowly reached out to casually finger one long corkscrew-shaped lock.

Deana had always hated her hair.

It hung down her back in long spirals to her waist. The fact that many women purposely permed their hair in an effort to get it to look the way hers did naturally, boggled her mind. The only reason she didn't cut it short was the fear of looking like Little Orphan Annie.

Lorgin did not seem put off by her hair. On the contrary, he seemed entranced by it.

He brought a lock of it to his face and deeply inhaled. "You smell like the *tasmin* flower, Little Fire." Those strange pink sparks started up in his eyes again.

What was this all about? And what the hell was a *tazmeen* flower? She felt like a complete fool, sitting here in her bedroom doorway, on the lap of a man who was smelling her hair. She grabbed the lock of hair away from him.

"Never mind that! What are you doing in the doorway?"

Lorgin smiled to himself. She smelled like the *tasmin* flower, but was as prickly as the *gharta*. He rather liked the combination, and idly wondered if she'd be as soft and sweet as the *gharta* was once you got beneath the spines to the fruit inside. His powerful hands settled warmly on her hips.

"I am guarding you." His voice was low and sultry.

"From what, the evil dead microwave?" He had the good grace to look sheepish over that. She started to rise, and he reluctantly let her go.

"Come on. We have a plane to catch. Let me find something to hold your stuff."

She located a duffel bag and helped him pack his new wardrobe. He insisted on taking his own clothes as well. She couldn't blame him for wanting his own belongings with him. She supposed she'd feel the same way in an alien place.

Deana got dressed while Lorgin used the bathroom, hoping the man remembered the demonstration she had given him last night on the plumbing. When he came out, he was dressed in faded blue jeans and a black T-shirt.

Mercy.

The jeans hugged his thighs, indecently showcasing his muscular legs. Never had a T-shirt looked so *regal*. She observed the brown boots on his feet, almost admitting that the pleasure of looking at him was worth the beating to her credit line.

Subtle as Deana thought she was being, Lorgin was not unaware of her pleasure of him. The woman was not skilled at hiding her feelings. This pleased him on numerous levels. The guileless trait, however, would make her very vulnerable to the unscrupulous. Despite her protestations to the contrary, such a woman definitely needed a Chi'in t'se Leau. Even so, he did not think this was the sole reason he had been brought to her.

When she dragged her ten-ton suitcase out of the bedroom, Lorgin was waiting for her patiently next to his duffel bag, his cape draped over his arm. Seeing her difficulty with the cumbersome luggage, he took her suitcase, tossing it under his arm as if it were nothing more than a mere annoyance. Deana was not going to argue; the stupid bag had wheels, but they all went in different directions.

They quickly left for the airport.

Everything at the airport terminal went smoothly until she recommended that he pack his cape in his bag. He did this readily enough, but that was when Deana noticed that damn dagger stuck in the waistband of his jeans. Her face blanched as she attempted to block him from security's line of sight.

"Are you mad? Put that thing in the suitcase."

"I will not. The Cearix stays by my side always."

"Look, now is not the time to be intransigent. They won't let us on the plane with that thing." Instead of taking her words in the serious vein they were intended, he seemed greatly amused. He smiled arrogantly.

"How would they stop me?" He ran the back of his hand down her cheek. "You worry for nothing, Adeeann."

She pushed his stroking hand away. "Do you see that security point over there? We have to walk through it. When it detects that weapon of yours, all hell is going to break lose. You have to trust me on this, Lorgin."

Lorgin ignored her brush-off, returning his hand to her face to lift her chin with a single bent forefinger. Did she really think they could stop a Knight of the Charl? He examined her face carefully, noting her belief in her words. It was not his desire to distress her. Sighing, he relented. "Very well. But I will retain my light saber." She started to object, but he was firm. "This I will *not* relinquish."

She gazed at the small black box. They'll never figure out what it is, she reasoned. "Okay, but if they ask you what it is, tell them . . . tell them it's a beeper."

He looked perplexed. "A *beeper*?"

"Just do it."

Pushing Lorgin in front of her, she held her breath as he went through the arch without a hitch. Then it was her turn. As she went through, she looked up at the monitor, noting the gate number of their flight with disgust.

"I wonder why my gate is always the last one in the terminal," she mumbled as she joined Lorgin, and they made their way through the crowded building.

Deana located their waiting lounge, gratefully sinking into a chair. Lorgin sat right beside her, his translucent eyes scanning the area, presumably looking for hidden attackers. He was guarding her like a junk-yard dog and it was starting to get on her nerves. He seemed to be quickly satisfied, though, that everything was in order, settling into his chair.

After several minutes, she noticed that he started looking slightly uncomfortable. "What's the matter?"

He looked down at his boots. "I . . . I have to relieve . . . use your bathroom."

She smiled. "Well, we're a little far away from it right now. Come on, I'll show you where the rest rooms are." He gratefully followed her.

She stopped in front of the door. "Public rest rooms are gender separated, Lorgin."

This puzzled him. "You use separate facilities in public but not in private?"

"Yes. See this little figure? The one with the little man on the door is the one you go into."

Lorgin peered at the stick figure. "How can you tell he is a man?"

"Because he's wearing pants."

He snorted. "You are wearing pants and *you* certainly are not a man."

He could be exasperating without even trying. "Okay. Think of it this way: don't go into the one that has the figure in a little skirt."

He shook his head in confusion. "This Disney is a most strange world."

"Ahem . . ." She cleared her throat, quickly changing the topic. "The plumbing is a little different than in a private bathroom, do you want me to explain—"

He raised a lordly eyebrow. "I believe I can figure it out."

"Fine. I'll wait for you here."

The next few minutes seemed interminable. Finally he emerged from the bathroom. A second later a little boy in a striped shirt ran out of the bathroom, calling at the top of his lungs, "Mommy, Mommy, that man just peed in the sink!" The mother grabbed her child and quickly disappeared in the terminal.

"You said you could figure it out!" Deana hissed under her breath.

He winced. "They all look like sinks to me."

She nabbed him by the shirt and yanked him away. "Pay attention. One is called a urinal, that is what you have to use. Got it?" she gritted out.

He looked sheepish. "I believe so."

"Come on, they're starting to board."

It was very crowded. Deana wouldn't be surprised to hear that they had overbooked the flight. She was very glad they had checked in as soon as they reached the airport; the last thing she wanted was to get bumped from the flight.

They boarded the plane, sitting in the first two seats behind first class. Lorgin squeezed his six-foot-four frame into the no-leg-room seat. He did not seem happy, but did not complain either.

As the plane started filling up, Deana noticed the flight attendant looking around the cabin. Her eyes lit on Lorgin and remained there.

Any female who is breathing, Deana sighed resignedly, watching the woman walk toward them. The stewardess purposefully approached Lorgin, bending over to talk to him as if she were about to impart the secrets of state.

"Good morning," she said in a breathy voice. "We overbooked the plane, and since you don't look terribly comfortable in that seat, would you like to come up front?"

Lorgin stared at her stonily, eyes slightly narrowed.

Deana giggled to herself. He probably thinks she's coming on to him, inviting him to join her up front. What a riot!

Deana leaned forward smiling sweetly. "Do you have two seats?"

"Oh, I didn't realize you two were together."

I'll bet you didn't.

The attendant hesitated briefly before continuing. "As a matter of fact, we do have two seats open; come on." The stewardess turned around and said to Lorgin, "I love your contacts—unusual color."

Lorgin furrowed his brow, confused at the woman's strange statement. He had not "contacted" her in any way. She had "contacted" him. He would have to ask Adeeann about men and women "contacts" on this planet. He had no desire to unintentionally invite advances. His interested gaze skimmed over the Little Fire next to him. With possibly one exception, he amended.

Deana didn't waste any time following the flight attendant into first class. Naturally, where she went, Lorgin closely followed.

"Aren't these seats much better, Lorgin? Here, you can sit by the window."

Deana sat back in the sumptuous seat, enjoying the spaciousness. Maybe having an alien around had its advantages after all. If he could get her into first class for nothing, she might keep him around. She helped him with his seat belt as he stared out the window at the ground crew.

"Adeeann, this plane does not resemble your car."

"Of course not." She opened a magazine and flipped through it.

"It has extensions on its side."

"You mean the wings?" She was studying a map of their air route, half listening to his remarks.

"Wings . . . like a"—he paused, waiting for the right word—"*bird*." Light was beginning to dawn.

"Yes, how else would it fly?"

He immediately unbuckled his seat belt and made to rise.

Deana grabbed him by the waist band of his jeans and yanked him back into the seat. "Whatever is the matter with you?"

"You fly in a *machine*?" He seemed revolted at the prospect.

She looked at him askance. "I'm not going to ask you why flying in a machine is upsetting you, because I just know I am not going to like the answer." She patted his knee. "You'll be fine."

He accepted what she had to say; whether he believed it was another matter.

The plane soon turned down the runway and took off. Lorgin clutched the arms of the chair tightly, but took it quite well, considering. Once they were in the air, he seemed to relax somewhat.

"The fight attendant will serve us breakfast soon. You must be very hungry, you haven't eaten since . . . You haven't eaten."

He agreed. "I am very hungry. Breakfast will not be . . . *greaseburgers,* will it?" That idea worried him.

A mischievous gleam sparkled in her eyes. "Not unless we're lucky." He shot her an I'm-not-amused look.

Breakfast turned out to be scrambled eggs, hash browns, toast, and orange juice. He ate everything, seeming only really excited about the orange juice. And coffee. The man loved coffee. He drank four cups before Deana warned him about the effects of caffeine.

"I would go easy on that stuff if I were you."

"Why?"

"Coffee contains a stimulant called caffeine. If you drink any more, I'll have to scrape you off the ceiling."

"I vow I would brave the effects of this caffeine if I could have more of this wonderful elixir."

Deana placed a hand on his arm, gently lowering the cup from his mouth. "Trust me."

He complied immediately, his intelligent gaze intently capturing her own. "I would that you also trust *me*, Adeeann."

Deana, flustered by his sudden intensity, returned to her tray of food.

After breakfast, they settled in for the long flight, Deana opening a paperback book, Lorgin leaning back in his seat, a look of stoic endurance on his face.

When Deana noted that Lorgin had been quiet for some time, she raised her head from her book, wondering if he had nodded off. Instead, she saw him staring intently out the window. He seemed fascinated by the wide blue yonder.

The plane bucked slightly in mild turbulence.

The captain's voice came over the loudspeaker, requesting the passengers to fasten their seat belts due to unexpected clear air turbulence. Deana leaned back in the seat and gazed out the window beyond Lorgin's golden mane. Just before she closed her eyes to take a nap, she idly noticed puffs of clouds fluffing by the window. Those clouds are moving rather fast, she thought as she yawned.

Too fast!

Deana bolted up in her seat and stared out the window, noting clouds rapidly and unnaturally converging together. Even as she watched, a bolt of lightning arced from cloud to cloud.

The plane bucked again.

The low rumble of thunder vibrated through the plane. She turned her horror-stricken gaze to Lorgin.

The plane took another hop and dive.

"Lorgin!" He turned to her.

"Are you doing this?" His smug look was admission enough for her. "Are you crazy? Stop it at once! Are you trying to get us all killed?"

He sighed and leaned back in the seat. The ride immediately smoothed out.

If she wasn't so shaken, she would be tempted to thump his head with her book. "What possessed you to do something so stupid?"

He shrugged. "You make too much of this, Adeeann. I was just . . . playing, to pass the time."

Playing? Causing a lightning storm was playing to him? Good grief! She'd have to watch him every minute to make sure he didn't cause a disaster. Chi'in t'se Leau my foot! Just who was guarding whom, she moaned. Cripes, an alien with a warped sense of humor! *And supernatural powers.*

Deana had never been so happy to land in her life.

They arrived at the hotel in the late afternoon.

Since there already was a line at the reservation desk, Deana sat Lorgin down in a chair outside the ladies room, and went in to splash some water on her face. She was patting her cheeks with a paper towel when Lori, an old convention acquaintance, walked in.

"Deana? Is that you? Wow, you look great! What did you do to yourself?"

Deana stared at her reflection in the mirror. Hey, she did look great! No, great wasn't it; she looked . . . *beautiful.* Her hair, always an auburn red, now looked somehow deeper, almost garnet, and it was absolutely luminous. Her features were the same, but in some undefined way, better. Her eyes, usually a drab gray, sparkled like crystals. Her light, rather dull skin tone glowed with a pinkish blush. Even her body felt slightly fuller and rounder. It was a magical transformation . . .

Magic!

She stormed out of the bathroom, leaving Lori talking to

the wall. Leaning over Lorgin, she placed her hands on the arms of his chair and glared down at him.

"What did you do to me?" she demanded.

He looked up at her, eyes half closed. "What do you mean?" he asked lazily.

"When did you make me look like this?"

Lorgin reached up and smoothed back a lock of silky hair which had escaped her braid. "You have always looked like this, Little Fire." His voice was husky as his hand came up and cupped the back of her head. He bent forward, knowing his eyes were beginning to spark. *She was a most pleasing prickly gharta.*

With a great effort, Deana twisted free of his hold. "You didn't put some spell on me?"

"I do not do spells. Only a sixth—"

"Don't start that business again. Why do I look like this?"

He looked genuinely perplexed. "You have always looked thus."

She pondered that statement. Perhaps to him. But something had happened to her. Obviously, Lorgin knew nothing about it, so she'd have to wait for an answer. Noticing that the line had thinned at the desk, she told Lorgin she was going to check them in.

Lorgin's heated amethyst gaze followed her to the desk. In truth, he had wanted to take her from the moment he had first seen her. Now he suspected it was something more. Much more. Of course, this he would know later, when he tasted of her.

Deana looked around the lobby, noting the indoor waterfalls, marble floors, and lush plants. It was beautiful. Getting a copy of the reservation confirmation out of her purse to give to the desk clerk, she briefly thought of getting two rooms, but the cost of even one room in this palace for the week was exorbitant. She also was afraid that if she got separate rooms, she'd wake up to find Lorgin sitting in the hallway in front of her door, guarding her from Darth Microwave.

The woman behind the desk scanned the form and punched her name into the computer. "So, that's one room." The clerk glanced at Lorgin. "King-size bed—"

"No! Two double beds."

The woman looked over at Lorgin again, her eyes traveling the impressive length of him as she raised her eyebrows. She leaned forward, whispering to Deana. "Are you sure, girlfriend? I'd take the king and tell him that's all we had left."

"You don't understand." She sighed. "The doubles will be—"

"*We will take the king bed.*"

Deana turned around to Lorgin open-mouthed.

"Am I not a Knight of the Charl and therefore entitled to sleep in a king's bed? I will take no other." He swept his hand through the air, as if to finalize it.

The woman behind the counter shook her head and tittered. "I don't know what he said, but if I were you, I'd go with the flow."

So, here she was in a lovely hotel room, sitting on a king-sized bed in her short cotton nightgown, *going with the flow.* Lorgin was in the bathroom taking a bath.

She looked down at the bed.

It was certainly wide enough for the two of them. She hoped he wouldn't get any ideas. No, that wasn't true. She hoped he'd get a lot of ideas, just not act on any of them. She didn't think she could deal with an intergalactic Don Juan.

Especially not one that looked the way he looked . . .

She shivered. Just the thought of anything physical with

him could turn her into a bowl of jello. And it wouldn't take him long to find it out either! No, she was not stupid enough to play with dynamite. She didn't have enough experience to handle a man like . . .

Her thoughts drifted off as the door to the bathroom opened and Lorgin walked into the room wearing nothing but that dangling crystal earring.

"What do you think you're doing?" she squealed.

He padded over to the vanity and retrieved her blow dryer, affording her a splendid view of his taut backside. He had the most perfect buns she had ever—

Lorgin looked innocently over his left shoulder at her, asking guilelessly, "It is not permitted?"

"No, it is *not* permitted!" She tried to make her voice project a firm, no-nonsense tone; what came out sounded rather shaky.

He turned toward her, giving her ample view of all of his generous assets.

Oh God.

He was awesome. She never would have imagined . . .

Deana flushed crimson. "Go into the bathroom and put a towel around you, or—or something!" she sputtered.

His hand covered his heart. "By your desire," he literally purred before he turned and padded back to the bathroom.

As soon as Lorgin was out of her sight, a devilish grin slowly creased across his handsome face. He pictured Adeeann's expression. No, she could not hide her emotions from him. He wondered what other reactions he could coax from her.

Deana heard the blow dryer go on, so assumed he had watched her dry her hair earlier. She lowered her still flaming face to her hands. She kept trying to think of something, anything, else, but it was no use. Her mind kept picturing him as he walked out of the bathroom, tawny skin still slick from his bath, with all the grace and beauty of a great golden tiger.

This would not do at all.

She heard the dryer shut off and braced herself for his reappearance, half expecting him to appear in the nude again. A moment later, Lorgin came out of the bathroom, graciously attired with a towel around his waist. However, his hair was going in every direction.

His face bore a thunderous expression. "What has that machine done to my hair?" The words were spaced and measured in an ominous tone.

Deana giggled. She couldn't help it. Great warrior, Knight of the Charl, done in by a blow dryer. He did not appear to appreciate her sense of humor. His next words confirmed this.

"I do not see the humor in this, Adeeann." He narrowed his eyes.

Still giggling, she patted the bed. "Here, sit down. I'll see if I can brush the knots out."

While he sat on the bed, she went to retrieve her hairbrush from the bathroom. Unbeknownst to her, his gaze followed her, flickering down the length of her bare legs in blatant interest.

Oblivious of his perusal, Deana sat down behind him cross-legged on the bedspread, saying, "You know, you're supposed to brush your hair while you dry." She looked at his head critically and smiled. "Unless you're aiming for the wind tunnel effect." He bunched his shoulders.

"Relax. I'm just teasing."

"Be glad I do not challenge you for such a remark, Little Fire." He spoiled the seriousness of his words by turning to grin wickedly at her.

She began brushing his long, silky mane, carefully smoothing any knots out. His hair was thick and straight, gleaming to the middle of his back. So beautiful . . .

Deana began stroking the length of his golden hair, letting the brush's bristles glide down his back, while her other hand followed the same path, smoothing down the strands. It didn't take long for her to lose all sense of time, getting lost in the activity.

Lorgin closed his eyes and leaned back into her small but capable hands, enjoying the sensuous tug and pull of the brush, the softness of her touch. He thought he might never master the use of this blow dryer, if the result would be Adeeann doing what she was doing for him now.

By Aiyah, such pleasure was almost pain.

She continued her long, sensuous stroking. The bristles of the brush lightly scraped over and down the skin of his naked back. Her sweet *tasmin* scent filled his nostrils. Occasionally her fingers lightly brushed against his bare skin, causing him to almost moan aloud. Enough!

Without warning, Lorgin grabbed her hand and brought it over his shoulder. He removed the brush from her nerveless fingers while holding her hand in his; then he turned his head to softly kiss the inside of her hand. Deana felt the tip of his tongue briefly touch the center of her palm.

Tiny ripples of electric current pulsed from his hot tongue to her fingertips.

Gasping, she tried to reclaim her hand, but he wasn't ready to release it just yet. Tugging her forward, tight against his bare back, he sweetly kissed the inside of her wrist. Some sane part of Deana's mind briefly wondered how such a strong man could have such soft lips.

Another shiver passed through her. What was that intriguing electric buzz she felt?

"Thank you, Little Fire," he murmured, kissing her wrist once more. Again, a little shiver.

49

"L-Lorgin?"

"Mmm . . ." His answer was muffled by the skin of her arm, which he was now nuzzling very affectionately.

"I think . . ." She tried to pull her arm away again. He reluctantly released her. "I think we should go to bed—to sleep!" She stumbled over her words. "We should go to *sleep* now."

He gave her a Mona Lisa smile—like a cat before it pounces on a hapless mouse, she thought.

She shakily got off the bed. This time she didn't miss his provocative perusal of her legs. Okay. This is one fire she was going to have to douse and douse fast.

"I'll take the right side, you can sleep on the left. Since there's plenty of room in the bed, I'll *expect* you to stay to your own side." There, that was plain enough.

Lorgin rose off the bed, going to the left side as instructed. He gave her a defiant look before he lifted the sheet, got into bed, and proceeded to toss the towel he was wearing onto the floor. Leaning back against the headboard, he crossed his arms over his powerful chest, raising an eyebrow in silent challenge, as if daring her to comment.

She ran her now sweaty palms down the front of her nightgown. Just go on with a normal routine, she advised herself, as if giving orders to a huge, naked, "consequential" alien in one's bed were a completely natural occurrence.

"Fine," she said in a little voice. "Now I'll say good night."

She moistened her lips nervously and dived into bed, quickly shutting the bedside light. Deana couldn't help but hear his low laugh echo in the darkness as he turned over and went to sleep. Did she say giving orders? Who was she kidding? She fumed silently. The man did whatever pleased him. *Arrogant beast!*

Unlike Lorgin, who slept soundly, Deana was not so trusting, tossing and turning half the night. She remembered thinking that she should've turned down the air conditioning before getting into bed. These hotel rooms could go arctic on you overnight. She briefly thought of getting up to turn it down, but then sleep finally overcame her and she drifted off.

Ahhh, her pillow was so warm, and smelled so cleanly of sandalwood . . .

She cuddled her cheek against the satin down, loving the smooth, taut feel of it against her skin.

Sandalwood?

She blinked her eyes and stared into a golden amber chest. Oh, no. *Please, no.*

Worse than that, in her sleep, her nightgown had ridden up to her waist, and her leg, probably looking for warmth, had insinuated itself between his thighs. *His naked thighs.*

She didn't want to know what her knee had been rubbing against.

As if that wasn't enough of a situation, she felt two large toasty hands cupping her bottom, *inside* her bikini underwear. She didn't move a muscle, praying he was still asleep and she could slowly untangle herself from him. Haltingly, she raised her head, apprehensively lifting her eyes to his face.

Lavender eyes burned down on her, sparking with passionate flame.

I'm in a fix here, she thought, swallowing.

Lorgin knew the instant she had awakened. He had been waiting patiently for her to do so for some time. It had not been easy. The woman had been rubbing and cuddling against him like a baby *zeena*. He had no intention of wasting the opportunity.

He swiftly dipped his head to claim her mouth. She tried

51

to squirm away. Not to be denied this time, he held her fast. Leaning toward her, he chose first to lightly brush his lips across her closed mouth, back and forth several times, to leave no doubt in her mind who was in control. Who would always be in control. He had not liked her thinking she could order him about like some untried youth. He was a seasoned warrior, a Knight of the Charl; best she know it and know it well.

He paused to regard her silently, with smoldering eyes, for several minutes. Her frightened gaze locked with his.

Deana thought he must hear her heart pounding in her chest. *This man is dangerous.* She was terrified of his strength, of his power over her, of his alienness. But most of all, she was terrified of his uncompromising masculinity.

He continued to regard her silently for several moments. Without warning, he abruptly released her, saying, "Go get dressed, Adeeann. I am of a mind for something to eat. Best for you if it is food."

Deana did not stop to question her reprieve. She leaped out of the bed and ran into the bathroom.

Lorgin rolled over in the bed and stared at the ceiling.

Aiyah, she was a woman who could surely test a Knight of the Charl. He sighed, knowing that if what he now suspected was true, eventually he would have no choice but to overpower her fear of him . . .

When Deana came out of the bathroom, he was sitting in front of the television watching, of all things, the Three Stooges. His look was incredulous as Curly started spinning horizontally on the floor, clucking, "Wub, wub, wub!"

Lorgin's head slanted to the side as he followed Curly's movements. "Is this a civil punishment of some kind?"

Deana thought of his overbearing behavior in bed. "Yes. So you better be careful what you do." She walked over to the television and turned the station. Bugs Bunny sashayed by in drag, batting his false eyelashes at Elmer Fudd.

Lorgin got up and stood in front of the set, clearly fascinated, his hand reaching out to the screen. "What is this? They appear alive, but are not. These are wondrous—"

"They're called cartoons." She felt she definitely owed him one, so added, "They live in a place called Toon Town."

His head whipped to her. "They exist? How could . . ." He noted her huge grin, which she could no longer hide. He wagged his finger at her, smiling. "One day I will return this mischief to you, Adeeann."

Of that, she had no doubt.

After breakfast, they walked to the convention center across the street. Deana purchased a membership for Lorgin, idly wondering if she could take all the money she had spent on him out in trade.

She looked over at him in his tight black jeans and cotton shirt. He had rolled back the sleeve cuffs exposing the sinewy muscles of his forearms. The crazy part of it was that she didn't think he'd have any objection to such an arrangement. And why should he? He was on a shore leave of a kind, albeit a permanent one.

I have to stop thinking like this, she groaned. It wouldn't do. Wouldn't do at all.

The guy behind the registration desk didn't even blink when he asked Lorgin's full name for his convention badge. After all, this *was* a science fiction convention. He grinned up at Lorgin. "Great name! Have fun!" He handed Lorgin his badge and program book, never realizing that here was the real McCoy.

While Deana registered, Lorgin looked around the room, his gaze falling on a man at the end of the line. His face broke into a huge grin.

"Ah, a Meephan!" he stated as he purposefully approached the man and began communicating with him in a series of clicks and whirs.

Deana strolled over while pinning her badge on. The confused man turned to her. "What is he doing?"

Deana took Lorgin's badge from his hand and pinned it on his shirt. She smiled over at the poor fellow. Let me take a wild guess here, she mused. "Talking Meephan to you?"

The man looked totally puzzled. Deana tapped Lorgin on the shoulder. "Sorry, Lorgin; he's Vulcan, not Meephan." Lorgin looked completely bewildered.

The convention had only just begun.

Chapter Three

Deana sat down in the main hall to look over her program book.

There was a lot to choose from—panel discussions, movies, workshops, costume displays, information tables on everything from NASA to special effects in cinema. They could visit the art show or the dealer's room. She spotted a panel discussion on a topic which she thought would especially interest Lorgin.

"Look, Lorgin, you might be interested in this." She pointed to her program book, then realized by his puzzled expression that he couldn't read her language. Apparently, his translating device did not work on written text. "It's called Magic: Myth and Meaning. Let's check it out."

She found the room on the second floor. It was already quite full, but she managed to locate two chairs for them on the end of an aisle. They took their seats as the moderator began with a lengthy introduction into the roots of magic in folklore.

After about ten minutes of self-indulgent palaver, Deana realized that the guy was in love with the sound of his own voice. She was going to ask Lorgin if he wanted to leave, but he seemed intent on the moderator's words, so she sat back stifling a yawn.

Without warning, Lorgin stood up, saying in a loud voice, "You know not whence you speak, you pompous fool!" Deana sunk into her chair, trying to make herself invisible.

The moderator, flustered, responded, "I'm a professor of mythology at Princeton. I think I have some authority to speak—"

"Bah! Can you cast runes? Do you read Signs of the Two even? What level of powers have you?" Deana decided then and there: *no more magic seminars for Lorgin.*

The professor answered Lorgin smugly. "One does not have to slay a dragon to understand the underlying—"

"And have you?"

"Have I what?" The professor was getting exasperated.

"Slain this dragon you speak of?" Everyone laughed. It seemed that Deana was not the only one who had been getting a little bored at the sound of the professor's voice.

"Not lately." His irritating tone was condescending.

"Not ever, I will wager. My friend Yaniff could turn you into a slimy zorph with the flick of his hand, and you could do nothing. It is not seemly for you to speak on matters you have no firsthand knowledge of."

That was it. Deana stood up. "We have to go. *Now.*" She took his arm, tugging him from his seat.

"I will find you later and finish with you," Lorgin warned the poor guy, as she hauled him out of the room.

"I can hardly wait," the professor sighed.

Once outside, Lorgin asked Deana why she wished to leave. "Because you were right, he was a pompous ass."

She decided to go to the dealer's room next to check out the merchandise before the heavy crowds got there and had first pick. Deana glanced wistfully down at Lorgin's new boots. Not that she could afford to buy much now.

They stood in the doorway to the vast dealer's den. About 500 hucksters had set up temporary shop in here, selling anything from art prints to collector's editions of rare science fiction books, from collectible science fiction toys to videos, from tarot cards to sculpted wizards.

Lorgin surveyed the scene. "It is much like the sacri on my planet." He walked over to a table displaying crystals. "Very similar," he murmured.

Deana didn't have the heart to tell him this was not a typical marketplace on earth. Not by a long shot.

They enjoyed themselves going through the various wares for sale. Deana spent some time looking through posters of old movies. Lorgin seemed fascinated by a wooden sculpture of an Ewok village. They slowly made their way up the aisles.

Deana had already met several of her friends, and they had agreed to meet for dinner later. Her friend Kristen seemed very curious about Lorgin. Kristen had always been too smart for her own good, Deana thought with a grin. She recalled how Kristen had tried pumping her for information on Lorgin. She couldn't blame her, seeing as she had never mentioned Lorgin to her friend in the past during their marathon phone calls. She would have to be very careful tonight at dinner.

Lorgin stopped at a table displaying unusual jewelry, admiring a French barrette with little white and pink porcelain-like flowers on it. He carefully fingered the tiny blooms.

"This is very beautiful." He observed Deana's reaction to it.

"It is pretty."

"The workmanship is so detailed. It must be very costly."

57

Deana swung her gaze to him, observing his interest in the barrette. *He doesn't know it's a cheap manufactured item.*

"If I were home," he continued, unaware of her scrutiny, "I would give this to you, Adeeann." He gazed appealingly at her. "But I do not have plastic."

Deana caved instantly under that sweet gaze. "I'll lend you the money, but I expect you to pay it back." She fished three dollars out of her pocket.

"No plastic?"

"Not for this." She gave him the money.

He gave the dealer the money, then motioned for her to turn around, placing the barrette in her hair at the crown of her head. Deana suspected that he could live the rest of his life in kingly style on just one of the smaller stones in the hilt of the dagger he called the Cearix. She also suspected that he would part with his life before he allowed the knife to be desecrated in such a manner.

Lorgin surveyed his handiwork, pleased with the result.

"Thank you. It's a beautiful gift, Lorgin. It was nice of you to think of me."

His hand warmly cupped her face. "I would give you more, Adeeann, much more."

Deana gazed into his beautiful eyes, feeling slightly disoriented. *Yes, more . . .* She blinked away her confusion. *By God, he's wearing me down! I can't let this happen. No way can I let this happen.* "L-let's check out the art show."

He smiled knowingly at her. "You lead; I will follow." His arm swept in front of her. As she went ahead of him, he intoned in a voice too low for her to hear, "*For now.*"

The art show was wonderful. Lorgin really seemed to enjoy this portion of the convention. Several covers of popular books were showing, as well as additional original art work.

Lorgin stood before a particularly austere rendering of an

alien landscape. The artist noticed his interest. "What do you think of it?" He asked Lorgin.

"It reminds me of Altarran Gaedre Two, in the Spheris sector. Have you been there?"

The artist grinned. "Occasionally."

"A starkly beautiful place to view, but treacherous for the unaware."

"Yes, I tried to capture that feeling on canvas."

"You succeeded. Once, I was robbed of every *croness* I carried by a *chaktan* in the olde city." Lorgin warmed to the memory. "I had imbibed too much, and I was completely disrobed. She took me—" He abruptly stopped as he remembered Deana's presence. She seemed avidly interested in the tale. Too interested. He decided it was best not to continue the story.

The artist chuckled. "You must be one hell of a writer. Hey, I'm tired of standing around here; why don't you let me buy you a beer?"

Lorgin turned to the artist. "Thank you, but I would not know what to do with a bear."

"A beer, Lorgin," Deana explained. "English is his second language." Or for all she knew, his thousandth language. "A beer is spirits, Lorgin. Fermented grain—"

"Ah—*keeran*. Yes!" He slapped the poor guy on the back, sending him five feet across the room. "Let us go, my friend."

Deana, thinking she'd take the opportunity to slip away, maybe see the Regency Dance, made to move discreetly away. Before she got two feet, Lorgin grabbed her by her shirt collar. "You are going somewhere, Adeeann?"

"Apparently not."

They had their drink, enjoying themselves with the artist, whose quick wit and ability to jump into what he assumed was role playing made the time a lot of fun. Of course, Lorgin had no idea he was participating in a game of sorts.

Since it was late afternoon, and she was tired from the night before, Deana told Lorgin she would like to rest before meeting the others for dinner. Noting the dark circles under her eyes, Lorgin readily agreed.

Once inside the hotel room, she could barely keep her eyes open blaming last night's anxiety over sleeping with him, as well as jet lag for her overtired state.

She quickly changed into her nightgown and plopped into bed, telling Lorgin to have fun watching the cartoons. Trying to decide how to instruct him on what time to wake her, she hit upon the perfect solution, informing him to wake her when the Flintstones came on. She was snoozing before her head hit the pillow.

Deana felt cold air hit her back and groaned a complaint into the pillow. As usual, her nightgown had hiked up, way above her waist, and if she wasn't so sleepy, she'd yank it down. She thought she felt the tip of a finger lightly glide down the indentation of her back to the base of her spine.

Lorgin whispered in her ear. "Adeeann, it is time to wake up." She brushed away his lips from her ear, mumbling something unintelligible.

He bent over her, his hair sweeping across her back. The tip of his tongue found the two little dimples at the base of her spine, above the band of her underwear. A small frisson lightly vibrated in its wake.

"Cut it out, Lorgin."

His answer was to graze her buttock with his teeth.

That got her up.

She rapidly flipped over, but he adroitly slid her under him, seeming amused at her expression of horror mixed with panic.

60

''Do you not like my wake up?'' he asked, way too innocently, while running his open palm down the length of her hair.

Deana froze, not certain what to do.

Lorgin dropped onto his forearms, leaning fully against her, his jean-clad thighs pressing warmly against her bare ones. His fiery gaze locked on her soft, full mouth. Her tongue, in response to a nervous reaction, barely came out of her mouth to lick her suddenly dry bottom lip.

He raised his eyes to capture hers as he ran his finger over the spot she had just moistened, and brought it to his own lips, as if he were . . . *tasting her?* His eyes flamed anew, and apparently he decided to come back for seconds, for he dipped his head intently toward her.

She silently shook her head no.

''I will have you, Little Fire,'' he murmured huskily.

Her eyes opened wide at that remark. She placed her hands against his chest in an effort to hold him off. He simply returned his finger to her lower lip, opening her mouth for him.

Deana stared at him, mesmerized. *He had captured her.* Very sure. Very knowing. Very male. When he spoke, his tone was raw and implacable.

''Have no doubt.''

Deana wasn't sure if she moaned or whimpered.

His sweet lips met hers in a brand of fire. Hot. Hard. Demanding. His mouth gave no quarter. She tried turning her head, but his hands locked her firmly in place. His tongue sought entrance to her mouth. She tried to tell him to stop, but when she opened her mouth to speak, he immediately took advantage by gaining entrance.

A bold warrior, he left no spot unconquered by the silky feel of him. His velvet lips and talented tongue expertly invaded her, taking her breath away, leaving strange tiny shivers of electric longing in their wake.

She was completely overwhelmed by him, as she had always feared she would be. Deana trembled helplessly under his commanding onslaught.

He broke off the kiss as abruptly as he had started, leaving her gasping for air. Explosively swinging off her, he leaped up and slammed the television off.

Lorgin was not unmoved by the exchange. His eyes burned like amethyst crystals, flashing and sparking pink with his heat. Her inexplicable fear insulted him. When he spoke, his cold, soft tone belied the fire in him. ''I can make you have desire, Adeeann.'' He whirled around, storming out onto the balcony to let the night breeze cool his ardor.

Make her have desire?

She was still lying in bed, shaken, her hand touching her throbbing lips. No one can kiss like that . . . *No one human.* Now she was more frightened of him than ever. And of herself. My God, if those electric-like currents were any indication . . . Good grief. It was . . . different. *Incredibly* erotic. And much worse than she had imagined.

Alien or no, he was too sexually sophisticated for her to cope with, way out of her league. Cripes, in her whole life, she'd only had one miserable experience. And it was miserable. She couldn't tangle with Lorgin, she just *couldn't.* There'd be no controlling him. She had just witnessed that. Besides he was arrogant beyond words. What would she do with a man like that?

What wouldn't she do with a man like that?

No. Absolutely not.

Her rational side took over. If he thought she didn't want him, that could only be to her benefit. Unless, a little voice inside said, he sees it as a challenge . . . a little nick to his male pride, perhaps? Ridiculous. It wasn't as if he . . .

She was getting a headache—a condition that seemed to be occurring a lot around him. *The best thing to do is to pretend it never happened, and make sure it doesn't happen again.* She would call housekeeping and tell them to bring up a cot for her.

Do I really think a cot is going to stop this warrior knight?

It had better, or they were going to have a parting of the ways. She got up and went into the bathroom to shower.

Later, while Lorgin was bathing, she picked out a caftan to wear to dinner. Since the sleeves were bell shaped, giving a medieval look, she decided to wear the torque. She fished it out of her bag and tried it on with the dress. Perfect.

Strange how she didn't recall the stone being such a bright green . . .

She shrugged. It wouldn't be the first strange thing that had been happening to her lately. Chilly, she donned a sweater jacket, zipping it up to her chin, and waited for Lorgin to finish getting dressed.

In the lobby of the hotel, Deana was delighted when she recognized an old friend of hers. "Jimmy!" she called to get his attention. When he spotted her, he bounded over as if he were her favorite pet.

"Deana!" His eyes widened as he took in her appearance. "You're looking good. But you always look good. So, what have you been up to, sweetheart?"

Deana's eyes briefly flicked to Lorgin. "Oh, the usual . . ." *I'm living with an alien now, did you hear?* She smiled at Jimmy catlike.

Jimmy had known her for too long to be fooled by the blithe statement. "Knowing you, that could be anything, hmm?" *Truer words were never spoken, Jimmy.*

"So, Jimmy, what's life like?" *What a stupid question!* She regretted it as soon as she uttered it.

Jimmy peered at her. "You are not acting yourself at all, dearest heart." He noticed her fidget and dropped the subject. "Are you going to the Scotland party tonight?"

"I'd like to."

"I hear the Scots brought cases of single malt Scotch with them—Glen Fiddich."

"Then I'll definitely be there."

"What hotel are you staying at?"

"This one. It's always easier to stay at the hotel closest to the convention center."

"Yeah, but more expensive. Say, why don't I come by your room before the party, then we can go together?"

"That would be grea—"

"*I think not.*" Lorgin stepped forward, placing a proprietary hand on Deana's shoulder.

Jimmy stepped back. "Oh, are you together?"

"No," she said.

"Yes," he said.

Jimmy looked from one to the other. Deana looked surprised, but the big guy looked like he was getting hot.

Lorgin's eyes narrowed ominously. "You will leave now and forget this woman."

Jimmy turned to Deana, clearly perplexed. "Deana?" Lorgin started forward. Jimmy was nothing if not smart. "I'll-I'll see you at the party." Deana gave him a half-hearted wave.

When he was out of sight, she turned to Lorgin, reached up on tiptoe, and grabbed him by his arrogant ear. She yanked and twisted it for good measure.

"Ouch! Unhand me at once!" Lorgin was shocked that anyone, let alone a mere slip of a girl, would have the audacity to touch a Knight of the Charl in such a manner.

Deana was not about to be intimidated like poor Jimmy.

She yanked on his ear again so there was no misunderstanding. "What did you think you were doing? I happen to like him!"

Lorgin clamped his hand around her wrist and applied subtle pressure to her hand, causing a reflex action which freed his ear from her grip. Still clasping her wrist, he turned to her, saying in a low voice, "You will not see this man again."

"What?" She could not believe his gall. She yanked her hand free.

"I have said what I wish to say. *I will not permit it.*"

"You won't permit—Listen, pal, what makes you think you've got the right—"

She stopped because Lorgin had grabbed her upper arms, furious. His luminous glare pierced her. "I have *taken* The Right. You will not do this."

"I never gave you The Right." What was she saying? She was starting to sound as crazy as him, for crying out loud.

He snorted at her foolish statement. "You do not give me The Right; I take it. We will talk no more of it."

"We will, too. I can do whatever I choose, I have my—"

"No."

"No? Excuse me, did I hear *no*?"

"At least there is nothing amiss with your hearing."

Now that made her mad. "Well, you can go back to your forest primeval and leave me alone. I don't like your attitude."

"This matters not to me." He shrugged arrogantly. It was impossible to have an argument with him, she fumed. He keeps changing the parameters to suit himself!

"Listen up, Lorgin, you may have ordained yourself my Chi'in t'se Leau but that doesn't give you the right to tell me who to keep company with."

"You are right." She gave him a surprised look, which quickly darkened with his next words. "I give myself that particular authority."

"Then I don't recognize it." Two could play at this game.

His look became thunderous. *"You will."*

She refused to talk to him for most of the meal. Not that he noticed. Apparently Lorgin had finally found food he enjoyed in the Chinese restaurant. She'd never seen anyone eat so much moo goo gai pan in her life.

Her friends found him strange enough to be interesting, and soon were drinking mai-tais with him as if he were a convention institution of some kind. She was beginning to suspect he could drink them all under the table and still be able to battle a microwave or two.

She was not at all happy about this sudden possessive attitude of his. Maybe he feared that she would abandon him. Maybe he was insecure, being in a new place, feeling strange . . .

The rich sound of his laughter broke into her thoughts.

That man never had an insecure day in his life, you idiot! He's just an arrogant beast!

She drummed her fingers on the table.

How to deal with him—that was the question. She looked over at him again. Lorgin was talking to her friend Kristen. He turned his head at that moment and coolly met her eyes.

Deana stared him down, lifting her chin a notch. Lorgin raised an eyebrow at her, an unspoken challenge.

Obviously he wasn't backing down from his stand.

And he didn't seem terribly wounded by her silent treatment. On the contrary, by the gleam in his eye, the man actually seemed amused by it. She turned away from his gaze in pique, not missing the sound of his low chuckle as he turned his attention to the other end of the table.

There was a name for men like him. She shuddered distastefully.

A horrible thought occurred to her. What would he be like in his own environment? She shuddered again. Thank God she'd never have to witness that display of swaggering lordliness. The very thought of it made her ill. No sense upsetting herself, for thankfully she'd never be in such a position.

Even though she was wearing her sweater, she inexplicably felt a chill run down her spine.

After dinner, everyone walked back to the convention center main hall area, deciding to mill about and mingle until party time. Lorgin was waylaid by the artist they had met earlier in the day.

Kristen decided to use the opportunity to grill Deana on the mysterious subject of Lorgin. Since the hall was warm, Deana unzipped her sweater and slung it over a couch. The torque gleamed brightly in the fluorescent lighting.

Lorgin felt a strange pulling sensation.

He slowly turned his head toward Deana, his eyes widening in shock. The Shimalee! By Aiyah, she wears the Shimalee! Lorgin stood transfixed, feeling its power even from this distance. There was no doubt in his mind now why he had been brought here.

So, the ancient prophecy was true.

Knowing that this was not the place where danger threatened the woman, he abruptly turned and walked away, leaving the artist talking to the air. There was much that needed to be done. He would avoid the nuisance of The Challenge and take care of the first now.

He headed back to the hotel.

Deana was being thoroughly grilled by Kristen. The girl

was like the Spanish Inquisition when she set her mind to it. *And no one knows when the Spanish Inquisition will strike!*

Deana smiled to herself while deftly avoiding answering some of the more pointed questions. She looked up, expecting to see Lorgin standing nearby and was surprised when she didn't spot him. That wasn't like him. He had made it a personal mission not to let her out of his sight. The last time she had seen him he was talking to that artist fellow . . .

There was a curious buzzing of voices down at the end of the hall by the doors, moving her way.

The crowd suddenly parted like the Red Sea and Lorgin strode through, wearing his original caped costume. The bright white of his shirt shimmered against his golden tan skin as his black pirate boots pounded forcefully across the cement floor. His midnight cape with the golden symbols swirled around him as he purposefully made his way to her.

Deana's breath caught in her throat. She had forgotten how magnificent he looked in his own raiment.

As he approached her, he whipped out the Cearix and went down on one knee, his cape floating about him. Bowing his head, he held the Cearix out to her, blade facing her, saying in a firm, bold voice, "Your servant."

Deana stood transfixed, looking down at the top of his golden head. He obviously expected her to do something. But what? Take the blade, perhaps? She reached out and gingerly took the blade from him.

Lorgin remained with his arms outstretched in front of him, head bowed. Now what did he want? It wasn't as if she knew what the damn alien wanted!

Annoyed, she started to return the dagger to him the way she had been taught since a young child. *Always hand a knife back to someone with the handle facing them, Deana.* Good advice, since this blade looked sharp as hell.

She was about to do just that when, for a reason she couldn't name, she abruptly changed her mind and handed it back to him exactly the way he had given it to her, the blade facing his heart.

Without looking up, his warm, powerful hands covered hers on the hilt, sending a wave of tingling heat up her arms and throughout her body. Then he reclaimed the dagger, swiftly embedding it in its sheath as he stood.

He gazed down at her, eyes heavy-lidded with a passion she didn't understand. "Your king," he murmured arrogantly.

Before she could ask what this was all about, he turned to Kristen. "Did you not witness this?" he demanded.

Kristen was stunned. "Y-yes."

"Your name, mistress?"

"K-Kristen. Kristen Brown."

Lorgin looked upward, throwing his arms wide as his compelling voice boomed throughout the hall.

"I, Lorgin ta'al Krue,
Knight of the Charl,
Holder of the Fourth Power,
Son of the line of Lodarres,
Whose destiny is about to speak,
Hereby claim Kristen Brown of this world
As Witness.
LET IT BE SEALED FOR ALL ETERNITY!"

There was dead silence in the room. Then spontaneous applause broke out all over the place. They think this is a skit! Deana looked around, not sure what to make of all this. She felt Lorgin's strong hand at her elbow.

"Come with me, *zira*." His tongue rolled the r on the strange word.

She looked up at him, recognizing *that* look. At any moment those little pink lights were going to start up.

Yes, they had definitely better leave.

69

*   *   *

They entered their hotel room.

Deana turned to confront Lorgin about that outrageous scene he had just enacted. She opened her mouth to let him have it, then abruptly closed it. He was approaching her with a purpose she was not sure of.

She backed against the wall, but he was not to be put off. He picked her up in his arms as if she were nothing more than a rag doll, his cape fluttering around both of them.

Then she felt a slight breeze and a strange prickling sensation. There was a peculiar light in the room. Suddenly a small circular hole of flashing colored lights appeared from out of nowhere. It grew and grew, almost engulfing half the room.

Deana was terrified and ducked her head inside Lorgin's cloak, seeking the security of his embrace. He wrapped his cape fully around her as he stepped into the portal. He inclined his head to hers, and his low, deep voice rippled over her like the pulses of light.

''Now do we go home, zira.''

She knew nothing more until her eyes opened onto a new universe.

Chapter Four

The bed was so hard!

The least this hotel could do was provide better mattresses for what they charged per night. Deana groaned. It felt as if she were lying on a slab of rock. She blearily opened her eyes.

Lorgin was leaning over her, his hands on either side of her hips, his expression . . . concerned. He was smoothing back her hair with a gentle hand.

"Lorgin." Deana weakly smiled up at him. What did he look so worried about?

"Adeeann, how are you feeling?"

How am I feeling? What a strange question. "I'm fine."

She started to sit up when a wave of dizziness washed over her. She cried out, and Lorgin quickly lowered her back down.

She put a steadying hand to her forehead. "Everything's spinning. Am I sick or something?"

71

"Not in the manner you have asked."

What the hell did that mean?

Her hand fell back down to her side, hitting the hard mattress. She blinked as her fingers felt along the rough, cool surface. It was a slab of rock!

Then she remembered . . . the strange pulsing lights, the whirring tunnel, and Lorgin carrying her directly into that maelstrom. Her eyes shifted warily to his.

"Tell me that what I'm thinking isn't true," she whispered.

Lorgin's hand brushed her cheek. "The effects of the phasing will pass," he said softly. "There is always this feeling of displacement the first time. Yours was more severe than our people's. I think this is because of your belief system as regards the nature of reality." He hesitated. "Although this is just a guess on my part, since no one from your world has ever transported through the tunnels. You will feel better in a short time."

Deana closed her eyes, fear making two tears track slowly down her cheeks as the significance of his words hit her. *He had taken her into another universe!* The enormity of it rendered her almost senseless.

Until she felt his fingers tenderly wipe the tears from her face, as if that could make her forgive him! Her eyes flashed open full of fire, leveled directly at him.

She brushed aside his irksome hand. "You told me you couldn't go back! Why did you lie to me?"

Lorgin tried not to smile as the *gharta* returned. "I did not lie to you, Little Fire. I said I could not go back. I did not say I did not know *how* to go back."

Her eyes narrowed in a fair imitation of him.

"Semantics? You knew very well how I felt . . ." She stopped as her eyes traveled about the room, or cave, they were in.

It was a small chamber with some kind of phosphorescent ceiling. The temperature in the room was fairly cool so she suspected that they were well underground. Behind Lorgin's right shoulder she could make out an opening which appeared to lead into a much larger cavern. A fur of unknowable origin partially covered the entrance. Strange-colored lights were coming from beyond the doorway, the source of which didn't bear thinking about. Her astounded gaze shifted back to his.

"Where am I, or should I ask what planet is this? Sound familiar?" she asked sarcastically.

Lorgin sighed. He'd rather battle a *hira* beast than have this conversation with Adeeann, and when she found out the rest of it, she would try to have his *kani* on a platter.

He rubbed the bridge of his nose with his thumb and forefinger. Travel the universe and women were still the same! There was no deciphering them. Lorgin learned long ago that the best thing was not to even try. Still, her response more than confused him. She should be grateful, should she not? Had he not removed her from her backward unenlightened world? Had he not offered the Cearix to her in the time-old tradition? What did she have to be angry about?

As these thoughts gained momentum, he pinned her to the rock with an icy glare.

"And if I tell you where you are, will it matter so much then? Will you know this place in relation to any other place?" He coldly clipped his words.

Deana raised her chin a fraction, trying to not let him see how his harsh but truthful words had affected her. "It would be a start—a focal point, if you will, to map my position."

A lot of good it would do her, halfway between here and nowhere. Her lips quivered at the thought, but she did not lower her eyes from his.

The slight tremble of her mouth did not go unnoticed by

73

Lorgin. The coldness of a moment ago melted within him, replaced by a sudden rush of tenderness. "You are frightened." He took her hand in his large one. "There is no need to be, *zira*. I will not let anything happen to you."

Deana drew in a deep breath, counted to ten, then came out shooting. "*You big dumb idiot!* You're what happened! I feel like punching you right in the kisser!" Intending to do just that, she looked up into his beautiful lavender eyes and shocked herself by bursting into tears.

"Adeeann . . ."

Not knowing what else to do, Lorgin gently gathered her in his arms, pulling her onto his lap. She sobbed all over his silky white shirt as he stroked her hair and tried to soothe her, while discreetly looking over his shoulder to make sure he wasn't being observed. After all, he did have a reputation to maintain. He *was* a warrior.

"We are on Ryka Twelve." The warrior's voice was now distinctly gentle. He spoke into her hair, his voice conciliatory in tone. "It is a small satellite of Ryka, an immense planet in the Graion System. This moon, one of fifteen, supports an atmosphere capable of sustaining life—barely.

"The inhabitants live underground in a series of interconnecting naturally formed caves that link the underworld of the planet. We are in what you would call a rural area—an outlying region. The population here is sparse, and made up of various clans. They are a simple people, but quite friendly to those they trust."

She sniffed and looked up at him, leaning back against his arm. "Is this where you live?"

He wiped her cheeks with the back of his hand, letting his fingers glide across the creamy skin. His action caused his hair to fall forward and tickle her nose. Deana crossed her eyes trying to focus on the lock of hair before blowing it away. Lorgin tried not to laugh out loud.

He looked down at her serious little face. "No, zira, this is not my home planet. I will take you to Aviara, but not for a while. There are . . . some things that have to be taken care of first, before we can go home. Word was sent to me that my mentor Yaniff is coming to meet with you. He should arrive shortly; I imagine he has much to discuss with you."

Before we can go home That didn't sound quite right. "Lorgin . . . you are going to take me back to *my* home, I mean after I've visited for a while, aren't you?"

Lorgin contemplated her with a thoughtful expression. His thumb rubbed the underside of her jaw before he answered her. "I—"

He was interrupted by a young woman who entered the room carrying a thin slab of rock on which rested a large steaming bowl. She was fairly tall, although much shorter than Lorgin. She had long black hair, sloe eyes, and a delicate face with elfin ears.

Exotically beautiful, Deana thought, wondering how well the alien woman knew Lorgin. From the looks she was giving him, Deana would bet that she knew him *very* well. In any event, the woman's appearance had prevented Lorgin from answering her question. Was it her imagination, or did Lorgin look grateful for the intrusion?

"Here is Miki with some nourishment for you. This broth will help your dizziness and make you feel better."

"What is it, chicken soup?" she asked facetiously.

Lorgin furrowed his brows, not knowing what chicken soup was. He decided to ignore the question. Placing her back on the slab, he stood up, saying, "I will be in the next chamber should you need me. Miki will see to your present needs."

He leaned over and whispered low in her ear. "Do not under any circumstances remove the Shimalee." That said, he turned and exited the chamber.

What the hell was a Shimalee?

Did the man ever make sense? And where could she possibly remove this thing, whatever it was, to? She could hardly sit up, for crying out loud. And another thing, this rock bed was getting as bad as a Sealy posturepedic. Didn't these people believe in padding?

While Deana was mentally going through her list of grievances, Miki's eyes followed Lorgin as he made his way into the main chamber. She kept her sights trained on him until he stepped out of view, entering a side tunnel. Sighing, she picked up the pranitei broth and gazed at the newcomer.

She was very beautiful in an exotic way. Miki had never seen that color hair before, but had to admit it was pretty to look at. She sighed again. Lorgin used to visit her often when he was in this sector. As a lover, she had known no better. And she had known many. Lorgin's force was powerful and his energy strong. Even she, who never weakened, could not keep up with him. She had, of course, never felt his *true* power, for this was not for one such as she.

Yes, she acknowledged to herself, this woman with the red hair would know Lorgin's power, and for that she envied her. But she could like her too, for in truth she seemed very nice and very alone.

Miki shrugged resignedly, knowing Lorgin would never come to her again. For she had heard the warrior call this newcomer of his *zira*. Truly, there would be no more nights for her or any other woman, except this one, with Lorgin ta'al Krue.

Miki stepped over to Deana and offered her the bowl of broth, smiling encouragingly at her.

Deana gingerly took the bowl from her. Although she could not understand the woman's language, she appeared to be genuinely friendly. Looking down at the strange brew, Deana sniffed it experimentally. Surprisingly, it had a pleasant aroma, but God knew what was in it. Vegetable, animal, or mineral?

Then again, did it really matter? She had to eat, and Lorgin had assured her it would help her dizziness. Shrugging fatalistically, she put the bowl to her mouth and drank. The broth had an herbal, fruity taste, and was actually quite tasty.

After drinking it down, she decided she might like some more, and feeling rather like Oliver Twist, held out the bowl to Miki, saying, "Please, I'd like some more."

To her surprise, Miki motioned a refusal, although softening it with a smile. Deana was wondering why she couldn't have any more when she felt a wave of drowsiness overtake her. Lying back down on the slab, she cursed herself for being all kinds of a fool. Lorgin had obviously had her drugged, she thought furiously as sleep overcame her.

She awoke abruptly, her eyes scanning the chamber as the residual effects of the broth left her. The outer cavern was silent, unlike earlier, when she had heard many voices out there. She supposed that by whatever system these people used to count out a day's period, it was their middle of the night. Even the unknown glowing substance emanating from the ceiling had dimmed, leaving a soft glow.

As she sat up, she noticed that Lorgin must have checked on her while she slept, for his cape covered her, warding off the chill of the stone. She no longer felt dizzy and disoriented, but her back was sore from the rock bed.

Noting that the animal skin now completely covered the doorway to the outer chamber, Deana started seriously wondering what alien plumbing would be like, and hoped that Lorgin would return soon to enlighten her. She didn't know how she would pantomime that request to anybody. Just as she was worrying over this, the curtain was moved aside and Lorgin entered.

"I thought you might be awake. Have the effects of the phasing diminished?" He sat next to her on the platform.

"Yes. They seem to be gone entirely." She ran her fingers through her hair in an effort to smooth it out. Lorgin started to help her by rearranging an errant strand, but she angrily slapped his hand away. "What was the idea of drugging me without telling me?"

Lorgin was amused by her senseless anger. "Are you not better?"

"That is not an answer to my question."

He looked down at her through half-veiled eyes. "I think that it is."

Arrogant *and presumptuous!*

Deana knew it was pointless to try to carry this any further. He would never understand the point she was trying to make. She gathered his cloak tightly around her and stared at the wall in a huff.

Lorgin's hand came up to clasp her chin, gently turning her to face him. "Would you not have done the same for me? If I were in your world, feeling ill, and you knew what to give me to make me feel better?"

How was he able to always defuse her objections, making her look childish in the bargain? Rather than answer him directly, she shrugged her shoulders noncommittally.

Lorgin's eyes glinted with humor. "Of course, my *gharta*, perhaps on second thought, you would prefer to let me suffer a little, hmm?"

Deana did not like the course this conversation was taking at all. In mounting distress she blurted out, "I have to go to the bathroom!" This time, Lorgin did burst out laughing.

"Stop laughing this instant! It isn't funny."

Lorgin valiantly tried to contain his mirth. "No, I can see that." He stood up, taking her hand. "Come with me."

He led her to a far corner of the small chamber where a tiny area had been curtained off with another animal skin. Pushing the skin aside, he pointed to a hole in the cavern floor. Next to the hole, a small stream trickled down the wall of the cave.

Deana looked at him horrified. "There?"

"There. It is a bottomless pit." His eyes twinkled. "At least everyone assumes it is. The caves are full of them. I agree that it is somewhat primitive. However, such is the world we are on."

"When in Ryka do as the Rykans do?"

He thought about her words, then nodded to her. "Exactly put. You may cleanse yourself in the stream; the water is pure." He turned and left the niche, closing the curtain behind him.

Deana finished her business quickly and left the area, having no doubt remaining why she had never liked camping. Lorgin was resting on the slab.

"That's one comfortable bed you have there, Lorgin."

He acknowledged her words with a murmur of agreement. Rubbing his eyes, he said, "This is not a world known for its comforts." He looked at her. "Come, let us retire. I am tired. It would be better for you to have more rest as well."

Deana put her hands on her hips. "And where am I supposed to sleep? That's a twin slab you're stretched out on."

"There is plenty of room here."

"There is no room there."

He sat up. "Adeeann, come to bed. I am weary and I am not going to argue with you over this."

"Fine, then we won't argue. Besides, I might as well just

sleep on the floor. They both share the same mattress filling.''

Before she could lower herself to the floor, Lorgin stood up and scooped her in his arms, carrying her to the platform. He talked over her objections.

"I have said I will not argue about this. I will be your mattress tonight.''

Deana's mouth fell open.

He stretched out on the slab placing her on top of him, then covered them both with his cape. Placing an arm at her waist, and the other cupping her head, he whispered a firm good night to her.

Deana nuzzled the warm skin beneath her cheek as she opened her eyes. This is getting to be a habit, she mused. Naturally, she had managed to find the vee of his shirt in her sleep, and her hand had slipped inside the shirt looking for warmth. Knowing Lorgin, she didn't doubt for a minute he was already awake.

She raised her sleepy eyes. He looked down at her lazily.

"I bet I'm more comfortable than you," she said smugly.

"Of this I have no doubt," he answered her wryly, adjusting his position on the rock.

It wasn't only the rock that was causing his discomfort, and as soon as Adeeann was more awake she would realize this. At that moment her eyes widened as she moved, making her own discovery.

Oh dear.

She looked at his eyes. Lazy pink sparks were appearing intermittently in the amethyst irises. She let out a sigh of relief. At least he didn't look like he was going to nuke. He spoiled that safe thought with his next words.

"Come," he murmured, placing his hand behind her head. "Give your mouth to me.''

She thought of refusing for all of a nanosecond. He looked so damned sexy lying there beneath her, his hair spread out over the rock, his eyes so sparkly and slumberous.

Oh, what the hey, one kiss won't kill me.

Unable to help herself, she leaned forward and lightly brushed her lips across his. Lorgin hit critical mass immediately.

A strong surge of current passed from him to her, causing her to gasp. His hands clamped on the back of her head as he used her surprise to deepen the kiss. His fiery tongue expertly swept inside her as his fingers threaded caressingly through her hair.

Even though Deana knew what to expect this time, the tingles that coursed through her still shocked her. Only this time was different. This time she enjoyed it. More than enjoyed it. *She craved it.*

When he removed his skilled mouth from hers and started to trail a molten path down her neck, she actually *needed* those shivers of current from him. Her breathing accelerated as his scorching lips, tongue, and—my, oh my—teeth feasted on her throat.

Yes. Oh yes. *Oh yeah . . .*

Her hands clutched his broad shoulders as Lorgin caught her earlobe between the edge of his teeth and gently tugged it, leaving a trace of special tingle there as well. She moaned softly.

Moving along her jaw line, he found her mouth again, kissing her with commanding skill. One of his masterful hands cupped her head, while the other moved to her buttocks, bringing her closer to his heat, his desire, his manhood. Deana shivered at the sense of being held captive against such raw power. Suddenly he was a favorite dish that she just couldn't get enough of. Her breathing became shallow as pulses of electric longing coursed through her.

The room was going strangely dark.

Lorgin blinked and pulled himself back. Like an unschooled youth, he had almost lost control, even though he had warned himself to limit the flow of his power to her. Such was his desire . . .

He cursed his lack of control, something that had never happened before. Even though he had taken the Oath for her, now was not the time or the place for this to happen. He wished to initiate her slowly into the joining, although he knew it would not lessen the impact of the Transference for her. In any event, he doubted he would be able to wait much longer as his need burned ever hotter in his blood.

It took a few moments for Deana to be able to focus again. She gazed at Lorgin blearily. *What had just happened to her?* She raised shaky fingers to her lips—lips that still hummed from the silky taste of his. Odd; she seemed strangely disoriented.

Lorgin sat them both up and, noting Deana's state, helped to rearrange her caftan for her.

"We must be up now, Adeeann. Yaniff will arrive soon." He gazed down tenderly at her confused expression. "Not that anything is liable to shock Yaniff at his years, but I think you would prefer to meet him on your feet. Am I not right, *zira*?" He raised an eyebrow as he awaited her answer. He could not help but feel a little pride in her response to him. Not that he ever doubted it.

Still slightly confused, she replied, "Yes, of course." Then belatedly wondered why she was agreeing with him on anything, especially when he had a look of arrogant mischief about him.

One kiss, she told herself. What had happened to her? Whatever it was, she couldn't let it happen again. My God, what must he think of her, losing control like a love-starved old maid? He probably was shocked at her exuberance, and backed off out of self-preservation.

She would put his mind at rest. "Lorgin, that will never happen again." His head whipped around.

"*What?*"

Deana looked down at her clasped hands. "That won't happen again. We—we can't allow that to happen again."

He was stunned. Did she not like the feel of him? She did and by *Aiyah*, he knew it! He stormed at her. "Whatever are you talking about?"

She drew back at the vehemence of his response. She hadn't expected him to react like this. "Just what I said. That can never happen again. When I leave here "

"It can and will. *Often.*" He towered over her, furious at her insult. "You are not going any—"

His words were interrupted by a glowing light at the end of the chamber. The brightness grew and grew, forming the now familiar circular passage that was used by these beings as a means of transport. Deana was almost becoming blasé to the event, except she was curious as to what Lorgin had been about to say. Never mind, she could always argue with him later. This promised to be very interesting. She had to wonder why this Yaniff dude was coming to talk to her.

Out of the light walked the strangest menagerie she had ever seen.

The focal point was a very, very old man. His silver hair hung down his back; his crimson robes hung to the floor. Like Lorgin's cape, his robes were covered in strange golden symbols. In his right hand he carried a long scepter, the end of which glowed iridescent. On his left shoulder perched a huge winged animal. The bird's head resembled an eagle's, but not quite; its body resembled an owl's, but not quite.

As the old man approached her, Deana noted that his eyes were pure black, neither giving nor receiving light, and she couldn't discern any pupils in them. She was startled as the bird thing on his shoulder turned its head to her and it had the very same eyes, black as night and just as fathomless.

Something about the man seemed vaguely familiar. Then it hit her. He looked just like numerous artists' renditions she had seen of Merlin.

Next to the man prowled an extremely large cat. Its fur was black, long, and fluffy; its eyes were quite strange, as one was ice blue, the other amber gold. The animal moved with a grace and beauty exceptional even for a feline. As the beast got closer, she wondered if it truly was a cat. It captured her in its hypnotic dual-colored focus and simply stared at her. Deana discreetly edged closer to Lorgin.

The old man spoke in a quiet but commanding voice.

"Lorgin, your . . . *frustration* emanates to me. Endeavor to control it."

She would have expected Lorgin to bristle at that remark, considering the way he reacted to her statements to him, so was surprised when he only nodded curtly.

The strange cat jumped up on the slab and swished his tail, as if he were enjoying Lorgin's set-down by the old man.

Deana wasn't at all sure she liked this Yaniff dude with the stern voice, until she caught his gaze and he winked at her. She smiled tremulously back at him. Damn if he didn't look like Merlin!

Lorgin's eyes flicked to the cat. "So, I see Rejar has come."

Yaniff noted the cat on the rock platform. "Yes. It was his desire to aid you in your quest."

More likely his desire to bedevil me, Lorgin sighed to himself.

Yaniff smiled, for he had heard Lorgin's thought. "Who was I to stop him from this noble gesture?"

Lorgin responded wryly, "Who, indeed?" As if Yaniff did not have the power to do as he wished.

Yaniff's eyes twinkled. "Have a care, he understands the words you speak."

It was not hard for Lorgin to figure out how the cat had acquired this power. Out of respect to Deana, they were conversing in her language; Yaniff would have learned the language from him telepathically, and then transferred this ability to Rejar. As a seventh-level mystic such abilities were commonplace to Yaniff.

The old man turned to Deana, holding out a withered, ancient hand to her. His eyes briefly fell to the torque on her neck. "Come here, child, let me look upon you."

She felt Lorgin's strong hands on her shoulders, propelling her forward. When she stood in front of him, he took her hand in his. Yaniff stared intently at her for several moments, sort of giving her the willies. Finally, he released her.

"You have done well, Lorgin ta'al Krue. *I add my seal to this oath, born of yesterday and tomorrow.*"

Lorgin seemed pleased with that statement, whatever it meant. People sure talked strange around here, Deana thought. Why didn't they ever say what they were really saying?

Yaniff chuckled, an ancient, rasping sound. "Because, child, it might give you the willies."

Deana gasped. How did he . . .

Yaniff clasped Lorgin's arm. "Come, Lorgin, we need to speak together. There are developments that have occurred since last I saw you."

"Very well." He faced Deana. "I will be back shortly. Rejar will stay with you." He turned to leave, then stopped

85

as if something important had occurred to him. He turned and spoke to the cat.

"Rejar, *behave yourself.*"

The cat swished its tail as Lorgin left.

Deana looked over at the strange cat. He seemed harmless enough at the moment. She decided to go over and try to befriend it. Sitting down next to the beast, she said, "Everyone is talking to you as if you understand, kitty. Do you understand?"

The cat swished his tail.

"You're awfully pretty; would you mind if I pet you?" The cat rubbed his face against her hand.

Deana began petting him, realizing he really was just a puss, no matter his great size. She began stroking the soft fur on his head, then scratched behind his left ear.

Rejar began a deep, contented purr.

Lorgin led Yaniff through one end of the main cavern to a private area where they might converse without being overheard. Placing one booted foot on a ledge, Lorgin leaned over his bent knee and waited for Yaniff to begin.

"You have not told her about the Shimalee."

Lorgin looked surprised. "Have I not? With all that has happened it is no wonder. Besides, that woman has a way of shifting my focus. I begin to tell her something, and before I know it, she has changed the course of the conversation. In any event, perhaps it would be best for me to retain this information for the time being."

"That 'woman' is *your wife,* Lorgin. Another fact you have neglected to inform her of. While you might be right in withholding information on the Shimalee, I cannot condone the other. She has a right to know. Even now, she expects to return to her world." Yaniff stroked his chin and looked slyly at Lorgin. "Due to the circumstances, I am not at all sure if this constitutes a proper union."

Lorgin relinquished his relaxed pose, standing in front of Yaniff with his fists clenched. "The oath was given and taken. She returned the Cearix to me in the time-honored manner." His eyes narrowed. "She is mine and I will hear no more on it."

Yaniff chuckled to himself, having accomplished what he set out to do. Lorgin, usually so much in control, had little where this woman was concerned. The old mystic decided to fuel the fire.

"Perhaps . . . perhaps not. In order for the oath to be *irrevocable*, you must complete the Transference. This you have not done."

Lorgin's gaze flicked to Bojo, who peered at him from Yaniff's shoulder like a nosy old woman. "She is not ready yet. She needs more time."

Yaniff sighed. "Time, my friend, is something we do not have. *Make* her ready. We cannot risk her falling under the power of another. She was meant for you, but destiny can play tricks on the unwary." Yaniff's eyes suddenly gleamed with humor. "Do not hesitate; I have complete confidence in your abilities in *this* area, Lorgin."

Lorgin grinned sheepishly. Yaniff could be embarrassingly direct at times. He decided to sidetrack the old mystic. "What was this development you spoke of earlier?"

Yaniff was not sidetracked, but he knew Lorgin had heard his words and would act accordingly. He answered the question put to him. "There is a man here on Ryka Twelve who recently returned from a journey to the far sector. Information was given to me that he might have some knowledge which might be of value to you. He resides in Pod 25."

Lorgin raised his eyebrows. "That is a long journey from

this cavern—on the border of what the inhabitants here call the Wilderness Reaches.''

Yaniff nodded. ''Yes. We should begin the journey without delay.''

Lorgin was surprised. ''You are accompanying us?''

''Only as far as the tunnel relay. As you know, there is a dampening field here. There are only certain fixed points from which the tunnels can be entered. Even I am bound by natural law. Another matter—Adeeann must be equipped with a translator device as soon as possible. It is dangerous for her not to understand what occurs around her.''

''I agree.''

''There is a healer in the direction we travel, in the Wilderness Reaches. She can do it.''

Lorgin nodded. ''What is the name of this man I seek in Pod 25?''

''He is called Greka al Nek. He is not to be trusted, but for the right amount of coin he will be honest enough for your purposes.''

Yaniff peered at the wall in the direction of the cave Deana was in. ''Let us return to your zira. Rejar is up to mischief.''

Lorgin did not wait for Yaniff to catch up with him as he bounded back to the cave he had left Adeeann in.

Chapter Five

Lorgin's voice boomed in the small chamber. "By the blood of *Aiyah*, woman! Do not scratch behind his left ear!"

Deana's head whipped up at the urgency in his tone. Horrified, she looked down at the cat, quickly standing to put some distance between her and it. Was it poisonous in some unknown way? Would she even now start seeing her life flash before her eyes? No matter how awful the truth was, she had to know.

"Why ever not?" she demanded of Lorgin, expecting the worst.

"Because he likes it too much!" Lorgin bellowed.

"Because . . ." she sputtered. "Now that makes a lot of sense!" She stormed over to Lorgin. "You scared me half to death, I ought to . . ."

And she did.

Kicked him hard on his shin.

Unfortunately the effect was spoiled by the thickness of his boot. "Ohhh!" She stormed off to the other side of the cave.

Lorgin leveled an angry glare at the cat.

Rejar gazed tranquilly up at him, as cats often do when they are being the most mischievous. "Meowww."

Lorgin took a step toward the cat, but Yaniff's hand on his arm stopped him. "We do not have time for this foolishness. We must make haste to depart."

Lorgin walked over to Deana, placing his hand on her elbow. "We must leave now, zira."

Deana *was* put out with him; nonetheless, she felt a frisson at the man's touch—a touch that was becoming all too familiar to her. She frowned up at him. "You are totally weird, do you know that?"

He smiled at her comment, while leading her from the chamber.

Deana could only gape at the outer cavern they entered. It was huge, perhaps the size of two football fields. Everywhere people were milling about in what looked to be a bazaar.

She could see several stalls selling various wares, some of which she had never seen before. There were carts brimming with all manner of items—beautiful sheer materials, jewelry, exotic foods, and much, much, more. Performers, dancers, and jugglers entertained the crowds. Strange music filled the air. It reminded her of stories she had read of the marketplaces in Elizabethan times.

Except for the aliens. There were all manner of beings here, presumably from other worlds. The sights, colors, sounds, and smells were overwhelming.

To think that she was probably the first Earthling to ever see this! To experience alien cultures coming together and interacting! She felt Lorgin's finger under her chin as he closed her gaping mouth.

Lorgin. He had done this for her.

Deana beamed at him. "Lorgin, this is wonderful! Thank you! Thank you! Thank you!"

Lorgin was momentarily spellbound by her radiant beauty. He had no idea what had made his Little Fire so happy, but he would be more than willing to take credit for it. He leaned toward her, lightly touching her lips with his own.

He murmured against her soft lips, "It is just a sacri, a marketplace—nothing compared to the wonders I will show you, Little Fire." Unable to help himself, he placed his arms around her, this time deepening the kiss.

Oh, he tastes so sweet, Deana thought, once again becoming somewhat dreamy. And a little spicy, too . . .

Lost in their embrace, neither heard Yaniff approach until he noisily cleared his throat. "Ahem! Now is not the time for tarrying, Lorgin."

Lorgin broke off the embrace as Rejar scurried forth into the fracas of the cave. "Come, *zira*, I need to purchase you clothing more suitable to our journey."

He led her to a stall which displayed various articles of clothing. Deana looked at several garments made of a beautiful, printed silky fabric, and was quite disappointed when Lorgin purchased a simple pair of harem type trousers and a tunic made of a heavy homespun material in a drab olive color. He also purchased a matching cape with a hood, and a pair of nondescript black boots.

Deana eyed the ugly garments. "Gee, thanks, I don't know what to say."

Lorgin patiently explained to her that these clothes were purchased with the specific purpose of *not* attracting attention. "Some of the areas we will be traveling through attract all manner of unsavory characters, including slavers from the Oberion colonies. We do not need to draw attention to your beauty, Adeeann."

Her beauty? Jeez, who would believe it? And put that way, who am I not to humor the man?

After she had changed, they continued through the marketplace as Lorgin made various purchases he deemed necessary for their journey. How he made this determination was a mystery to her, as his list of purchases reminded her of scavenger-hunt booty.

He bought them all, including Rejar, small pastries filled with something grainy that tasted spicy. After they had eaten, Lorgin placed all of his purchases on the ground and nodded to Yaniff.

The old mystic extended his now glowing scepter, closed his eyes, and so help her, the items vanished! Deana noticed several bystanders giving Yaniff discreet looks and a wide berth. She correctly guessed that such ability was not a usual occurrence here.

"Where did the stuff go? And why did you go to the trouble of buying all of that if you were just going to have Yaniff make it disappear?"

Placing an arm around her shoulders, Lorgin explained, "Yaniff sent everything up to the next dimensional level. How do I convey this? In this next dimensional level, everything folds in on itself, and exists in a different spatial plane. When we need the items, Yaniff will bring them out of that dimensional plane into this one. Is this clear to you?"

Deana scoffed. "As mud! All I got out of that is that you've got plenty of closet space that follows you around." A brilliant thought occurred to her. "You know, you, ah, I mean . . . we, *we* could make a fortune with that idea back on . . . *Disney.* You see, they have these things called self-storage places, where people rent space for storing their stuff and . . ."

As she was talking, Lorgin led her through a throng of

people to a side tunnel, throwing an amused glance over her head at Yaniff, who just raised his eyes to the ceiling while shaking his head.

Rejar scampered behind, his tail swishing.

It wasn't long before they left the sounds and bustling activity of the large cavern far behind. The tunnel passage they traversed was not as brightly lit as the cavern. And it seemed to Deana that the further they got away from the main cavern, the darker it became, until all that remained of the light was a dull green glow emanating from the ceiling and walls.

Lorgin insisted that they travel in single file as he led, followed by Deana, then Yaniff, with Rejar bringing up the rear. What good a cat would do if they needed protection from behind was beyond her, but amazingly, the cat stayed to the back of the line.

When they had first left the market area, the tunnel had been fairly wide, allowing for the many travelers to this sector to converge into the city from the various tunnels. However, the farther they traveled, the narrower the tunnel became, until there was only room for two people to walk abreast.

Deana realized the reason they traveled in single file when they passed several parties going in the opposite direction. At these times, it seemed that Lorgin was very tense and watchful, often glancing behind him at the rest of the party to be sure nothing was amiss.

They walked for hours, crossing intersecting tunnels every now and then. Deana wondered how anyone could know where they were going in this seemingly endless maze, marveling that Lorgin did not hesitate in his movements at all.

She also wondered when they were going to stop and rest; her feet were starting to hurt. Putting one foot in front of the other in robotic fashion, she gazed at the beautiful crystalline structures on the ceiling and idly wondered if they were composed of gypsum. Since this was not Earth, there was no way of knowing.

"We will rest soon, child." Yaniff's kind voice came from behind her.

She turned and gave him a grateful smile, noting that the orb on the end of his staff was glowing, giving the old man a little more light for his steps. It rather endeared him to her.

After a while, the tunnel began to widen, and soon they found themselves in a cavernous room abundant with stalactite and stalagmite formations. A few stray wayfarers were resting and eating.

Lorgin led his group off to a far corner behind some large columns, away from the other travelers. Yaniff slowly lowered himself onto a rock while Deana gratefully sank to the floor at his feet. She rested her back against the side of the rock the old man had perched on. Lorgin leaned against a pillar, and motioned to Yaniff, who used his staff to produce some of the supplies Lorgin had purchased.

Surprisingly, the old mystic proceeded to cut up a bunch of odd-looking vegetables with a little knife, threw them into a caldron-like pot, and added some liquid from a pouch. Deana couldn't help grinning at the incongruity of it.

"Something amuses you, child?" Yaniff asked her, his gaze never leaving the pot.

Deana was almost getting used to this man's uncanny ability to know her moods—even when he had his back to her, as he did now.

"I was just wondering why you don't wave your magic wand and produce the soup already made."

Yaniff chuckled. "Never tastes the same that way."

"I think I know what you mean. It would be like using a microwave to bake bread."

Lorgin sauntered over to them. "With all this talk we will be here till the morrow before we eat." He waved his arm across the caldron and a fire sprang up under it. Deana's eyes widened.

"Do not look so surprised, Adeeann. Did I not tell you I had power over fire?" He walked off to a curtained area, presumably to use the facilities. Deana made a face at his retreating back.

Rejar, who had been watching her, sauntered over and curled up next to her, placing his head on her lap. She absentmindedly stroked his fur, her thoughts still on Lorgin.

"Sometimes he is so obnoxiously arrogant!" she fumed.

Rejar purred his agreement.

"If only he weren't so devastatingly gorgeous." Rejar picked up his head and stared at her. "Well, he is, so don't look at me like I've just lost my mind."

The cat blinked.

"I've never met anyone like him before." She gazed down at the cat. "I'll tell you a secret," she whispered.

Rejar stopped purring and, as if intent on her words, leaned closer to her.

"He is the sexiest man I have ever seen. When he looks at me in a certain way . . . I absolutely melt."

Rejar widened his eyes.

Deana didn't think a cat could look amused, but this one certainly did. "So, you think it's funny, do you?"

Rejar put his head back on her lap and started purring again.

"See if I scratch behind your left ear again," Deana grumbled as she petted his head.

While the soup was cooking, Yaniff sat next to them, his gaze falling on Rejar. "You do enjoy stirring up your own soup, eh, Rejar?" The cat swished his tail without changing his comfortable position. Yaniff chuckled. "Best be off before he comes back, if you know what is good for you, scamp."

Rejar begrudgingly picked himself up and moved off to lie in front of the fire.

Deana knit her brow. "What's with Lorgin and his cat?"

Yaniff seemed amused by her question, but declined to explain, choosing instead to question Deana about her world.

Deana had a few questions of her own. "Yaniff, when you made the items Lorgin purchased disappear, I noticed that many of the people near us seemed in awe of your ability. I was under the impression that magic was a rather common occurrence here. Why did they seem so fascinated, yet fearful?"

Yaniff reached up and stroked Bojo as he thoughtfully replied, "Magic is a common occurrence here, Adeeann, but the ability to perform it is not. Very few have such ability in our worlds, as the training is long, the discipline required strict. The supplicant must also be born with a latent ability to 'sing' to the forces which comprise our existence. And of course, some have more innate talent than others."

Yaniff gazed thoughtfully at Rejar. "Then, there are some that have great abilities, but refuse to acknowledge the gift in themselves."

"So, what you're saying is that those that can 'sing' to these forces are looked upon as specialists here, as we, in my world, would view a doctor or engineer?"

"Specialists, yes, but there is also a mystical 'respect' involved. I believe that is what you perceived as the fearfulness amongst the villagers."

"Did you teach Lorgin?"

"*Teaching*. It is an ongoing process throughout one's existence in this plane."

Deana shook her head. "This is very different from my world."

"Not really. Yours is a world based on technology. Our world is based on mystical principles you call magic. The machines from your world which I have seen in Lorgin's mind would be as legends to our people. They would regard your devices as you would stories of the unicorn. Although there are similarities, what is real for us is not always real in your world, and vice-versa. For this reason, our universes must exist independently of each other. Knowledge of each other would disrupt the very fabric of existence, the basis of reality for each of our spaces, causing total annihilation."

Deana gulped. "Sort of like matter and anti-matter combining?"

Yaniff nodded. "A very similar concept."

"Basis of reality . . . a great scientist of ours talked about reality in frames of reference; he called it relativity."

"Then he was a great mystic."

"Um, I'm not sure he would've viewed it that way."

Yaniff smiled wryly. "Perhaps not."

An uncomfortable thought occurred to Deana. "Yaniff, I am aware of your existence. Wouldn't this constitute a threat to our universes?"

Yaniff looked at her thoughtfully. The fact that he knew she would not be returning to her world must not figure into his response. He had a trust to Lorgin, and it was the younger man's responsibility to guide her to her destiny. His reply was measured.

"Not necessarily. You would have no proof of our existence, other than your word. While one's word is good enough in our land, in a world based on fact and science, I believe it will not be enough. They will need irrefutable evidence, and even then belief would be slow in coming. Such is the nature of the existence of your kind.''

Deana sighed. He was right about that. No one would believe her in a million years. Worse, they'd probably throw her in Chumley's if she became too vocal about it. The best she could do was enjoy the adventure, and when she was back in her own living room, convince herself that she hadn't imagined the whole thing. Perhaps if she wrote it down as a story . . .

As her thoughts wandered along these lines, something occurred to her. ''Yaniff, if your universe is based on magic as you say, why does Lorgin have a translation device?''

Yaniff smiled. ''The device is not based on technological principles, Adeeann. It is''—he paused, searching for the right way to explain it to her—''for lack of better words, an intricately contained 'conjure' of the Guild. The Guild of Aviara produce many such devices for the Alliance, a useful tool in trade and negotiation.''

''That's interesting; like what?''

''Well, for instance, the clothes you are wearing.''

Deana gazed dismally down at her drab outfit. ''They made this stunning creation?''

''No, but the merchant told Lorgin that the Weavers' Guild of Aviara cast a spell on it so that it would continually cleanse and renew itself.''

''Terrific,'' Deana responded dryly.

Yaniff stroked his chin. ''I see what you mean; one might not necessarily want such an outfit to renew itself. But, in spite of the appearance, I assure you Lorgin insisted on the Weavers' Guild stamp. Such a stamp marks the cloth as being of the highest quality.''

And costly, no doubt. Devices, Yaniff called them. They would explain many little questions she had, oddities that stuck in the back of her mind; things that didn't quite jell with the way things worked in the world as she knew it.

Lorgin approached them, leaning down on one knee in front of Deana. "After we eat we will resume our journey. There is an inn about half a day's journey from this point. I hope to arrive there before evening, so that we may have a more secure place to bed down for the night. Do you think you can make it that far, Adeeann?"

"I don't know—that's a lot of walking on top of what we've already done today. Are there no places to rest along the way?"

Lorgin smiled sympathetically. "There are a few. I know this will be a hard journey on you, *zira,* but believe me when I tell you it is of the utmost importance that we have a safe resting place for the night. We are headed to a region the locals call the Wilderness Reaches. The closer we get to it, the farther away we are from civilized behavior. The area abounds with cutthroats and scoundrels. Your safety is always my first concern." He reached out and gently stroked her hair.

He's looking at me like that again. "Th-thank you, Lorgin. I'll try my best."

He leaned forward and affectionately kissed the tip of her nose. "Good. If you get too tired, you must tell me, Little Fire."

She nodded, and he abruptly rose to check on the soup.

Deana had been able to endure four hours of the walk before she collapsed and could go no further. Lorgin had been very upset with her, not for tiring, but for not telling him she was tiring. Picking her up, he carried her the rest of the way, berating her foolish pride for not admitting to her dwindling strength. For a good portion of the final part of the journey he told her exactly how he felt about that. If Deana hadn't been so tired, she would have punched him in the stomach.

Instead she had to endure the dressing down in silence.

The worst part of it was that Yaniff showed no signs of being fatigued, and she was embarrassed that she couldn't keep up. She felt somewhat better when Yaniff approached her later to explain that he had different resources of strength to draw upon when he needed to and she shouldn't blame herself for her exhaustion.

The "inn" turned out to be a large cavern off which many smaller caves opened on different levels. A rock pathway wound around the walls of the larger cave leading to the various "rooms." In the center of the cavern was an eating area. Deana mused that a good name for it would be Tavern in the Cavern.

Several unsavory-looking characters were huddled around the few slab tables. Lorgin apparently didn't like the looks of the riffraff in the main cave, and after putting her down, decided it would be best for them to remain in their room. Yaniff agreed.

Deana looked around their "room."

It was just an empty cave! No beds. No chairs. No furniture of any kind. It didn't even have a raised dais, like their other cave had.

"I hope they didn't charge you too much for this exquisite accommodation," she murmured sarcastically.

Lorgin turned around from the fire he had started and grinned ruefully. "As a matter of fact, they did. As this is the only lodging around here, they can command what they like for their price and have no trouble getting it. The only alternative is to sleep in the tunnels, a dangerous proposition."

For their evening meal, Yaniff prepared a stew. Deana dared not ask what was in it. It wasn't delicious, but it was palatable. After they had eaten, Lorgin retrieved a small vial from his cape and led her through a second doorway in the rear of the chamber.

The hallway twisted down and around a rock formation and opened up onto a small room from which there were no other exits. Deana noted the perennial hole in the rock floor. A natural stream cascaded down the side of the cave, forming a gentle waterfall which flowed into a small pool.

Lorgin removed his cape, saying, "We may bathe here." He began to take off his shirt. Then his hands went to the waistband of his pants.

Deana was shocked. He was stripping! "Stop!" she yelled.

Lorgin reacted instantly by grabbing the Cearix out of his waistband and whipping around, half crouched. "Something is amiss?"

Apparently he expected an intruder, not an objection. When his eyes could find no threat, he frowned at her. "Why did you yell out, Adeeann?"

"Because you were undressing!" she replied indignantly.

He looked at her as if she had lost her mind. "And how else am I supposed to bathe?"

"By yourself, of course." She raised her chin at him.

Lorgin leaned against the wall and crossed his arms over his naked chest. His dark look seared into her. He remained silent for a few moments, clearly annoyed with her. Then, in a low, firm tone, he said. *"Get undressed, zira."*

There was no way she was going to get undressed with him in the same room. "Not until you leave."

"That is not an option. I have told you there are all manner of criminals lurking about this sector. I will not leave you unguarded. Now get undressed! We waste time with this foolishness."

"I won't."

"You will."

He came away from the wall and strode purposefully toward her. Deana started backing away from him. Her eyes darted to the hallway, and she made a sudden break for it. Lorgin reached her before she had gone two steps, confirming her earlier assessment of his capabilities.

His arms came around her from behind and he lifted her bodily off the floor. Deana began kicking and yelling, which had absolutely no effect on him. She knew he was strong, but hadn't realized how strong he was until he shifted her weight to one arm, and while still holding her aloft, squirming and thrashing, he used his other hand to quickly divest her of her clothes, leaving her donned in nothing but her necklace.

She gave a yell of outrage, then a squeal of protest as he unceremoniously dumped her into the cold water of the pool.

Deana surfaced, sputtering, pushing back the sodden hair from her face. "You swine! I'll never forgive you for—"

He wasn't listening to her. He quickly removed his boots and pants and jumped into the pool next to her. She could tell by his tightly controlled expression that he was close to losing his temper.

He bore down on her from his great height, eyes narrowed. "You wish to say something to me?" His voice was ominously low.

Deana closed her mouth, knowing not to push him further. She crossed her arms protectively over her chest and, looking down at the clear water, shook her head.

"A wise decision," he intoned.

Lorgin reached over to the ledge, retrieving the vial. Deana noted that the water was crystal clear and did nothing to hide him from her eyes. She quickly closed them, lest he think she was staring at him. She opened them just as quickly when she felt his hand on her arm.

"Use this oil to cleanse yourself. It works much the way

your soap does." Deana gingerly took the vial, opening the cap. It smelled of sandalwood. "A small amount is all you need. One drop will lather your body. Another for your hair." Trying not to look at him, Deana quickly soaped her body, noting that when she rinsed off, the bubbles disappeared.

"It does not pollute the water. Something your world should learn about. Turn around, I will help you with your hair." Deana meekly obeyed. She had just experienced a side of Lorgin she didn't want to test again. At least for a while. Besides, he seemed totally oblivious to her nudity.

When she turned, Lorgin swallowed in an effort to maintain his control. The feel of her naked in his arms, thrashing about, had almost been his undoing. But when he caught his first glimpse of her, the beautifully formed full breasts, the narrow waist, the sweetly rounded hips, and long tapering legs, he almost moaned aloud. It was all he could do not to lower her to the floor by the edge of the pool and take her right then and there.

The only reason he had been able to maintain some semblance of control was his anger toward her. He had hoped she would be more comfortable around him by now. But such was not the case. He suspected that her experiences with men were limited, a thing unheard of among his people for women who had reached their maturity.

His earlier thoughts came back to haunt him. He would have to overpower her fear of him when the time was right. Yaniff believed that sooner was better than later, and Lorgin was wise enough not to disregard the mystic's insight.

But now was not the time. Tomorrow, when they reached the house of the healer . . .

Deana felt Lorgin's strong fingers massaging her scalp as he lathered her hair. He did not linger over the task, but briskly went about his business, instructing her to duck under

103

the water to rinse off. With economy of movement, he then took care of his own ablutions, rinsing his hair in the same manner. Then he levered himself out of the pool and leaned over to give her a hand out.

Deana tried to look anywhere but *there*.

She must have been obvious, for he smiled slightly at her discomfiture as he helped her out. As soon as she was clear of the water, she ran to retrieve her clothes, but he stopped her by coming up behind her and wrapping his powerful arms around her waist.

Deana froze as she felt his slick skin, cool from the water, slide tight against her.

"Lorgin!" She tried to pry his arms loose.

He bent forward whispering in her ear. "Shh . . ."

She felt warm air gently caressing her ankles. It traveled up her body, this gentle breath of air. Then the soft breeze flowed around them, drying the cool moisture from their bodies. The feel of the soft, warm breeze combined with Lorgin's smooth, cool hardness behind her, mesmerized Deana. She didn't realize that her head had fallen back against his chest, or that she had closed her eyes, overtaken by the sensuality of the moment.

Lorgin stared silently down at her, wondering if he should take advantage of her lapse. It would not be hard for him to ignite her senses now; this he knew. Just as he thought it, he quickly discarded the idea. The area was too accessible, the surroundings too primitive.

When they were dry, he turned her to face him, raising his hands above and to either side of her head, creating a breeze through her hair. The light wind curling through the tendrils of her hair was a direct extension of Lorgin. As he created and controlled the wind current, drying her locks, Deana couldn't help but feel that it was his fingers running through her hair, lifting it, caressing it, entwining with it . . .

It took her a few moments to realize he had finished and was now drying his own hair. She quickly donned her clothes, her back to him. Lorgin soon finished, put his garments on, and silently led her back to their room.

As Deana entered the chamber, she realized that Yaniff had retrieved three pallets from his "spatial" closet. She also noted three furs which she assumed were for blankets. At least she would have her own bed tonight. Although she had to admit that Lorgin had made a very nice mattress last night. She sneaked a peak at him and blushed as she thought of his good morning to her. Better to avoid that happening again. Although after the bathing session they had just shared, she was beginning to wonder why she was avoiding it.

She sank down on the nearest pallet, weary to the bone, as Yaniff called Lorgin over to him. Yaniff grinned cheekily, and something he said made Lorgin actually blush. Deana shrugged her shoulders, too tired to even wonder about it . . .

Yaniff fed Bojo a strip of meat, smirking at Lorgin.

"When I told you to get on with it, boy, I did not anticipate your enthusiasm." Yaniff fairly cackled with his mirth. "Try wooing her, Lorgin, not terrorizing the poor child."

Lorgin flushed, his gaze falling on Rejar, who swished his tale, obviously enjoying the entertainment. He squared his shoulders. "I did not terrorize her!"

Yaniff scratched his head, seemingly puzzled. "No? Half the inn heard her yells, I am sure."

Lorgin started to object, but the old mystic cut him off. "I admire such technique, my young friend." Yaniff guffawed. "You must teach me this way you have with women!"

Yaniff's laughter rang through the cave. Even the cat

seemed unable to contain his mirth, rolling onto his side, eyes gleaming.

Lorgin just shook his head and turned to the pallet where Adeeann lay. Sometimes, for all his years, Yaniff could be amazingly juvenile. Removing his cape, he lifted the fur and got into bed.

Deana shot up. "What are you doing in here?"

Lorgin stared at her. Was everyone going to give him a problem tonight?

"Sleeping." He sighed. "Just sleeping."

"Well, why don't you use one of the other pallets?"

"What other pallet? You wish me to sleep with *Yaniff*?" he asked incredulously.

"Of course not! There is another pallet." She pointed to the bedroll next to the fire.

"That belongs to Rejar."

"A cat needs a whole bedroll for himself? I don't—" She stopped, hearing a strange slithering sound coming from beyond Yaniff's pallet. "Wh-what's that noise?" She edged closer to Lorgin.

He gazed up at her, eyes innocently wide. "What noise?"

"There—did you hear it?"

"Yes," he breathed. "I hope it is not . . . it is!"

She edged closer to him. "What?"

"Look!" He pointed to a strange creature slowly making its way across the floor. It dragged itself along, using a series of suction cups beneath its wormlike body. Slime oozed out of it, and it made a sickening sucking sound as it traversed the floor.

"What *is* it?" she hissed, horrified.

"Oh no! A cave zorph."

A zorph! That was the creature Lorgin had threatened the mythology professor he could be turned into by a flick of Yaniff's fingers!

"Are—are they dangerous?"

"Yes, very. At night they slink the caverns looking for prey. You see the fluid they exude? It digests their food for them. I have heard they especially have a taste for human flesh."

"Oh, God!" Deana was totally backed against Lorgin now.

"Of course, they detest fur of any kind and have a tendency to steer clear of it." His arm snaked up and dragged her underneath the covers, fitting her backside tight into the curve of his body.

Deana gulped as she stared at the horrid creature. "So—so it will leave us alone tonight?"

Lorgin rested his chin in the crook of her shoulder. "Probably. Do not be frightened if you hear screams in the night. *Human screams.*" Deana shuddered, and Lorgin's arm came securely around her.

"Human sc-screams?" Deana clasped his arm firmly to her waist.

"After they finish their nightly feedings they return to their homes," he whispered in her ear. "To a place called Toon Town."

His teeth captured her earlobe, which he playfully tugged.

"Lorgin! How could you!" His low laughter caressed her ear, sending tremors down her neck.

"Go to sleep, Little Fire. You will be safe here. They are harmless." He kissed the side of her neck and settled in to go to sleep.

Despite Lorgin's assurances, Deana remained awake for a while, her gaze trained on the repulsive zorph.

Chapter Six

Deana stretched her stiff muscles as she awoke the next morning.

She vaguely remembered Lorgin murmuring in her ear that he and Yaniff were going down to the main cavern to check out the eating establishment, saying they would be back shortly.

Sitting up, she yawned loudly, reluctantly rising from her bed. If it had been a bit more comfortable she would have been tempted to linger under the covers longer. Without Lorgin's warm presence, there didn't seem to be any point. She flushed when she recalled how he had held her all night. For a warrior, he sure liked to cuddle.

Pressing her hands to the small of her back, she turned toward the entrance. She was intending to peek out the door down into the tavern below when she detected a slight movement out of the corner of her eye. It stopped her dead in her tracks.

Even though Lorgin had assured her those wretched zorphs were harmless, she had no desire to confront one alone. As she had pointed out to Lorgin, they didn't have to actually *do* anything to you, they could build a reputation on repulsiveness alone. He had found her reasoning quite humorous.

She slowly turned to the source of the movement, stunned to see an intruder in their room.

A man was sleeping on one of the empty pallets under a fur, his naked, muscular back facing her. Apparently, he must have entered the room after Lorgin and Yaniff had left and had decided to crash in here. Remembering what Lorgin had said about the dangers of sleeping unprotected in the tunnels, she was thankful that all the man wanted was sleep. Anything could have happened to her as she was fast asleep herself when Lorgin left.

She could still be in danger. As that thought occurred to her, the man rolled over in his sleep onto his back. Deana stared unabashedly. She knew now why his chest was bare. He was too sexy for his shirt.

The man was incredible.

His hair was silky black. Thick and long like Lorgin's, it seemed to have a texture that was . . . *fluffy.* His face was nothing short of beautiful, the intriguing features so utterly sensual, they were breathtaking. He must have sensed her appraisal, for his eyes suddenly opened.

He turned his riveting gaze directly on her.

Up until that moment, Deana would have had to say that Lorgin was the most handsome man she had ever seen. She reluctantly admitted that this strange man before her was equally devastating, his sleek presence undeniably magnetic. She was captivated by his assessing stare, mesmerized by the fact that he had one blue eye and one amber eye.

One blue eye and one amber eye . . .

109

She blinked. It couldn't be! It just couldn't be! Her mouth dropped open, aghast at the incredible notion which had seized her.

As if he knew her thoughts, the man's face curved into a slow, sensual grin, his perfect white teeth gleaming wickedly in the low light. It was a totally sexual smile, the feral potency of which nearly robbed her of her senses. Until his thoughts penetrated her mind.

{Good morrow, my brother's wife.}

"Oh, my gawd!"

Her hands flew to her head as if she could physically prevent his words from reaching her. She began to back away from him, scared half out of her wits, and ran right into Lorgin. His strong hands grabbed her shoulders, steadying her.

"What is it? Has Rejar been bothering you?" Lorgin looked over her shoulder with a thunderous expression.

Deana gazed up at Lorgin, realizing that her incredible notion was quite credible after all; she started laughing hysterically.

Lorgin gently shook her. When that had no effect, he gathered her in his arms, rubbing her back to calm her. "Shhh . . . it is really all right. We have brought clothes for him."

Deana stopped laughing and looked up at Lorgin dumbfounded. What? "Clothes for him?"

"Yes. When he embodies himself into his corporeal form, he is always nude. I apologize if his nakedness offended you."

"His nakedness? What are you talking about?"

"The transformation leaves him in this state. Is this not why you are distressed? I only go by how you have reacted to *my* nakedness."

She blinked at the ridiculousness of his words. A cat had changed himself into a man, and Lorgin thought it was the guy's naked chest that was upsetting her! Now that was maddening. Her eyebrows lowered as her patience snapped.

She looked Lorgin straight in the eye and firmly said, "This is a stupid world and I want to go home!"

Lorgin grinned while tenderly removing a lock of her hair that had fallen forward into her eyes.

"Do not be silly, *zira*." He looked engagingly at her. "You would leave me lonely here by myself?"

Deana's expression was distinctly suspicious. As if a man like Lorgin would be lonely for a minute! Why, there'd be women queuing up for the privilege of that steamy lavender gaze.

Suddenly she felt very irritated with that particular notion.

It wasn't as if he belonged to her or anything. But just the same, the thought that he would call another woman by one of the many nicknames he had for her made her feel . . . bad. Real bad. Especially the way he called her *zira* sometimes— his voice sultry and low as he let his tongue roll the r in the word. That special way he looked at her, as if he really *enjoyed* her . . .

Not that any of this mattered. She swallowed. She couldn't allow it to matter. Resolutely she refocused on Lorgin and ignored his last question to her.

Pointing to Rejar, she said, "What *is* that?"

Lorgin had observed the emotions flicker across her face as his seemingly careless words impacted her. He knew with every extrasensory perception he possessed, with every fiber of his being, with every breath he took, *she wanted him*. He felt a responding surge of powerful emotion.

Tonight, he would be only too happy to show her just how much she wanted him. His eyes briefly sparked before he answered her question.

"That is my brother. I believe you have met."

111

"*Your brother*?" Deana swung her gaze around to the incredible man lying on the pallet. His intriguing eyes twinkled with mirth as he watched her confusion. "What do you mean your brother? That man is a cat!"

Lorgin sighed. "Only sometimes."

"Only . . . This is bizarre, Lorgin! I mean really bizarre. Why do you have a cat for a brother?"

Lorgin took a deep breath. "He is not a cat!" She raised her eyebrow at him. "Well, he is not *really* a cat. He is a Familiar."

Deana did a double take. "What? You don't mean like . . . no, no—"

"I will try to explain. Rejar is a what we call a shape-changer. He inherited his ability from his mother, who is also a Familiar."

Cripes, a Familiar! What next?

Deana tapped her chin. "We have legends of this in my world." She thought of her earlier conversation with Yaniff regarding the legends in her world. "Does he—" She looked at Rejar and lowered her voice. "Does he work with a witch?"

Lorgin laughed. "No. Obviously your legends are different from our reality. Rejar has the ability to shape-change into the catlike form you have witnessed. This allows him a certain freedom that is unattainable to those not of the Familiar. Familiars walk this plane in two forms, thereby learning and experiencing things that others can not. They have other traits that are different as well. Because of their special abilities they will often align themselves to wizards of the Guild, forming a partnership that is mutually beneficial."

"So Rejar works with Yaniff?"

"No. Rejar walks alone. He is somewhat different from other Familiars."

Deana looked at Lorgin squarely. "Do you have this ability also?"

Lorgin shook his head. "I do not have Familiar blood. My father met Rejar's mother, Suleila, many years after my own mother passed from this plane. My mother was young, and her untimely death a tragic event most uncommon among Aviarans.

"My father grieved deeply and would have no other until he met Suleila. She did not reveal to him her true nature for fear of losing his love. It was not until much later that he discovered she was a Familiar. He was very angry at her deception, but he forgave her, for he loved her deeply. Besides, she presented him with Rejar, who, despite his"—he looked at his brother—"*peculiarities*, we are all quite fond of."

"Where are your parents now?"

"They live on Aviara. My father is one of the Coven, a council of thirteen which governs the planet. My nextmother, Suleila, has all of us wrapped around her finger. I was young when she came to my father's home. In truth, she has become my mother."

Deana tried to digest what Lorgin had told her. She cautiously told him, "Before you came in here, I thought I heard Rejar speaking in my mind."

Lorgin flicked a glance at Rejar. "He can send his thoughts, when he chooses, to an individual, or he may send thoughts to many individuals at once, at his discretion. However, he cannot receive thoughts in this manner, unless of course, it is another Familiar sending him thoughts. Familiars can converse with each other through their minds, but they cannot read each other's minds.

"When Rejar was a boy, he used to anger me by sending thoughts to Suleila about mischief that I had supposedly got-

113

ten into. Of course I had no idea what he was telling her and could not defend myself. Suleila caught on very quickly to his game, though.''

Deana chuckled at the thought of what growing up in that household must have been like. ''So Rejar can't speak?''

A sizzling, sensuously low voice purred from the pallet on the floor. *''Yes, he can speak.''*

And what a voice! Dare I drool? Deana looked at the dark-haired man and flushed. They had been talking about him as if he weren't there.

''He does not favor conversing in that manner.'' Lorgin threw his brother a smirk. ''I think it is because he is lazy.''

{Smart, dear brother, smart.}

Deana jumped as she heard Rejar's sultry voice in her mind.

Lorgin walked over to Rejar's pallet. ''Yaniff has left these clothes for you. We will meet you in the tavern below.''

As he was leading Deana down to the eating area, she asked him why he was willing to eat in the common room now when he wouldn't last night.

''Since the tavern is fairly empty at this early hour, it would be best to save our supplies as there are no other *sacri* where we are going.''

They joined Yaniff, already sitting at a table. The first thing the old man said was, ''Has the rogue woken up yet?''

Lorgin grinned at Yaniff, sharing the private joke as he nodded.

They ate a breakfast consisting of various fruits and a thick, pasty liquid that was poured freely by a young serving woman every time she passed their table. Deana didn't like the taste of the drink, and politely declined the refill.

''Not nearly as good as your coffee, but very nourishing. You should try to drink some more.'' Lorgin picked up his cup and swallowed another glassful.

"No, thank you." The stuff was bland and gluey.

Yaniff raised his head from his bowl. "What is this coffee you speak of?"

Lorgin leaned forward, excitement shining in his eyes. "A marvelous elixir, Yaniff. It has an aroma unlike anything I have experienced, and it fills one with strength. It is very popular in Adeeann's world."

"Yeah, what I wouldn't do for a cup right now," Deana sighed.

Yaniff stroked his chin. "Perhaps I will look into this elixir. I may be able to reproduce the brew from your memories of it."

Deana's face lit up. "That would be great!"

Yaniff rose from the table. "I will store the pallets for you, Lorgin." He headed off to the room, muttering to himself, "I wonder what spell would work best in recapturing such an essence."

Lorgin fondly watched the old man leave and smiled regretfully at Deana. "Do not get your hopes up regarding that coffee, Little Fire. Yaniff is notoriously absentminded in regards to spells involving recipes. In short, as a wizard, he is a terrible cook."

Deana giggled. "So that's why he made the soup the old-fashioned way."

"At least we did not find a boot in it!" Lorgin and Deana both started laughing.

{Now this is an improvement, Lorgin. Perhaps you have not lost your skills after all.}

Rejar had approached the table, and from the look of Lorgin's lowered brows, had obviously sent a thought to him. Rejar gave his brother a gamin grin, and sat at the table.

While Rejar ate, Deana discreetly observed him. Now that

the shock of his existence was wearing off, she was able to note a strong family resemblance between the two men.

They were of a size for one thing—both large men. She thought that Rejar's sultry features bore a strong likeness to Lorgin's. Although, where Lorgin had a cool, regally handsome appearance, Rejar possessed a very sensuous, earthy quality.

He was dressed similarly in style to his brother. His shirt and boots were black, his leather pants dark green. His cape was of a simpler design than Lorgin's, being maroon in color, but with none of the elaborate gold appliqués on it. Rejar must have noticed her perusal of his cape for he gazed over at her.

{I am not a Knight of the Charl, and do not wear their raiment.}

Lorgin had heard his words and put down his cup. "You could be of the Charl if you would only focus yourself. Yaniff has been hoping for years that you would change your mind and join us."

The serving woman came over to fill Rejar's bowl. His beautiful eyes flicked to the young woman momentarily before he answered Lorgin.

{Then Yaniff hopes in vain.}

Deana sat back, listening to the exchange between the two brothers. It was a new experience, overhearing a two-sided conversation where only one person was actually speaking out loud.

"You can deny your true being to yourself, but you cannot deny it to Yaniff. He has sensed something in you."

{As he has in you, brother. Interesting are the sons of Krue, are we not?}

The serving maid refilled his cup and Rejar fastened his feral gaze on her. She was young and pretty, and more than

116

interested in him. He could sense the difference in her surface temperature as she looked on him.

He casually let his arm stroke her backside as he sent her an enticing thought. The maid, overcome by anticipation, agreed with the incredibly handsome man before her. She would very much like to try that with him. Standing, Rejar put his arm around the girl and began leading her off to a chamber. Lorgin called after him.

"Rejar, we must leave shortly!"

Rejar turned back to his brother, grinning. *{Ten moments, Lorgin, just ten moments.}*

They passed Yaniff as the old man made his way back to the table. As he sat down, his ancient eyes followed the dark-haired man.

Yaniff sighed deeply. "He squanders himself." He turned back to the table. "Your brother is a great trial to me, Lorgin. It is a pity I am so fond of the lad."

Lorgin grinned ruefully. "He has a certain way about him. Hopefully he will not be too long."

Deana was mortified. "Your brother just went off with the waitress to . . . to . . ."

Lorgin raised his eyebrows. "Quite. Familiars have a sensuous nature. It is best to let them express it."

"But your, what did you call her, your nextmother, surely she doesn't . . . ?"

"Of course not. She is mated. A state Rejar claims will never happen to him."

Deana did not understand these people at all, and doubted she would in the time of her visit. The best she could do was nod at their strange behavior while observing it.

Rejar returned not very much later, still smoldering as he adjusted his cape. *{Shall we depart, then?}*

Lorgin took Rejar aside, whispering to him, "And where

is that pretty maid you went off with?''

Rejar grinned like the satyr he was, carefully sending his thoughts only to his brother. {*I imagine it will take her some time to compose herself. Indeed, when I left her, I do not think she could speak her own name.*}

Lorgin laughed out loud. ''You are incorrigible, brother.''

{*And not the only Krue who has been called such. Shall I tell your new wife about the time you visited the sirens of Mayra? They still remember you fondly to this day. All twelve of them.*}

''Yaniff is right, you are a scamp!''

Lorgin discreetly looked over at Adeeann, who was engaged in conversation with the old mystic. He pointed a warning finger at his brother. ''Not one word, or you will live to regret it.''

Rejar only smiled.

They continued on their journey, once again entering the seemingly never-ending tunnels.

Deana noted that they passed fewer and fewer travelers on the 'road', and assumed that they were now in the Wilderness Reaches that Lorgin had mentioned. The few scruffy travelers they came across gave them a wide berth. She suspected that the intimidating sight of Lorgin and Rejar was enough to dissuade any would-be attacker.

As they plodded along, she had plenty of opportunity to let her mind drift. Unfortunately, she had time now to recall when she had confessed to the ''cat'' that she thought Lorgin so sexy he could make her melt. Her faced flushed as she remembered her careless words.

But then, how could she have known she was talking to Lorgin's brother!

Would he reveal to Lorgin what she had confided? That was an appalling thought. She turned and looked at Rejar, her face mirroring the embarrassment she felt. He winked at her, obviously realizing what had just occurred to her.

{*I will say nothing, Adeeann. You need not worry.*}

She threw him a grateful look as she continued along the path, thinking back to the first time she had seen him in the cave. What a shock! The way he had sat up and stared at her, telepathically saying, "Good morrow . . . *my brother's wife?*"

Yes, that was what he had said.

With all the excitement, she had forgotten his initial words to her. Deana stumbled over her feet. Lorgin quickly turned to help her. She viewed him with horror.

"Are you all right, Adeeann?"

"Y-yes. Yes, of course." He looked inquiringly at her, then shrugged, and continued leading them through the tunnel.

Why had Rejar called her Lorgin's wife? It was obvious that he had mistaken their relationship. Should she correct him? That might be rather embarrassing. Suppose they were doing something against their strange customs? It could put Lorgin in a difficult position. Should she mention it to Lorgin? *Absolutely not.* Let the two of them work it out. She wasn't about to stick her foot in her mouth.

The morning passed slowly as they continued to trudge along. Once, the tunnel widened, leading them into a magnificent cavern which had a massive, frozen waterfall. The temperature dropped significantly in this area. Lorgin motioned for Deana to come walk beside him so he could enfold her in the warmth of his cloak. He then used his power to form a slightly warmer current around them as they walked. Rejar disappeared around a column, reappearing in cat form, wisely deciding to let his thick fur protect him. Yaniff obviously could take care of himself.

Soon the temperature began to rise again, and they resumed their normal rank in file along the path, with Rejar once again walking on two legs. In the distance, Deana thought she heard the sound of rushing water intermingled with the sounds of people.

The tunnel eventually opened up onto a larger cavern, and sure enough there were several beings milling about the area. They looked like a seedy lot. Most appeared to be drinking something out of large animal horns. In the distance, Deana noted an underground river passing by the main body of the cave.

Lorgin led them to the bar, requesting food from the none-too-clean-looking alien behind the counter. He had a snoutlike nose and beady eyes. He rather reminded Deana of her ex-boss. The alien snorted at Lorgin, then spit a huge wad of slime onto the floor. Yep. Her ex-boss.

Lorgin reached into his cape, then turned his hand over onto the counter, spilling out several gemstones. The alien snorted again, quickly snatching up the gems. He shoved a platter at Lorgin, along with four horns of liquid.

It didn't seem to Deana that Lorgin had really gotten his money's worth, considering the fortune of gems he had thrown down. But since she had no idea what anything was worth here, who was she to judge? She had no trouble judging the quality of food before her, even though she was no gourmet, especially in this cuisine. She gave the platter a wary eye.

Lorgin encouraged Deana to eat.

''I don't think so. It looks like it's been hanging around here awhile.'' She took a sip of the drink, surprised to find it delightfully refreshing.

Lorgin eyed the food, then shoved it away. ''Perhaps you

are right. I think I will stick to the *keeran*.'' Yaniff and Rejar concurred.

So they drank *keeran*.

Deana was starting to feel much better. She didn't even feel tired anymore. Yaniff was securing a boat for the remainder of their journey to the healer's house, and Rejar had gone off somewhere with a set of giggling twins.

Deana took a large swallow of the brew, remembering how Rejar had a possessive palm firmly planted on each shapely bottom while he smoothly led the breathless women away. She turned to Lorgin.

''Your brother has the morals of an alley cat.'' Her eyes widened as she realized her unintentional pun. She started giggling, then surprised herself by hiccuping.

Lorgin looked down at her, amused. ''Adeeann, you have not had *keeran* before. I should have remembered that.''

She looked at him and giggled some more.

''I think you have had enough for now, *zira*.'' He tried to take the horn away from her. She was not about to give it up.

As they were wrestling with the horn, Deana felt something snake around her upper thigh. Looking down, she noted it was a tentacle belonging to the purple guy standing next to her. He looked at her and grinned, revealing several sharply pointed teeth.

The intergalactic geek was trying to hit on her! It was too much! She broke into uncontrollable laughter.

Lorgin had finally wrested the keeran from her, now noticing that a Seckla had her in an embrace. He spoke to the alien in his own language, ''Remove your touch from my woman at once.''

The Seckla answered, ''I have no reason to.'' He snickered at Deana's laughter. ''The woman obviously enjoys my touch.''

121

Lorgin, having given what he considered adequate warning, whipped out his light saber. "I will give you a reason." He neatly sliced through the tentacle, severing it from the Seckla in an instant.

The barroom became very quiet, eagerly awaiting the Seckla's reaction. He gazed carefully at Lorgin for a long tension-fraught moment, sizing up the opponent. Then he abruptly bowed to the blond man, quickly leaving the cavern. The noise level resumed as if nothing had happened.

Deana, in her fuzzy state, was not sure what had occurred until she looked down to see the severed limb slide off her leg. She stared at Lorgin horrified.

"You—you cut his arm off!" She started swaying toward him.

Lorgin was clearly irritated. "Do not be so upset, Adeeann; it is not as if he will not grow another."

Her surprised look was cut off as she passed out in his arms.

She came to in the boat to the sight of the cavern ceiling rapidly whizzing by.

It took her a few moments to realize that they were the ones moving, not the ceiling. She had a horrendous headache. Sitting up, she clutched her forehead, groaning. Yaniff crouched down beside her, sticking a cup of brew under her nose. The strange substance hissed and bubbled.

"Drink this, child. It will clear your head."

She warily took the cup from him, grimacing at the thick, smelly liquid. "Definitely not hair of the dog. What's in it—eye of newt?"

Yaniff smiled slightly. "Toe of dog is the accepted remedy."

Deana wasn't altogether sure he was joking. Her head hurt

too much to worry about it. Holding her nose, she downed the concoction.

As her head began to clear, she noted Lorgin and Rejar at opposite ends of the boat, steering through the fast-moving water by the use of long poles. The underground river carried them swiftly along, causing the men to make quick sudden adjustments with the poles to prevent the currents from careening the boat into the rock structures they passed. The cave walls sped by at dizzying speeds as they were hurled forward by the powerful currents. It was a task that required utmost concentration, so Deana thought it prudent not to talk to either of the brothers.

After what seemed like hours, she quietly asked Yaniff when they would reach their destination. Unbelievably, the old man was snoring! How he could sleep through this whirling maelstrom was beyond her. Even that weird bird thing on his shoulder seemed to be snoozing.

Yaniff opened one eye. "His name is Bojo and when you have lived as long as I have, child, you develop the virtue of being able to sleep through anything."

Deana looked sheepish. "You can read my mind. I thought you might have that ability."

Yaniff stretched, causing several old bones to creak. "Does it bother you?"

"I thought it might, but it doesn't. I think it's because you're so non-threatening."

Lorgin snorted from the bow of the boat, having overheard their conversation. "No one in fifty quadrants with a micron of sanity would believe Yaniff non-threatening."

{Half the universe quakes in fear at the very mention of his name.} This from the back of the boat.

Yaniff patted her hand in a comforting gesture. "If the child wishes to view me as a kindly oldfather, I have no objection."

Lorgin shook his head as he pushed the pole against a passing boulder. "Yaniff, you are beginning to worry me."

Yaniff grinned wickedly before sending out a small bolt of lightning, hitting Lorgin squarely on the backside. Lorgin jumped, turning a fulminating glare on the old man.

Yaniff calmly replied, "I would not want to be the cause of too much worrying for you, Lorgin ta'al Krue."

Rejar's rich, sultry laughter rang out across the water.

"The passage is coming up, Lorgin. It is a small tributary branch to the right. Do not overshoot the entrance lest our journey become much more difficult." Yaniff leaned on his staff, peering ahead in the cavern.

Lorgin nodded. "I will not miss it, Yaniff."

Suddenly the tributary was upon them. Deana thought they would surely overshoot it as the raging river carried them forward.

"There." Yaniff pointed, but Lorgin was already turning the boat, using the pole to gain leverage. His arm muscles bulging, he displayed an incredible amount of strength as he battled the pull of the water, successfully bringing them away from the main current of the river and into this small, relatively calm waterway.

They traveled up the little canal for a ways, both Lorgin and Rejar now using the poles to push the boat forward in the calm water. Soon they approached a small mooring area, where a few other boats were secured.

Deana scanned the plaza of the small outpost, noting a few traders, travelers, and locals milling about. Though rural, this outpost did not seem as lawless as the others they had passed through. She mentioned this to Yaniff as the men secured the boat.

"You are right. We can all rest a little easier here." His

eyes landed on Lorgin. "Since this pod has the only healer in the Reaches, it is generally acknowledged as a safe zone, respected by citizen and outlaw alike. Anyone may come here for treatment without fear of being victimized." Yaniff stroked his chin. "Surprisingly, it is the criminal element which ensures this."

"Probably because they so often need treatment." Lorgin had come up beside them, adding his wry thoughts to the subject. He took Deana's hand in his own, leading her down the main esplanade. "There are exceptions to this unwritten attitude. I still want you to stay near me at all times."

"I hear and I obey, mastah!" Deana began walking like a zombie.

Lorgin raised an eyebrow. "I like these words you speak, but what are you doing?"

"I am a mindless zombie, who only lives for the sound of your command," Deana responded in a low monotone voice, suitable for the walking dead.

Lorgin had no idea what a zombie was, but he knew when he was being mocked. He scratched his chin as if deep in thought. "I am very surprised."

Deana continued her act. "Surprised at what, mastah?"

"That you have realized your reason for existence so quickly." He firmly led her down the street, inwardly laughing at the outraged look on her face.

After taking several side tunnels at Yaniff's direction, they finally came to the abode of the healer. They were ushered into the residence by a servant who asked them to wait for the healer to come.

Deana immediately noticed a difference in this domicile from the others she had seen on this world. For one thing, there actually was furniture here. Although rustic in design, at least it wasn't made of rock. Deana spotted a chair in the corner that had a real cushion. She didn't waste any time gratefully sinking down into the soft, padded seat.

"Ahhh! This is more like it."

Yaniff agreed as he joined her on a matching chair. "Laeva decided that if she was going to leave the culture of the larger pods, she was at least going to be surrounded by some comfort. Most of her patients gift her with items such as these fine furnishings. A rarity in these parts, to be sure."

Stretching her legs out, Deana leaned back in the seat, her mind wandering. Closing her eyes, she pictured a large pepperoni pizza. Her stomach growled. "How's the food here?"

"The food here is fine, thank you very much." Deana jumped at the sound of the authoritative feminine voice. "To what do I owe this visit, Yaniff? I am sure it is not just my sweet presence you have come to see." The gruff voice snickered.

Deana was surprised at the appearance of the healer. She was a large woman, tall, and in her later years. Like Miki, her ears were pointed, but unlike Miki's, they were not delicate. In fact nothing about this woman could be called delicate. Her eyes were brilliantly alive with humor. Deana decided she liked her at once.

Deana discreetly glanced at Yaniff, interested in his apparent embarrassment at Laeva's words. The old mystic was making a great to-do about straightening the folds of his robe. Deana guessed that he was fond of the old gal.

Lorgin spoke, saving Yaniff from having to answer her.

"Laeva, I am sure that your presence alone is enough for any man to brave the Reaches. However, we do have need of your services."

Laeva turned from Yaniff to gaze upon Lorgin. "Well, what do we have here besides an honest man?" She inspected Lorgin, shifting her gaze to Rejar. Her face took on a thoughtful expression when she noted his eyes. "A wizard and his Familiar. How quaint."

Rejar moved away from the wall he was leaning against. *{I am not his Familiar.}*

Laeva looked at Yaniff, then back to Rejar. "You are his, all right."

Lorgin spoke up. "What do you mean? My brother and I—"

"Your brother?" Laeva smiled at Lorgin. "Yes, the two of you . . . Yaniff follows his—"

"Enough!" Yaniff stood, facing Laeva. "You have always had this keen ability to irritate me beyond belief, healer."

Laeva didn't seem at all shocked by Yaniff's rudeness. Quite the opposite; she seemed to be enjoying it.

"Hit a nerve, have I? Good." Ignoring Yaniff, she turned back to Lorgin. "Who are you, my dear man?"

Lorgin introduced himself, Rejar, and Adeeann to her, all the while wondering at Yaniff's strange behavior.

"What is this service I can do for you? Excuse me for saying so, but you all look healthy to me." She eyed Lorgin cheekily. "More than healthy."

"We need you to perform a translator insertion on Adeeann."

Deana's head snapped up. "Whoa! I never agreed to this. What do you mean *an insertion*? An insertion where?"

"In your mind, of course. Do not be concerned, *zira*; it is a minor procedure."

"Minor to you maybe." She put her hands on her hips. "No one, I repeat, no one is going to mess with my mind. I don't want some alien device in my brain."

Lorgin was somehow not surprised at her reaction. She was, after all, his *gharta*. "Come, there is no need for worry. It will be over very quickly."

"I told you no. Besides, I don't need a translation device. I won't be here that long, and we've managed okay up till now."

Lorgin ignored her comment about not being here long, concentrating on her other remark. "You need the device. We will be leaving this world soon. You will need to know what is being said around you."

Deana had an awful feeling he wasn't going to relent on this one. She decided to be firm. "You can tell me what's being said. The answer is no and that is final."

Lorgin sighed. Then began advancing on her.

Chapter Seven

Deana started backing up, then crazily decided to hold her ground.

"Lorgin, I mean it! I will not have this . . . *thing* put in my head." She crossed her arms over her chest to show she was serious. "That is the last I will say on the subject."

"Promise?" Lorgin continued to advance on her.

Deana began backing away from him again. She started looking for an avenue of escape, missing Lorgin's nod to Rejar. Which probably was the reason she turned right around and ran straight into him.

"Rejar, let me go!"

"He will not let you go because he knows you are being foolish." Lorgin was in front of her now. She tried to kick out at him, but missed. He managed to grab her leg, though. Then the other one. "Where shall we bring her, Laeva?"

Laeva raised an eyebrow. "Through these doors here."

Deana let out a howl of protest as the two men carried her,

kicking and squirming, into the next room. Laeva turned to the silent Yaniff. "You never bring me the easy ones, do you, old man?"

Yaniff's twinkled. "Pfft! A woman like you needs a challenge every now and then." A particularly loud wail came from the other room. "We best help my young friends else you will need to treat their hearing as well."

Laeva smirked and led the way into the treatment room.

"Place her on the table there in the center of the room."

"No!"

"Adeeann, stop this now. You will have Laeva think we are not appreciative of her skills." Lorgin held her shoulders down to the table. Rejar gripped her ankles.

Deana stopped thrashing to pierce Lorgin with a heated glare. "If that woman so much as touches me, I'll sue! Do you hear me? I'll sue all of you! Now let me go."

{What is she talking about?}

Lorgin shrugged. "I have no idea. I think I am going to need your assistance, Rejar."

{Very well.}

Deana's focus shifted to Rejar. "Don't you dare touch me, you . . . you . . . cat in a hat!"

Rejar grinned. Instead of insulting him as she intended, she apparently was entertaining him. He leaned over her, his multicolored eyes dancing with mirth. *{You are tired}*

Was he trying to hypnotize her? "I am not!"

{You are tired . . . }

Deana blinked. "I am n—"

{You are tired . . . }

"Yes . . . I am tired." She tried not to close her eyes, but her lids seemed so heavy.

{Sleep now . . . }

Rejar straightened up *{She will sleep for a short time}*

Lorgin smoothed Deana's hair back from her forehead. "Good. The procedure will not take long."

{*Why was she so opposed to it? It is but a simple method to benefit her.*}

"I do not know why she behaved in this manner." Lorgin sighed. "I only hope her anger is short-lived."

{*Yes.*} Rejar grinned. {*Anger would make things so much more difficult for you, brother.*}

Lorgin gave him a rueful look. "You need not enjoy it so much, Rejar."

{*That is what a brother is for.*}

Laeva clapped her hands briskly together. "Everyone leave. I'll call you when I am finished."

Yaniff and Rejar gladly departed. Lorgin, however, stayed behind.

"You, too, Lorgin."

"I will stay here."

"She will be fine. Now go along."

"I expect her to be fine. Nonetheless, I will stay here."

Laeva looked at the man before her in exasperation. "You are no different than your wife. Both of you stubborn beyond belief! Truly, it is a good match you have made."

Lorgin responded with a wry grin.

Once again, Deana opened her eyes to the sight of Lorgin leaning over her, a concerned expression on his handsome face. It briefly occurred to her that he wouldn't have to wear that expression so much if he didn't cause so much trouble! He took her hand, the warmth of his skin making her realize how cold she felt. She began shivering.

"I-isn't there any h-heat in here? I-I'm f-freezing." She looked around the room, noticing that she had been placed in a bedroom. Hesitantly she felt the surface beneath her, sighing when her hand confronted a real mattress. "Is there another blanket?"

"No. Here; use my cloak." He stood up, removed his cape, and placed it gently over the blanket covering her. "It is the aftereffects of the sleeping potion you were given. It causes your body temperature to drop."

She eyed him out of the corner of her eye. "I thought Rejar put me to sleep—for which I will never forgive him." Her teeth began chattering from the cold.

"He did, initially. Laeva decided to administer a sleeping draught when the procedure took longer than we had anticipated."

"So, it's done then?" Her hand reached up to her forehead. Although nothing felt any different, a tear tracked its way down her cheek.

Lorgin sat on the edge of the bed. "What is this? Why does it disturb you so?" He wiped away the tear with his finger. "Children have this done all the time in my world. It is nothing."

"To you, maybe. Now my mind's been tampered with. I'm not the same as I was. For all I know, I'm a different person entirely."

Lorgin's look was ironic. "Believe me, you are the same person. This I can tell you with complete confidence."

"But I can never know that for sure, can I?" Her expression was mutinous.

"Woman, there was nothing done to your mind! All you had was a simple translation device inserted." Her expression did not waver.

Lorgin exhaled a long-suffering breath of sound "If you could have been altered, first, I would have made you more agreeable. This, as you can see, was not done!" Lorgin rubbed his temple. "You are giving me a headache."

Deana was hardly listening to him. She was getting colder and colder by the minute, her body wracked with chills. "Lorgin, I'm so cold. Help me; I'm scared."

Lorgin stopped rubbing his forehead, noticing her distress. "It is the medicine clearing from your body." He stood and got under the covers next to her, enfolding her in his arms. His voice was gentle. "I will try to warm you." He kissed the top of her head as he rubbed her back, his soothing hands leaving a trail of heat. "Do not be frightened, Little Fire. I would not permit anything bad to happen to you."

"I believe that, but who's going to stop *you* from happening to me?" Her chills were starting to subside, but her feelings of helplessness in the face of Lorgin's will frightened her. She was truly at his mercy in this strange land he had brought her to. Her secret fears were confirmed with his next words.

Lifting her chin with his forefinger, he firmly replied, "No one."

She pushed out of his arms and turned away from him in the bed. His words upset her. She thought they were . . . well, friends. Now, in her mind, he was abusing their friendship. In the future, her behavior toward him was going to be quite different. If this was his attitude, he would learn that no man lorded himself over Deana Jones. With those thoughts, she allowed herself to drift into a nap.

She never felt Lorgin's protective arms encircle her waist, pulling her possessively close as he too fell into slumber.

Lorgin heard Yaniff's voice whispering in his ear like an insistent insect.

"If all you intend to do is lie there and sleep, Lorgin ta'al Krue, you might as well get up and come to the evening meal."

Lorgin opened his lavender eyes, gazing straight into Bojo's beady ones. "Get that beast out of my face, old man." Bojo squawked at the insult.

"There, there." Yaniff stroked the animal, soothing his ruffled feathers. "Just because this woman has you in knots is no reason to insult Bojo." He gazed at Deana sleeping peacefully in Lorgin's arms. "Hard to believe such a little thing wields such power over a Knight of the Charl." The wizard grinned slyly. "Perhaps Rejar—"

Yaniff never finished his words as Lorgin held the Cearix to his throat. "You were saying?"

Yaniff's eyes gleamed. "Take that dagger away from my throat, you insolent pup, before I turn you into a snail." Lorgin complied. "Much better, thank you. Now, as I was saying, Laeva sent me to bring you down to the evening meal. You may wish to come." He turned to leave, then stopped, turning cunningly back to Lorgin. "After all, you may need to keep your strength up for the terrible ordeal you have to face later."

Lorgin's deep, throaty laughter filled the chamber as Yaniff left.

Deana woke to the rich sound of his laughter. The man never took her seriously! Even now, he was laughing at her. Perhaps he found her attitude regarding the translating device humorous; she did not. He was about to find out how serious she was. Disengaging herself from his embrace, she afforded him a cold stare.

"You are awake? Good. Laeva has prepared a meal for us. I recall you saying you were hungry some time back." His lazy glance flicked to her hair, which fell about her in a cascade of red curls. He wanted to run his fingers through the silken strands, watch the incredible little curls wrap around his fingers.

"Yes, I am." He's probably going to make fun of my hair, as well, Deana thought sourly. Giving him another chilling look, she got out of bed, exiting the chamber without giving him a second glance.

Lorgin watched her departure with interest. He rubbed his chin in thought. So, that was the way of it, was it? The *gharta* thought to hold him off with a spiny exterior. Lorgin shook his head and chuckled. A prickly front was no obstruction to him. She could sting him all she liked, but in the end, the sweetness would be his. He got up to follow her below, looking forward to the confrontation.

All during dinner, Deana made it a point to ignore Lorgin. She talked gaily with Laeva, whom she liked but did not really forgive. She winked at Yaniff, and laughed with Rejar, whom she also did not forgive. But to Lorgin, the person who was really to blame for the whole fiasco, she gave the cold shoulder.

After the meal, which was the first appetizing one she had enjoyed since coming to this place, she excused herself and headed back to her bedroom.

She kicked her boots off, flopping down on the top of the bed. She was surprised when Lorgin entered the room.

"Get out! This is my room. Your presence here is not wanted."

Lorgin grinned at the little gharta. "No? Perhaps I should make it *wanted*." Deana hopped off the bed.

"This is not *your* room, Adeeann. It is *our* room. I will come and go as I please."

Deana put her hands on her hips. "Why do I always have to share sleeping arrangements with you? There must be another room for you. I don't want you here."

Lorgin approached her, peering intently down into her face through half-closed eyes, responding to her quip in a tone all

135

the more threatening for the quietness of it. "Even if there were a thousand rooms in this dwelling, I would still sleep in this one."

Deana looked away from him. Now she had done it! He wasn't cowering under her cold treatment like other men she had known. In fact, it seemed to have the opposite effect on him, fueling his aggressiveness. That wasn't what she wanted at all. What should she do now? This whole episode confirmed her belief that she was wise to steer clear of any entanglement with the man. There was no controlling him. She bit her lip while she concentrated on her next move.

"Come here, *zira*."

His words interrupted her thoughts. He had called her *zira* again. This time she suddenly knew, just *knew*, what the word meant. The translating device! Her look was one of utter horror.

"You called me . . . *wife*." She flung the accusation at him. Actually, he had called her "beloved wife," but she chose to ignore the endearment attached to the translation.

Lorgin leveled his amethyst gaze on her. "*You are my wife.* Mine by right of succession, as well as sworn oath. It is past time we join."

"What are you talking about? I don't belong to anybody but myself!"

Her words angered him more than she would have believed. "We are mated!" He slashed his hand through the air. "The oath has been given and taken."

Deana looked nonplussed. She blinked. "I don't recall any oath between us."

His eyes pierced her. "Do you not? Recall, if you will, my kneeling before you, offering myself and my line to you, offering the Cearix of the Lodarres, a noble line of sixteen generations!"

136

He stood before her now, towering over her. "Recall, if you will, your acceptance of this sacred symbol; binding us for all time, *joined as one.*"

Deana took a step back, noticeably paler. "Are you telling me that . . . when you gave me that dagger of yours, you were . . . *marrying* me?"

"Precisely."

"And according to your customs, the woman isn't allowed a say in this?"

"Of course she is. By our customs, I told you in the sanfrancisco I had taken the Right. You, *Adeeann zira'al Lorgin*, accepted my troth when you returned the Cearix to me in the time-honored manner, its point to my heart. You have taken the oath. I expect you to honor it."

At this point, Deana decided to put the space of the room between them.

"But how was I to know? I have no knowledge of your customs. I didn't even know what you were doing!"

Lorgin said nothing, only grinned wickedly, reminding her of his feral brother. His crystal earring flashed as it dangled from his ear.

She gulped. A thin film of sweat broke out on her forehead. "You planned this! Tricked me into marriage. You . . . you . . ." she sputtered. "It's not legal! It's called entrapment or something. It would never stand up in a court of law. What am I saying? This doesn't mean anything on my world."

"Ah, but we are not on your world."

"How dare you! You arrogant, presumptuous, overbearing . . . intruder!"

Lorgin furrowed his brow. *Intruder?*

"Coming into my house, my home, totally uninvited, forcing your way into my life! Who asked you to?"

Lorgin opened his mouth to answer, but Deana cut him off.

Crossing her arms over her chest, she emphatically stated, "I'm not staying here another minute. Take me back this instant!"

Lorgin snorted at the ridiculous statement. Taking off his cloak, he tossed it onto a floor cushion.

"I want to go home, Lorgin."

"You are home." *He removed his shirt.*

Deana could not believe she actually stamped her foot in anger at the man.

"I do not desire to be your wife!"

"No? I am about to show you exactly what you desire."

She didn't need a translating device to interpret those words. She stuck her stubborn little chin in the air.

"You'll have to take me if you want me!"

Lorgin shrugged, removing his boots. "I intend to."

He was totally ignoring the meaning of her words, stalking her with determination.

"I mean, you'll have to rape me." Just to clarify the issue.

His eyes twinkled as he chuckled low in his throat. "You are so dramatic, Little Fire," he whispered, shaking his head at her theatrics.

She clearly wasn't getting through to him. Hell no, she was amusing him! Her last shot. The outraged Victorian Maiden gambit. "Touch me and I'll kill myself." It sounded a lot stupider said out loud than when you read it in books. Hopefully he wouldn't know she was bluffing.

He looked surprised, but not by her words. "Behind you!" He pointed. "A *zorph!*"

Deana turned, jumped, and screamed at the same time. "Where?!"

Lorgin grabbed her from behind, falling on the bed with her. He quickly rolled over, pinning her beneath him. A slow grin spread across his handsome face as he looked down at her, his white teeth flashing in the low light. "Here." A tiny dimple appeared in his left cheek.

"You rat!"

He blinked innocently at her, his long black eyelashes a stark contrast to his pastel eyes. "What is a rat?"

"A rodent-creature, it comes out and nibbles on things. Get off!"

Lorgin was clearly amused. He wickedly nudged against her just to let her know how hard he was. Her eyes widened.

"What kind of things?" he purred.

Oh God. "All—all kinds of things. Lorgin, let me up!"

He devilishly nudged her again. "What things?"

It was awfully difficult to think with him looking at her like that. With him feeling like that. *He was positively sizzling.* "I don't know . . . food, and fingers, and toes, and stuff . . ."

He drew her hand away from the bed, bringing it to his mouth. Heated lips briefly seared her palm; he playfully nipped her index finger before drawing it deep into his warm mouth. His silky tongue provided the electric sparks as his teeth slowly scraped the length of it, all the while his penetrating, fiery stare never leaving hers.

His action was blatantly suggestive.

Deana's breathing noticeably speeded up. When he captured her eyes again, she almost became spellbound by the brilliance of the fire in his gaze. *Like little pink fireworks.*

She closed her eyes for a moment to clear her head and regain her resolve.

"Am I a rat?" he lazily asked.

"Yes!" He bent toward her neck, sweetly nibbling the soft skin with tiny love bites. Chills ran down her side. "No! I . . . I mean you're acting more like a vampire. Stop that!"

Lorgin raised his head, his silky hair brushing across her taut nipples. She swore she could feel the sensuous texture of his hair right through her tunic.

"What is a vampire?"

"A monster! A monster who sucks . . ." His eyes widened. "Oh God! Lorgin, stop!"

Lorgin's eyes sparkled with mirth. "I definitely think I will be a vampire . . ." He captured her breast in his mouth, tunic and all, flicking the swollen tip with his tongue; he rolled it back and forth gently between his teeth.

Deana arched up, clutching his bare shoulders. "Please, Lorgin, don't." Her plea came out a wispy rasp as the feel of his mouth through the material combined with the feel of smooth, rippling male flesh under her hands. She gasped for breath, overwhelmed by the potent force that was this man.

He paused to look down at her, eyes now bright with iridescent pink sparks. He rested his lower body fully against her as his hands cupped the back of her head, his bent elbows raising her face to him.

"Give me your mouth." His tone was implacable and raw, all earlier traces of humor gone.

Deana gazed upon his beautiful countenance, so masculine and alive with passion. She knew in that moment, no matter what she said or did, he would not stop. He meant to have her.

"Give me your mouth," he repeated, his glance falling to her full, soft lips. When she did not respond to his words, he pressed his lower body tight against her, his hips rocking seductively in the cradle of hers. She shivered at the intimate feel of him. Raising his eyes from her lips, he captured her with his brilliant, heated stare. His ragged breath caressed her face.

As he looked upon her, Lorgin could barely think. He almost moaned, his need was so intense. He wanted this woman to the exclusion of anything else. The heat of desire was upon him. His heart pounded in anticipation of the Transference to take place. He felt his power building and growing within him, driving him to the edge. Her being sang within him; he could hear only her in his future. The touch of her pulsed and skipped along his nerve endings, setting up a fire in his blood. The scent of her entwined in his heart, choking him with pleasure. He *longed* for the taste of her. The taste of her . . .

"Kiss me." he whispered hoarsely. "Kiss me, my Adeeann."

Deana could feel her heart pounding in her chest. Or was that his? It was no use, every fiber of her being wanted him. She couldn't deny herself another minute. He was made for her, a fantasy in the flesh. Just this once. She had to. She'd sort out the marriage nonsense with him later.

Just this once . . .

With a choked cry, she raised her mouth to his, joining them together in a burst of frenzied longing.

Lorgin's response was immediate and intense. His large hands threaded through the hair at her scalp, holding her prisoner for the fierce plunder of his mouth. His tongue dived between her lips as if craving the very taste of her. And taste her, he did.

Deana became senseless as the full impact of his sensuality hit her. Wild and tender, raw and spiritual, his nature pierced her very soul as he stormed his way through every defense she had in that one moment.

His heated hands found their way under her tunic, and she felt their scorching warmth on her back and the tender skin of her belly. They were a man's hands—large, firm, and slightly rough, with a gentleness that did nothing to disguise the determination and experience in every stroke. Lorgin

141

knew exactly what he was about; there was no hesitation or unschooled fumbling in his sure caresses. This was a man who brought his confidence into the bed with him. His expert touch made her feel as if she were the only woman he had ever embraced; the only woman he had ever clasped in such tender abandonment. In a brief moment of clarity, Deana thought he played her like a master musician, keying every note to the perfect pitch.

She had never stood a chance.

He lifted the tunic from her and flung it across the room. Once again, he covered her mouth with his own, drowning her in the wildness of his kiss. He brushed his chest against hers, allowing the differing textures of their skin, one soft and full, the other hard and sinewy, to slide against each other, sensitizing her for his touch. Little pulses of electric desire skipped from him to her, turning her mindless.

"Lorgin, Lorgin . . ." She recited his name, a breathless mantra.

"Yes, Adeeann. Yes . . . Do you want me now, *zira*? Do you feel me coming to you?" His hot breath whispered against her lips.

He began to slowly invade every sense she possessed until all she could feel, all she could see, all she could taste was Lorgin ta'al Krue . . .

"You taste like my tomorrows, Adeeann."

Lorgin's soft love words in what she assumed was Aviaran were spoken breathlessly in her ear, causing her to sigh. She definitely would have to set him straight. But not now. No, not now. She shivered as the tip of his tongue swirled around her earlobe, then gently teased the canal.

He mapped her with his tongue, down the side of her neck to her collarbone, around her necklace, following a trail to the center of her chest, between her breasts. Every spot he loved sang with residual vibration as he passed.

He swirled his tongue around her navel, stimulating the sensitive nerves, before moving back up to the flat plane above her stomach. Using his teeth and mouth, he suckled on her there, leaving love marks in his wake. Deana gasped at the rawness of his actions, wondering if she was capable of taking on such an uninhibited, feverish lover.

Lorgin never gave her the time to ponder it further.

His intoxicating caresses swept away any misgivings she might have harbored when he traveled to her breast. Taking the turgid, rosy peak full in his mouth, and using just the tip of his tongue, he sent a small jolt through her.

Deana reared off the bed, crying out in a choked sob, *"You'll kill me with this pleasure!"* Nevertheless, she clutched his head to bring him closer.

The corner of Lorgin's mouth lifted. "I will do my best, Little Fire," he promised.

He cupped her full breasts in his masterful hands, noting with a tender smile that they filled his palms rather nicely. He bent his head to her other breast, once again sending her a small love jolt, taking the peak in his mouth and playing the vampire that Adeeann had accused him of being. Letting his fingers drift lightly down her sides to her narrow waist, he continued sucking the hard little nub as he stroked his thumbs in tiny circles on the yielding flesh beneath the underside of her breasts.

"Lorgin. . . ." Deana choked out, her fingers clenching in the strands of his hair.

He did not think a verbal response was necessary.

Purposefully, Lorgin spanned her waist with his hands, smoothly sliding her pants down her legs. He tossed them in the same corner as her tunic. Briefly, his adept fingers rubbed the soft skin of her calves, coaxing her pulsepoints to quiver under his touch. He got up to quickly to shed his own pants, standing at the foot of the bed for a moment to gaze down the naked length of her. Despite her resolve not to cave in under that intense sexual regard, Deana found herself blushing.

"You're making me feel shy."

"There is no need of this."

But it was all she could do not to cover herself as his burning gaze traced every line of her body. Did she ever really think this man was indifferent to her? Last night, in the pool. . . . How naive could she have been? Her eyes dropped to his manhood. It was fully erect, large and swollen with passion.

He was enormous. How could he . . . It would never . . .

Easily reading her thoughts, he smiled as he said confidently, "It will."

Her face flamed at her transparency, but Lorgin did not hesitate. Firmly grabbing an ankle in each of his hands, he spread her legs apart, placing a knee up on the bed. The strands of his hair lightly brushed against her calf as he leaned over her.

"Be assured, *zira* You will know me like yourself, and I, you." Then his teeth grazed the inner skin of her lower leg—a message of intent and promise. Deana couldn't help but moan out loud.

Holding her ankles firm, Lorgin worked his way slowly up her inner leg, employing his tongue, lips, and teeth in a combination of relentless sensuality. He kissed. He lathed. He bit. Using a timing known only to him, he would pause intermittently. Deana's whole body was shuddering both from his touch, and from *his lack of it.*

Lorgin was not unaffected himself. His pulse rate had increased, he was finding it more and more difficult to concentrate, and his blood fairly sizzled. When he reached her upper thigh, he raised his head to regard Deana in a haze of heat. He observed her erratic breathing, her glazed eyes, her shivers of pleasure. He dropped his gaze to the juncture of her thighs. The glistening red curls had originally been his destination. He noted her present state and doubted she would be able to take that experience on top of everything else facing her. Not now, but definitely later . . .

He moved up and covered her mouth with his own.

At the sweet taste of his lips, Deana plunged her hands into his hair, running her fingers through the long, silky length. His overwhelming potency almost robbed her of the strength to move. She had never felt like this before, curiously drained yet thrumming with energy. He bit her neck sharply, then lapped at the spot to soothe it, then sizzled it again as he sent tiny currents to her. Then, in exquisite contrast, he blew on it. Deana reared off the bed.

"Please, please, Lorgin, I can't take much more."

This he could believe. He did not think he could take much more either. Her responses were innocently sweet. Again it occurred to him that she was very inexperienced. This was an unfamiliar concept to him, having been raised in a world where a certain amount of sexual freedom was a way of life.

Gently, he inserted his middle finger in her. Her velvet slickness surrounded him with a little caress. She was incredibly small and tight. He knew now that she wasn't completely untouched; but she was so small . . . He wondered if somehow he was wrong about his supposition.

He lifted his mouth from hers. "You have been with a man before?"

Her face flamed. Did he think she was a babe in the woods, totally inexperienced? "Of course I have! Lots of times!"

Lorgin raised a skeptical eyebrow at her. So much for the world-weary act. She turned away from him. "Once. It wasn't . . ."

145

He drew her face back to his. "It is all right, Adeeann. This will be."

Her revelation did not surprise him. What surprised him was his own response to it. He was *grateful* for her lack of sophistication. He could always lead them where he wanted them to go, but strangely, the thought of another man touching her made his blood boil. After tonight they would only know the touch of each other. Tonight—tonight he had concerns, despite what he had told her, that his great size would hurt her. The Transference alone would be more than enough for her to take without added discomfort.

There was no help for it.

He nudged her opening with the tip of his erection, carefully inserting himself a few inches, only to withdraw and repeat the act several times, each time entering her a little more. In this manner, he attempted to widen the narrow passage as gently as possible for his ultimate penetration.

Deana felt a hard bluntness throbbing between her legs. It pushed against her, creating an intense pressure. Lorgin thrust into her slightly. He withdrew. He bore into her again. He withdrew. His intermittent thrusts were driving her over the edge. She was in no mood for a game of parry and thrust. *She wanted all of him.*

"You're tormenting me," she cried.

"No. You are too tight." His ragged reply was lost in a cry as she met his next thrust with an upward movement of her hips.

So be it. Lorgin filled her. And filled her. *And filled her.*

There was acute discomfort as her skin stretched taut to accommodate him. Damn, but it stung! A tear inadvertently slipped from her eye.

Lorgin, who was trying his best to remain motionless while deeply embedded in her, caught the tear with the tip of his finger. Smoothing back her hair, he whispered, "Why did you not wait?"

Her eyes locked with his. "I couldn't." Lorgin groaned. Deana felt him flex deep inside her.

"Forgive me, Little Fire, but I can wait no longer either."

He began to move in her. What had been discomfort quickly turned into burning pleasure. This was something she had never experienced in her brief sexual past. Again, he followed his own timing, his controlled stroking actions driving her crazy.

Wrapping her legs around his waist, she brought him as close to her as she physically could. Sensing her need, he slowly ground his hips from side to side, while imprisoning her with his mouth and hands.

"My beautiful *gharta* . . ."

He tasted her with unbridled passion, nearly sending her over the edge. Then his stroking increased as he held her virtually motionless beneath him. His powerful, steady thrusts, combined with his relentless kisses drove her almost completely mad.

He was sending her sparks of current now, one wave following another. Timed to his strokes. Not timed to his strokes. It was way, way too much. She shouted into his mouth as her first orgasm hit her in powerful ripples, her waves combining with his waves . . .

Lorgin felt the coming close upon him. His whole body was humming with his power. It flowed and skipped through his veins, amassing, building. Breathing raggedly, with hands that trembled he grabbed Deana's face, his voice amazingly strong, considering his state; he uttered the Aviaran ritualistic words of the Transference.

"Be apart from me no more, forever."

Deana screamed as his power hit her full force. It flowed

into her in a never-ending torrent of strength.

Just before she passed out, Lorgin was pleased to note that in the shock and pleasure-pain of the Transference, she had not turned away from him. No, she had clutched him yet closer.

Yaniff sat up late in his bedchamber, reading an ancient tome of wizardry. Abruptly, he stopped his perusal of the page to look at Bojo. He had felt a slight shift of power on the Fourth Plane. The Transference had taken place. Smiling, he returned to his reading.

Chapter Eight

"Absolutely fantastic!" Deana's eyes fluttered open, her gaze falling dreamily onto the passionate face of her lover.

Still entwined with her, Lorgin looked down at her with eyes heavy lidded from the passion they had just shared.

Intermittent sparks still flashed lazily in his eyes. He reminded Deana of a fine racing engine, temporarily in idle. She had the silly idea that if she gave him a green light, he could easily boost the r.p.m. and go into overdrive. She giggled.

He gave her a slow, sated smile. His hands were still clasped around her head, his fingers locked in her hair. He dipped his head, lightly brushing his lips across hers several times, his hair tickling her chest with each movement he made.

"What are you laughing about, *zira*?" His voice was a soft caress against her lips. "You think my lovemaking humorous?" She could feel his smile against her mouth. And something else between her legs. Growing.

Deana's eyes widened. "Lorgin, you can't!"

His eyes crinkled at the corners in amusement. "Apparently, I can."

Nevertheless, she didn't think *she* could. What they had just had was wonderful, intense, overwhelming, and very frightening. Deana didn't know if she wanted to experience his brand of lovemaking again. Well, at least not for a while.

"L-Lorgin, I-I don't think I can do that again."

His look was somewhat indulgent and damned sexy. "Do not worry, Adeeann. I am sure I can repeat my performance to your satisfaction."

She flushed. "No! I-I mean I can't . . . I don't . . . I'm not . . ."

He breathed softly, warmly, in her ear, whispering low. "You can. You will. You are . . ."

He nuzzled her neck with his open mouth, letting his tongue flick lazily across her skin. Not in any hurry. It was obvious he was just enjoying the taste of her.

Deana froze, knowing very well where he was leading. She sucked in her breath as he hit a particularly sensitive spot. He acknowledged her reaction with a tiny scrape of his teeth before resuming his casual meandering.

"Lorgin?"

"Yes?" His voice was muffled and languorous.

"I'm afraid."

He stopped instantly, rising to meet her eyes. His expression one of concern, he smoothed her hair away from her face. "Of what?" His quiet voice echoed a soft note in the room.

Unable to meet his eyes, she turned away. He brought her focus back to him by gently cupping her chin. "Of what?" he repeated softly.

She had to tell him. Unfortunately this type of thing required a great deal of tact. Something she was not well known for. "Um—it was . . . great, but . . . I mean . . ."

His eyebrows lowered ominously. She obviously wasn't handling this with the proper finesse. "But what?" His voice was stony.

Squirming beneath him in embarrassment, she blurted out, "It was uncomfortable, all right?"

A curious expression came into his eyes. "All of it?"

Avoiding his gaze, her hand reached over and idly twirled a lock of his hair. "N-no, just the last part."

If Deana had been looking at him, she would have noted the light of comprehension dawning on him, as well as a brief flash of relief. "You mean the Transference."

She looked up at him with a puzzled expression. "The transference? You mean when you—well, when you finished . . ." She could feel her cheeks flaming.

He ran his thumb across her flushed cheek, smiling gently. "No, that is not what I mean." He went on to explain. "The Transference occurs only once, the first time an oath couple join."

"Oh." She thought about that for a moment. "Then the . . . discomfort I felt won't happen again?"

He threaded his fingers through her hair, then lightly kissed her forehead. "Only pleasure from now on, Little Fire."

Now that the problem was cleared, Lorgin thought it only proper to prove his words. He lowered his mouth to hers. She surprised him by placing her hands against his chest to stop him.

"What does it do?" Her question was cautious and leery.

A little dimple popped up in his left cheek. "*What does it do?*" His eyes were glinting with suppressed amusement. "Has no one taught you?"

151

Her expression of total puzzlement was answer enough. He frowned and looked away. Did they not teach their women anything on the Disney World? He remembered her sweet naivete during his lovemaking, answering his own question. What a provincial planet!

He sighed. Apparently he would have to teach her this as well. He had never heard of a warrior being called upon for this task. It was . . . a little embarrassing. Would that the Astral Alliance appreciate all that he endured for their cause!

He swallowed, clearing his throat. "When a couple joins, they do what we just did."

"Yes?"

She still appeared perplexed. Lorgin swallowed again and bravely forged ahead. "A Transference occurs during the . . . the culmination of the act."

"Always?"

"No, only if it is a true union."

"I don't understand."

He was afraid of that. "During the Transference, the man gives his power to his mate."

She gasped. *"All of it?"*

Lorgin couldn't help it. He burst out laughing. He knew he should not make light of her ignorance, but her bewildered look was his undoing. Wiping a tear from his eye, he knew that for the rest of his life, he would never forget this moment. Gazing down at his unique *zira*, he felt his heart swell.

Still grinning, he answered her. "No, not all, just some."

She furrowed her eyebrows, not having a clue as to what he found so humorous. "But why?"

His light eyes veiled. "Thus it is a Transference. She will return it to him when the time is right."

"Then they are not joined anymore, like a divorce?"

"What is a divorce?"

Deana explained. He slashed his hand through the air. "No! Nothing like a divorce. A joining is forever."

Deana shook her head. It was as clear as mud. She still wasn't getting it. "I still don't understand."

Lorgin smiled secretly. "You will."

Deana peeked up at him through her eyelashes. Was she in over her head? What was all this mumbo-jumbo about anyway? None of it applied to her, in any case, simply because she was not of these worlds. Surely Lorgin knew she wouldn't be bound by customs not of her choosing. She would have to make him see that.

Something else disturbed her. When he talked about them together, it was almost as if he had known it would happen—that it was a foregone conclusion. His words did not sound like vanity talking. Rather, it sounded as if he were following some type of alien ritual she knew nothing about.

Suddenly she remembered him saying that he couldn't leave her world. But when she had questioned him about it back in the first cavern, she recalled him saying something about her misinterpreting his words. Since he definitely did know how to get back to his worlds—her being here was the very proof of it—he must have meant something else. But what? She tried to recall his exact words.

"I do not like this expression on your face." His words brought her out of her reverie.

"Hmm? Why not?"

He chucked her chin with his finger. "Because this is the face you wear when you are about to make me angry."

She pushed his hand away. "Don't be ridiculous." Then she remembered! He said he could not leave, but then he must have decided that he *could* leave. Which meant that whatever reason had prevented him from leaving was no longer valid. So, what was it? *He brought you back here, you dolt! Personal or business?*

153

These thoughts were making her very uncomfortable. Up to now, she had just assumed that he had brought her here as a visitor, sort of a recompense for her hospitality. All of his other blather about joining and oaths, she shrugged as a communications barrier. Alien lingo for a desire to tussle between the sheets. But what if it wasn't? What if . . .

"Lorgin, why did you come to my world? I know you said it was a mistake, but—"

He shook his head. "Not a mistake, Adeeann. Hardly a mistake. Unexpected, perhaps." His eyes fell to the Shimalee around her neck. Now was the time to tell her; this he knew. He pointed to her necklace.

"Know you not what this is?"

"No, I do not. I mean, I don't."

"This brought me to you." He fingered the heavy stone. Deana felt a pleasing hum vibrate through her. "It is called the Shimalee."

Shimalee! He had mentioned it to her before, but she had no idea what he was talking about. "How could this necklace bring you to me?"

"It is a divining stone—an amplifier. They sing to very few. Those that hear its voice can bend space and time. They say that each stone of every Shimalee matches exactly, each crystal aligns to a perfect atunement. Flawless beauty. To hear the voice of the stone is to know the sublimeness of perfection. They are the link to all existence." Lorgin's voice reflected the reverence and awe he felt.

This junk-shop find? She wisely kept that thought to herself, saying instead, "Where did it come from?"

"No one knows. There were twelve originally in existence. It is said that countless millennia ago, nine of the Shimalees linked throughout space and time, forming a complex matrix in the fabric of the continuum. We call this matrix the tunnels.

You experienced the tunnels when I brought you here.''

"How did it come to the hotel room?"

"Some mystics have the ability to call the tunnels to them.''

"You have this ability?"

"Yes, but you must understand that I can only do this under certain circumstances. In our worlds, the entrances to the tunnels are largely at fixed points. Those that can call the tunnels have the ability to bring forth the opening to the pas sage.''

"You said nine of the Shimalees—what happened to the other three?"

"Up to a thousand years ago, the remaining Shimalees were under the protection of the Guild. They were not happy about the entrustment. The Old Ones worried constantly about the grave consequences should a stone fall into the wrong hands, for its power is limitless. So great was their concern, it overshadowed everything they did, until they felt they were ineffective in their work. It was then they decided it was best to 'lose' them in the tunnels forever.''

Deana was fascinated by the story. "Did they?"

"Yes. But Yaniff had a vision of prophecy. He foretold of a Shimalee that would sing to a voice not of our plane of existence.''

"Yaniff? But you said this was a thousand years ago!"

"Yes.''

Deana expelled a breath. What a fantastic story!

Lorgin continued with the tale. "Yaniff saw much that day. He foretold of the ancient Lodarres line and the intricate web the forebears of this line would weave in the far future.''

"Lodarres line? Isn't that your ancestral background?"

Lorgin nodded curtly, his eyes locked with hers.

Deana was starting to get the picture and she didn't like

155

the form it was taking one bit! "Are you saying this—this necklace brought you to my world, and that you joined with me because of some ancient custom you were bound by?"

Lorgin flicked his hair back over his shoulder. "Yes and no." She waited for more. "Yes, the Shimalee brought me to you; and as foretold, since you wore the Shimalee, and I am the first in the line of Krue, you belong to me. I *joined* with you because I desired it."

Deana did not look pleased. Lorgin felt compelled to add, "I warned you in the sanfrancisco I had taken the Right. You did not take me seriously; you have no one to blame but yourself."

Disgusted, Deana turned away from him. He brought her back to face him. "Do you understand what I am saying to you? You have *always* been mine. You *will* always be mine. It is sealed. The choice was never yours to make."

Deana thought back to that day in the resale shop when she had stumbled upon the necklace. It was true that she found the necklace under a pile of junk, unearthing it to the light of day. The purchase itself was just an impulse buy on a rather bleak day. Try as she might, she couldn't recall anything unusual about the scene. And she definitely hadn't heard anything "singing" to her.

Her face was rather sad as she confronted Lorgin with what she knew to be the truth. What was he going to do when he realized he had joined with the wrong person?

"You have made a terrible mistake, Lorgin. This purchase was nothing more than an impulse. There is nothing special about me."

His hands cupped her face. "There is everything special about you," he whispered as his lips descended sweetly on her own.

It was all she could do not to cry.

* * *

Deana was following Lorgin.

She had been surprised when, after he had given her that bittersweet kiss, he had rolled off her, gathering their clothes which he had flung about the room. "Get dressed, Adeeann; there is something I wish to show you," he had said.

She was still pretty depressed about what he had told her. Soon he would realize the terrible error he had made. She felt bad for him. Perhaps it would lessen the blow for him if she got him to return her to Earth soon. It would be bad enough to know you had made a mistake of momentous proportions; to be shackled to it indefinitely didn't bear thinking about. For his sake, she had to convince him to return her to her home, the sooner, the better.

It wasn't as if there were any emotional attachments between them, other than friendship. By Lorgin's own words, he saw their relationship as some kind of duty he was bound to by their strange beliefs. There had been moments while they were making love when she had actually believed he had a real affection for her. What could she have been thinking of? The fact that she was involved at all with a man like him was unbelievable.

She swallowed the lump in her throat.

This is what she had been afraid of back in San Francisco. The man was getting to her. No. *The man had already gotten to her.*

Already, she was thinking of making love with him again. Her vulnerability frightened her. If he knew, it would give him power over her. There was no way she could ever let him see she was starting to have . . . *feelings* for him. Good God—he would use them against her to act out his crazy fantasy. He would ensure a self-fulfilling prophecy.

No!

She knew she wasn't this "voice" he had spoken of earlier. He had given her an incredible adventure, made heart-stopping love to her, but she knew she would have to leave him and soon. For his sake and hers.

What if she got pregnant?

Deana stumbled.

How stupid could she be? She hit her forehead with the heel of her hand. She wasn't on any birth-control medication because she wasn't involved in any relationship. Besides, most of her friends who were involved with someone used condoms these days. In her brief visit here, she hadn't noticed anything that even remotely resembled the corner drugstore. What an idiot! What a complete idiot!

Deana took a deep breath to steady her fraying nerves. She was losing it. Nothing had been right since that man had intruded into her life! But perhaps she was putting the cart before the horse, and besides, maybe their two species weren't fertile together. There was always that hope. In any case, she firmly decided against any more romps with her sexy alien friend. She looked over at him as he led her through a rabbit warren of passages. Pity he had to be so damn good to look at. She sighed heavily.

At that precise moment, Lorgin turned around, giving her a heart-wrenchingly beautiful smile. The dimple popped into his cheek, showcasing lips she knew felt like satin on heated skin. It was not going to be easy, she thought, shaking her head. Not easy at all.

"Where are you taking me, Lorgin?"

He reached over, taking her hand. "You will see. Right through here."

He led her through a concealed doorway in the rock wall, then down some narrow, twisting passageways. In the distance, she could hear what sounded like gurgling water.

The passage widened out, and suddenly they were in a large cavern. Facing them was one of the most beautiful sights Deana had ever seen. She was spellbound by the scene before her.

Lorgin came up behind her, placing his hands on her shoulders.

"What is it?" Her breathy voice seemed to bounce gently off the walls.

"It is called the Cave of Many Colors."

"I've never seen anything like it."

Multicolored waterfalls cascaded gently down two opposite sides of the cavern, joining together in a pool of swirling hues. "It's beautiful. What causes the colors to form?"

"No one knows." His voice came from over her left shoulder. Gently, he squeezed her shoulders. "Sometimes it is better to just enjoy the magic in life, not to analyze it."

She nodded, too moved by the beauty before her to speak.

"Yaniff made this for you." Lorgin's words broke into her thoughts as he thrust a vial into her hand.

"What is it?"

"Cleansing oil. I thought you would prefer a more womanly scent to my oil, which you used last night." He didn't add that he had asked Yaniff to create this oil in the scent of the *tasmin* flower, which so reminded him of her.

Deana unscrewed the top, taking a whiff of the oil. "It's lovely. You must thank Yaniff for me. It was kind of him to be so thoughtful." Lorgin's answer was a brief nod.

They stood enjoying the view for quite awhile. Deana was aware that Lorgin had moved off when she heard the rustle of his garments as he undressed. Surprised, she turned to him. "We can bathe here?"

He smiled. "Yes, of course."

Looking down at the vial in her hand, Deana wondered if

it was wise. Lorgin noticed her hesitancy. "Tell me you are not still shy of disrobing in front of me, Adeeann." His words echoed in the chamber as he approached her completely divested of clothes. His voice lowered. "Not after what we have done."

Her face flamed. "A-a little."

He was standing in front of her now. He reached up, gently running his fingers through the long, curling strands of her hair. "You are an unusual woman," he murmured. "Sometimes I have no idea what is going on in that mind of yours; other times, you are only too obvious."

She backed away from him a few steps, eliminating the contact. Her expression serious, she asked, "When am I obvious?"

Lorgin moved closer. "When your emotions are involved. You are not adept at hiding your feelings. Your thoughts are another matter. They continually surprise me."

He could see her feelings? How disastrous! Gramps had always told her she was a lousy poker player. She would have to be more careful. Raising her chin, she looked him right in the eye.

"Oh really? And what emotion am I giving away now?"

His low chuckle bounced off the walls. "You are nervous. I do not know why."

"You should be standing here." Her eyes flicked to his tumescent arousal.

He followed the direction her eyes had taken, raising an eyebrow. "I would hope you would be flattered, not nervous."

She turned and sat down on a boulder. "I am nervous, Lorgin."

He stood behind her, again lacing his hands on her shoulders, giving them a little squeeze. "Why?"

Refusing to look at him, she thought it best to just tell him. "We can't do that anymore."

The hands on her shoulder tightened. "Why not?"

"I—I don't want to get pregnant."

Lorgin let out a sigh of relief. Leaning over, he whispered in her ear, "Then you will not."

She turned to look up at him. "I won't?"

He gently kissed her. "Of course not."

She looked perplexed. "Oh? Are you sure?"

He smiled slightly. "Positive. You need not worry about this."

Well, she must look like a first-class ninny. He obviously had some type of birth control she knew nothing about, or perhaps she was right in thinking that the two species might not be able to reproduce. Somehow that thought didn't make her joyously happy. At any rate, he seemed somewhat amused at her concern, so he must not have any worries over it. Maybe she would look less of a ninny if she explained a few things to him.

"We use condoms." He had leaned over and was nuzzling her neck. Now he stopped.

"What is that?"

She didn't expect him to ask her that! "They—um—they're made of a material that is waterproof, and they—um go over the man, you know, when—"

Lorgin looked at her aghast. "Why do you do this?" What a horrible sexual custom, he thought. "Do you not like the feel of each other?"

"Yes, but it is used as a preventative, both for disease and—"

"*Disease?*" He looked appalled. Deana didn't think she was doing a very good job of explaining this to him. "What do you mean, disease?"

Deana explained as best she could, which probably wasn't very good because he looked rather sick when she finished.

"We do not have disease here, Adeeann. Our well-being is part of our very makeup. Illness here is only of a spiritual kind."

"That's amazing. No disease of any kind?"

"No. Not like you spoke of. Of course, anyone can come under the influence of a spell, but such magic is strictly enforced and watched over by the Guild."

Lorgin watched her as she thought about what he had said. By Aiyah, he was glad he had removed her from such a horrible world. Disease! Who had ever heard of such a thing!

Deana was thinking about what Lorgin had said as she rolled the vial between her hands. Now that her fear of unwanted consequences had been resolved, should she allow Lorgin to remain her lover while she was here? She remembered the smile he had given her in the passageway and crossed her legs. *All I have to do is think of him and I'm squirming. Does that answer your question?*

She felt him nuzzling her neck again; his warm hands on her shoulders seared through her tunic.

"Come, *zira*, bathe with me."

Zira! She had to at least straighten that out with him. "Lorgin, if we do . . . bathe together, it doesn't have anything to do with my going back to my planet."

Lorgin hid his smile. "I agree. It has nothing to do with it."

Deana, pleased with his response, got up and undressed. When her last garment fell away, Lorgin scooped her up in his arms, carrying her to the pool.

She flung her arms around his neck, leaning back in his arms to look at him.

"We—we are just friends, aren't we?"

162

Now he did smile. "We are friends."

"And . . . you will take me home soon, Lorgin; won't you?"

His eyes were heavy-lidded with passion as he went into the swirling water with her. "Of course, *zira*. I will take you home." His mouth swooped down to capture hers.

Lorgin prided himself in the honesty of his responses.

Some time later, Lorgin lay by the edge of the pool on his back, his hair flowing over the rock rim into the water. He could feel the mildly swirling current tugging on it. How he had let Adeeann talk him into this, he knew not.

He felt her fingers glide through his hair as she gently washed it. Perhaps it was not such a bad idea after all. Her soothing ministrations produced a tranquil effect on him; he closed his eyes, letting his thoughts wander over the pleasure they had just shared . . .

He had set her down in the water, watching her delight as the beautiful colors swirled around her, telling her she looked like the center of a living rainbow. He remembered the tinkling sound of her laughter as she scooped up a handful of water and watched it trail down her arm, the colors separating and combining as it flowed over her skin.

"How beautiful, Lorgin!" She scooped up another handful, fascinated by the liquid spectrum.

Lorgin watched the colorful droplets of water separate and flow down her arms to her breasts with interest. A pale turquoise droplet rolled slowly toward her aureole where it seemed to hover for a moment on the tip of her nipple before dripping off. It was followed by a lavender one. Then pink. He felt his manhood throb.

"Where is your tasmin oil?" She looked up at the hoarse sound of his voice. He knew his eyes were sparking.

"Here. Why?" He held out his hand for the vial. She gingerly placed it in his palm. He put a drop of oil on his hand, then slowly reached for her breast.

The feel of her skin beneath his massaging fingers was like the finest *krilli* cloth, smooth and silky, and soft as only a woman can be. He let his fingers glide along the path of the crystal water, slowly. His fingertips, like the droplet, separated as they moved down her; they seemed to flow around her, echoing a gentle vibration.

When he reached her nipple, he slowly circled the tight nub with the tip of his index finger, taking his time to reach the crest. As he arrived at his destination, he coiled his arm around her narrow waist, bringing her closer to him while he smoothly took the luscious peak in his heated mouth.

He heard her light intake of breath, an exclamation of wonder. It moved him, this innocent sound of delighted pleasure. Taking her breast full in his mouth, he wrapped his other arm around her waist. The embrace seemed appropriate to him, somehow; the fact that he had to cage this woman, demanding her to have pleasure.

This subduing was a new experience for him.

Other women he had known did not need to be coaxed into being with him. Just the opposite. But this woman—she resisted him on many levels. Her fear of him, which he knew to be fear of herself. Her stubborn talk of returning to her world. Her refusal, even now, to admit to being his wife. Her physical resistance to him when he entered her—that slight muscular barrier that tried to stop him even as it welcomed him.

Lorgin knew how to take what he wanted. His training and his experiences, both as a warrior and a mystic, served him well. Each of these pathways would be adhered to. As a warrior, he would conquer her. As a mystic, he would bind her to him.

She was, after all, his.

He had claimed her in every way possible. And if she had any doubts, well then, he would just have to find a few new ways of claiming a woman. He smiled sardonically at the intriguing thought.

He felt her tremble as he suckled her.

She was very responsive, his Adeeann. Moving upward, his lips traced a searing path. He kissed her ardently, opening his mouth on hers, inviting her to come inside.

The first tentative touch of her tongue rocked him. He lifted her higher against him in the swirling water to give her better access to him. Tightening his embrace of her, he silently urged her on.

She entered his mouth like she did most things, he thought: in a rush of passion. She was fiery and feisty, and, occasionally, playful. She probed and toyed and nibbled. Her arms wrapped tight around his neck as she lost herself in her pleasure of him.

Lorgin groaned. She tasted so sweet!

He easily held her to him with one arm, letting the other slide down her slick skin. He caressed her bottom under the water, gently running the edge of his hand along the crevice of her rounded buttocks.

She gasped into his mouth.

Letting his hand glide lower, he continued to allow her access to his mouth.

His fingers found her under the water, and he gently nudged her legs apart so that he could have better access to that which he sought. His finger glided against the inner folds of her soft womanly passage, smoothly like the flow of water around her. He wondered if she was even aware of what he was doing, so light was his touch.

When he inserted a finger gently into her, she stopped kissing him, blinking her surprise.

"Lorgin . . ."

"Yes, Little Fire?" He moved his finger in her, stroking her. She braced her hands on his shoulders.

"Lorgin . . ."

"That is my name." He bent his head to run his open mouth up her neck. She trembled in his arms. He brought one of her legs up around his waist. Then the other.

She was completely open to him now.

He brought the tip of his erection to her passage, sealing his mouth to hers at the same moment. While he kissed her, he slowly lowered her down onto him. As before, there was a moment of resistance before he was invited in. He smiled against her mouth. And thrust.

"Lorgin!"

She threw her head back, gripping his shoulders. Her long hair trailed behind her in the swirling colored water. Her voice shook with her passion.

"Did you think it was another?" His large hands clamped on her buttocks, pulling her fully onto him.

Her gasp echoed across the cave.

He took her breast in his mouth again, tugging on her, drawing on her, as he moved inside the sweet, hot canal. A ripple of current flowed from him to her *and back again.* It was a first for him. The pleasure of it moved him deeply because it was a pleasure that came only after a Transference.

His broken whisper bespoke his deep emotions. "*Aiyah*, Adeeann . . . such . . . pleasure . . . you give me." He laced his fingers through her hair, kissing her with abandon.

As he continued to steadily thrust into her, the currents began flowing back and forth between them, ripples of power and pleasure. He could feel Adeeann trembling in his arms as she started the coming.

In the throes of her passion, she tried to pull her mouth

away from his, but he would not let her. He kept her locked to him as the coming approached him. So that when it was upon them, they moaned into each other's mouth: breath for breath, shiver for shiver . . .

Lorgin stretched on the rock surface, his thoughts returning to the present and Adeeann's pleasant massaging of his scalp as she washed his hair. Her flowery scent reached him on a gentle waft of air. He loved the scent of—

He sniffed the air again.

His indulgent mood vanished instantly. His expression thunderous, he abruptly sat up, yanking his hair away from Deana.

"By the blood of *Aiyah*! You are using *tasmin* oil on my hair!"

Deana looked down at the vial in her hand. She had been so absorbed in the massage, she really hadn't been paying much attention to the cleanser. She didn't see what all the fuss was about. It was just a scent, for crying out loud. Admittedly, a very feminine scent.

"Look, I'm sorry. But it's really not that noticeable." He threw her a look. "Believe me, you'd have to be standing this close to you to smell it." He still didn't seem to be buying it. Time to use a feminine wile. "No one but me is going to be this close to you, are they, Lorgin?" She smiled at him coquettishly. It appeared to do the trick.

Lorgin sighed. "I suppose you are right." He stood up, retrieving their clothes. "We should be leaving. It is late, and we need to depart early on the morrow."

They quickly dressed, exiting the beautiful cavern. As soon as they had rounded the corridor, Lorgin told her he had forgotten his cleansing oil in the cave. Instructing her to wait for him, he re-entered the pool cave.

His lilac eyes briefly scanned the beauty of the scene before him; then he passed his arm in front of him, turning the colorful waterfall back to the ordinary one it had always been.

It had pleased him that Adeeann had enjoyed his secret gift to her.

As they were making their way back to their chamber, they came across Rejar in a corridor. He was coming toward them, tugging on a boot and fastening his cloak about his shoulders.

"Every time I see your brother, he's adjusting his clothes," Deana whispered.

"That is because he takes them off so much." A corner of Lorgin's mouth lifted as he thought of his rascal of a younger brother.

Deana shook her head in awe. The man was a sex machine.

As Rejar came abreast of them in the hallway, he sniffed the air, grinning. "Mmm . . . *tasmin* flower. Very nice, brother," he said aloud as he passed them in the corridor.

Lorgin's thunderous expression followed him down the hallway, then turned on Deana.

She shrugged sheepishly. "A fluke. How many people have a cat for a brother?"

He took her by the arm dragging her down the hallway. He was not amused.

Chapter Nine

She could hardly walk.

Deana gingerly stepped down into Laeva's feasting room, wincing with each tiny movement she made. The source of her discomfort was sitting at the table, blithely wolfing down what looked like a flat loaf of bread.

Lorgin reached for a cup of that gluey paste drink everyone around here seemed to be mad about, noticing she had entered the room. Motioning for her to seat herself in the empty chair next to him, he poured her a large cup of the godawful stuff, placing it on the table in front of her chair.

Sitting down very carefully, Deana stared dismally at the paste. Under the best of circumstances she was not a morning person. This was not the best of circumstances. Resignedly, she took a sip of the gooey junk. A twinge of protest echoed between her legs. She winced.

Then she became aware of Lorgin watching her over the rim of his cup.

Their eyes met.

He flashed her a knowing look which spoke volumes of insufferable male pride. He casually ran a hand through the length of his hair on the right side of his head.

"You are sore, Adeeann?"

She almost spit out her drink.

Lorgin addressed the table at large. "Our journey has been tiring for her. She is not used to so much physical exertion."

Deana didn't miss the mischievous little dimple that creased Lorgin's cheek. Nor did she miss Rejar suddenly showing an interest in examining his plate, the corners of his sensuous mouth twitching as he tried not to burst out laughing. She threw Lorgin a venomous look.

"Gharta." Lorgin mouthed the word at her, his eyes crinkling at the corners in amusement. He so enjoyed igniting his Little Fire. In every way. Ignoring her obvious irritation with him, he placed his arm around the back of her chair, letting his fingers dip inside her tunic under her hair. He idly stroked the sensitive skin at the nape of her neck as he resumed his conversation with Yaniff.

Deana turned and stared at him in disbelief.

It was a blatant act of possession.

Did the man never listen to her? Had she been talking to the rock wall last night? Apparently she might as well have been. Of all the nerve!

She clenched her teeth, muttering under her breath, "Lorgin ta'al *Arrogant* Krue."

She didn't think he'd heard her because he continued on with his conversation with Yaniff. That is, until she felt his finger slide vertically down her neck, followed by a sharp little jolt. She jumped in her chair. "Yeow!"

He briefly glanced her way, speaking to her in a low, authoritative tone. "Behave yourself." She narrowed her eyes at him. Unconcerned, he turned back to Yaniff. "I am hoping to find al Nek this day so that we may continue on without delay."

"Yes, that would be the course." Yaniff broke off a small piece of flat bread for Bojo. The beast daintily nibbled the crumbs from the old man's fingers.

Laeva looked up from her bowl of fruit. "Greka al Nek? Are you talking about that slimy trader from the Oberion colonies?"

"The very one." Yaniff took a sip of his drink. "Do you know him, Laeva?"

"I have treated him once or twice. A man like that always has somebody out to kill him. A couple of times they nearly succeeded. I swear, the trader has more lives than a cat." She quickly looked at Rejar. "Sorry." Rejar inclined his head.

Laeva turned to Lorgin. "What do you want with riffraff like him?"

Lorgin's eyes met Yaniff's. "He has some information I need."

"I see. Well, if you hurry, you might catch him in the square. He sometimes comes early to peddle his wares to the merchants here. There was talk recently that he had just returned from a caravan to the far sector—if you believe it."

Lorgin, Rejar, and Yaniff immediately stood.

"Thank you, Laeva. For everything," Lorgin said as he pulled Deana out of her chair. "We must make haste to depart at once."

"I haven't finished eating!" Deana protested.

"I will purchase something for you later—hurry, Adeeann! We must not miss him." Waving goodbye to Laeva, Deana was quickly ushered out the door by the three men.

They found al Nek about a half hour later in the middle of the square, sitting at a small cafe type table. Deana tried not to stare at the alien. It was not easy. His skin was a patchy, bumpy, grayish hue. He was small, probably only about five feet tall. His three hands each had eight long, thin fingers, sporting even longer talons at the ends. He was one ugly dude.

Al Nek was drinking a bubbling hot brew from a tiny cup. The smell of it almost made Deana gag. His beady little eyes assessed them all silently, finally resting on Deana. His lascivious perusal made her skin crawl; she moved closer to Lorgin. A flick of his eye was the only indication she got from Lorgin that he was aware of her action.

"What can I do for you, esteemed travelers?" Al Nek's voice was nasal and tinny. It grated on Deana's nerves.

Placing a booted foot up on an empty bench, Lorgin leaned toward the slimy trader. Deana didn't doubt that Lorgin's stance was purposely chosen to be intimidating. From the look on Greka al Nek's face, it was working.

Lorgin's steely lavender gaze pierced him. "I have need of some information from you, al Nek."

The trader's eyes instantly took on an avaricious gleam. He motioned to the empty benches around the table, inviting them to sit. No one did. He didn't seem the least insulted. "I see. And what is this information you seek of me?"

"It is said you recently returned from a journey to the Rim. Is this true?"

Al Nek shrugged his narrow shoulders. "Ah, truth—what a relative concept." He slowly sipped his drink, taking his time before he replied, "Information dependent on truth . . . could be costly."

Lorgin narrowed his eyes. "How costly?"

Al Nek's eyes trained on Deana who was unconsciously clutching a piece of Lorgin's cloak. "The girl?"

"What about her?" Lorgin's tone was stone cold.

"Perhaps we could work something out. She is very comely in an exotic way. There are many who would pay highly for her. What if . . . you trade her for this information you seek."

In the blink of an eye, Lorgin was holding the Cearix to the man's throat. "What if, instead, al Nek, you give me the information I seek . . . *and I let you live.*"

Al Nek swallowed nervously. When he spoke, his voice was even higher. "This could be agreeable also."

"Were you at the Rim recently?"

"Yes—a small caravan, you understand. We almost did not make it back. A most inhospitable region, that."

"Did you hear anything that might be of interest to the Charl?"

The little man's eyes shifted apprehensively from Lorgin to Yaniff. "Th-there was something. But I thought at the time it was nonsense. Surely, you do not—"

Lorgin pressed the blade tighter against his throat. "Tell me."

"There was a rumor—just a rumor, mind you—that someone had found a phasing stone." Lorgin looked at Yaniff over the trader's head.

"Do you know who has the stone?"

"I-I saw a man there. On one of the Rim planets. He was a mystic like you. By his cape—power of the Six."

Lorgin took a deep breath. "What was his name?"

"I do not know th that he has such a st stone . . ." The trader was clearly terrified of what this man might do to him should he find out about this conversation.

"What was his name?" Lorgin repeated. Deana could see he was beginning to lose patience.

"He—he said his name was Theardar."

Lorgin sucked in his breath, his eyes meeting Yaniff's once

again. He reached into his cape and threw the slimy little man a gem. "For your *cooperation*."

Greka al Nek was clearly surprised by the payoff. He was glad to still be alive. He did not doubt that the man with the golden hair would have killed him in an instant if it suited his purposes. These Charl were a breed apart. Most knew better than to ever cross one.

Al Nek tried not to think of what would happen to him should Theardar come across his path again. He looked at the golden-haired man speculatively. Perhaps it would be in his best interest to befriend this knight. One could never be too careful.

"Sir, perchance I can be of further assistance to you?"

Lorgin's head whipped around. "What do you mean?"

"Some pleasure after a long journey, perhaps? I have many fine *chaktan's* available for hire." He looked hopefully at Rejar. "Even the Familiar would not be disappointed."

Rejar leveled a searing glare at the disgusting little man. "This Familiar does not pay for his pleasure, trader." He turned his back on him in disdain, walking away.

Yaniff spoke for the first time. "If I were one such as you, Greka al Nek, I would not be overly concerned about a Familiar's pleasures. No, I think I would spend my time wondering if it is possible to avoid a sixth-level mystic and, if so . . . *for how long*."

As they left the square, Deana glanced back at al Nek, noticing his hand shook as he raised his drink slowly to his mouth.

Once they had reached the esplanade, Lorgin led them into a small eating establishment, securing a table in a quiet corner. Yaniff wandered off with Bojo, saying he would be back shortly.

"I will bring you something to eat, Adeeann." Deana

perked up in anticipation, until Lorgin returned with a cup of the dreaded glue.

Her shoulders sagged. "Is this all they had?"

"You are not fond of *Rasking*? On my home planet, Aviara, this is considered a delicacy."

Rejar looked up at Lorgin's words, his dual-colored eyes twinkling. The two brothers exchanged glances.

{*Yes, Adeeann. Rasking is considered quite a treat on Aviara. Then again, most things are considered a treat on Aviara.*} Rejar sighed mournfully.

Deana looked up from her drink, trying to decide whether to swallow it or go hungry. "What do you mean?"

Rejar nodded to Lorgin. {*Has he not told you?*}

"Told me what?"

Lorgin looked at the ceiling. "Now you have done it, Rejar. I was going to break it to her gently, but, as usual, you have spoiled my methods."

"Break what to me?"

Lorgin shrugged. "There is no hope for it now. I will have to tell her." He took a deep breath. "This is considered a delicacy on Aviara, Adeeann, because we have *nothing* to compare to it."

Deana's eyes widened. Was he telling her *this* was a gourmet selection on Aviara? If so, what kind of gunk did they eat?

{*So true, Lorgin. Our food is . . .* } Rejar let the thought trail off, content to let Deana draw her own assumptions.

"It is because of our weather, of course."

Deana turned to Lorgin. "What's wrong with the weather?"

"Bitterly cold all the time."

{*Except when it is scorchingly hot.*}

Deana looked from one brother to the other. They both

returned a bland expression to her. She chewed her bottom lip.

"Did you say we were going there soon?"

Lorgin looked at her straight-faced. "Absolutely."

Jeez, this place sounded like a pit hole. Maybe she could talk Lorgin out of it. "Do we have to?"

He looked at her through veiled eyes. "Yes."

Deana slumped in her seat.

Yaniff returned, sitting on the bench opposite her, speaking directly to Lorgin. "So . . . the time has come for us to deal with Theardar. I tried to warn the Guild of the repercussions when they excommunicated him, but they would not listen."

Lorgin seemed surprised by Yaniff's admission. "You did not agree with their actions?" Although he had overheard his parents discussing it often, in hushed voices, he was a young boy at the time and had no real memory of the event.

"No, I did not. I wished to counsel Theardar, but they would not hear of it. They wanted him removed from their presence for the terrible deed he had committed and would not relent. I warned them that their actions that day would come back to haunt them."

"They say he is mad." Lorgin looked questioningly at Yaniff. "They say he has been mad for years. That he could not control his power and went insane. Is it true, Yaniff?"

Yaniff did not immediately respond. When he did, his voice was laced with sorrow. "It is the boy who suffered."

Lorgin closed his eyes. "Traed."

"Yes, Traed." Yaniff wiped a hand across his eyes. "Even now I think of him."

"Why was nothing done at the time to prevent it from happening? He was so happy with us."

"One cannot separate a man from his son so easily. It was Theardar's right—he chose to exercise it."

176

Lorgin's fist crashed against the table. "At Traed's expense!"

Yaniff nodded sadly. "You must seek him out, Lorgin. Find him on the barren world of Zarrain where he has exiled himself."

Rejar's eyebrows raised. {*He is on Zarrain? Why would he go to such a bleak place?*}

Yaniff's shoulders sagged. "A man who has suffered as Traed has will often take himself to a place which outwardly mirrors his inner spirit. Find him, Lorgin, and convince him to return to Aviara with you. I see now his presence is essential to the outcome of this quest."

Lorgin leaned his back against the wall. "If what you say is true, he will never leave Zarrain. He loathes Theardar."

"He will remember your friendship, Lorgin. Use it to make him come." Lorgin reflected on Yaniff's words, not at all comfortable with using their boyhood friendship to manipulate Traed. Yaniff's eyes pierced Lorgin. "It must be done, Lorgin, or all is lost."

Lorgin turned away, then nodded curtly.

Deana, who had been listening to the whole exchange, was fascinated by what she had heard. Not that she understood most of it. "What's a phasing stone?" she whispered to Rejar.

{*Phasing stones make up the Shimalee—like the one you wear, Adeeann. Each Shimalee is somewhat different from the others. The one you wear, for instance, has one stone. Some have many stones, depending on the design matrix and how they line up to atunement.*}

Deana thought about Rejar's words. "So, if this Theardar guy only has one stone, what could he do with it?"

Lorgin answered her. "In and of itself, nothing. Phasing stones, like the Shimalee, can fold space and time. But in order to do this they need a diviner—one who 'sings' to them. Theardar does not have this ability.'' He glanced at Yaniff. ''However, should Theardar somehow *unlock* the secrets of the stone, there is no telling what could happen. We might see—''

''—all manner of disturbances,'' Yaniff finished for him.

Lorgin exhaled heavily. ''Such as rifts in space and time.''

''Yes, Lorgin.'' The old mystic bowed his head. The knowledge of what was occurring on the Rim was all too clear now.

Lorgin stood up. ''Adeeann, finish your drink. I do not know when we will be able to stop to eat again, and you need this nourishment.''

Deana was not about to balk at a drink when they all seemed so deeply concerned about a grave matter. She held her nose and quickly drank it down.

''I will accompany you to the tunnel point.'' Yaniff stroked Bojo thoughtfully. ''From there I will await you on Aviara.''

The boat bobbed in the swirling current as the raging river carried them along. Yaniff had explained to Deana that the underground river would eventually bring them up to the surface of the satellite. From there it would be a short journey to the tunnel point. She did not look forward to entering that maelstrom of pulsating energy again.

Soon, Deana heard a roaring sound up ahead of them. Fearing the possibility of approaching rapids, she asked Yaniff what it was. Before he had a chance to answer her, the swiftly flowing water carried them forward, and they emerged with a jutting bob onto the surface of Ryka Twelve.

She didn't have to ask what the sound was now. A roaring wind blasted her, almost toppling her from the boat. It grabbed the tendrils of her hair, whipping it about her face.

Now she knew why the population here lived underground. She quickly retrieved the little barrette Lorgin had bought for her at the convention, using it to tie back the two front sections of her hair.

Lorgin battled the water and the wind, eventually bringing the boat to the bank of the river. Rejar agilely leaped out, his boots splashing into the frothing water as he held his arms out for Deana.

{Hurry, Adeeann, I do not know how much longer Lorgin can control the boat.}

Deana looked to the bow of the boat.

It was a sight she knew she would not soon forget.

Lorgin stood in the wind, his cape and hair whipping about him. He looked magnificent. The light of two Rykan moons backlit him as he battled the forces around him. Using the long pole and what must be a great deal of strength, he anchored the boat to a small piece of shore which jutted out into the river.

{Hurry, Adeeann!}

Her attention returned to Rejar. He was waiting for her to leap out of the wildly rocking boat into his arms. She looked down at the churning water below her, swallowing.

"You—you won't drop me, will you Rejar?"

{Never. Now come—quickly!}

Closing her eyes, she jumped from the boat.

Rejar's secure embrace enveloped her. He carried her to the shore, gently depositing her on the bank. Then he turned back to the boat to aid Yaniff.

As Yaniff stepped from the boat, Bojo gracefully spread his wings, lifting into the air. He did not go far from the old mystic, hovering concernedly near him. Rejar put his hand under the old man's arm, assisting him to shore.

Noticing that everyone had made it safely to land, Lorgin

used the pole in his hands to vault over the edge of the boat onto the shore. Without Lorgin's control, the little boat careened wildly in the currents, rapidly bobbing down the river out of sight.

Deana briefly wondered why Lorgin had not used his abilities to tame the wind and the water. Yaniff spoke to her, leaning heavily on his staff, Bojo once again on his shoulder.

"There is a dampening field here, child. We are both, Lorgin and I, at somewhat of a disadvantage." He stopped a moment to catch his breath. "Always at tunnel points a dampening field." He nodded to Lorgin, who turned in the direction of the moons, closing his eyes.

"What's he doing?" she whispered to Rejar.

{Calling forth the tunnel.}

"He didn't do it that way on my world."

Yaniff replied, "Things work somewhat differently here, child."

Suddenly the ground beneath their feet shifted. A violent tremor rocked the earth, knocking them all sideways. Yaniff was right—things sure were different around here!

Lorgin's eyes snapped open. "*Xathu!*"

In a heartbeat he grabbed Deana around the waist, hauling her backward. He dragged her under a rocky overhang, Rejar and Yaniff right on his heels.

Deana turned in Lorgin's arms. "So where's the tunn—" Her eyes widened as the ground before them broke apart.

Something was coming out from under the ground.

A wailing shriek rent the air, raising the hackles on the back of her neck. An enormous bulk unfurled out of the earth, rocks and dirt flying in its wake as the ground trembled.

The beast hurled itself from the bowels of Ryka Twelve.

It was hideous. Deana cowered against Lorgin as the monster gained its full height, towering over them at least fifty feet, hissing and screeching into the howling wind.

An enormous body supported a thick trunklike neck which sported five heads. The heads reminded Deana of pictures she had seen of Tyrannosaurus rex, except for the sharp fang-teeth which dripped greenish saliva. The thick fluid hissed and smoked as it hit the ground.

"What is it?" she yelled over the wind and noise.

Lorgin put a protective arm around her. "*A xathu.* Sometimes on this world, such beasts make their home near a tunnel point. Probably in the hopes of dining on some unwary travelers."

She shivered in his arms. "Such as us?" He squeezed her shoulder, a small gesture meant to reassure.

"It will never let us enter the tunnels. I will have to try and kill it, Adeeann."

"No!" Suddenly she was terrified for him. How could a man fight that thing? Even Yaniff had said there was a field here dampening his abilities. She clutched the front of his shirt in her fists. "Lorgin, don't!"

He gently but firmly extricated himself from her grip. "I must." Reaching up, he removed the crystal point from his ear; he placed it in her palm, closing her hand around it. "Stay here with Yaniff. If I am . . . unsuccessful, he will take care of you."

"No!"

But it was too late. Lorgin nodded to Rejar, removing his light saber from his waistband.

They circled the beast.

Deana could see that Rejar was trying to gain the xathu's attention, probably to allow Lorgin a chance to deliver a blow. Rejar moved with his characteristic lithe grace, but Deana doubted it would help him much. The man didn't even carry a light saber.

Three of the xathu's heads focused on Rejar. He barely managed to jump out of the way as the powerful jaws snapped at him. At that moment Lorgin struck, slicing off a head in an instant. The creature bellowed in pain and anger, turning back toward Lorgin.

Deana put her hands over her ears to block out the deafening sound.

Rejar waved his arms in an attempt to attract the beast again.

It worked.

The *xathu* focused on him and advanced. Rejar stood stock still staring down four throats of inevitable death.

"What's he doing?" Deana yelled. "Why doesn't he move?"

Yaniff placed a hand on her arm. "He attempts to mesmerize the beast. It is an ability some Familiars have. If he can do it, he will not be able to hold him for more than a few moments."

They watched with bated breath as Rejar stood his ground in front of the *xathu*, not moving a muscle. Deana wondered at the courage it took to stand so still in the face of certain death.

It appeared to be working.

The *xathu* stopped suddenly, staring at Rejar like a charmed cobra. Deana noticed Lorgin moving behind the beast out of the corner of her eye. He raised his arm to strike, but in that instant the xathu broke free of Rejar's hold. He whipped his gaze to Lorgin, teeth gleaming and dripping in the moonlight.

Deana screamed.

Lorgin jumped back in the nick of time.

Or so it seemed.

He suddenly clutched his chest, grimacing in pain. Something hissed, and she saw smoke coming from his shirt.

Some of the saliva had struck him. Probably a burn, but, thank God, nothing too serious. Deana started to exhale her pent-up breath, when, unbelievably Lorgin sank to his knees in the dirt. He was writhing on the ground in agony. She heard Yaniff suck in his breath. The *xathu* was coming in for the kill on Lorgin.

The old mystic helplessly watched the scene unfolding before him. "He will die."

Deana could not believe it. Lorgin die? It—it couldn't happen. Not like this! They had just discovered each other—they needed more time to . . . She couldn't let this happen!

She wouldn't let this happen.

Without stopping to think, Deana ran to Lorgin, placing herself between him and the *xathu*.

"Adeeann . . ." he gasped. "Get back!"

Deana ignored him, focusing on the beast. Its beady eyes surveyed her like a specimen under a microscope. This close she could smell its fetid breath. Out of the corner of her eye she saw Rejar preparing to place himself directly in the path of the beast in an attempt to save her.

She felt curiously detached as the scene played out before her. A humming began to vibrate through her body.

Its source was the necklace.

The Shimalee! Deana's hand touched the cool stone. It vibrated under her skin, as if . . . as if it were singing to her! She could hear it in her blood, this cosmic voice calling to her. It gained in pitch and tone, pulsing through her body like a second heartbeat, singing of other places, other times. Deana closed her eyes as alien landscapes, the birth of stars, the death of galaxies revealed themselves to her in rapid succession as if she were flipping the pages of a cosmic picture book.

It was a fabric! Woven by the threads of the song she was hearing.

Faintly, somewhere in the back of her head, she heard the roar of the *xathu* as it bore down on her. The Shimalee sang to her.

Send it away . . .

She suddenly wished she *could* send the horrid beast to one of the alien vistas she was seeing.

Yes . . . the song whispered in her mind. *Send it away . . .*

She touched both hands to the stone, feeling its soothing tones in every point of her body. Then, for a reason unknown to her, she stretched out her hands, palms up, in the direction of the *xathu*.

Suddenly there was a loud clapping sound, a flash of light, and the *xathu* was no more.

The beast had been displaced in time and space.

She could not believe what had occurred. Both Rejar and herself should be dead. How had she done it? Or did she do it? Perhaps it was Yaniff or . . .

Lorgin groaned in pain. Deana dropped to her knees beside him, placing his head in her lap. She would worry over what had occurred later. For now, Lorgin needed her.

"Are you badly burnt, Lorgin?"

"Not burnt . . ." he moaned in agony. Deana could sense Yaniff and Rejar approaching them.

"What's wrong with him, Yaniff?"

Yaniff gazed sadly down at Lorgin ta'al Krue, in truth, his favorite of all students. "He dies."

Deana's head whipped up. "Why? What do you mean?"

Rejar knelt by his brother, placing a hand on his arm. He spoke aloud. "He has been kissed by a *xathu*. It is a poison there is no cure for."

"No! There must be something we can do! What can we do, Yaniff?"

The mystic turned away, shoulders slumped. At that moment, he did not look like a great wizard; he just looked like a tired old man.

Rejar watched his brother dying. A tear tracked slowly down his sensitive face. "It will not be long, now. The poison drains him even as we speak."

"Yaniff!" Deana ran to the mystic, grabbing his robes. "Yaniff, think of something! You must!"

Rejar rose. Beneath his pain of impending loss, he could not help but admire his brother's wife for her courageous act on Lorgin's behalf. Not many would place themselves in the direct path of a *xathu* beast. Now, however, she needed to accept that the fight was all but over. "There is nothing, Adeeann. Go to Lorgin to say your fare—"

Yaniff's eyes flew to Rejar, a speculative gleam in them. "Wait! There might be *something* . . ."

Rejar and Deana focused on Yaniff. The old man went to stand over Lorgin. "Come here, Rejar." Rejar did as he was bid. "There is a moment," Yaniff said, "when you transform yourself that you are neither man nor animal. Is this not so?"

Rejar looked at Yaniff confused. "Yes, but—"

"At this precise moment, this split second in time, your form is pure energy, is this not correct?" Rejar nodded. "It might be possible then, at that exact moment in time, for you to pass through your brother and take the poison with you."

"But then Rejar would die!" Deana was appalled. She dearly wanted Lorgin to live, but not at the expense of his brother.

"Not necessarily. Rejar, if you can disperse the poison while in your energy state before you complete the transformation, it may work."

Lorgin broke into Yaniff's words. His pain-wracked voice was weak. "No! This I cannot allow!" He tried to focus on his brother. "Rejar . . . you must not do this . . . it is . . . suicide."

Yaniff motioned Rejar over to him, talking quietly to him. "Do you wish to attempt it?"

Rejar nodded without hesitation.

Yaniff placed a hand on the younger man's shoulder. "If you cannot disperse all of the poison from Lorgin and yourself, Krue will lose two sons this day."

Rejar nodded again, shielding his thoughts from Yaniff. As a Familiar he could do this. The import of Yaniff's words was known instantly to Rejar. There was a good chance that either or both of them would die. If only one of them were to live, he would make sure it was Lorgin. He unshielded his mind and spoke.

"Yaniff, I have never held the between state more than a moment. I do not know if—"

"If you need me, I will help you."

Rejar stood above Lorgin. His brother was very weak now, laboring for breath. Rejar closed his eyes and began to metamorphose. Deana watched, part of her terrified for Lorgin, part fascinated by what she was witnessing.

Rejar began to glow from within. Steady streams of photons flowed and arced around him. He seemed to shimmer, *melting* into a gleaming phosphorescence. As Deana watched entranced, he became an amorphous pulsating body of light. It was . . . *beautiful.*

Yaniff spoke in her ear. "Not many witness the transformation of a Familiar, Adeeann. It is a private thing amongst them. I know you will not speak of it in the future." Deana nodded her agreement, wondering why such a beautiful thing was kept hidden.

"There are those who fear that which they do not understand. Familiars have learned to guard themselves over time."

The light moved toward Lorgin. As it became one with him, Deana noticed it begin to weaken and dull. She turned questioning eyes to Yaniff.

"He is in trouble. He cannot hold the state." Yaniff extended his staff. An arc traveled from the glowing orb at the end into the center of the light. As she watched, the light seemed to grow in intensity, gaining strength.

It passed through Lorgin, shimmering in the night.

Lorgin was breathing easier. He slowly sat up, his eyes going to the light which was his brother. "Rejar!"

As they watched, the light began to flow and meld; a shape was attempting to form. It coalesced, then broke apart.

"Rejar!" Lorgin tried to stand but was still too weak. "Help him, Yaniff. He grows faint."

But Yaniff was already helping him.

A stream of energy flowed directly from the old man into the center of the now fading light. For an instant nothing happened, then the light sparked, its luminosity intensifying. Soon, Deana could discern a shape coalescing out of the brightness. Rejar!

The glowing stopped when his form acquired substance.

Nude, Rejar slumped to the ground in a heap. Lorgin crawled over to him, quickly draping him with his cloak.

Lorgin intently checked Rejar for any signs of poisoning. He detected none. Seeing that his brother was going to live, Lorgin let his anger out.

"Rejar! I distinctly told you not to do this! As I am the elder brother, you should have heeded my words. Have I not trained you thus? You—"

Rejar smiled wanly up at Lorgin. "So, the poison has not killed me, but you will?"

Lorgin started to respond, then gave it up. Instead, he ruffled Rejar's hair—a gesture Deana guessed went back to their childhood. "You do realize that if anything had happened to you, Suleila would skin me alive."

"That would make dying worthwhile." Rejar grinned at Deana.

Deana couldn't recall ever hearing the man speak so many words out loud.

"He is too weak to send his thoughts." Yaniff knelt beside the dark-haired man on the ground, placing a hand on his arm. "You have done well, Rejar. That is, for someone not of the Charl. Of course, had you been of the Charl, you might have been able to call the forces upon yourself—"

"Please, old man, do not badger me now about joining you. I am too tired to ignore you."

Yaniff smiled slightly, then stared straight ahead into nothing. "There will come a day when you will be moved to try this technique again. Do not attempt it by yourself, Rejar; it is too dangerous for you."

Rejar regarded the mystic strangely. Finally he spoke. "I can assure you, old man, I will never be tempted to try that again."

Yaniff said nothing.

The ancient wizard took Lorgin aside, slapping him on the back. "This old mystic is pleased he has not lost such a promising pupil as you, Lorgin ta'al Krue."

Lorgin raised an eyebrow at him.

The old man suddenly seemed embarrassed by his display of fatherly affection. He cleared his throat. "Ahem, yes, well, you cannot imagine how tiresome it is to constantly have to train new students from scratch."

"I imagine after the first four hundred years it becomes tedious," Lorgin responded wryly. Nonetheless, he clapped the old man on the shoulder, telling him silently that he understood what he was trying to say.

Deana smiled, hearing Yaniff say, "I must tell you some things of Traed . . ." before the two of them walked out of earshot.

They said their goodbyes to Yaniff as he and Bojo entered the tunnels for Aviara. Lorgin and Deana waited awhile for Rejar to regain some of his strength, before they, too, entered the tunnels heading for Zarrain to seek out a man who wanted nothing to do with guests, invited or otherwise. From all accounts, a lone, wounded wolf. Son of a madman.

Traed ta'al Theardar.

Chapter Ten

It was a weary party that arrived on Zarrain.

The tunnel point deposited them on the outskirts of a frontier town. Deana surmised the town probably served as a way station to the tunnels.

It was night here, as well, on Zarrain.

Deana looked up at a clear sky, alive with stars. In every direction around the settlement was desert. A cool breeze gently wafted her hair.

"This isn't such a bad place."

Lorgin looked at her askance. "The nights on Zarrain can be pleasant enough. It is the days which are difficult." He peered down at his booted feet as he heard a scurrying sound in the sand. "You will find that everything comes out at night here in Zarrain: the stars, the people, and the wildlife. Watch where you step, *zira.*"

Deana looked down, suddenly noticing that the sand was moving below the surface. Just what was under there, she didn't care to speculate. She thought of Earth deserts, and their snakes and scorpions. "Is anything poisonous here, Lorgin?" Her voice went up a notch at the end.

He did not answer her directly. "Do not worry. I will keep an eye on you."

How he was going to do that when he was holding up his brother, she didn't know. Rejar was still very weak. He sagged against Lorgin's shoulder, the effort of walking seeming almost too much for him. Deana got on his opposite side, hiking his other arm over her shoulders. He leaned heavily on them both.

Deana was concerned. "Are you sure the poison is gone from him, Lorgin?"

"Yes. He would be dead if it were not. His energy level is very low. He just needs some time to recuperate his strength. He should be fine by the morrow."

The three of them headed slowly toward the town.

When they were almost there, Lorgin suddenly whipped out the Ccarix and hurled it at Deana's feet. There was a whooshing sound, then a little shriek split the air. The blade was sticking upright in the sand not an inch from her toe. It impaled a flat, black disc that had a lot of legs. Lorgin bent awkwardly while propping up Rejar, retrieving his blade. Deana stared at him behind Rejar's back, eyes wide.

"Do not look down, Little Fire. Just keep walking."

They entered the town a short time later. As Lorgin had predicted, everything appeared to come alive at night in Zarrain.

The joint was really jumping.

Discordant music filled the air; people danced in the streets, several of them drinking from those horns Deana recognized as containing *keeran*. There was a lot of partner-exchanging. Several establishments had their doors flung open to the night revelry. Merchants were hawking wares while sweet/acrid smoke filled the air.

"What's that sweet smoke?" She sniffed the air.

Lorgin looked away, while Rejar weakly chuckled.

"Well, what is it? Hey, what is that woman with the two mouths doing to that man?"

Lorgin reached across Rejar to pluck at her shirt collar, effectively turning her around.

"Do not gaze upon that. And do not breathe deeply of the smoke, either."

What a place! Deana peeked down one alleyway and saw what appeared to be a slave auction. She involuntarily shuddered.

Rejar sent her a weak thought *{Oberion slavers. Do not stare, Adeeann, lest you gain their attention.}*

She turned away from the horrid sight.

"Why do they allow it, Rejar?" She kept her voice low.

Rejar spoke aloud, his small store of strength rapidly depleting. "This is . . . a lawless world in a lawless sector. Such despicable activities . . . are . . . not . . . permitted in the Alliance."

Lorgin cautioned his brother to keep his head down. "We do not wish to draw attention to you here, Rejar. Especially when you are in this weakened state." He explained to Deana, "Oberion slavers have been known to abduct male Familiars on rare occasion."

Deana was surprised. "But why?"

"The reputation of their sensuous natures is well known throughout the sentient worlds. There are . . . twisted individuals who would pay highly for one."

Male love slaves? "But—wouldn't their abilities protect them?"

"Yes, but they are kept drugged, of course. Eventually they

escape. No one can keep a Familiar for long who doesn't want to be kept. However, I have heard stories of them being hunted down and destroyed.''

"How awful!" She turned horrified eyes to Rejar. "Is he in danger here?"

"No. When he has rested, he can protect himself. They would not dare tangle with him."

Lorgin led them to an establishment farther down the street which was marginally quieter than the others they had passed. Once inside he requested one room with two beds. "We cannot leave Rejar alone tonight," he said aside to Deana. She nodded her agreement.

The room was something of a surprise. Both beds hung from the ceiling by ropes. Deana was about to ask about this when she saw something scurry across the floor. The Cearix whizzed past her face striking home.

Great. Just great.

I'm going to be getting a lot of sleep tonight.

No wonder the beds didn't touch the floor. She wondered if she was going to be hearing that all night: *thwack* of the blade, *squeak* of the victim. She sighed deeply.

Lorgin deposited Rejar on one of the beds, helping him remove his boots. The weary Familiar sank back onto the cushions with a grateful sound. At least the beds looked clean and comfortable.

Deana hopped up on the other bed. It swayed back and forth, back and forth. She was getting seasick.

Thwack—squeak.

Oh no. "Lorgin, are you getting into bed?" *Please, get into bed.*

"In a moment." *Thwack—squeak.*

"Lorgin, get into bed this minute!" *Or I will strangle you.* She felt the bed dip and sway as he got in.

193

He rolled over to her, causing the bed to rock again. "Why is it you are only anxious for me to get into bed when I cannot do anything about it?" His voice was low in her ear.

"Don't be ridiculous." She turned her back to him, burrowing under the covers. He curled around her, enfolding her in his arms. Soon they were all asleep.

Several times during the night Deana awoke to the bed rocking wildly as Lorgin turned over in his sleep. Finally, she elbowed him in the stomach. All she got was a mumble for a reply.

"Quit moving around!" she hissed.

His answer was to roll over and cup his palm territorially over her breast in his sleep. The bed swayed some more.

Great. Just great.

Deana opened her eyes to the sight of a long snout with snaggle teeth not three inches from her face. She let out a bloodcurdling scream.

All hell broke lose.

Both brothers had lightning-fast reflexes. Lorgin rolled over on top of her to protect her. Rejar leaped from his bed, tackling the alien. They went down with a crash and rolled across the floor. She heard the sound of pottery shattering, Rejar cursing, and Lorgin laughing. Then she heard a loud, whiny, plaintive wail. Of course she couldn't see anything because Lorgin was crushing her into the mattress.

"Get off of me! I can't breathe!" Lorgin quickly rolled over, grinning from ear to ear at the scene in front of them.

Rejar was sitting on the floor on top of the guy with the snout. Food was flung everywhere, dishes smashed. The alien under Rejar wailed ceaselessly. Rejar gave Deana a disgusted look as he flicked a dollop of what looked like oatmeal off of his nose.

Deana couldn't help but giggle. "I take it this is Zarrain's version of room service?" Another wail came from the floor. "The poor thing! Rejar, let it loose." She hopped off the bed to help the unfortunate bellhop.

Lorgin chuckled as Deana helped the Zot to its feet.

"I'm terribly sorry for screaming," she said earnestly. "You just gave me such a scare." The Zot gave a little snort of disgust. "Would you like me to help you clean up this mess?" The alien turned his back on her, whipping his tail furiously as he stormed from the room. She turned to Lorgin. "What did I say?"

Lorgin stretched his muscles as he got out of bed. "On top of everything else, Adeeann, you insulted him."

"How did I do that?"

"By offering to help him, you implied he wasn't capable of cleaning up the broken dishes. Zots are very sensitive about their responsibilities. I do not think you are his favorite patron today, Little Fire."

{I empathize with him.}

Deana looked at Rejar. He was covered in food of various hues.

"Oh, Rejar, look at you! I'm so sorry. The past two days haven't been very pleasant for you, have they? How are you feeling? You look a lot better."

A glob of goo dripped off his forehead. He gave Deana a stony look.

Deana covered her mouth as she giggled again.

Rejar could just imagine what he looked like. His eyes began to twinkle as he saw the humor in it. Suddenly they were all laughing.

"Did you see the Zot's expression when you sat on him, Rejar?" Lorgin laughed to his brother. "I wager he will not forget it anytime soon."

{I do not think he will tangle with a Familiar again. He kept screeching he brought food; he was not the food.} Rejar laughed out loud at the ridiculous words of the Zot.

Lorgin and Deana ate breakfast in the main room of the inn while they waited for Rejar to clean up. He joined them when they were just finishing, his beautiful personage looking none the worse for the ordeals he had been through.

Deana kept Rejar company while Lorgin went out to purchase supplies and equipment for their journey. Since Yaniff no longer accompanied them, they had to carry all of their supplies with them—no inter-dimensional storage space. Lorgin returned a short time later, sitting down at the table.

"I have purchased all the supplies we will need. The merchant is loading the *prautaus* now."

Rejar put down his drink. "Were you able to gain any information about Traed's whereabouts?"

Lorgin leaned forward. "Yes. The merchant knew of him. He resides several days' journey from here in the direction of the main morning sun."

"Just a sec!" Deana threw up her hands. "What do you mean 'the main' morning sun?"

"Zarrain has binary suns. The larger of the two is referred to as the main, the smaller, the minor."

"Of course." She smirked at Lorgin. "I should've guessed. So, how hot is it out there?" She nodded toward the doors and the desert beyond.

"Hot enough even for a Little Fire." He tugged a lock of her hair. "I think it best to travel in the day despite the heat. There is more of a chance of avoiding desert tribes and other . . . things."

Deana knew what other things could be around at night in Zarrain. She had seen a few scurrying around last night. Which brought her next question. "If it takes us a few days to reach Traed, where will we sleep? Are there any outposts along the way?''

''A few. They are not as luxurious as this one, though.''

The man was a master of subtlety, Deana thought, viewing the spartan accommodations.

''I have purchased sleeping huts for us as well.''

Sleep in the desert? On the ground? At night—with those *things* squirming around? ''I don't think that's such a good idea.''

''You will be perfectly fine.'' He ushered her outside into the heat of the day. ''We have nothing to worry about. Rejar can always sit on anything that dares to attack us.'' He chuckled as Rejar gave him a smile of chagrin.

The heat of the suns bore down on them as they crossed the desert terrain.

Deana had balked when she had found out what prautaus were—great, plodding pack beasts which lumbered along with a swaying, rolling gait. Lorgin had purchased three of the beasts.

First, Lorgin explained to her that the beasts were perfect for this type of travel, requiring little maintenance or water and having great stamina. Then he effortlessly swung her up onto the *prautau's* back and, before she could object, smoothly mounted behind her.

''Before you ask me why, I will explain.'' He adjusted her cape around her. ''I am concerned about bandits and slavers. If need be, I think I can better protect you if we are on the same mount. Rejar will take the other beast. The third is for our supplies.''

Perhaps that had been his primary reason. But as the trip progressed, Deana found Lorgin's hands straying under her cape. She turned, looking back at him over her shoulder.

197

"What are you doing?"

He turned a guileless face to her. "What?" His hand caressed her midriff, just under her breast.

"You know what!" She placed her hand over his on top of her cape. His was still underneath. He stroked his middle finger against her ribs back and forth in a tickling motion as he bent forward to speak in her ear.

"I have never before known a woman who would challenge a *xathu*." His thumb rubbed the underside of her breast. "So, you would go to battle for me, Little Fire? Not many Knights of the Charl can boast their mates would defend them thus."

"I did not exactly go to battle for you, Lorgin. I'm not sure what happened with the *xathu*. And I am not your mate."

He continued on as if he hadn't heard her, idly cupping her breast; he ran his thumb across the peak. "Although I do not know if it is such a good thing for you to take on such a role."

The idea of her fighting for him was ludicrous and they both knew it. He seemed to be considering it, though. "Perhaps in time you will wish to beat me, also." His thumb and forefinger caught the hardened peak, giving it a little tweak.

"Lorgin!"

He nipped her ear, ignoring her slapping hand.

"On Aviara, you will have many an opportunity to defend me. All manner of beasts roam the streets—"

"The *streets?*"

"Yes, right out in the open. One never knows. Even a simple journey to a *sacri* can be fraught with peril. Beasts which make a *xathu* look like a kitten."

She peered at him aghast. "Are you serious?"

"Yes. Men gobbled up whole for a meal, right in the middle of the boulevard." He shrugged fatalistically. "It makes for a good character, a warrior character, to grow up in an environment such as this.''

Deana was appalled.

Rejar sent his thought only to his brother. *{What nonsense are you telling her?}*

Lorgin threw a wicked grin to his brother over Deana's head.

Deana wasn't paying attention now to Lorgin's hand. She was contemplating a world where monsters roamed the streets looking for snacks, the weather was horrid, and the food, by all accounts, sucked. Terrific vacation spot. She wondered if she'd survive to show the snapshots. She'd have to talk Lorgin out of taking her there.

''Lorgin, we don't have to go—''

''Yes, we do, *zira*.'' Deana hunched her shoulders, staring straight ahead into the desert. Blasted male!

Hours passed as they traveled the land. It was hot. The beasts didn't seem to mind as they plodded along. Once, they saw a caravan in the distance, but it quickly disappeared from view. Distances were deceiving in the desert. They did not stop to eat. Lorgin handed her a rolled flat bread, something that resembled cheese, a piece of fruit, and a skein of water. They continued on. Deana drifted off to sleep.

Rejar surveyed the unending desert before him with a mournful eye. Not a female in sight! *{Do you think it will be long before we reach an outpost?}*

''Ages,'' Lorgin teased Rejar. They rode on.

{I wonder what the women are like here?}

''Of this I am certain, Rejar; it will not take you long to find out.''

Rejar grinned, his thoughts going to pleasantly rounded hips and curving thighs. *{Perhaps we are not too far from an outpost.}*

"Far enough."

Like everything else on this planet, Rejar's good mood evaporated.

Deana woke up in Lorgin's arms a few hours later to the same unending vista. She leaned back into his chest, yawning. Lorgin's low voice rumbled in her ear.

"Did you enjoy your rest, zira?"

"Mmm. Did I miss anything?"

"Sand. Then there was . . . sand; and let me think—ah, yes, more sand."

She smiled faintly. "Are we near an outpost yet?"

"I have been hearing this question all afternoon." He glanced toward Rejar. "No, not for a while—maybe not this day." That meant camping out overnight in the desert. Big yuck! Deana made a face.

{Did I hear you say not this day?} The life seemed to wilt out of Rejar.

Since Deana was now awake, Lorgin decided to pick up where he had left off. He began by rubbing her midriff with his palm under her cloak. She fidgeted on the *prautau*. Then he ran his hands down the outsides of her thighs and back up the insides.

"Cut it out," she gritted out. He smiled into her hair.

It was when he cupped her breasts in his palms, sending her a little frisson of desire, that Deana decided enough was enough.

She removed his hands. He playfully returned them.

Deana was getting irritated. He was dealing the cards but there was no game. In an effort to make him stop, she turned, saying to him, "Look, either put up or shut up."

Lorgin's flashing gaze dropped to her mouth; slowly his lashes raised and his incredible eyes locked with hers. A shiver of desire raced through her. Without breaking his visual hold on Deana, he spoke to his brother.

"Rejar, go on up ahead and scout out the area."

Rejar immediately kicked his mount, galloping ahead. Lorgin reached under her cloak, his nimble fingers going to the fastening of her pants. She felt his other hand between them, unfastening his own.

"Wh-what are you doing?" she squeaked.

"I am about to 'put up' as you so aptly phrased it." He easily pushed her pants down.

"You can't be serious? Not here!"

"Put your legs up on the *prautau's* neck."

"No!" She was mortified.

"Very well, let us try it this way." He lifted her onto his lap, smoothly hooking each of her legs over his own.

"You can't do it this way!"

In the next instant he proved to her *he could*.

He pushed her slightly forward, then pulled her back onto him. His hands firmly planted around her waist, he sank into her. Deana sucked in her breath.

"My God!"

The only place skin touched skin was where they joined. It was an intoxicating, erotic sensation. Material slid against material; velvet stroked honey.

Initially, Lorgin let the pack animal set the pace; its rolling, rocking gait provided more than sufficient movement. Deana gasped for breath as he surged into her with every step the prautau made. She felt Lorgin's hot lips on the back of her neck, the puffs of heated breath against her skin. The desert was silent except for the plodding thuds of the *prautau's* hooves and their combined labored breaths.

Lorgin began working into the forward motion with every step the beast took. She was well aware of his powerful thigh

201

Dara Joy

muscles controlling the animal beneath him as well as his own movements.

"How—how far does sound travel in the desert?" she gasped.

"What?" Lorgin was somewhat preoccupied and could not believe her question. "Why . . . do . . . you . . . wish . . . to . . . know?" His voice was ragged. Was he actually attempting to carry on a conversation with her now? By Aiyah, this woman—

He groaned as she unexpectedly augmented his movement.

"Because I think I'm going to scream and I don't want Rejar to hear," she panted.

Lorgin's low chuckle vibrated against her neck. "Scream all you like. I am sure Rejar will understand."

"Lorgin!"

He nipped the nape of her neck. "What do you think he thinks we are doing?"

Deana tried to turn around. "He doesn't!"

Lorgin paled significantly at her movement. He quickly turned her back around. "Please. Do not turn again. This could be an . . . intricate . . . situation. I do not wish to be unmanned on the back of a *prautau*. And I assure you, he does."

"How could he? This is a standard mating position here? Backwards on the back of a beast crossing the desert?"

Lorgin started laughing behind her.

"Adeeann, you are going to make me lose . . . this *mood*."

Deana pushed back into him. "You put in the ante, Lorgin, don't you dare fold on me now." She rubbed against him, feeling him twitch inside her.

"Ah, as I suspected, a bluff."

Lorgin's hands at her waist pulled her down, tight against him. He wasn't laughing now; he was quite *focused*. With a couple of incredibly sensuous moves, he took them both over the edge.

Deana's head fell back against his chest as she fought to regain her breath. Lorgin refastened her pants, then his own. He leaned over and sweetly kissed her on the mouth before he softly whispered against her lips.

"Be warned, Little Fire. I always answer a challenge."

"Yes, I have noticed that about you," she mumbled as his mouth once more covered her own.

They made camp shortly before sundown. Once the two sleep huts were set up, Lorgin brought out some rather bland fare for their evening meal. No one was very excited about it. Even Lorgin lamented the deprivations one had to endure while on a quest.

Rejar seemed pretty forlorn, enclosing himself in his hut soon after they finished the meal. Deana and Lorgin entered their hut soon after, having no desire to be out in the desert after darkness fell. Deana was relieved to see that the hut had a floor, and once the door flap was closed, they were completely sealed from the outside.

They quickly undressed, getting under the fur of their pallet. The temperature was rapidly dropping, and it seemed the hut didn't protect them from the temperature change. It was getting cold. They snuggled together cuddling under the fur. Until Deana felt something.

"Lorgin, something's moving under the pallet!"

He grinned rather raunchily at her. "What do you mean?"

She gave him a double take. "Not that! I mean *under* the pallet."

"Do not concern yourself with this. Nothing can penetrate the hut."

Something squished under her. She shuddered, horrified.

"But it's moving!"

His arms came around her, partially lifting her onto him.

"Here. Is this better for you?"

It was. Marginally. "Yes," she mumbled into his chest.

"Good." His hands cupped her face. He raised his head, brushing his mouth across hers. "Is this better?"

"Yes, but—"

His hands moved down to her derriere, cupping her buttocks, gently squeezing the rounded globes as he enticingly brushed her mouth again. "Is this better?" he breathed close to her parted lips.

"Lorgin, I hear shuffling sounds outside and I thought I heard—"

He swirled his tongue inside her mouth, his large palms stroking her back as he whispered against her. "I could show you another way of riding that is just as pleasurable as the one we shared earlier—"

She broke away from his roaming lips. "Lorgin, I hear something out there!"

There was a distinct shuffling sound.

Lorgin instantly raised his head, lowering her beside him. He was just reaching for the Cearix when the hut door was unfastened and four heads peered in. They did not look friendly. Lorgin uttered what Deana assumed was a potent epithet in Aviaran.

One of the heads spoke. "Come out now, Off Landers, and no tricks."

Lorgin faced the man, towering over him. "Let my woman and me clothe ourselves first."

The man grinned, showing an assortment of odd teeth. "And why should I let you do that, Off Lander?"

Lorgin regarded him coolly. "Because I will kill any man who gazes upon my naked wife." Deana raised her eyebrows. That was succinct. A little extreme, but then, this was Lorgin.

The other man's eyes flicked to their clothes on the floor,

widening slightly as he noticed Lorgin's cloak. "So, you are of the Charl. No tricks from you, now, Off Lander. Give me your word and you may clothe yourselves."

"My word."

The man narrowed his eyes. "Your word as a Charl or we kill you both, and then the Familiar."

"My word as a Charl."

"Be quick about it." The men retreated, and the flap closed, but did not seal.

Lorgin did not seem happy at having been maneuvered by the man into the promise. Deana wondered why Rejar hadn't sent them a warning telepathically. A horrible thought entered her head. She clutched Lorgin's arm.

"Are they Oberion slavers?" Her worry was mirrored on her face. Lorgin reached up, brushing her cheek.

"No, *zira*. They are desert nomads. Very fierce, very brave, and very greedy. They will try to steal everything we have, and then leave us in the desert to rot. They will take Rejar and sell him to the slavers."

"What can we do? Why didn't Rejar warn us?"

"They must have rendered him unconscious somehow. A small number of them have the Sight. One of them must have seen a Familiar amongst us. That alone would have prompted them to pursue us. He would be quite valuable to those who live a hand-to-mouth existence."

A harsh voice penetrated the flap. "Stop that talking! Hurry up in there or we will come in and get you, Charl, threat or no threat."

Lorgin clenched his powerful fists. "If you do, I will take many down with me—starting with you. And if you know anything about the Charl, foolish man, you know we never make threats . . . *only promises.*"

Dead silence followed that remark.

Lorgin took her hand, leading her into the desert night. Deana tried not to look down as she walked across the sand. She felt Lorgin kick something away from her path. A slithering sound came from her right. She started to shake. Lorgin picked her up in his arms.

His steely gaze went to the same man he had talked to earlier. "Let my wife sit upon a *prautau*."

The leader nodded curtly.

Once she had been placed on top of the beast, Deana drew a deep breath to calm her failing nerves. Her gaze raked over the campsite, searching for a glimpse of Rejar. Her hand went to her mouth in horror when she spotted him.

He was lashed to a *prautau*. Even from this distance she could see that his phenomenal eyes were glazed and disoriented. They obviously had drugged him.

Deana had seen Rejar in many moods: happy, mischievous, smoldering, anguished by his brother's poisoning, courageous, and selfless. But she had never seen him like this.

He was a wild tiger.

He thrashed at his bindings, his eyes spewing venomous hatred at the men who had captured him. Deana could feel his rage. It was a palpable thing. She wouldn't have been surprised if he began howling at the moons. But his was a calculated rage. His glazed eyes noted each man as they sat around the campfire they had lit, as if marking them for a future hunt. Many a man, noticing the Familiar's penetrating stare, turned nervously away, marking a sign in the air. She supposed it was a sign against the evil eye.

Lorgin, too, had noticed his brother. His expression was at once angry and deeply empathetic. "Above all else, Familiars cannot abide to lose their freedom."

"Why doesn't he transform himself to escape?" she whispered.

"This drug they have given him disorients him so that the transformation is impossible for him."

"You mean he can't change?"

"He can. But to do so would most likely result in death, for the drug debilitates him. He cannot focus on the process and could possibly lose the ability to become his cat self, or the ability to change back into a man. The result would be disintegration."

"This is terrible!" Her heart went out to the man who was tied up like a wild animal.

Lorgin squeezed her hand. "I have heard stories of male Familiars choosing disintegration, rather than be taken as slaves."

"You don't think Rejar would—"

"No, for he also has the blood of Krue, and a son of Krue would not take this path. It would not be honorable to the Lodarres line. Rejar will fight—to his death if need be."

A powwow appeared to be going on between several of the men, including the leader, a man they called Searan. Some arguing ensued. Finally Searan got up and approached Lorgin.

"Your Familiar is making some of my men nervous. They will not travel the night desert with him for fear he will call to the beasts to attack them. We will remain here until daybreak, then head east. There is a small oasis often frequented by Oberion traders on their journeys. All of us agree it would be wise to unload the Familiar as soon as possible, even if we could get a better price for him elsewhere. My men feel the risk of keeping him contained is too great. We have decided to sell the woman as well."

Searan watched the golden-haired man carefully for a response. The Charl had said nothing. But his eyes promised much. Searan knew that a man such as this Off Lander would not rest until he avenged himself against his enemies. Searan must make sure this would not happen.

Searan knew that it would be foolish to murder a Charl. To do so would be to invite horrors down upon his head, the likes of which he did not care to think about. And it would only cause another Charl to seek him out and destroy him.

No, he had a better way.

"You, Charl, will be taken to the Waters of Tomorrow. There you will be immersed in the springs, and all that you have known in your lifetime will be wiped from your mind."

The man did not react as Searan had expected. In fact, he did not react in any visible way. But his woman did. Indeed, the little female Off Lander seemed more upset over the Charl's fate than her own. Perhaps Searan could use that to his advantage in the future.

Lorgin's icy eyes became warmer as he regarded Deana. She was so kindhearted, his Adeeann. He was not concerned over his own supposed fate. The stupid Searan did not even realize that Lorgin was a fourth-level mystic and so had power over water, even spellbound water. He needed to come up with a plan to help them escape from these nomads. He would bide his time. It would come to him. Thus Yaniff had trained him.

Lorgin stayed by Deana all night. Against her protests, he removed his cloak, placing it over her own when the cold night air flowed around them. Discreetly, Lorgin directed a warm stream of air to both Deana and Rejar, who had been dragged from his hut wearing nothing but his pants and boots and now was tied to a post.

Deana watched Rejar. His head was slumped forward, and he sagged against the bindings which held him. The drug had finally overcome his monumental efforts to keep it at bay.

Deana closed her eyes against the heartrending sight of Rejar held captive. She waited for the dawn with Lorgin.

Something unexpected happened at first light. The nomads were attacked by another band of nomads.

Blades sliced the air; blood stained the sand; yells and war cries rent the air. Deana covered her ears and tightly closed her eyes to block out the violence around her.

Lorgin quickly gathered her to him, shielding her with himself while he protectively hid her face in his chest lest she see the horror of the battle.

The three of them, obviously prisoners, were left alone by the invaders.

When the battle was over, there was a different tribe surrounding them; Searan and his group had been run off. The leader of these men looked them over to see what he had won.

He walked purposefully toward Rejar. Grabbing a hank of Rejar's hair, he roughly pulled back his head, peering into his bloodshot dual-colored eyes. The leader spat upon the ground, then swiftly removed a huge blade from his waistband. Alarmed, Lorgin started forward, but the leader whooshed the blade through the air, slicing Rejar's bonds in an instant.

Rejar sank wearily to the ground.

"I do not abide with slavery, Familiar, but be warned. We are still thieves and murderers."

Rejar slowly got to his feet, massaging his stiff muscles. "Better a thief and a murderer than a slaver."

"Hah!" The leader slapped his thigh. Then he turned his gaze to Deana. His eyes lit up. "Perhaps we do have a treasure here after all." His gaze fell to the necklace around her neck.

Lorgin, seeing the recognition in the man's eyes, stepped forward. "Let us go. We mean you no harm and can offer you nothing."

The man regarded Lorgin. "No? There is something around her neck that is worth much . . . some would say it is priceless." He turned to his men. "She wears the Shimalee!"

A chorus of "Ahs" greeted his statement. He focused on Deana, but spoke to Lorgin. "Is she a true wearer or an infidel impostor?"

"She is true," Lorgin responded. Deana wisely kept silent.

The leader scratched his chin. "Tell her to cast a spell. If she casts a spell, I will let you all live and you will be free to go. If she cannot, you all die where you stand."

Lorgin calmly turned to Deana. "Cast a spell, Adeeann." Deana looked at him as if he had lost his senses. "Do it. Now."

"Are you nuts?" she hissed back at him. "I can't—"

Lorgin grabbed her to him to muffle her words. He spoke low in her ear. "Say something—anything. Recite something, sing something. I do not care, just sound like you mean it." He released her.

A high school football cheer her grandfather used to chant popped into her head. Now how did it go? She thought for a moment, not remembering it exactly, but that wouldn't matter to these guys.

Suddenly, she leaped in the air, waving her arms like a cheerleader, hopping and jumping.

"Brackety-ax! co-ax! co-ax!

Hi-ho! Hi-ho!

Wallego-wallego wax!

Yah team! Yah team!

Tou. . . . .ch down!"

She attempted a split at the end and flopped over face first into the sand.

A chorus of 'Ahhhs' followed her.

Lorgin's eyes flicked over her, an incredulous look in them. He shook his head briefly, not believing what he had witnessed.

The leader was not so easily swayed as his henchmen. "What kind of a spell did you cast?" he spoke directly to Deana.

"What kind of spell did I cast?" She turned beseechingly to Lorgin. "What kind of a spell *did* I cast?"

Lorgin quickly answered. "She cast a spell on you to doubt her ability to cast spells."

"What?" The leader didn't seem to be buying it.

"Is it not true? Do you not have such doubts?"

"Yes, but surely—"

"There, you can see her powers."

The chorus concurred with their "ahhhs."

The leader was becoming flustered. His men were entranced by the ridiculous display. It was clear he had no choice but to let his captives go now. He stroked his beard, coming to a decision.

"You are free to go. Take your things and leave."

They quickly gathered their belongings. Before they left, the leader grabbed Lorgin's arm taking him aside. "I think it was more your swift mind and sharp tongue which saved you, Off Lander, and not any spell from this woman."

Lorgin smiled at the crafty old desert fox. "Not true; for any fool can see that this woman has indeed cast a powerful spell over this Charl."

The nomad laughed heartily, slapping Lorgin on the back; he sent them all on their way.

Chapter Eleven

Traed ta'al Theardar looked up from the book he was reading to coolly stare at his manservant. The man knew better than to interrupt him when he sought solitude. If Traed were in a frame of mind to be fair he would acknowledge the fact that he often sought solitude these days and considered just about everything an interruption. But he wasn't in such a frame of mind. After all, this was his home; he was not obligated to be fair.

"What do you want?" His frigid tone froze the poor servant to his spot by the open door.

"I-I most humbly beg your forgiveness for disturbing you, b-but there are some visitors at the gate demanding entrance."

Traed crossed his arms over his chest, leaning back in his seat. The caravans which sometimes traveled this way often traded with his people who lived inside the keep. But they were never called visitors. There was only one person who had ever visited him in all the years he had lived here. The blood in his veins turned to ice. "It is not my father, is it?"

The servant backed up a step at the fierce expression on Traed's face. "N-no, my lord Traed. They did not say who they are."

Traed's features relaxed slightly with the news that these visitors were not his dreaded sire. "They seek me?"

"Yes, my lord Traed."

"Send them away. I do not wish to be disturbed." Traed turned back to his book, dismissing the servant.

"B-but, Master Traed, they said it was most urgent, and that they needed to see you—"

Traed exhaled noisily. *"I said send them away."*

"Yes, my lord Traed." The servant scooted from the room.

Traed looked down at his book again, not really seeing the words before him. Sometimes when he sat lately, the hours would sort of slip away as if he were in a trance. He wondered if a man could let all his hours slip away, until, blissfully, there would be no more.

Such thoughts gave him reason to live. He smiled at the irony of it, wondering if he was not already half mad.

It had taken them three days to finally reach Traed's keep.

The trip had been tiring and difficult; they had never once crossed an outpost during the journey. Rejar was becoming sullen, Deana was irritable, and Lorgin remained . . . Lorgin.

They were sitting by the gate in the broiling sun waiting for the gatekeeper to let them enter.

"I wish he would hurry up. I'm about to fry out here," Deana complained.

"It will not be much longer, Adeeann." Lorgin's calm response seemed to irritate her even more.

"Doesn't anything ever bother you, Lorgin? My God, this has been the most hellacious trip I've ever been on." She wiped the sweat off her brow with the back of her hand. "What I wouldn't do for a nice cool bath . . ."

Lorgin's mouth lifted slightly in a faint grin. "You will get your cool bath soon, *zira*. Perhaps we can share it." His eyes sparkled with sexual mischief.

{Must you talk of such things now? I vow I am getting tired of it.}

Lorgin raised an eyebrow. "Rejar, it is not like you to be so edgy."

Rejar rubbed his eyes. *{Forgive me, Lorgin. I am . . . wound up.}*

Lorgin chuckled. "Yes, it is not usual for you to go so long without your *comforts*. Yaniff says sometimes abstinence is good for the soul. It can renew your heart and spirit."

{Yaniff is an extremely old man. He has probably forgotten exactly what such comforts feel like to a man. Besides, you are a student of his, yet I do not see you practicing this philosophy he preaches.}

"I am his student, this is true"—Lorgin grinned slowly and wickedly at his brother—"But I think a man must also have his own beliefs to follow."

Rejar grinned knowingly back to his brother.

"What are you two talking about?" Deana had only heard Lorgin's side of the conversation, as Rejar had shielded his thoughts from her.

Lorgin answered her. "Rejar is thinking of joining the Charl."

{Not in this lifetime, brother.}

Deana looked from one to the other, somehow doubting by their very male expressions that that had been the topic of conversation. She was about to inquire further when the gatekeeper returned.

"He will not see you. Go—be gone from this place!" He

was about to go back inside the keep when Lorgin grabbed him by the scruff of his neck, turning the man back around to face him. Lorgin's voice was deadly low.

"Then you will go back to your master again. We have come a long way. It is hot in the sun here. *I grow annoyed at being kept waiting.*" Well, Deana, thought, Lorgin is human after all! She chuckled to herself.

The gatekeeper began babbling. "B-but he will not see you!" He wrung his hands together.

"Tell him Lorgin ta'al Krue is on his doorstep. Tell him I have come to challenge him to a game of *dizu*." The gatekeeper hedged. "*Do it.*" At Lorgin's forbidding tone, the servant ran to do Lorgin's bidding. When he was out of earshot, Lorgin turned to Deana. "I wonder why I do not have that effect on you, Adeeann?" He raised a commanding eyebrow at her.

"Because I know you are all bark and no bite."

He rubbed the back of his head as if thinking over her words. "This is not what you said last night." Deana's face flamed as her hand went unconsciously to a spot on her neck. Lorgin winked at her.

{Why did you challenge him to dizu?}

"When we were children we played the game constantly. I never beat him. Not once. Of course, it never stopped me from challenging him."

"Of course not," Deana said dryly. Now, this sounded more like the Lorgin she knew. He threw her a look.

"It became something of a joke between us." Suddenly Lorgin became serious. "Before he left us the last time, he said to me, 'I will never refuse your challenge.' I replied that I would never stop issuing it."

The servant slowly made his way back to Traed, dreading the confrontation. The gatekeeper had given him a ridiculous message to relay. He took a deep breath, squared his shoulders, knocking on the door. There was no response for a full minute.

"What is it?"

The servant tentatively opened the door. "The man at the gate asked that a message be sent to you."

"Yes? Come on, man, be quick about it."

"He said his name is Lorgin ta'al Krue and he is on your doorstep to challenge you to a game of *dizu*," the servant finished apprehensively.

For an instant, the corner of Traed's mouth lifted in what could have been the beginning of a smile. But it passed so quickly, the servant was sure he had been mistaken.

Traed ran a weary hand across his eyes, rubbing at the bridge of his nose. Lorgin! What was he doing here? He did not want to see him, or anyone else for that matter. But . . . he could not turn him away.

He shocked the servant by saying, "Bid him to enter. Tell him I will be down shortly."

"Yes, my lord Traed. But he is not alone, he has a woman with him, and—and a Familiar."

Rejar. It could only be Rejar. And the woman? He would find out soon enough. "Show them in."

When the servant left, Traed stood looking out of the tower window onto the desert below. The suns were sinking in the sky. Night fell quickly on Zarrain. *Mirroring life.* He desperately tried not to think of a time long gone when he had been so innocent and his life had been happy. A time before his father had come out of the night to take him away. When the darkness began . . .

They were shown into a large sitting room and told to wait. A servant came in and lit a fire in the stone fireplace. They didn't have to wait long. A side door opened and Traed ta'al Theardar entered the room.

He was tall, although not as tall as Lorgin and Rejar, Deana thought. About six two. He had a beautiful body. Muscular, but not brawny, he moved with a characteristic sleekness that Deana had observed in the brothers. In fact, something about him reminded her of them, though he didn't bear an actual physical resemblance to either of them.

As she observed him, it suddenly occurred to Deana that nothing about this man was as it seemed, and *everything* about him required a second look, a deeper look.

Traed was a man of contrasts.

His hair, at first glance, would be mistaken for black. On closer inspection, it revealed hidden highlights, the color a deep mahogany black/brown. Long, straight, and silky, it was pulled away from his face to hang down his back to his waist in a ponytail.

His eyes, a compelling light green, the color of clear peridot, appeared emotionless and flat, reflecting only what they saw. But further examination revealed them to be deep and fathomless—the eyes of a man who had been forced to see more than what was visibly apparent.

The expression on his face was no less than forbidding, perfectly suited to his angular, chiseled features. But, Deana curiously noted, when the firelight reflected on those features, they were sensual and promising.

The man was a strange brew of enigmatical changing facets.

Traed stood before Lorgin, and at that moment the firelight caught all three of the men in its glow. Deana raised her eyebrows as she took in the view. *If this is an example of Aviaran manhood, perhaps it wouldn't be so awful to visit the wretched place. The scenery would certainly be en-*

ticing . . . She grinned mischievously. Lorgin caught her expression, throwing her a "behave yourself" look. She blushed right where she stood. *How did the man do that?*

Lorgin broke the silence by stepping toward Traed, a genuine smile breaking across his face. "Traed!" He slapped him soundly on the back. Unlike the unfortunate artist so long ago at the convention, Traed did not move an inch.

Nor was he smiling.

"Why have you come here, Lorgin?"

Lorgin chose to ignore Traed's rudeness. "You do not offer me *keeran* in your house?" Traed waved his hand in the general direction of a side table, implying that if Lorgin wanted *keeran* he could damn well get it for himself.

Deana sighed. This was not going well at all.

She stood beside Rejar as Lorgin poured himself a horn of *keeran*. He hadn't asked her if she wanted any, but she wasn't going to berate him for it now. The last thing he needed was her passing out on Traed's floor. Her attention shifted to Rejar, who had a strange look on his beautiful face.

When Lorgin came back with the horn, he tried engaging Traed in conversation. It didn't seem to be working. Deana took the opportunity to whisper to Rejar, "Is anything wrong?"

{No . . . I do not know . . . }

Uneasy, Rejar left Deana to walk over to the sideboard, slowly pouring himself a horn. He took the time to discreetly study their reluctant host. When last he had seen Traed, Rejar had been a young boy, years away from coming into his full Familiar senses. In fact, he was so young, he barely remembered him. Now what he sensed was making him uncomfortable.

He sensed Lodarres blood in Traed, and the bloodline was strong.

218

How could this be? he thought. Where is the connection? His thoughts strayed to his father, Krue, unacceptable possibilities presenting themselves to him. Rejar knew his father to be a man of honor, so what he was thinking could not be true. The answer must lie elsewhere. *It had to.* But his senses could not be deceived.

It had to lie elsewhere. . . .

Rejar continued to observe Lorgin and Traed, realizing that neither of them could sense what he sensed. He downed half his horn of *keeran* in one swallow. He would keep his silence. He would not tell Lorgin of this until he had a chance to counsel with Yaniff. The old mystic would guide him.

It would not be the first time Rejar had to turn to Yaniff for help. If he thought about it, the old man had been there to help him throughout his life. Whenever he got into a scrape or trouble, he always went to Yaniff. Strange, he never realized it until now.

He relied on the old man.

Rejar finished his horn of *keeran* with the revelation. He mentally shook himself. It was not as if he were the wizard's Familiar or anything. They were just . . . friends? That did not seem quite right either. Why had he not thought on this before? he wondered.

Rejar was quickly overloading himself. He cleared his mind, focusing back on Traed.

"For what reason do you stare at me so, Rejar?" Traed's expression was cold, removed, and faintly condescending.

"I have not seen you since I was a young boy, Traed. I was trying to remember you." Rejar purposely spoke aloud. For some reason, he did not think Traed would want him to enter into his mind with his thoughts.

"And have you?" The words were coldly clipped.

Rejar put down his horn. "In truth, I have not, Traed. The

young man I remember was not you."

Traed narrowed his eyes at the thinly veiled reference to the different man he had become.

Lorgin threw his brother a disgusted look. He had been trying to thaw Traed for several minutes. With one carelessly thrown comment, Rejar had destroyed the ground Lorgin thought he had made.

Traed leaned back against the stone mantel, crossing his arms. "Lorgin, you have not told me why you have come here."

Lorgin smiled at him. "Yes, I have. I challenge you to a game of *dizu*."

"You came all this way out here to Zarrain for a game of *dizu*? I think not."

"You *refuse* the challenge?" Lorgin locked eyes with him, awaiting his answer.

Traed blinked once, as if he were not sure how he could respond. Caught in a quandary, he turned to stare at the fire in the grate. In that moment, Lorgin knew he had won. Traed would allow them to stay. It was confirmed with Traed's words.

"No," he exhaled, "I do not refuse."

Lorgin inclined his head. "I expected no less." He motioned to Deana to step forward. "This is my zira, Adeeann." A glimmer of surprise flashed in Traed's eyes.

Deana waved her fingers at the stern man before her. "Hi, how ya doing?"

Traed nodded to her, acknowledging her presence but not deigning to say anything to her. He spoke to Lorgin.

"You have mated?" He glanced at Deana's neck, seeing the Shimalee. "So, Lorgin ta'al Krue, your destiny has spoken, as you believed it would when we were children. You are a fortunate man. Most men do not have a destiny to speak of."

"I do not think you are amongst those men, Traed," Lorgin replied quietly.

Rejar wondered if Traed had sensed the full scope of Lorgin's prophetic words when the man visibly flinched. Despite Traed's comments, it was obvious the man wanted no part of a destiny, his or otherwise.

Traed showed them to their rooms, his manner neither gracious nor inviting. He opened a door, ushering Deana and Lorgin into their room. Deana was surprised to see a regular bed, floor mounted. She peered at the floor looking for critters.

"You need not worry," Traed's voice behind her surprised her. It was the first time he had spoken to her. "On one of his unexpected visits"—his voice became bitter—"my father could not abide it, so he did his wizardly duty, banishing anything from the keep which is not invited to enter."

Lorgin was surprised. *"Your father visits you here?"*

"On the rare occasion." Traed ended the topic immediately. "My servants have brought food for you." He pointed to a table against the wall before he exited the room, abruptly closing the door behind him.

"Jeez. He's about as gracious as Dracula. Come to think of it, this place does sort of look like Dracula's castle."

"Who is this Dracula?" Lorgin removed his cape, swinging it over his shoulder onto the bed. A *prautau* snorted in the courtyard below.

"Listen to them, the *prautaus* of the night—what sweet music they make . . ." She tried to imitate Bela Lugosi.

Lorgin laughed. "What are you doing?"

"It's—oh, never mind."

"Tell me." He patted the bed for her to come sit next to him.

221

"It has to do with vampires and—"

"Vampires?" His eyes flashed, recalling when she had last used the word. "I remember these—you called them monsters who—" She put her hand over his mouth. His tongue shot out to tickle her palm.

Deana giggled. Turning back into Bela, she salaciously eyed Lorgin's strong neck. "I never drink . . . *keeran*, Mr. R-R-Renfield ta'al Krue." She swooped down on him, causing them both to fall over onto the mattress. In true vampire fashion, she latched onto his neck, pretending to bite into his jugular.

"Adeeann, stop!" Lorgin was really laughing. Well! It seemed she had found a ticklish spot on the big guy. Hmm . . . now this was power! She moved in for the kill. He quickly rolled over, pinning her beneath him. Something sharp stuck into her side.

"Ow! Lorgin, get up, something's sticking into me!"

"Not yet, but it soon will be." In retaliation, he tickled her midriff in a spot he knew reduced her to mindless giggles.

"Pl-please!" she gasped between laughing. "I mean it."

He had his doubts, but released her just the same, sitting up in the bed. She dug into the pocket of her tunic, finding Lorgin's crystal earring.

"Aha!" She held it out to him to return it.

His lashes formed a dark crescent against his cheekbones as he looked down at the crystal in her palm. "The mark of a Charl."

"I suspected as much. I noticed Yaniff wore one also."

"Yes. It is a symbol of initiation. Such symbols often carry great meaning to a man, Adeeann. I want you to have it." He looked up at her, his expression earnest.

"No, I can't do that. It belongs to you—you should be wearing it." He started to protest, but she placed it firmly in his hand. He reluctantly took it, placing it back in his ear.

"Lorgin, are there any women in the Charl?"

"You do not understand what the Charl is."

"Then tell me."

"This is not so easy. I can tell you the Charl are warriors, as well as mystics."

"There are no women warriors?"

He smiled slightly at her question. "I have seen entire planets with nothing but women warriors. On my planet, however, the women are not warriors."

"They cannot join the Charl?"

"They can, if they desire it. They choose not to. The women follow their own mystical pathways. Aviaran women do not desire to be warriors. They have no need to be. Their men protect them from any danger."

"What if a woman doesn't have or want a man?"

He shrugged. "She would still be protected."

"No woman has ever decided to join the Charl?"

Lorgin shook his head.

Deana was surprised. "You'd think one of them would— just to say she did."

He reached over, lacing his fingers through hers. "It is not that simple. One cannot decide to join the Charl. The decision is first made by destiny."

"What do you mean?"

"The inherent abilities must be there. Most often such abilities run in lines of descent. Rarely, a new line is created, and someone whose ancestors were not of the Charl comes forward."

Deana digested this information. "Why is Rejar so opposed to joining the Charl?"

"There has never been a Familiar who was Charl also."

"But your father—"

"Is Charl. A fifth-level mystic. Rejar fights this side of himself. You must understand, he is totally of the Familiar. A child born of a Familiar which bears the mark of them"— he pointed to his eyes as he spoke, referring to Rejar's dual colored eyes—"this child will be Familiar, inheriting all of their abilities."

"Then Rejar has no . . . abilities from your father?"

"Not outwardly. But he has them. And more. Yaniff has sensed it in him. I have told you Rejar is unique. There has never been a child born of Charl and Familiar before."

"How come? Familiars seem like a randy enough bunch." He smiled at her observation.

"Except for casual relations, Familiars most often mate amongst themselves. Their abilities and strangeness sets them apart. In matters of permanent bonding, they have a tendency to keep to themselves. I think it is much the same on your world, Adeeann. In my brief time there, I have seen people shun that which was different or unknown."

Deana nodded, knowing his words were, unfortunately, true. "Do the beings here realize what a rare and beautiful people these Familiars are?"

"They do. But still, the Familiar is both revered and denigrated, sought after and shunned."

"You told me your father did not know Suleila was a Familiar. How could he not know?"

"It is a long story. Suffice it to say Suleila wanted to experience life for a while without being labeled. She disguised herself—but her intention was not to trick anyone; she just wanted a new experience." Lorgin smiled ruefully. "She found it; or I should say, Krue found her. She was able to experience many new things." He chuckled, remembering the stories Suleila had told him of Krue's pursuit of her.

"Do you think Rejar will join you?"

"He says he will not. Yaniff has hopes." Lorgin examined her face intently. "Perhaps our children, Adeeann, will be Charl." Deana's eyes widened.

Lorgin smiled poignantly, missing her shocked expression. "A daughter of yours might very well wish to be the first woman warrior of Aviara."

Our children? Deana swallowed, suddenly very nervous. He was still enacting this fantasy of his. What if . . . "Lorgin—you said I wouldn't have to worry about that."

Lorgin looked away, shielding his hurt at her reaction to his words. He had all but asked her . . .

"You do not," he said quietly.

She visibly relaxed. What was the matter with the man? Children. *With him.* She peeked over at him from beneath her lowered lashes. He was looking toward the window and did not see her studying him. Her heart began to pound in her chest as she gazed at his averted profile. So strong!

The perfect—

No.

She was not the right woman.

Not the woman destined to be his by a prophecy as old as time.

Not the "maestro" of the space/time continuum.

Her lips curled in poignant amusement. She was just Deana Jones. She didn't belong here. She didn't belong with him. She blinked the sudden dampness from her eyes.

If she had been this woman he had mistaken her for . . .

A vision popped into her mind: Lorgin, pastel eyes shining, laughing in delight as he lifted their child high in his arms, up, up above his head, while the child screamed in mock fear between giggles. The beautiful child turned to her, holding out its arms, as if to say, "Take me."

Yes . . .

She reached out to the child . . .

A strange pulse flowed from the top of her head to the tip of her toes. For an instant it glowed around her and within her, subsiding as quickly as it had come. Deana gasped at the weird sensation as the vision dissolved.

Lorgin turned back to her. "What is it?"

She shook her head; she had to have imagined it. "Nothing." She placed her hand over his on the bed; he turned his hand, warmly clasping hers. "Lorgin, about the *xathu*—I think Yaniff must have done something."

Lorgin's eyes shuttered. He knew where she was heading. She still did not accept who she was, or her life with him. "Yaniff did nothing. He told you of the dampening fields. Think you Yaniff would let me die if he could prevent it?" He stated all this very coldly, removing his hand from hers.

He leveled his intense lavender gaze on her. "It was you, Adeeann."

Irritated by the situation, confused by conflicting emotions, Deana glared at Lorgin. "No! No! No! You're wrong, you know. I am not who you think I am. *Deana*. My name is Deana. Why don't you say it, Lorgin? I know you know it. *Dee-ann-ah*."

Lorgin stared at her for several moments, not even blinking. It was rather unnerving. She wondered if he was going to completely lose his temper. He didn't. After a moment, he calmly suggested, "Perhaps we should have something to eat before retiring."

Deana let out a pent-up breath and nodded, strangely relieved he had chosen not to engage in a confrontation. She was terribly tired and not up to confronting him now about their situation.

Throughout their meal Lorgin said little, seeming very withdrawn. Deana wondered if he had concerns about con-

vincing Traed to leave Zarrain. Traed did not seem the type
to be easily convinced. She knew how important it was to
Lorgin that he bring Traed back to Aviara. She broke the
silence between them.

"Are you worried about Traed?"

His glittering eyes lanced her. "Partly."

His poignant answer unnerved her. She lifted her cup to
her mouth, noticed her hand shaking, and lowered it silently.

Her reaction did not escape him. Although he was dis-
heartened at her continued non-acceptance of her situation, it
was not Lorgin's desire to upset her so. He reached across
the table, covering her hand, steadying her.

"Yes. I am worried about Traed."

Their eyes met. He was no longer removed from her; his
expression as he watched her was once again warm. Deana
blinked back the tears in her eyes. *It was going to be all right.*
She smiled tremulously back at him, relieved.

Lorgin gently traced his thumb over the soft skin above
her wrist.

"He is not the same, Adeeann. He has changed. The kind,
laughing boy I knew has become a cold, distant man. I do
not know if I can reach him. I do not know if there is anything
left to reach." Lorgin spoke the words regretfully, as if it
pained him a great deal.

"I'm sorry, Lorgin."

After they had eaten, Deana was relieved to discover a
bathing room off their bedroom, gratefully immersing herself
in the water. When she came out, crossing the room, she
noticed that Lorgin had pulled a chair up to the window. His
booted feet were crossed on the stone windowsill. He clutched
a horn of *keeran*, staring into the night, seemingly thousands
of miles away.

Not wanting to disturb him, she crawled under the covers,

falling asleep almost immediately.

Hours later, Deana felt the bed dip as Lorgin got in. He rolled over to her at once, enfolding her in his arms.

"Adeeann . . ." he whispered.

There was anguish in his voice. Deana instinctively knew he was coming to her for solace. Not because he might not accomplish his quest, but because he feared his friend Traed was lost.

She embraced him, running a soothing palm down his naked back. He was still slightly damp from his bath. His mouth covered hers in a bittersweet kiss. She returned the kiss, hugging him tight to her, if for no other reason than because he needed it and she wanted to alleviate his worries; she wanted to soothe him. He was her dear friend and more . . .

"Adeeann . . ." She put her fingers against his lips in the darkness.

"Shhh. It's all right. Just love me tonight, Lorgin."

He clutched her to him. "I love you every night, Adeeann."

His mouth descended sweetly on her own.

When he entered her, she eased the way for him.

The woman entered his room, leaving the door open behind her. She boldly crossed the floor to stand before him. He gazed at her silently above the rim of his *keeran.*

She smiled seductively at him, releasing the catch on her robe. It shimmered to her feet in a satiny golden pool. No outward expression crossed his glacial features as he clinically observed her nude form with curiously flat eyes.

The woman's spicy, sultry whisper caressed the room. "What is your wicked pleasure, my lord Traed?"

Traed's ice green eyes briefly sparked, hinting at the powerful emotions boiling beneath the surface of this man.

Setting down his drink, he rose from his chair, his boots clinking across the stone floor. He kicked the door shut.

Soon the woman's wanton moans of pleasure filtered through the thick door.

She begged him to stop.

But he would not . . .

Chapter Twelve

They had been at the keep a little over a week and the melting of Traed ta'al Theardar was not remotely on the horizon.

The man did not bend.

His routine, if such behavior could be called a routine, followed a disturbing pattern. He usually slept most of the day away, joining them in the late afternoon. He spoke only when spoken to, maintaining his distance with remote coolness. While not exactly insulting, he was barely civil. Just what the man did all night was anybody's guess, as he retired to his chambers shortly after the evening meal.

Since their first night here, Lorgin never mentioned his despair over the situation, but Deana could tell he was concerned. In typical Lorgin fashion, he had decided to approach the problem patiently, hoping that over time some of the old Traed would surface. So far, the strategy wasn't working. Since he had used much the same approach on her, Deana

230

knew what the next step was. Confrontation Lorgin style. She wondered how long Lorgin would wait before he started pushing buttons.

She hadn't seen too much of Rejar either. The wildcat had taken himself off to ignite the female population in and around the keep. Yesterday, he had mentioned something about a caravan camping outside the walls and she hadn't seen him until dinner this evening. He was still smoking.

After their evening meal, Traed had excused himself and Lorgin had asked Rejar to accompany him for a walk around the keep. Just why anyone would choose to walk outside at night on Zarrain was a mystery to Deana.

She looked around the empty room, extremely bored. There wasn't much to do here. She couldn't read the language, there was no television or videos; hobbies were difficult to maintain while on a quest; and Lorgin was otherwise occupied. She sighed.

Earlier in the day, Lorgin had taken her into the square in the center of the keep. She had been fascinated by how these people lived. There was a small *sacri* for trading. Various craftsmen offered their services, depending on what you needed. Some of the women from the caravan were making interesting little pots out of a claylike material, although no one from the keep seemed interested in them, refusing to buy when the women tried to sell them. Perhaps she would see if she could buy some clay from the women tomorrow. At least she would have something to do in the evenings.

The nights were another matter. Then, she had *plenty* to do. Her face took on a dreamy expression as she thought about Lorgin's lovemaking. She never forgot his words to her the first night they arrived here: *I love you every night, Adeeann.* He did, too. Mornings could never be ruled out. Sometimes in the afternoon. And, in between, whenever the mood struck him. She had never met anyone like him. *The man had energy.*

The scope and breadth of his knowledge amazed her. His inventiveness and spontaneity took her breath away. Every night with him, it was as if he were on his own personal quest with her. He rediscovered her every time he made love to her. What was the best just kept getting better. He commanded, demanded, cajoled, beguiled, enticed, and bewitched her. Lorgin was an incredibly passionate man. Some nights he was downright insatiable.

Face it, the man had a talent for being naughty.

A servant entered the room to light a fire, interrupting a fantasy she was having that involved Lorgin, whipped cream, and ropes. Her face flamed guiltily. Well, it wasn't as if she had anything else to do! Except for Traed, she was the only person left here who—*Traed.*

Why not?

He was here. She was here. Maybe—just maybe—she could see something, do something Lorgin had missed. It was worth a try. She was starting to get tired of Zarrain. It was not the vacation spot of the year. Deana turned to the servant who had just finished making the fire.

"Where does Traed go in the evenings?"

The servant seemed surprised by her question. "He retires to his chambers."

Deana's idea didn't seem so promising now—there was no way she would enter the man's bedroom. "He goes to sleep?"

"No, mistress, he reads in his study." At least the servant thought that was what he did. With a master as strange as his, one could never be sure.

His study! Good. "Could you show me how to get to his study?"

The servant blanched. "You cannot go there! No one goes

there. He does not wish to be disturbed.''

Deana waved her hand. "Pfft! Anyone can be disturbed." Especially Traed. Pun intended, she thought. "Just show me where this sanctum sanctorum is and you can go on your merry way disavowing any knowledge of the deed.''

" 'Tis a most strange way you have of speaking, mistress.''

Deana gave the man an ironic look. "Relative, I'm sure. Now, which way is it?''

The brothers walked around the outside perimeter of the keep, paying no attention to the little squeaks and squishes beneath their boots.

"What do you think, Rejar?''

{I think I must be crazy to be walking around with you when I could be better occupied.} His heated eyes roamed a caravan campsite where a young woman was warming herself in front of a fire.

Annoyed, Lorgin chucked his younger brother on the side of his head to regain his attention. "This is important. Rein in your hungry ways to listen to me a moment.''

Rejar rubbed the side of his head. *{I am listening!}*

"What can we do about Traed?''

{We? I was under the impression this was your problem.}

"Then why are you here?''

Rejar grinned flippantly. *{To annoy you.}*

Lorgin gave him a stony look. "You are succeeding." Rejar made a satisfied sound. "Rejar, I am losing my patience.''

It was a warning Rejar knew better than to ignore. He knew from a lifetime of experience with his brother that he would only get one warning. Rolling around in the night sand of Zarrain engaged in a fight with his brother held little appeal.

{Very well. You wish my opinion? I think the man is beyond your reach. He has locked himself in a wall of stone. How can you reach such a man?}

233

"There must be a way."

{If there is, I know not of it.} Rejar's eyes once more strayed to the girl by the fire.

"What could we do to make him more approachable? Surely the man has some—" Lorgin noticed that Rejar's attention had strayed again. His eyes followed the path of his brother. Hmm. . . . might it work? He chucked Rejar on the head again.

{Ow! Will you stop this!}

"You have given me an idea."

{I have?}

"Yes." Lorgin nodded in the direction of the young woman. "You will take Traed carousing with you."

{What? I will not!}

"Why not?" It seemed like a good idea to Lorgin. "He is a man—what better way to renew your friendship than to gift him with a night's pleasure?"

{Have you lost your mind? First, I have never been friendly with Traed. He was your friend. Second, the man could freeze water with a glance—what kind of woman could I find for him? Third, you ask much of me to expect me to spend an entire evening in his dour company. If you are so enamored of this idea of yours, you do it.}

"I cannot go out for a night of carousing! I am mated, or have you forgotten?"

Rejar sighed. *{I will not do it. Think of something else.}*

"There is nothing else. You will do it."

Rejar's shoulders sagged as his head dropped forward. He stared at the ground morosely. Why could he not have been born the elder son? A night with Traed! Perhaps he could reason with his brother one more time.

{I tell you, Lorgin, the man is odd.}

"Which reminds me—The night of our arrival here you

acted strange when Traed came into the room. Why?''

Rejar's eyes skittered away from Lorgin's. For someone who did not possess Familiar sense, Lorgin was amazingly acute. What could he tell him? "It was nothing . . . just . . . I have not seen Traed for so many years . . . I . . . thought he . . . looked different.''

Very convincing, Lorgin thought sarcastically. Besides the ridiculousness of his words, there was one thing Lorgin had always known about his brother. Whenever he was prevaricating or angry, he spoke aloud. And Rejar never even realized he did it. Not that Lorgin had any intention of giving that little piece of insight away to his brother. Well, whatever it was, Rejar would tell him in his own good time. He decided to let the matter drop for now.

The brothers headed back to the keep, one pleased with the outcome of their talk, the other totally dismal.

Deana drew up her courage, then knocked on the door. She held her breath. Nothing happened. Either Traed hadn't heard her or he had gone to bed. She knocked again, louder.

Traed's voice boomed from behind the door. "By the blood of *Aiyah*! Can you not leave me in peace? Enter!'' Deana must have jumped three feet. She hesitantly opened the huge door, timidly stepping into the room.

Traed sat in a chair, staring into the flames in the fireplace while absentmindedly stroking a round, fuzzy object in his lap. Deana stood there for several minutes before she realized Traed had forgotten he had told whoever was at the door to enter. He just kept staring into the flames. This did not appear to be a healthy pastime to her. Especially if it was done for hours on end.

"Are you looking for the phoenix?''

Traed turned to her, a slight lifting of his eyebrow the only indication that he was surprised to see her in his study. "What is the 'phoenix'?" he calmly asked her, still stroking the fuzz-ball on his lap.

"A mythical bird which lived a very long time, and then consumed itself in fire, rising renewed from its own ashes."

Traed turned back to the flames. "If I were this phoenix, I would stay consumed," he said quietly.

Not healthy. Not healthy at all. "Why do you say that?"

He shrugged, not answering her. Score nothing for Deana.

She tried again. "What is that?" She pointed to the fuzz-ball on his lap.

"It is called a *phfiztger*."

"A what?" Before he could reply, the ball rolled off his lap toward her. She backed up. "It's alive!" The thing stopped in front of her feet. It pivoted slightly, revealing a gaping maw with three rows of very sharp teeth. "Eek! Does it bite?"

"Not unless provoked." The ball hurled itself up into her arms. Deana dropped it like a hot potato. The ball issued a little cry. "Do not hurt it!" Traed sprang out of his chair, bending down to the creature.

Deana's head snapped up. A pet! Traed had a pet. Who would have guessed it? And what's more, if the concern on his handsome face was anything to go by, he *cared* about it.

He gathered the *phfiztger* carefully in his arms. "They are gentle creatures; they would not harm anyone." He stroked the fuzz reassuringly.

"I'm sorry; I didn't know. Is it all right?" He nodded curtly. "I'm not from around here, so I'm not very familiar with the fauna, or the flora for that matter." She smiled at him with her best "let's be friends" smile.

"I did not think you were from Zarrain. And I know you are not from Aviara."

She shook her head. "No, definitely not from Aviara. Lorgin says I come from a different universe. Sometimes I don't know if he means that figuratively or literally."

Traed blinked as if not quite sure what to make of her. "A different universe—truly?"

"Truly."

That seemed to fascinate him. "What are your worlds like?"

"I don't think I'm supposed to talk about it—at least that was the impression I got. All I'll say is, boy, you are really missing out."

He seemed to ponder her words.

"Perhaps, when I return home, you can visit me sometime. Sort of a return of hospitality."

He seemed surprised, but not by her invitation. "Lorgin is letting you return to this universe of yours?"

"Sure. He's taking me. Well, when he's finished—" She had almost said *with his quest.* Stupid. Stupid. Stupid. "When he's finished with me," she ended lamely.

"When he is finished with you?"

Deana nodded.

That had got a rise out of him. His voice got significantly louder. "Has the man lost his honor? What can he be thinking of to shame his line in this manner? How will he face Krue with this?" Deana threw up her hands to stop the tirade.

"Hey, easy! It's not what you think." She never would've guessed Traed would get so hepped up on this honor jazz. Whatever he was ranting about, he was upset. At least she had succeeded in piercing his cool reserve. Now to get him back on the right track.

"We're going for a visit—just a visit, so cool it." As if it should matter to him what they went back to earth for. These Aviarans were downright weird.

What she said must have appeased him, for he simmered down at once, slipping back into his cool reserve. He stroked the fuzzball again.

"It looks like a tumbleweed. That's a—" What exactly was a tumbleweed? "Well, it's a thing that looks like that." Traed looked at her strangely. "Does it have a name?" He shook his head. "How about Tumbles? May I hold it? I'll be careful this time."

Traed went down on one knee to place the fuzzball on the floor. "First, you must get used to the way it feels. Here, give me your hand."

Deana gingerly placed her hand in Traed's. Surprisingly, instead of being cold and rough as she had expected, it was warm and strong. He knelt with her in front of the little beastie.

"Now, stroke your hand slowly down from the top, yes, like that."

Lorgin, who had heard those words as he rounded the doorway in search of Deana, was wondering what was going on in there. He stopped short at the scene in front of him. Traed was on the floor with his wife, holding her hand.

Traed's head snapped up as Lorgin bounded into the room. He dropped her hand like a hot poker, immediately standing. "Your wife came to me. She wanted to—I was just showing her—"

Lorgin's glance took in the *phfiztger* on the floor. He smiled. "What are you so worried about, Traed? I trust you." Lorgin pushed his first button, implying that the reciprocal couldn't be said. Traed had yet to open to him. Their eyes met. Traed was the first to look away. He spun on his boots and stormed from the room.

"Nice going. Remind me to nominate you for a Nobel Peace Prize," Deana said.

Disgusted with his failure, Lorgin turned and strode from the room. Deana was left with Tumbles. She bent down, softly stroking the ball of fuzz. "Well, aren't you a revelation, though?"

The little pet rolled against her.

"Don't you get it, Lorgin?"

"I am getting *it*. I think." He continued nuzzling her neck.

"No!" She yanked his hair. "Listen to me; he has a pet."

"So?" He dropped his head back down to the crook of her shoulder, his tongue swirling a pattern across her collarbone.

She pushed at his shoulders. He did not appear happy with the interruption. A frustrated expression crossed his regal features.

"I am listening. He has a pet—I do not see the significance you place upon this."

She brought her hand up to the side of his face, cupping it. "It has a lot of significance. He *cares* about this little fuzzball." Lorgin placed his large hand over hers, turning his head to kiss her palm.

"How do you know this?" he mumbled into her hand.

"If you could've seen how he was stroking the thing—he was so gentle. Then when he thought it might be hurt, he was really concerned."

He removed her caressing hand from his face. "So, you were fascinated by the way he strokes the phfiztger, were you? And why were you paying so much attention to this?"

The big idiot was jealous! She balled up her fist, socking him in the stomach. He wasn't prepared for her punch; he grunted. "Will you get real! I am trying to tell you I think there might be something under all those layers of icy reserve. Oh, and he also got quite angry."

Lorgin bristled. "With you?"

"No, with you."

"With me? Why?"

"I don't know. It was weird—he just sort of blew up after I mentioned that you were taking me back to my world after you were finished with me."

Lorgin looked at her aghast. *"You what?"* he bellowed.

She put her hand against his chest, totally misinterpreting his anger. "Well, I couldn't very well tell him about your quest, could I?" He settled down somewhat.

A speculative look came over Lorgin's face. "Tell me how he reacted."

"He started spewing off about honor and how could you do that to Krue—What was he blathering about?"

A spark of hope flowed through Lorgin. "Yes. I believe you are right. Traed has not forgotten who he is or his responsibilities."

"He's in there, Lorgin. The Traed you knew—I feel it."

Lorgin looked down at her, considering her words. "I would not discount a woman's senses in this. Perhaps tomorrow my plan with Rejar will work."

"What plan?" Lorgin stared down at her; for some reason he was suddenly speechless. "What plan?" she repeated.

He quickly covered her mouth with his own in an attempt to distract her. The *gharta* was not going to be distracted. She broke away from his searching lips.

"Well, I'm waiting." Sitting up, she crossed her arms over her naked breasts, unknowingly pushing them up. Lorgin's eyes fell to her chest, sparking pink flames. He pushed her back down onto the bed.

"It is nothing. If it works, you will know." He covered her with himself. She squirmed out from under him.

"You haven't cooked up some stupid scheme with Rejar to take the man on a woman hunt, have you?"

His silence was answer enough for her.

"It will never work."

Lorgin raked his hair back. "Really? You are such an authority on this?"

"I know what I know. It's the wrong approach with this man."

"Would you like to wager on this? He is a man; it will work."

"It won't."

He glanced sideways at her, tongue in cheek. "What do you wager?"

It wasn't as if she had a lot to bet with. She pointed to the barrette he had given her on the bedside table.

"What would I do with it when I win? I have a better idea."

"What?"

He rolled over to whisper in her ear.

Her eyes widened and she giggled, "It can't be done that way!" He raised one of his eyebrows. "It can? Okay, you're on. But what do I get if I win?"

His husky laugh vibrated over her as he lowered his head. "Same thing."

Seemed like a fair bet to her.

The next evening, the two brothers all but dragged Traed out for a walk with them. Deana had no doubts that Lorgin was trying to put his genius of a plan into motion. She smiled to herself. There was no way it would work. Traed was too tense, too guarded, and too damn smart. They'll find out, she smirked.

Sitting down on the middle of the main sitting room floor, she carefully unwrapped the cloth which held the clay. Earlier in the day she had told Lorgin she wished to purchase

241

something at the *sacri*. He had simply said, "Of, course, zira," then filled her hand with an assortment of gemstones.

At first, the woman in the sacri was leery of trading with her, but when she realized that Deana was a real customer, the sale went smoothly enough. Now, what to make with the clay? A lascivious thought went through her brain. No, not that. Besides, if memory served her accurately, she didn't have enough clay to do it justice. She grinned at the idea. Better stick with the little pots she had seen the women making.

Lorgin, Rejar, and Traed strolled around the perimeter of the keep. So far, no one was talking. If Traed wondered at the strange behavior of his companions in insisting on his company, he was silent about it. Lorgin nudged Rejar's shoulder to get him started. Rejar cleared his throat.

"Traed, what do you do for entertainment here?"

"What do you mean?"

Rejar threw Lorgin an exasperated look with a personal opinion. *[I told you—it is hopeless.]* Lorgin was not of the same mind; he discreetly motioned to his brother to continue. Rejar resignedly turned back to Traed.

"You know—for *entertainment.*"

Traed knew exactly what he meant. Crossing his arms, he rocked back on the heels of his boots. "You cannot find your own amusements?" His voice was distinctly suspicious.

Rejar scratched his chin, at the same time throwing his brother a dirty look. "Yes, of course, Traed. I just thought—"

"What did you think?" Traed's eyes were now distinctly narrowed.

"I thought you might wish to accompany me this evening. We could have some keeran, and perhaps"—Rejar was floundering under Traed's glittering green gaze—"perhaps we could reminisce; and then, who knows? The caravan is here. There are many delightful—"

"You thought wrong, Familiar." Traed turned, swiftly heading back to the keep.

The brothers watched his rapid departure silently.

Then Lorgin chucked his brother on the head.

"Have you no sense, Rejar! You do not just approach a man like this with your intentions. You were too obvious!"

Rejar's eyes took on a strange light. He was getting angry. *{And how else was I supposed to do it? Let him guess my meaning?}*

"I never should have listened to this foolish idea of yours. Now I will have to devise something else."

"My idea! What do you mean my idea? It was your idea! If you recall, I wanted no part of it."

Lorgin threw him a quelling glance before he turned and strutted inside. Rejar followed on his heels, ready to do battle.

They were still arguing when they came into the main sitting room, their voices preceding them. Lorgin was first to enter. Deana, arms elbow deep in clay, looked up from her spot on the floor, a smudge of clay on her face.

Lorgin stopped short.

Rejar, not expecting this, barreled into him.

Both men gazed at her in horror.

Lorgin found his voice. "Adeeann, know you not what this is?" He gestured to the clay covering her.

Deana held her muddy hands up in front of her, shrugging her shoulders.

"It is *prautau* . . ." He let the sentence drag out meaningfully, allowing her to make her own conclusions. It didn't take her long. She jumped to her feet, shrieking.

"Ugh! Are you telling me this is *prautau* poop?!"

Lorgin and Rejar just stared at her, their revulsion plain in their faces for what was all over her hands.

Then the three of them turned amazed faces back to the door.

Traed was leaning against the door frame, arms crossed, one leg crossed over the other, and *the man was laughing*. Deep and rich, his laughter echoed across the room, shattering the dark shadows like a door flung open to sunshine.

Lorgin's eyes lit up. This was the Traed he remembered!

He joined his friend in laughter as he recalled the expression on Adeeann's face when she realized what she had been molding. Soon Rejar was laughing with them.

Deana looked at them stunned. She didn't see anything funny about this at all. She only prayed the stuff wouldn't be too difficult to get off.

It had taken her 45 minutes and two baths to get the wretched stuff off of her. When she got into bed, Lorgin experimentally sniffed her.

"It's gone." Her lower lip pouted mutinously, as if she dared him to rebut the validity of the statement. Lorgin dropped his head, gently suckling that pouting lower lip into his mouth.

"Did you not notice the strange odor, Little Fire?" He smiled against her lips.

"I thought it was just—smelly clay." Against her will, she felt her eyes start to water. He noticed at once.

"What is this? Do not be foolish." He wiped away the single tear that had escaped her eye.

"Oh, Lorgin. I can't believe I did something so stupid! I'm terribly embarrassed."

He gathered her in his arms, letting her burrow her face into his chest. "Forget this. How could you know?" As he patted her back consolingly, he rolled his eyes to the ceiling, not believing what she had done.

"Rejar and Traed must think I'm a nutball," she mumbled into his chest.

"They do not think you are a—what is it?"

"A nutball," came the mumbled response.

"They do not think you are a nutball."

She looked up at him, her face streaked with tears. "Are you sure?"

He wiped her face with the back of his hand. "I am sure."

She sniffed. "Well, how did your scheme with Rejar go? By the way Traed was laughing, I guess I was wrong about that too."

"No, you were right about that, *zira*. He took affront at Rejar's suggestions and left us. Rejar and I were discussing it when we came into the room and saw you . . ."

Deana remembered their raised voices. "You mean you were arguing about it. I bet Rejar didn't think the plan had any merit either, did he?"

Lorgin stopped rubbing her back, annoyed at her accurate observations. "The point is, it did not work. It was the sight of you covered in your clay that did it."

At the mention of the humiliating fiasco, her eyes teared up again. "I can imagine how I looked!" Lorgin couldn't help but smile as he thought about it.

Deana reached around him, grabbing a pillow. She walloped him on the back of the head with it. "Don't you dare laugh at me again."

Lorgin raised his hands, palms up in surrender. "I would not, Adeeann. I swear." He broke his promise immediately by collapsing into laughter.

She went to swing at him again with the pillow, but he neatly fielded it this time. In the blink of an eye, he pinned her to the bed, holding both her wrists over her head.

Bending low, he murmured in her ear, "I noticed you had quite a number of those little pots lined up across Traed's floor. Perhaps you intended to serve us our keeran in them tomorrow?"

"That's not funny." She bucked against him, having no effect on his hold on her whatsoever.

He continued on. "I had not realized how artistic you are until now. This creative genius must not be allowed to lie fallow. I especially admired that one pot which sagged to the left. I said to myself, this is brilliance! What is she saying through her miraculous creations?"

Deana pursed her lips. "Oh, you are terrible! I planned on giving one of those to you as a gift. Now you can forget it."

He dropped his head forward, as if in humility, his hair swinging onto her chest. "I am deeply moved you would think of me in this manner, Adeeann. I truly do not know how I could repay such thoughtfulness."

That did it! "Get off of me right now, you ungrateful wretch!" She broke free of his hold while he was laughing. She leaped out of the bed, storming across the floor, her bare feet making slapping sounds on the stone.

"Where are you going?" He grinned at her from the bed.

"I am going downstairs until you get over this little fit you are having at my expense." She headed for the door.

"Like this?" He gestured to her.

She looked down, gasping when she saw she was buck naked. Lorgin clutched his stomach as he fell back on the bed laughing. Deana's nostrils flared. Did he think she wouldn't do it? She threw back her head, her long red hair flowing around her.

"Yes, like this!" She started to open the door. One moment he was on the bed, the next moment, his hand was slamming the door shut from over her shoulder. *The man could move.*

His arms came around her, lifting her bodily off the floor; he easily shifted her weight to tuck her under one arm as he headed back to the bed.

"Put me down!" She thrashed against him.

"I think not."

She turned, trying to nip his waist.

"I would not do this if I were you." She stopped immediately. When Lorgin used that tone of voice he meant business.

When he reached the bed, he deposited her back under the covers, getting in himself. He turned to her. "I will not laugh about your pottery. I see it has a disturbing effect on you."

She crossed her arms over her chest, grudgingly throwing in the towel. "All right."

His arm reached up to pull her down beside him. Running his hands smoothly down her legs, he asked, "What else did you purchase at the *sacri* today, *zira*? A *krilli* robe, perhaps, bright with color and soft to the touch?" He nuzzled her neck as he continued to stroke her.

"No, that's it. Just . . . the stuff."

"What did you do with the rest of the stones?" He caught her earlobe between his teeth, gently tugging.

"What rest of the stones? I gave them to the woman for the clay."

All nuzzling ceased.

"You gave this woman *thirty* clarified stones for *prautau skrut*?" Rolling onto his back, Lorgin groaned as he slapped the heel of his hand against his forehead.

Deana peeked over at him. "Was that a lot?"

He groaned again.

Chapter Thirteen

The situation with Traed improved after the "clay incident," as Deana preferred to think of it. Not that the man would soon be voted Mr. Congeniality, but he seemed to be opening up to them more. Especially to Lorgin.

The two men spent more time together, often taking walks around the keep. One afternoon, Traed took Lorgin on a tour of the castle itself, telling him of its history and the improvements he had made. Infrequently, he actually smiled. Almost.

Of course, with Traed, you never knew when he was serious or not. Just that evening, toward the end of their meal, he turned to Rejar, a stern expression on his chiseled face.

"Rejar, it has been brought to my attention that you have availed yourself of half of the women in my keep."

The sensual Familiar was not particularly concerned. "Be patient, Traed; I have only been here a short time. I will get to the rest of them."

Deana almost spit out the water she had just swallowed.

She looked incredulously at Rejar. The rogue meant it! *Tomcat.*

Lorgin grinned at his brother's response, but Traed did not smile. Although it did seem that his eyes were glowing with faint amusement. He turned to Lorgin.

"How do you put up with him?"

Lorgin shook his head. "It is not so easy."

When they had finished their meal, Traed led them into a cozy sitting parlor. A soothing fire burned in the fireplace, taking the chill out of the room as the nightly temperature dropped in typical Zarrain style. He poured them each a small cup of brasus, which he explained to Deana was a liquor made from the fruit of a desert plant. It was smooth, and slightly sweet. Definitely a sipping drink. They all sat around the fire in companionable silence, gazing at the flames while savoring the exotic liquor.

"Now it is you who is searching for this phoenix of yours, Adeeann." Traed cradled his drink in his well-shaped hands, warming the liquid.

Lorgin raised an eyebrow. "Phoenix—what is that?"

Deana smiled. "A mythical bird, Lorgin. Traed understands." Traed saluted her with his cup.

Lorgin looked from one to the other, not at all sure he liked their understanding each other so well. True, Adeeann had succeeded in thawing some of Traed's icy reserve, but then how could she not? He knew firsthand the power of her appeal. Unconsciously, he placed his arm around her shoulders, bringing her closer to his side.

Traed, noticing Lorgin's protective gesture, endeavored not to smile. It was only too obvious that his old friend was totally besotted with his wife. Traed was pleased for him, for there was no one he knew that deserved happiness more than Lorgin ta'al Krue. The man was a true knight in every sense of the word, his character above reproach. It suddenly struck Traed how much he had missed his friend over the years. For, in truth, they had been like brothers.

Traed's attention focused on Lorgin and Rejar as they bantered back and forth, teasing each other in good-natured sport. He remembered when it had been the three of them, all those years ago. Rejar, a scamp even then, was forever getting into mischief. When Lorgin wasn't around, Traed watched out for the boy as if he were his own younger brother. Not that anyone could ever truly safeguard the lad; the best one could do was try and save his youthful hide when his playfulness backfired.

Traed suddenly remembered the time when Rejar had told a local confectioner that his spun honey was being insulted by a man outside his shop. The little imp confided to the merchant that the man had said his confections were the worst he had ever tasted. The irate merchant raced outside to do battle, while Rejar helped himself to a generous portion of the sticky sweet.

By the time the merchant had returned, over half of his supply was in the boy's stomach. In an effort to make good on his crime, Rejar had transformed into his cat self. The only trouble was, the evidence was all too visible in the sticky strands caught in the cat's whiskers.

Fortunately for Rejar, Traed happened to come by. Although barely a young man himself at the time, he quickly assessed the situation and told the furious merchant that he had instructed the lad to help himself to the sweet as a natal day gift. He told Rejar to go someplace to transform himself, and to return at once.

While Rejar complied, Traed gave the man a substantial payment for the missing honey crystal. Whereupon he dragged the returning Rejar out of the shop, giving him the same stern lecture Lorgin would have. Then he promptly spoiled the effectiveness of his lecture by laughing out loud at the gamin expression on Rejar's sticky face.

As Traed recalled, the boy's main concern was that his father, Krue, not find out about this latest mischief of his.

Traed smiled slightly at the remembered incident as he slowly sipped his *brasus*.

He suddenly realized what he was doing. What was wrong with him? No good could come of this. Did he not know this by now? No good ever came of it. Best to dampen such memories as these thoughts only brought pain . . .

Lorgin had discreetly observed the play of expression on Traed's face. By his training, he was attuned to mark any changes which could unlock the secrets of an opponent, or in this case, simply a man. He was sure that for a moment when Traed had gazed on Rejar, he had been lost in the past.

Deciding to reinforce what he had noticed, Lorgin stood, slowly stretching his muscles. He sauntered about the room, as if examining this and that, letting the three of them carry on their conversation. When his circuitous route took him to Traed's side, he idly removed his light saber from his waistband, releasing the blade of light.

All conversation stopped as three pairs of eyes looked at him questioningly.

Lorgin lifted the saber and twirled the hilt nimbly across his fingers, causing the blade to whirl and spin, as if it were balanced on nothing but the air. Not paying the least bit of attention to the deadly weapon as it scalloped about his hand, he asked Traed in a bland voice, ''Tell me, are you still as weak with a saber as you always were?

Rejar grinned devilishly at Lorgin's imputation while Traed raised a supercilious eyebrow. He tilted his head as if thinking deeply on Lorgin's words.

"Your memory fails you, Lorgin. *I* was not the one who was weak with the blade. Mayhap . . . it was *you*."

Then the man smiled. Actually smiled.

Deana looked from one to the other of them, once again pondering the vagaries of the Aviaran race.

"Perhaps we should see?" Lorgin flicked the blade through the air. "So there is no doubt." A subtle grin inched its way across Traed's face. "Or do you *conveniently* not have a saber in your possession?" Lorgin was deliberately baiting him now.

Eyes flashing with spirit, Traed slowly sauntered to a cabinet in the corner of the room. With a steady hand, he removed the familiar black box that served as the hilt of the extended blade. Traed was definitely mocking Lorgin as he deftly tossed the saber up in the air and caught it several times with one hand.

Deana's breath caught. They were challenging each other! "What do you guys think you're doing? You aren't really going to—"

"Shall we?" Traed interrupted her as he spoke to Lorgin.

"By all means." Lorgin motioned for Traed to lead the way.

The men followed Tread through the castle maze with Deana tagging behind. As she trotted along behind them, she nagged from the rear of the line.

"This is so stupid! I can't believe you're going to do this! What am I saying? You're men! You have a license to do stupid things." Lorgin frowned at her over his shoulder.

After turning a corner in a long corridor, Traed kicked open a huge wooden door. It banged against the stone wall, the sound reverberating off the walls of a cavernous room.

The room was mostly empty except for a few long wooden tables which had been pushed to the walls, probably ages ago as they were covered in about an inch of Zarrain dust. A narrow rusty wrought iron circular stairway stood in one corner of the room, leading God knew where.

At the far end of the room, a massive stone fireplace covered almost the entire wall. The grate was empty, the room cold. Rubbing her arms to ward off the chill, Deana guessed that at one time in the keep's history the room had served as a great function hall. Too bad there was no central heating.

Lorgin swung his cape off his shoulders and placed it around her.

"Here, *zira*. Do not let the chill bother you." He threw Traed a smug look. "This should not take too long."

Traed made a scoffing sound as he deftly released his light blade.

Lorgin paced to the center of the room, smoothly releasing the blade in his hand. He motioned with his free hand to Traed. "Come now, Traed. Do not be shy."

Traed's answer was a bold lunge toward Lorgin.

Lorgin's blade arced through the air, meeting the forward motion.

The light blades crackled against each other, little arcs of lightning issuing from them with the force of the strikes. The men broke apart. Lorgin spun around, meeting a lateral cut. The men began circling each other slowly, leisurely twirling their blades around their hands.

Deana groaned. "I can't believe they're doing this."

They looked like two pirates caught in mortal combat as the light of the moons shone through the high windows, casting an eerie whitish glow about the room and the dueling men.

The blades sizzled as they struck again and again.

Traed leaped back out of Lorgin's reach, then feinted and closed. Lorgin sidestepped him, swung around, attempting his own lateral cut. Traed blocked it.

Their swordplay took them around the room as they thrust, parried, lunged. Each time barely missing the other. Each time becoming more aggressive.

{They are evenly matched. Krue taught them both.} Rejar came to stand beside Deana.

"You don't carry a saber, Rejar?"

{A Familiar prefers to rely on his senses.}

"So you don't fence?"

Rejar shrugged. *{Some.}*

Out of the corner of her eye Deana saw the crackle and flash of the blades. "It's a good thing they're not trying to hit each other."

{Why do you say that?}

Deana's eyes widened. "Are you telling me they are trying to wound each other?"

{What would be the point otherwise?}

"I think I'm going to be sick."

Reluctantly she turned back to the spectacle before her. They were going at it fast and furious now. Traed advanced on Lorgin, lunging. Lorgin leaped back, but the blade caught his chest, slicing across his shirt, instantly rending the fabric. A thin red line appeared on the white fabric.

Deana screamed.

Both men ignored her as they continued.

"Sorry about your shirt, Lorgin." Traed smiled slowly as he parried a thrust. "I should have compensated for your lack of ability."

Lorgin grinned as he neatly returned the favor by slicing across Traed's shirt. *His* skin was not even broken. "Unlike you, my friend, I have compensated."

Traed laughed, rushing a charge. Lorgin jumped out of the way onto the circular stairway, backing up the stairs as Traed advanced on him.

"It is almost over, Lorgin. You will soon have your back to a wall."

"Not quite." Lorgin parried, then, using the handrail, vaulted over the staircase and down onto the stone floor twelve feet below.

"My God!" Deana blanched, then gasped as Traed followed Lorgin's path over the railing to land in front of him. The clashing of the blades picked up momentum.

In an incredible display of skill, Lorgin struck his blade against Traed's in a lightning-fast maneuver—one, two, three. Parry. Cut. Lunge. He saw an opening, pivoted, and literally stomped the saber right out of Traed's hands with the heel of his boot. The sound echoed off the stone floor.

Deana was stunned. "How could he—"

{The flat of the blade cannot injure—only the edge. It will slice through anything.}

Deana felt faint and slightly nauseous. If Lorgin had miscalculated, he would have sliced off his own foot. *Men* What a stupid and senseless thing to do!

Traed nodded to Lorgin, catching his breath. "A good match, Lorgin. I will have to remember that move. It must be one of your own, for Krue never taught it to us."

"It is. It saved my life once when I was on a mission for the Alliance. The last opponent I tried it on did not fare as well as you."

Traed shook his head. "I can imagine."

"You have not lost your skill, Traed. Few can match it. Perhaps you would like another challenge. Or are you spent?"

Traed scoffed.

Lorgin smiled.

Without looking in his brother's direction, Lorgin called out, "Rejar!" at the same moment he threw his brother the saber. It arced through the room, end over end, the light blade flashing as it spun. Rejar's arm shot into the air, catching the barrel fast.

Deana swallowed. If Rejar had caught the blade wrong, it would have sliced his arm off. *What was wrong with these Aviarans?* Did they have some kind of death wish? She turned to ask Rejar what Lorgin thought he was doing, but noticed that Rejar was already halfway across the floor, a predatory expression on his roguish face as he stalked Traed.

Traed circled him slowly, making tiny, taunting, circular movements with the tip of his light blade. "Come, Rejar." He beckoned the younger man. "And none of your Familiar tricks."

Rejar stepped forward testing the saber in his hand. His face displayed a very feral smile. "I *am* a Familiar." He began circling Traed. "How do you propose I forget it?" He lunged suddenly, narrowly missing Traed's arm. "You take what you get."

"Really?" Traed parried Rejar's next thrust with little effort. "You are a son of Krue. Do you think to mesmerize me into dropping my saber or will you fight like a warrior?"

Rejar smoothly jumped forward, feinted left, spun around, and engaged Traed in a series of adept maneuvers. His characteristic grace of movement served him well.

"I will fight like a warrior"—Their blades crackled as they struck off each other in rapid succession—"who is *also* a Familiar."

For a man who claimed he only fenced "some," he was pretty damn good, Deana thought as she watched them fight.

"He has a talent for it." Lorgin had come up beside her. "It is unfortunate he denies his abilities. With practice such skill could become legendary."

"I happen to think Rejar shows remarkable insight in choosing the high road. He believes in using his senses instead of swords."

"Familiars have that luxury—sometimes. I will point out to you, Adeeann, that it is a philosophy which over time has gotten many of them slain. But you misunderstand Rejar. He can and *will* fight. Familiars can be fearsome and ruthless adversaries when they pick up the gauntlet." When Deana did not respond, he turned his attention back to the match.

"Traed is an artist with the blade," he murmured.

"And you were brilliant, Lorgin," she said through clenched teeth as she gazed at the singed gash in his shirt. "But if you ever do anything as stupid as that again I will kill you myself!" So saying, she stormed off back to their chamber.

Lorgin's amused gaze followed her retreat.

"Something troubles Adeeann?" Traed wiped the sweat off his brow. It had not been an easy thing to get Rejar to yield.

"It seems my wife cannot live without me and is ready to kill me to prove it."

Traed nodded sagely. "Women," he remarked dryly, "are easily understood."

The two men burst into laughter.

Lorgin clasped Traed's shoulder. "It is good to hear you laugh again, my friend."

Traed smiled. "Forgive me, Lorgin, but your woman is . . . very entertaining."

Lorgin raised an eyebrow. "Do not let her hear you say this. Think you it was so easy for me to get her to play with skrut solely for your amusement, Traed?"

He chuckled. "It really was not fair of you, Lorgin. And such a sacrifice."

They both laughed again.

"Now, Traed, I will give you a chance to even the score. My challenge to dizu still stands."

Traed smiled. "A safe challenge for you, Lorgin, for well you know I have no *dizu* board here."

Lorgin nodded his head in agreement. "Hmm—this could be a problem." His crafty eyes assayed Traed. "I suppose we shall have to go to Aviara to play the game."

Always sharp, Traed knew at once the intent behind Lorgin's ploy. His chiseled face became devoid of all expression, except for his eyes, which were suddenly throwing sparks of green anger.

"If you so desire this game, Lorgin ta'al Krue, you need return to Aviara. I am sure you will find someone else who plays the game as well as I."

Traed's meaning was all too clear.

Lorgin's response was measured. *"There is no one who can play this particular game but you."*

Traed placed the retracted saber in his waistband and walked out.

Deana sat in front of the mirror of the dressing table in her room, not really paying attention to the comb in her hand. A thoughtful servant had left her a robe, which she had immediately donned as soon as she had thrown off her pants and tunic. She was beginning to hate that outfit. It never got dirty and it never wore out!

She saw the room reflected in the mirror: the large bed with its massive scrolled headboard, the few odd tables, an oversized chair in the corner, and this very old-fashioned dressing stand she was sitting at. It looked as if she had gone back in time to the days of the Round Table.

What was she doing here?

Unconsciously, she began combing her long hair, stopping when her hand began to shake. Briefly she closed her eyes, then opened them to stare at her reflection.

Lorgin.

He was the source of her problems, and she was beginning to fear he was the cure to them as well. It couldn't have been more obvious to her than if she had slapped her own face. Tonight when he was fencing with Traed and the blade had sliced across him, she had almost thrown up. That nauseous feeling could only mean one thing: she cared too deeply for Lorgin ta'al Krue.

If the very thought of him getting injured could scare her silly, it was time to do something about it. She was in too deep. It was definitely time to go home.

Deana frowned at her duplicate in the mirror.

The man was acting out some crazy self-fulfilling prophecy.

He had kidnapped her from her world, told her she was his wife, seduced her, and dragged her halfway across a universe on some nebulous quest.

What was she going to do with him?

She shouldn't allow this to continue. It wasn't fair to either of them. She would have to make him see reason. She would have to make him pledge to take her back to Earth right away. Because the thing that was in the utmost danger around here was herself.

And she was not going to feed his fantasy anymore.

She cared too much for him to do that. In time he would realize the mistake he had made and go on from there. He would forget—

The heavy wooden door to the bedroom crashed open.

"That man is the most difficult person I have ever dealt with! He is stubborn beyond belief."

"Don't you think you ought to close the door before you wake up half the keep?"

Lorgin kicked the door shut and threw up his hands in exasperation.

"He will not be swayed one micron unless he desires it!"

Deana raised her eyebrows. "Why does that sound familiar to me?" She looked pointedly at Lorgin.

"I am nothing like that."

"Really." She didn't even try to swallow the sarcasm.

He walked further into the room. "Explain yourself." He crossed his arms and peered down at her arrogantly, missing the point.

"All right, I will." She turned in her seat to gaze up at him—a long way up. ".I want to go back to my home." For an instant he looked thunderstruck.

"Why would you say this?"

Why would she say this? Where should she start? The kidnapping? The seduction? Her eyes fell on her pants and tunic draped over the chair. As good a starting point as any.

"I don't like those clothes." His mouth actually gaped open for a moment.

"For this you wish to leave me? I will buy you a castle full of clothes when we reach Aviara."

"You're missing the point. It's time for me to go home."

Lorgin stared down at her through half-lidded eyes. He had thought that she would soon get over these foolish notions of hers. Had he not been the most patient of husbands with her? Had he not taught her the joy of Transference? Had he not always given her everything he had for her pleasure?

Perhaps Yaniff had been right. He had been too indulgent with her. This ridiculous talk of returning to the Disney World! Did she think he would remove her from such a backward, *diseased* world only to place her in jeopardy again? Did she think he would disregard his honor? Did she, *who was above all others to him,* think he could let her leave him!

He fastened a steely, searing glare upon her.

Deana watched Lorgin's expression go from shock to confusion to anger. This was not what she wanted. Tentatively, she reached up to place a soft hand of his rock-hard forearm.

"It's not as if you—" She swallowed. "You don't really care about me, it's—"

He didn't allow her to finish. Grabbing her shoulders, he turned her back to face the mirror. When he spoke next to her ear, his voice was chillingly quiet.

"I do not care about you?"

She made to rise, but his firm touch at her shoulders held her down.

"Look in the mirror, Adeeann."

She ignored his words, looking down into her lap instead. Her shoulders tensed as she felt his cheek softly rub against the side of her face, his tongue lightly tracing a sizzling path along the side of her throat.

"Look in the mirror, Adeeann." His words vibrated against her skin, but she continued looking down.

She felt him loosen the top of her robe, sliding it just off her shoulders. His open mouth latched onto the sensitive spot where her neck met her shoulders. The tip of his tongue sent her a tiny frisson, coaxing a response from her. She couldn't help the little moan that escaped her throat.

"Look in the mirror, zira," he whispered against her.

She silently shook her head no.

His hands left her shoulders to come around her, cupping her breasts through the silky fabric of the robe, his thumbs stroking across the tips. The heat of his large hands electrified her as he continued with his ardent ministrations to her throat with his mouth.

She shivered, taking in a large gulp of air. He gently raised her chin with one finger, steadily meeting her eyes in the mirror. "Look."

Her gaze shifted from his passionate regard to her own

face, shocked by what she saw. Her eyes were sparking! Little pink sparks, such as she had seen in his eyes. She leaned forward to examine this phenomenon more closely, her hand coming to her lips in astonishment.

"Oh, Lorgin, what have you done?" Her voice was barely a whisper.

He tenderly kissed her shoulder. "Even now, I am inside of you." Her gaze flew to his image in the glass.

"How?" she breathed.

He stroked the side of her neck, his warm fingers threading through her hairline. "We are joined. I have told you thus. There will be no more talk of leaving."

She scrunched the fabric of her robe between her hands. "Why, Lorgin? Why? You said you would take me home. You promised me."

He squeezed her shoulders. "And I spoke the truth. I am taking you home—to *our* home on Aviara."

"I cannot go with you. It is a mistake!"

Lorgin sighed deeply. He would have to convince her completely and utterly that it was no mistake. *Once and for all.*

He bent over her, releasing the tie on her robe. It fell around the base of the chair in a soft puddle. He spoke in a hushed, intimate tone, leaving Deana no doubt as to what he planned.

"You have challenged me."

"No, I haven't! At least I didn't mean to." She vividly remembered the last time he thought she had challenged him and what the outcome had been. "What are you doing?" She turned quickly in her chair.

Lorgin had already kicked off his boots, removed his torn shirt, and was in the process of dispensing with his breeches.

Deana stood, facing him. "You wouldn't!" she gasped.

He shrugged. Then smiled in an altogether calculating way.

He approached her with a determined glint in his eye.

Before she could come up with another word of objection, he had scooped her up in his arms and carried her to the bed. He gently placed her on the mattress, then immediately came down on top of her, his mouth searing hers in an intoxicating kiss.

As so often happened with his expert touch, against her better intentions, Deana immediately turned to mush. His wonderfully adept hands began stroking her in all the right places; his lips were tender and stimulating as he breathlessly awoke her hunger for him.

Deana moaned, "No, Lorgin, no . . ." even as she sought out his provocative embraces.

As expected, he paid little heed to her words and more attention to her reactions. Reactions she was powerless to control under the onslaught of his attentions. His mouth grazed down her throat as his fingers brushed across nipples that were already pebble-hard. Fingers explored. Teeth nipped. Hands caressed. Lips bewitched . . .

He had aroused her to the point of madness and still he continued against her protests, his heated mouth trailing an erotic path down to the indentation of her belly, and lower still.

Suddenly, through a haze of passion, she realized what he was about to do. She panicked. This she had never done. This was way too personal. This she was not ready for. She tried to scoot away from him on the bed.

"No, you can't!"

He brought her firmly back.

"Of course I *can*." His warm breath feathered against her inner thigh.

"I-I mean you shouldn't!" she squealed as his hot tongue licked the inside of her leg, trying once more to scoot away.

"And here I thought you were going to teach me something new." He smiled wickedly as he dragged her back down to him. His strong palms pressing above the inside of her knees held her uncompromisingly open for him.

"Lorgin, pl-please!"

His eyes shot up, piercing her. "What can I do, Adeeann?" It was a question he did not expect an answer to. "You keep talking about returning to this world of yours." He paused, intentionally holding the moment. "It is only right I convince you otherwise. I do not believe you will have any doubts"— he gave her a determined look—"*soon*."

That said, he dropped his head between her legs.

She sobbed and begged and screamed and hollered.

Still he would not stop. He loved her with his mouth in a way that was totally indecent. Totally intoxicating. The first touch of his tongue, silky hot against her, made her reel off the bed. But that was just the beginning. He flicked. He licked. He suckled. And he thoroughly loved it.

His tongue caressed her, his lips kissed her, his teeth scraped against her. Through it all he sent her his electric current of desire, a steaming shockwave of vibration echoing through her as he continued his onslaught of surging, quivering, pulsating challenge. As her own waves returned to him, they seemed to fuel his intense ardor, inspiring him to greater heights as they further ignited him.

When she literally screamed her release, he watched her, his fevered eyes sparking in arousal.

"I do so enjoy convincing you, Adeeann." His voice was a husky ripple purring against her glistening mound. He licked her one last time as if reluctant to stop.

But he was not done yet. Not by a long shot.

Her bones were still jelly when he neatly flipped her over onto her stomach. Clasping both her arms over her head in one of his hands, he skimmed his other hand possessively down her back, softly massaging as he went. He kneaded her buttocks, lightly running the edge of his fingers down along the cleft until they found the still throbbing folds of her womanly passage.

Deana sucked in her breath, already anticipating what was in store for her.

Lorgin did not hesitate.

Grabbing a pillow, he placed it under her hips, slightly raising her. She felt the pressing heat of his body as he covered her with himself. *She was under siege.*

"You can't do this, Lorgin!"

"I *am* doing it."

"You have no right—"

"I have every right."

"No!"

"You will stop this ridiculous talk of returning to your world. Understand this, Adeeann zira'al Lorgin, *you belong to me.*"

Unclasping her hands, he spread her arms beside her, placing his broad palms over the backs of her hands; he interlaced his fingers with hers, literally pinning her to the bed. He purposefully nudged her legs apart with his knee and ever so slowly entered her from behind.

His thick shaft filled her slick, wet canal, pulsing inside of her. Deana choked on a sob at the sheer pleasure of it. This was sexual domination; Lorgin was completely and irrevocably staking his claim. *And it was to die for.*

"Say you belong to me, Adeeann. Say it . . ." His hot, breathy whisper was right behind her left ear.

"No, I won't!"

He flexed and surged inside of her, the firm muscles of his thighs bracing her.

"Oh my God, *Lorgin* . . . that feels incredible."

His response was to kiss the back of her neck, rubbing his face in her fragrant hair.

"Say you are mine, sweet Fire; you know in your heart you are."

"Don't you dare mention hearts to me when you're doing this out of some crazy fantasy you have!"

He smiled shamelessly against her skin. "I admit it is somewhat of a fantasy. I vow I have never had to take a woman thus."

It was the wrong thing for him to say, for it conjured up images of him in her head—images of him in bed with scores of willing women.

"Stop this right now!" But there wasn't a thing she could do to enforce her words and he knew it.

"Make me." He bit her sharply on her nape, and plunged deeper into her.

"I hate you!"

Her liquid honey increased around him, belying her words. He chuckled against the side of her neck. "No, you do not."

"Just you wait, I'll—"

"Shh . . ." He traced his sizzling tongue around her earlobe. "Stop talking and *listen,* Adeeann. Listen to this surging, flowing thing between us." His actions mirrored his breathless words as his shaft glided against and into her.

"Listen to it pounding in our blood, our hearts." Strong fingers entwined tightly with her own. She could feel the pulse of his blood rushing against her hands.

"Listen to the power in me awaken *for you.*" Without warning, he sent her a surge of incredible power inside where they joined.

"Oh, God . . . Lorgin . . ."

His breath grew ragged as he stroked into her again and

again, still pinning her to the bed. Deana moaned with each thrust, catching his wildness, his sheer eroticism. His quickening.

"Can you hear it? Can you hear this savage warrior in me, coming to you?"

"Yes!" she gasped.

He released her hands, clutching her tight around the waist, bringing her even closer to him as he buried his head between her shoulderblades.

"Can you feel this powerful magic in my heart entwine around you?" he whispered against her.

She clutched the sheet beneath her, whimpering. "Yes, yes, yes . . ."

"Now you taste of my passion, Adeeann."

Chapter Fourteen

Deana was senseless.

Lorgin had made love to her the entire night.

He was relentless.

He had been totally without mercy, extracting every word he wanted to hear out of her.

Yes, she would not mention returning to her world to him again.

Yes, she didn't really want to leave.

Yes, she wanted him.

Yes. Yes. Yes.

He had confused her with his powerful lovemaking, his heart-stopping caresses, and his whispered entreaties: *Was she not his Little Fire, his gharta, who he placed above all others?* Yes.

Did she not crave him the same way he craved her? Yes.

Did he not entrust her with his power to keep safe inside of her? Yes! Yes! Yes!

Deana pulled the sheet over her head. She had caved like a house of cards on an active fault line.

Earlier this morning when he had taken her in his arms again, she all but whimpered. All she could think of was, *He's going to start up again.* She must have made some sound, for all he did was kiss her on the forehead, saying, "Hush, Adeeann. I am just getting up. Go back to sleep."

He had used sex against her.

Her brow furrowed. No, that wasn't quite right—he had used sex *for* her.

Then he had used sex *with* her.

It was a very potent technique. By now, Deana knew that Lorgin was a man who had a multitude of techniques. Depending on the circumstances, he would draw on the one he thought most apt to accomplish his goal. She believed this trait had to do more with the man himself rather than any Charl training of his.

It really wasn't sporting of him. She hadn't had a lot of experience in the past and had no defenses against his expertise. All right, so even if she had been very experienced, she was honest enough to admit that she probably wouldn't have been able to put up much of a cold front. He was just so overwhelming.

The man had stormed the citadel.

What was she going to do now?

Bringing up the subject of returning to Earth was totally out of the question. There was *no* subject, as far as Lorgin ta'al Krue was concerned. That left her with only one option. She would have to go with him to that wretched Aviara of his. But when they got there, she intended to seek help from Yaniff. She was almost sure the kindly old wizard would help her once she explained the situation to him.

She only prayed she wouldn't be gobbled up in the streets

by one of the monsters Lorgin had mentioned before she got the chance.

Deana was getting dressed when Lorgin returned to their chamber.

For some reason, after what they had shared last night, she felt terribly shy. He did not suffer from any such affliction as he came up to her, softly kissing her on the forehead.

"You must be hungry, Adeeann. It is well past the midday hour. Would you like to accompany me to the little *sacri* in the center of the keep? I am sure we can find something to eat there."

"Okay," she mumbled, not quite meeting his eyes.

"Come." He took her hand and led her outside.

For Zarrain, the day was a pleasant one. The heat was at a bearable level; occasionally there was a faint puff of air which could almost be classified as a breeze.

Lorgin led her to a stall where he purchased some turnovers which resembled the ones they'd had on Ryka Twelve. Only these were a lot spicier. Deana wondered if the spice was masking the age of the meat. She eyed the pastry dubiously.

"It is fine, I assure you. Although perhaps not best on an empty stomach. Would you like something else?"

Deana scanned the stall. "How about some plain baked dough?" Close enough to a donut, she thought.

He handed her one of the brick-shaped loaves. "You do not care much for the food here." His eyes traveled over her form. "You have lost some weight."

She took a bite of the dough. It not only looked like a brick, it was as hard as one. "I'm not used to it."

"I admit the choices must seem alien to you, but you must overcome such problems. You would not wish to appear provincial, would you?" He winked at her.

She laughed. "That is the least of my concerns, Lorgin."

After they had finished eating, Lorgin led her through the alleyways of the keep into several tiny shops. They browsed a bit, looking at the items in companionable silence.

Deana glanced his way every now and then, when he wasn't looking her way. His handsome profile. His beautiful eyes. His sensitive hands. *Those hands* . . .

It was hard to believe that the regally contained man next to her had been an uncontrollable, erotically wild lover just a few short hours ago.

Her heart skipped a beat.

She was getting excited just thinking about how he had made love to her last night. Her gaze strayed to his lips—those smooth, silky hot lips—and she couldn't help but think of where *they* had been just a few hours ago. She blushed, turning quickly to look at some merchandise lest he notice.

There was more variety in the shops than Deana would have thought, considering they were at the end of never. Lorgin told her the caravans had brought the items from all over Zarrain, as well as a few off-planet items. He motioned to the proprietor to bring a silky jewel-toned robe for his inspection.

"Do you like it?" He turned to her.

"It's very pretty," she replied without thinking.

"I agree." He handed the shop owner several gems. "Send it up to the castle," he told the little man.

"Lorgin, what are you doing?"

He ignored her question, turning back to the proprietor. "Let me see those caftans in the corner."

The little man hesitated. "Those are pure krilli, sir. They are very costly."

Lorgin motioned impatiently for him to do his bidding.

There were four caftans. Each was obviously hand-made and exquisitely embroidered. Deana had never seen or felt

271

such beautiful cloth. It was softer than the softest silk. The color combinations of the threads were extraordinary, each dress displaying a tonal combination rather than a particular color.

Lorgin watched her face as she viewed the *krilli* caftans. He spoke to the man. "Send those as well." Deana gasped, her eyes flying to him.

"All"—the man cleared his throat—"*all of them?*" They were outrageously expensive.

"No, Lorgin!" Deana knew what he was doing. It was his response to her comment last night regarding her clothes. But she hadn't meant for him to spend all this money on her; she had simply tried to make a point, which actually had nothing to do with clothes.

Lorgin looked down at her through half-veiled eyes as he spoke to the shop owner. "Yes, all of them."

"Lorgin, it's not necessary. You don't have to do this."

"I do have to do this, Adeeann. It was remiss of me to be so unthoughtful of your needs."

"You're being ridiculous; you're the most thoughtful man I have ever met." It was true. She recalled how he always was concerned over her comfort and well-being. He really was a very gallant man. And a very stubborn one once his mind was made up. He seemed to read her thoughts as she was about to voice another objection.

"It is done. Besides, I vow I look forward to seeing you in them, although you must promise me to wait until we reach Aviara before you wear them. There will still be the danger of slavers on the way back to the tunnel point."

"Thanks for reminding me. I forgot all about the return journey through that awful desert."

They left the shop, continuing with their walk.

"Perhaps it will not be so bad. Traed will be able to provide us with adequate escort. At least we will not have to fear being so outnumbered in an attack, should one occur.''

''Do you think Traed will be joining us?''

''I do not know. But . . . the time has come for me to confront him directly. I cannot afford to tarry here any longer. The situation with Theardar grows critical.''

''He doesn't know his father is involved, does he?''

''No, and I wish it to remain thus. I will leave it to Yaniff to explain the situation to him. If I mention to Traed that Theardar is involved, there will be no chance of Traed agreeing to come back to Aviara with us.''

They walked on awhile in silence, holding hands. Deana asked the question she had been wondering about for some time.

''Lorgin, did Theardar abuse Traed?''

''Abuse him?'' Lorgin looked at her confused, not understanding her question. ''He blamed Traed for his mother's death.''

''Did he have anything to do with it?''

''No, he was just a babe at the time, newly born, when his mother died.''

Deana was surprised. ''She died in childbirth?''

''Yes.''

''That doesn't happen very often anymore on my world.''

He glanced her way. ''Nor here, *zira*. There were . . . extenuating circumstances.''

''So Theardar blamed Traed for his mother's death—wasn't that rather irrational?''

''Yes. As you have heard, it is said Theardar is mad. As a boy, nothing Traed could do was ever right enough or good enough for him. My father, Krue, guided Traed when he could, trying to undo the damage that Theardar inflicted. The tragedy is that Traed was exceptional in so many ways, but

Theardar was blind to his son.''

Deana swallowed, hesitant to ask, but knowing she had to. "Did Theardar beat him?''

Lorgin looked away. "He punished him severely,'' was all he would say.

"How terribly sad.''

"His spirit is not broken. Traed has the seeds of honor and courage, and, I believe, great compassion in him. He has the makings of a Charl if he would but seek it.''

"But he won't?''

"No. He will not do anything which even remotely follows in Theardar's footsteps.'' Lorgin exhaled resignedly. "Knowing what I know, I cannot blame him. He needs to find his own way.''

"How can he do that hiding away on this hideous world?''

"He cannot. The time has come for Traed to leave. Not just because of the quest, but for himself as well.'' Lorgin gazed up at the sky. "I will just have to convince him of it.''

Deana smiled ironically, speaking quietly. "I shouldn't worry too much, Lorgin. You have a certain talent for convincing.''

It was the only reference she had made to their previous night. His mouth turned up slightly at the corners as his gaze fell to her.

"Mmm.'' He bent over to brush her lips with his own.

Traed did not join them for the evening meal, which was not a good sign. Lorgin didn't comment on his absence, but Deana could tell that he was concerned. Rejar elected not to bring up the subject either. As if he sensed the tension in his brother, Rejar sought safer, more lighthearted topics.

{A man delivered many colorful caftans here today. Perhaps I will offer one to a pretty maid I have seen in the caravan.}

Lorgin raised an eyebrow. "No, you will not. They are gifts to my wife. If you wish to make such a generous offering to this maid, might I suggest you provide it?"

{You might, but it lacks my subtle touch.}

Lorgin snorted. "And what subtle touch is that, brother? I vow you do not have a subtle *bone* in your body when it comes to women."

Rejar grinned. *{I did not mean that subtle touch; I meant having a maid give her favors to me because of a gift you paid for.}*

Deana giggled, putting her hand to her mouth.

Lorgin looked at his brother, surprised. "You have allowed her to hear your less than honorable words?"

"Oh, Lorgin, lighten up. Rejar is just teasing you."

Lorgin looked totally perplexed. *"Lighten up?"*

Rejar and Deana both burst out laughing.

Lorgin sought out Traed after their meal. He found him in his study, sitting before the fire, staring into the flames. This time he did not hold the *phfiztger* in his arms. Unconsciously, his hands clutched the arms of the chair, mirroring the upsetting thoughts he was obviously having.

Lorgin entered the room without knocking, quietly closing the door behind him.

"I thought I would find you here, my friend."

Traed did not respond, did not even look his way. Lorgin found another chair and pulled it up to the fire next to him.

"What troubles you so, Traed?"

For a long while Traed did not answer. When he did, his voice was very low. "You, of all people, must ask me this?"

Lorgin did not don the mask of pretense, even to spare Traed's feelings. "You must put aside these thoughts for now. I tell you, Traed, you must return to Aviara with me."

Traed looked up at the ceiling, then closed his eyes. "It is impossible. I cannot do this. Even for you, my friend."

"It is not just for me; there are those who must depend upon you now."

"I want no one depending upon me. That is why I came here. That is why I shall remain here."

"Such choices are not always ours, Traed. Sometimes choices are made *for* us whether we want them or not."

Traed rested his head back against the rim of his chair. "I cannot, Lorgin."

Lorgin remained silent for a few moments. "Sometimes, you remind me of my brother . . ."

Traed looked at him in surprise. "Rejar and I have very little in common."

Lorgin stretched his booted feet out to the fire, crossing his ankles. "More than either of you thinks."

"Explain yourself."

"Neither one of you wants to recognize your birthright. Both of you deny who you are and what you can become. Rejar hides himself behind his carefree, frolicsome Familiar ways while he denies his Charl background. You hide out here, as Adeeann would say, in the back of nowhere, hiding from what you fear, denying your own heritage."

Traed raised an eyebrow. "You would make a terrible diplomat, Lorgin. You have never learned to temper your words."

"Then it is fortunate I am a warrior, is it not?"

"Most fortunate."

Lorgin rose, going to a sideboard; he poured them each a horn of *keeran*. He handed one to Traed before retaking his chair.

Traed gestured with his horn. "I take it this means I am in for a siege here?"

Lorgin shrugged, grinning faintly. Traed knew him all too well.

"It will not do you much good, Lorgin, for I tell you I will not set foot on Aviara again."

"There are things you do not know." Lorgin glanced at Traed, reflected in the firelight, realizing that there were probably things *he* did not know as well. But such things did not concern him now; he had a particular task to accomplish. It was not a time to let his thinking be sidetracked.

Traed cupped the horn between his hands. "What if I tell you I do not wish to know of these things? Will it make a difference?"

Lorgin ignored his words, plowing on. "Yaniff told me your mother was of the Tan-Shi."

"A Tan-Shi?" Traed looked perplexed. "How does he know that?"

"How does Yaniff know anything? Believe me, if he said it, it is so."

Traed shook his head. "It is impossible. Tan-Shi take an oath of chastity. They devote themselves to the Rites of Passage. When they take this oath, they divest themselves . . ." Traed sucked in his breath.

Lorgin finished the thought for him. "They divest themselves of the right of the Transference. All power which flows into them will flow out, taking with it their very lifeforce."

Traed was clearly stunned. "But . . . how? My father—"

"Your father *knew* she was Tan-Shi."

"I do not understand any of this." He took a large swallow of his *keeran*.

"Your father met your mother when he was but a young man. Even though she was a young girl at the time, I am told he loved her even then. While he waited for her to come into her maturity, she had discovered that she had a different calling. She loved Theardar, but only as a friend.'' Lorgin paused.

''Continue.''

''While Theardar was on a mission for the Alliance, she took the oath. When he returned, he was enraged, refusing to let the matter go. Even though they were the best of friends, my father could not reach Theardar or make him see reason. His behavior . . . his behavior concerned Krue who sought out Yaniff's counsel.

''When Yaniff and Krue returned to find Theardar, it was too late. He had already kidnapped your mother from the Holy Sanctuary. He took her against her will.''

Traed paled. ''*By Aiyah!*''

Lorgin sipped his drink, giving Traed a moment to digest the terrible story. ''The Transference was completed.''

Traed leaned forward in his seat, dropping the horn to the floor. It bounced off the stone with a heavy clang.

''Are you certain my father knew she had already taken the oath?''

''Yes. He knew, but he took her anyway. Do you understand? Your father knew this but could not face the fact that it was he who killed her, killed that which he loved above all else. So, when her lifeforce left her at the moment of your birth, he blamed you. It was for this the Guild excommunicated him.''

''Because he killed her.'' Traed's voice was a mere whisper.

''No. *Because he blamed you.*''

Traed's head snapped up. ''What are you saying?''

''The Guild would have punished Theardar for the terrible thing he had done, but not excommunicated him. It was a crime of passion, and very possibly unbalanced behavior. They would have tried to heal him. He is, after all, a sixth-level mystic. Such power demands a certain respect. But when he blamed you, they could not allow this dishonor to continue. I understand Yaniff was opposed to their decision but was overruled. He believed your father needed a healing, not a breaching. Krue begged Theardar to leave you with us permanently, but, as you know, he refused. Although he did let you stay with us from time to time."

Traed stared into the flames again. "Did you know there were days when he would forget I was there? Then suddenly he would look at me as if he were just realizing he had a young boy who needed to be cared for. I lived for those moments. It was as if he would briefly come to his senses and leave me on your doorstep. I am ashamed to say I used to pray he would never return to take me away. My own father . . . But he always did."

There was nothing Lorgin could say.

"In a sense, Lorgin, you have just confirmed what my father has always blamed me for. My mother did die because of my birth." When Lorgin made to protest, Traed cut him off. "Anyway, it does not matter now. The fact remains that Theardar was mad. When did this come upon him? Before or after he decided to take her? Or did he always have the seeds of madness within him, festering, waiting to grow?"

Traed's hands covered his eyes as if he could not stand these tortured thoughts another moment. His voice became a raw, painful sound. *"Waiting to grow in me?"*

"No!" Lorgin knelt in front of Traed, pulling his hands away from his face. "Yaniff told me this will not happen to you."

Traed flung Lorgin aside, pacing the room as if he were trapped. "Yaniff! Yaniff! What does that old man know!"

Lorgin stood. "More than either of us care to speculate."

Traed slumped back down into the chair. Lorgin stood over

him. "Yaniff wants you to leave this wretched place and come back with me to Aviara."

Traed sighed. "For what reason?"

"He wishes to speak with you. He will not come here."

"In case my *loving* father decides to pay his favorite and only son a visit? So, Yaniff fears to confront the Beast."

"Yaniff fears nothing. It is you he thinks of. He would not battle your father on your own doorstep."

"Does it matter?" Traed scoffed.

"It matters to him."

"You said he opposed the Guild's decision. Why would he wish to fight my father?"

Lorgin looked away. "For what he did to you. He robbed the Charl of you, and by his actions, interfered in your destiny."

Traed was surprised. "Yaniff still speaks of me?"

Lorgin smiled softly. "Often and with great fondness. Traed, you must come with me."

Traed bowed his head, hating having to deal with these strange emotions. Yaniff and the family of Krue were the only kindness he had known in his young life. They had taken him in, making him one of their family. Krue had almost called him son. Suleila had been like a mother to him. And Yaniff . . . In truth, he would not mind gazing upon the withered face of his old teacher again. *Yaniff wanted to see him.*

As if one could refuse the venerable mystic's summons. It was over. Lorgin was right; there had never been a choice, now or before.

He looked up at Lorgin, eyes bright. A man caught between honor and self-preservation. The mettle of the man spoke volumes in just three small words.

"I will come."

Lorgin said nothing, but placed his hand on his friend's shoulder.

* * *

It was late when Lorgin entered the bedchamber. He had stayed with Traed for some time. It did not seem right to leave the man alone after revealing such truths to him, so they drank *keeran*, sitting side by side in front of the fire, mostly silent. Lorgin knew that ofttimes more was said with silence than with words. He believed this was such a time.

They agreed it would be best to leave at daybreak. Traed told Lorgin of a little-known tunnel point his father had told him of, a day's journey to the west, high in the mountains. Although more difficult to access, its proximity to the keep, and Lorgin's need for haste, made it the better choice.

At least their trek through the desert would be lessened considerably.

Lorgin gazed down at Deana fast asleep under the cover, curled into a tight ball in the middle of the bed. The nights of Zarrain were, indeed, chilly. Quickly he shed his clothes, getting under the warm blanket.

He was not surprised when she rolled right over into his arms.

Smiling to himself, he waited for her to push her knee between his thighs. It was her favorite sleeping position with him, since their very first night together in the sanfrancisco; and he did not think she was even aware of it.

Ah . . . yes. He felt her leg slide between his.

His palm ran down her back, enjoying the feel of her soft skin as he idly stroked her saucy curls, trailing them with the tips of his fingers down her back. She made a little sound and cuddled her face deeper into his chest as she slept.

Lorgin gazed down at Adeeann lying peacefully in his arms, his thoughts wandering back over his conversation with Traed.

For the first time, he thought about Theardar, not only the

suffering the man had caused, but how he must have suffered as well. Having to watch his child grow within his woman, knowing that with its life came her death. Did a man pray for the death of his child or his wife? How could he choose? Combine that with the knowledge that he was the executioner of that which he loved above all else . . . It was enough to drive a man mad . . . if he was not already mad.

His hold on Deana tightened as he tried to place himself in the mind of Theardar. It was a technique Yaniff had taught him as a means of gaining understanding and perspective. The mystic believed that only in such a way could one truly understand the intricacy of a situation. The large picture, Yaniff would tell him, shows much, but tells little. Look for the small pictures, the details within—there lies the pathway to the truth.

He tried, but it was impossible to have a full sense of Theardar, for Lorgin was not of a like mind and would never have committed the deeds that Theardar had. Nonetheless, on one level he could feel significant compassion for the man. Lorgin did not think he could bear to lose this Little Fire in his arms and wish to live. Only on that level could he empathize with Theardar.

Yes, he fully understood the consuming passion a man could have for a woman.

A passion that became life itself.

The rest, like Yaniff, he could not forgive.

Lorgin awakened Deana before daybreak with a soft kiss on her lips.

"We must arise now, Adeeann. We leave this day for Aviara."

Deana sleepily opened her eyes, noting the dark shadows in the room, as well as the dark shadows under Lorgin's eyes.

"It's still night." She burrowed back under the covers against his warmth. "Let's go back to sleep."

"We cannot, much as I would like to. Come, wake up." He squeezed her derriere. She rubbed against him in protest.

"I can't wake up—see, my eyes won't open." She raised her face to him, eyes tightly shut.

His low chuckle vibrated against her forehead. "I think I know how to open your eyes."

"How?"

He adjusted her leg with his thigh and slipped inside her.

"*Lorgin.*" Her eyes popped open.

"You see? If you have a problem, you need but ask me." His hands pressed against her bottom, bringing her closer to him.

She placed her hands around his neck. "What am I going to do with you?"

"Kiss me," he breathed.

She did.

Later, after they had dressed, Lorgin removed something from his cape, asking Deana to join him on the bed. When she did, she noticed he held three black strands embroidered with gold. She thought she recognized a few of the symbols as the same ones on his cape. He sat behind her, motioning for her to turn around.

"What are you doing?" His fingers threaded through her hair, smoothing it down.

"You will see." His capable hands began sectioning out her long hair.

She tried turning around. "Are you braiding my hair?"

He placed his hands on her shoulders, turning her back. "I am weaving your hair. Be still." She felt her hair being very intricately styled. Every now and then, he interwove one of the black and gold ribbons. His touch was very gentle as he

283

silently worked, seemingly enjoying whatever he was doing.

"Why are you doing this?"

"There." He leaned forward, lightly kissing the side of her neck. "Look in the mirror—tell me if you like what I have done."

Deana gave him a strange look as she got up to walk to the mirror. Just when she thought she was beginning to understand him, he always did something weird. She cautiously looked in the mirror.

"It's beautiful! How did you do it?" Her red hair was pulled back in a weave design, the ribbons laced all through the intricate pattern. The black and gold shot through her hair with each cross section.

Lorgin walked over to stand behind her. "Aviaran boys learn this at a young age. I am honored I have pleased you."

"Wait a minute—is this one of those weird customs of yours?"

He smiled slightly. "Aviaran men weave their wives' hair. It is a sign of pride and respect. The ribbons mark my house, my line, and that you are the mate of a Charl."

"I don't know that I like being marked like some—Hey, wait a minute! You mean you have to do this for me every day?" She grinned flippantly at him. "That's different. I think I rather like the idea of you playing lady's maid."

"As usual, I think you twist the meaning to your liking. But there is another reason the men do this, *zira*."

"Why is that?" She patted her hair in the mirror.

"So that we can *undo* it in the evenings," he whispered.

She threw him a look over her shoulder. "So, why did you do it now? It will be days before we reach the tunnel point."

"No, by this evening we will be in Aviara. Traed knows of a tunnel point within a day's journey from here."

"I'm glad to hear of it. Is he coming with us?" She had

hesitated to ask, but since Lorgin had mentioned Traed, she had to know.

"Yes, he will come." Deana beamed at him. "And why are you smiling so?"

"I never doubted it."

His expression was incredulous. "How could you not?"

"Because I know *you.*"

Lorgin's arms came around her. "Do you?

Before they left, Rejar sincerely told Deana he thought her hair looked very pretty. Even Traed had stopped for a moment on seeing it. He had told her it had been a long time since he had seen a woman whose hair was woven. He had forgotten the beauty of it. Deana graciously accepted the compliments, realizing that what she had assumed to be a simple custom obviously held deep meaning for Aviaran men.

A contingency of Traed's men escorted them through the desert, up into the mountains. Deana was not surprised that Traed had brought his *phfiztger* with him. Tumbles rested comfortably behind Traed in a little basket on the back of a *prautau.*

At day's end, they reached the mountain pass and Lorgin called forth the tunnel.

Chapter Fifteen

They emerged into a giant hall.

The whiteness of the walls almost blinded Deana after the strobe lights of the tunnels. She felt rather than saw Lorgin take her hand.

"Where are we?" She put her arm across her eyes to shield them from the brightness.

"It is called the Hall of Tunnels. Come." He led her through the vast cavernous space. After a moment, her eyes adjusted to the light. She noticed many people, most human, some not, going in all directions. Every now and then the hair on the back of her neck would rise and a great maw would appear, seemingly devouring the people.

"It's-it's like Grand Central Station, isn't it?" She stared openly at what was going on around her, like a country bumpkin in the big city.

Since none of the three men escorting her had a clue as to what Grand Central Station was, no one bothered to respond.

They led her to one of the large stone portals which flanked the walls.

Rejar and Traed stepped through to the outside. Lorgin started to lead Deana through, but she held back.

"You can't just go out there!" Deana was wondering if it was dinner time for those hungry monsters in the street.

"Come—we need to go this way." Lorgin yanked her arm, pulling her into the street with him.

Deana got her first look at Aviara.

They seemed to be in the midst of a quaint village.

The streets were of paved stone, wide and immaculately clean. There were some shops flanking the streets, each one unique and interesting-looking. Some sold flowers of incredible beauty; others jewelry, art work, all manner of handcrafts, perfume, and more.

It appeared to be late afternoon. Blooming trees and plants were everywhere, their scent sweetening the air with exotic, lush fragrances. The sky was a clear, light blue with not a hint of pollution.

People were strolling about, stopping to talk to others, or sitting down at small cafes.

The temperature felt like a perfect 72 degrees, with a light breeze. Little trilling creatures were singing in the trees, and crystal chimes hung from every conceivable place, issuing harmonious tinkling sounds.

It was utterly beautiful.

But Deana knew from her travels with Lorgin that looks could be deceiving. They had encountered many things that could not be judged by their appearance. Indeed, she was standing next to one right now: Rejar. So she continued to eye the surroundings very carefully as they walked along.

Traed had also been viewing his surroundings, not with the eyes of a stranger, but with those of someone coming home after a long absence.

"Adeeann, what are you looking for?" Traed asked.

"The monsters!" Deana spun around to make sure they weren't sneaking up on her. She never noticed Lorgin trying to hide his grin.

"Monsters? What monsters?" Traed seemed genuinely perplexed.

"The ones that gobble you all whole for dinner when you walk the streets."

Rejar leaned toward Lorgin. "Do you think she means the Guild?"

Lorgin chuckled as he pictured the ancient, austere body of mystics. "Most definitely."

Deana smelled a rat—a six-foot-four rat with golden hair and amethyst eyes. "All right, Lorgin, what gives?"

Lorgin tried to appear innocent, failing miserably. "What?"

"Don't give me that 'what' routine! You snookered me!"

Rejar raised a fascinated black eyebrow. "Does that mean what I think it means?"

Lorgin laughed out loud.

Deana turned, pointing an accusing finger at Rejar as well. "Don't think you're free and clear of this either. I don't see anything wrong with the weather. I know Lorgin's a lost cause, but how could you, Rejar? I thought you liked me."

Rejar draped his arm around her shoulders as they walked. "I do like you, Adeeann. That is why I did not tell you about the dancing poisonous plants."

She shrugged off his arm. "You are both impossible. I'm walking with Traed." She looped her arm through his, leaving the two brothers to follow. "At least he's sensible."

Lorgin looked on, still grinning. "As you desire, gharta." He winked over to Rejar, adding, "But I warn you, Traed; do not even think to 'snooker' her."

The two brothers roared in laughter.

Even the corners of Traed's mouth lifted slightly.

"Do not worry, Lorgin," Rejar chimed in, "mayhap Traed does not remember how to 'snooker.' "

Traed coolly assessed the younger man over his shoulder. "What I have forgotten about 'snookering' you have yet to learn."

This caused another round of raucous laughter. Deana was getting steamed.

"That's it! *All* of you are impossible!"

She disengaged herself from Traed's arm, quickening her stride to leave the men behind her. Until she realized she had no idea where she was heading. Her step faltered slightly. It was difficult to leave in a huff when you had no idea where you were going. Her shoulders hunched when Lorgin calmly called out to her, inquiring as to the directions to his family home. More laughter.

She didn't say one word as she waited for the men to come abreast of her, overhearing Traed's low aside to Lorgin which sounded suspiciously like "most entertaining."

Lorgin approached her, putting a conciliatory arm around her shoulders.

"You must overlook our teasing, Adeeann. We are all so happy to be back on Aviara."

She squinted up at him. "I can understand that. It always feels good to come *home*." Her look was pointed.

Lorgin gazed at her through lowered lids, his eyes momentarily flashing in anger. He lifted her chin with a proprietary finger. "Then you, too, must share in our joy, zira."

Stubborn, arrogant man! This was not her home. But she was not about to bring that point up to him again, and well he knew it. She gazed at the surrounding beauty of the land, sighing. She supposed there was no reason for her not to enjoy the place while she was here. Lorgin drew her closer, causing her to smile slightly. How the man was able to sense her moods had always been a mystery to her.

Following an ancient roadway, they left the little hamlet behind, entering a heavily wooded area. Afternoon sunlight dappled through the trees onto dense wildly flowering foliage which carpeted the forest floor. It was cooler here. Cool and green. The same little tree creatures she had noticed in the village hopped from tree to tree singing sweet trilling songs.

The path/road continued to zigzag through the forest.

In the distance she heard a gurgling brook. It was a beautiful spot, hushed and cool; it was a place of peace such as many sought on earth, but few found. Often, when she had read stories of medieval England, she had pictured a forest like this one. She wouldn't have minded staying in it for the rest of the day and into the night.

Occasionally along the road, they passed small stone cottages, some almost hidden in the trees, others near the road. Several times the inhabitants called out to them, waving, or inviting them to stop for refreshment. The men politely declined, anxious to reach their home and family. Deana smiled to herself as she noticed several young women specifically trying to get Rejar's attention.

As they continued walking, Deana noticed that the cottages ceased altogether. After a while, they rounded a bend in the dirt road.

Set far back into the woods, yet still visible from the road, was an enormous stone mansion. It was reminiscent of Tudor houses she had seen around Massachusetts, except this one was entirely made of stones. Mullioned windows with long shutters graced the facade. Somehow she was not surprised when Lorgin turned down the pathway which led to the estate.

"I take it this is your humble abode?" She stood before

the enormous double wooden doors, feeling dwarfed by their size.

"This is my—*our* family home, *zira*."

Before anyone could knock on the door, it flew open and a beautiful dark-haired woman threw herself into Lorgin's arms.

"You are home at last! I was so worried about both of you." Her dual-colored eyes flew to Rejar, sweeping him in a glance as if to ascertain the state of his health.

"You worry too much, Suleila." Lorgin patted her back affectionately. "What could happen to the sons of Krue?"

"What indeed?" The woman smiled. "Come in, come in. Your father awaits you. Yaniff told us of your impending arrival." Suleila's eyes momentarily flew to her son, noting Rejar's questioning expression as his intelligent Familiar eyes met hers.

He knows, she thought. *So, now he knows.*

She turned to seek Traed standing slightly behind everyone. "Traed," Suleila whispered, holding out her hands to him.

Traed came forward to clasp her hands. "Suleila. It is good to see you again."

"Yes. Welcome home, my special son." It was a Familiar term used for a well-loved child. Suleila had bestowed it upon him when he was a young boy. It moved Traed greatly that she had remembered and greeted him in this manner. He gently squeezed her hands in recognition of the singular distinction she afforded him.

Deana waited for Lorgin to introduce her to his nextmother Suleila, noting that the woman's long black tresses were woven with purple and gold ribbons. When Lorgin failed to make the introduction, she gazed at him quizzically.

"I must introduce you first to my father," he informed her as they followed Suleila into the house.

"Why?"

"Because it is the way it is done."

"You've got to be kidding."

"Suleila has seen my ribbons in your hair. She knows who you are, though she cannot acknowledge you yet."

Deana shook her head, muttering, "Bizarre, truly bizarre."

They entered into a huge foyer. Deana had a brief glimpse of a vast hollow space, scores of gorgeous hanging tapestries, and colorful woven rugs as she was rapidly ushered into what looked to be a sitting room.

A tall man stood in front of the window, turning as they entered. Deana could tell at once that this was Krue, for he was an older version of Lorgin. His hair was mostly golden, silvering only slightly around the edges. Still in his prime, he was a vital and commanding presence.

As they approached him she could see that Rejar had also inherited much from his father. The sultriness in Rejar, however, was obviously bequeathed to him from his mother.

Then she noticed Yaniff standing in the corner, the perennial Bojo on his shoulder. She smiled warmly at him, realizing she had missed the kindly old wizard.

Lorgin stepped forward with Deana in tow. Suddenly he went down on one knee before Krue, yanking her down next to him. He withdrew the Cearix from his waistband, handing it to Deana.

"Father, I continue your line. Do you accept this offering?" He turned and whispered to Deana, "Hand him the Cearix, Adeeann."

Deana hesitated. She wasn't at all sure she wanted to do this. It would be like deceiving his parents. Perhaps she should try to explain to Krue what Lorgin failed to acknowledge: he had the wrong woman.

Just as she opened her mouth to speak, she caught Yaniff

out of the corner of her eye. He was shaking his head, as if to tell her no. Obviously, he had read her mind and did not think it was such a great idea. She had seen enough of the mystic to know when to defer to his judgment. She gingerly handed the blade to Krue, who gazed down at her with intense amethyst eyes so like his son's.

When he immediately accepted it from her, she heard Lorgin exhale.

"I accept this offering, my son. You honor my line and your name." He handed the Cearix back to Lorgin.

Lorgin got to his feet, bringing Deana with him. "I present Adeeann to you, Father."

Krue turned to her, surprising her by wrapping her in a bear hug. "Welcome, daughter. Long have I awaited this day. Your presence is a gift to this house." He indicated his wife. "This is your mother, Suleila."

Just her presence was a gift? Jeez, these Aviarans had a way with a phrase. Not to mention a way of confusing someone with their strange rhetoric. She turned, bewildered by Krue's effusiveness, only to be confronted with a beaming Suleila, who clasped her hands in joy.

"I am so happy you have come to our family, Adeeann." She leaned over, kissing her cheek. "How lucky Lorgin is to have won such a pretty bride. I know I shall enjoy having another female in this family."

Krue's eyes wandered to the third man in the room. "Traed." He walked over to him, clasping his shoulder. "I vow it is good to see again. Welcome home." Then he surprised the younger man by hugging him as well. "Your room in this house awaits you, as it always shall." Traed nodded, too moved to speak.

Yaniff stepped forward. "The lad will remain here this eve, but on the morrow he will reside with me."

Traed turned at the sound of Yaniff's voice. "Yaniff . . ." He approached the old man, tears in his eyes.

Yaniff placed a withered hand on his shoulder, his voice suspiciously gruff. "I am pleased you have come, Traed. Despite what you believe, my belief in you is not misplaced."

Traed chose not to respond.

Suleila decided it was time to shift the emotion-charged scene. She linked arms with Deana, leading her to a settee. "Come, let us all sit and enjoy a sweet drink before the evening meal. Are you very off time?"

Since Deana had no idea what the sensuous, stunning creature beside her was talking about, Lorgin answered for her. "Not very. It was early evening on Zarrain when we left."

"Then you must be very hungry. We will eat shortly. I have prepared many of your favorite dishes."

"*Calan* stew?" Rejar asked hopefully.

Suleila smiled indulgently. "Not tonight, my son. But I am sure you will find a dish or two to delight you."

"You had better," Krue said to his younger son as he handed each a tiny glass of liquor. "She has been cooking all day for you."

They sipped their drinks, engaging in idle chat. Deana noticed an instant relaxing effect from the incredibly delicious liquor, immediately putting it on her Aviaran shopping list. As they were conversing, a light knock sounded on the sitting room door, and a man entered. He was obviously a servant.

Krue looked up. "Yes, what is it, Malkin?"

Malkin cleared his throat. "There is a young lady at the door for Master Rejar. She insists on seeing him." Krue's stony glance fell on his younger son.

Rejar abruptly stood. "I will see to it, father." He quickly left the room.

Lorgin, sitting on the other side of Deana, tried not to smirk as he spoke low in her ear. "Back only a short time, and already they seek him. I wonder how long my father will last before he loses his temper."

"I take it he doesn't approve of Rejar's ways?" She whispered.

"He is in firm agreement with Yaniff. Krue would like to see Rejar take up Charl ways. It irritates him to see his son squander himself so."

Rejar returned shortly, finger-combing his hair. The "someone" at the door had mussed it up pretty good. Deana could just imagine the fond reunion.

Krue's eyes narrowed at his son, but he said nothing.

The conversation resumed, but was interrupted by a high-pitched chitting sound. Suddenly a small animal raced pell-mell across the floor directly at Rejar. It was about the size of a ferret with a head like a small otter. The little beast scampered up Rejar's leg, tweaking all the while. When it reached his throat, it rubbed against him several times, then flopped across his shoulders.

"Sookah! Did you miss me?" Rejar stroked the fury little head with one finger.

"She pined for you the whole time you were gone, Rejar," Suleila said.

Krue put down his drink with a distinct clink. "Of course she did, she is female, is she not?"

"It will not be long now," Lorgin whispered to Deana.

Seeing Krue's mood, Suleila suggested they all go in to the dining room.

Yaniff discreetly clapped Lorgin on the shoulder, his gaze falling on Traed's back. "Once again you prove to me that my faith in you is well placed."

Lorgin seemed slightly embarrassed by the wizard's praise. He nodded curtly, walking with him into the dining room.

Dara Joy

An enormous table of burled wood almost filled the room, surrounded by heavily padded chairs in a silken brocade fabric. The table was beautifully set with colorful plates done by a very talented artisan and goblets to match. Candlelight illuminated the room, casting an inviting glow.

As soon as they took their seats, servants brought out a staggering array of food, each dish on its own uniquely crafted platter. The brothers' faces lit up.

"Suleila, you have outdone yourself." As was customary, Lorgin filled Deana's plate with an assortment of the dishes, then served himself.

Traed took his first mouthful in seeming ecstasy. "I have never forgotten your culinary skills, Suleila."

Deana tasted a red concoction on her plate. "Ohh, this is delicious! What is—never mind, I don't want to know. I think I'll just enjoy it."

Suleila smiled at her. "I will teach you how to make these dishes. Lorgin loves—"

She was interrupted by the intrepid Malkin, who once again cleared his throat.

"There is another young woman at the door for Master Rejar. She says it is most urgent she—"

Before he could finish, Rejar jumped out of his seat. "I will see to it, Father."

Krue slammed his goblet down as Rejar left the room.

"Now it comes," Lorgin mouthed to her.

Krue's hands clenched into fists. "Women have ruined my son!"

Suleila quickly reached over to clasp his fist on the tabletop. "He is only just returned, Krue. Let it be tonight."

Krue contemplated his wife for a moment, his lavender gaze softening. He slowly unfolded his fist, gently squeezing Suleila's hand. It seemed he was not immune to her entreaty.

"As you wish, Suleila. For your sake and our new daughter's"—he nodded toward Deana—"I will let the rascal be tonight."

Beaming, Suleila leaned across to quickly kiss her husband. Deana suspected that the female Familiar had her husband wrapped around her dainty little "paw." But it was also apparent that a man such as Krue was indulgent with his wife only because he desired it. Lorgin's parents obviously enjoyed a loving relationship.

Rejar returned to the room treading cautiously. He risked a glance at his father as he resumed his seat at the table. Krue's penetrating stare pinned his younger son to the spot.

"I take it there will be no further interruptions this evening." It was not a question.

"No, Father." Rejar's expression was somewhat sheepish.

After that, the meal went by in companionable ease. Deana learned a great deal about the family of Krue as she partook of Suleila's myriad delicacies. This was a family with a strong father figure, closely knit, and bound by love. That love was evident in every interaction which occurred at the table. Even Yaniff and Traed were included in the familial bond which existed between these people; Yaniff was treated with the respect due a venerable patriarch, Traed as another son.

Deana was not excluded either. At every opportunity, they attempted to make her feel welcome and part of the family. She was deeply touched by their open affection and warmth, thinking what a truly nice family they were. If she had been in the market for an adoptive family, this would be it.

After the meal, they all retired to the sitting room.

Deana noted that Krue and Suleila were careful not to mention Lorgin's quest. She assumed that Yaniff had cautioned them to say as little as possible in front of Traed. She supposed the old mystic would reveal all to the green-eyed man in his own mysterious fashion. Her heart went out to Traed, sitting so complacently across the room. It seemed as if he were destined to be battered about by forces he had no control over. What would he do when he found out he must face Theardar again? Would he help these men against his own father, or would he walk away, once again removing himself from life?

She hoped she would never be confronted with such heart-rending decisions.

Krue and Suleila did question the sons about their run-in with the xathu, Suleila turning positively white when she heard the details of how very close they had come to losing both of them. Krue said nothing, but Deana noticed that he contemplated Rejar with a father's pride. She could see in that moment that for all his gruffness with his younger son, Krue loved him deeply.

Later, when the spices in the exotic foods were making her thirsty, she asked Lorgin if she could get a glass of water. He obligingly led her to the rear of the house into the kitchen. It was a large room, but cozy. Faint delicious aromas still tantalized the nose.

Lorgin poured her a glass of water, quickly stealing a kiss.

She smiled, pressing her palms lightly against his chest. "What are you doing?"

"They are very pleased with you, Adeeann." He took one of her hands and brought it to his lips. "As am I."

"How do you know they like me?"

He grinned. "I know."

She disengaged herself from his arms, drinking the water. She was going to hate to hurt these people. And the longer she put it off, the worse it would be. Resolving to see Yaniff privately as soon as possible, she put her glass down, noticing an odd-looking object resting in a bowl on the large wooden trestle table. It was about the size of a coconut, with a hard brown shell and a very sharp-looking inch-long spines.

"What is that?" She pointed.

Lorgin looked over to see what she was pointing at, instantly bemused by what had caught her attention.

"A *gharta*." He replied drolly. Deana was shocked.

"This is a *gharta*? This is what you've been calling me?" And all this time she thought he was complimenting her! Her cheeks stained red as she observed the ugly-looking fruit in front of her.

The corners of Lorgin's mouth twitched as he picked up the *gharta*. Placing a booted foot up on the bench, he removed his Cearix, using it to slice into the spiny fruit. His triangular cut revealed a soft, fleshy pink interior.

His eyes never leaving hers, he carved off a chunk of the flesh and suggestively popped it into his mouth, slowly licking the sticky juice from his fingers.

His smoky eyes lazily traveled down to the spot between her legs. "Delicious . . ." he whispered.

Deana's whole face flamed red.

She turned away from his blatantly erotic allusion, feeling his low, sexy laughter skip along her nerve endings.

"You are terrible!"

He came up behind her, placing his palms on her shoulders, drawing her back against him. His husky words breathed against her ear. "Terrible good or terrible bad?"

"*Both!*"

She broke free of his light hold and immediately returned to the sitting room.

Deana eyed Lorgin dubiously as he lifted the covers and climbed naked into the enormous four-poster bed which graced his room.

"Are you still angry with me, my *gharta*?" He scooted next to her, taking her into his arms.

"For heaven's sake, Lorgin, don't call me that!" Her face still reddened at the thought of his earlier blatant actions.

He nibbled her mouth, tenderly sipping at her lips. "I will call you this because it is so."

"Don't you—"

His tongue dipped into her mouth as he delicately sizzled her senses. Whatever she had been about to say was immediately forgotten.

She couldn't argue with him; somehow she had lost the will. The truth of it was, she wanted him very much. The fact that he had molded her into this wanton, passionate creature somehow didn't bother her at all.

She threaded her hands through his hair, her fingers splayed against his scalp, pressing him tighter against her mouth. She was ignited, that was all there was to it. He was both the cause of her heat and the remedy.

"I'm burning . . . Please, put out this fire, Lorgin." Her choked words spilled into his mouth. She instantly felt the shock of her declaration ripple through him. He went rock hard in an instant.

"Yes . . . yes, I will put it out, Adeeann." He ran his tongue lightly along her bottom lip. "But first I will fan this flame slowly . . ." His teeth grazed along her collarbone as if to lend truth to his words. She shivered. "I will take each ember and treasure it, nurture it, build on it . . ."

Moving down to her breast, he took her nipple into his tingling mouth, sucking lightly at first, then with more and more insistence. As he increased the drawing pressure, he sent her a love jolt with the tip of his tongue. A line of fire shot down to the center of her desire, causing her to groan.

Fueled by her response, his wide palms scored her body,

stroking and caressing; the light touch so at odds with the firm insistence of his mouth. The heat from his magic touch seared her. The power and demand of his body engulfed her. She moaned deep in her throat, belatedly concerned that someone in the house might hear her.

In the same breath, his silken lips moved down to her feminine core, and soon she was beyond caring if anybody heard her.

"Lorgin."

Once again he proved his mastery of her with his velvet lips and gifted tongue. When he inserted a long finger into her and actually suckled on her, she lost it completely and would have screamed her release to the world, but fortunately Lorgin had the presence of mind to cover her mouth at the right moment with his own.

When her breathing calmed down somewhat, she became rational enough to realize he was still stroking her idly with his fingers.

"Lorgin?"

"Yes, *gharta*?" He chuckled against her throat as he kissed her too-sensitive skin.

"Aren't you going to . . . ?"

"Yes, *gharta*." He nudged her limp legs apart with his knee.

Deana blinked, quite surprised. "You mean you want to do this in the missionary position? I can't believe it." Considering her past encounters with him it could actually be called novel.

A furrow appeared on his smooth brow. "Missionary position—you have a name for this?"

"It's just what we call a standard mating position." A dimple appeared in his cheek. He snickered, obviously finding this tidbit extremely humorous.

"You have a standard position on this Disney?"

"Well, yes." It did sound odd when she thought about it.

He grinned seductively. "Lucky for you I brought you here, is it not?"

"You don't understand—"

"Where every time is a . . . new adventure." He rubbed his erection along her cleft before swiftly entering her.

He impaled her with an exquisite fullness.

They both moaned as he slid to her very womb, his sex swelling incredibly at the erotic sounds. Even though her liquid honey immediately cushioned him, he throbbed almost painfully. He locked his teeth for a moment as a violent tremor shook him. He had caught the fire.

Lacing her head between his palms, he kissed her ardently on the lips while gasping heated words and phrases in so many different languages she could not understand him.

He was feverish yet totally in control.

He took what she gave and then he took more, moving in her with a calculated slowness designed to drive her into a frenzy. His compelling movements made her absolutely brazen.

"More, Lorgin, more!"

"As much as you want, Little Fire. It is yours."

His hands cupped her bottom, bringing her up to meet his powerful downward thrusts, while he buried his face in the fragrant hair he had so recently released from its woven design.

Lorgin did exactly what he claimed he would: he fanned every flame, nurtured every ember, treasured her responses and intensified them. Deana held him to her tightly as she was completely swept away by his passion.

"Do you know what you do to me, Sweet Fire?" His ragged voice was breathless. "I vow it is the finest feeling . . .

the best moments of my life here . . . again and again with you . . . a special place I can only find in your arms."

She knew it was probably just passion speaking, but his words were so beautiful she could feel tears forming in the corners of her eyes. Who *was* this unknown woman who was destined for a man like this? Would she have a sense of his greatness? Would she be passionate enough for him? For this man, she prayed it would be so.

"Oh, Lorgin."

She rained kisses all over his face as they reached the pinnacle together, holding each other as if they would never let go.

Afterwards, for a long while Lorgin remained on top of her, supporting his weight on bent elbows while he tried to regain his breath. He kissed her, then collapsed on the bed next to her, taking her hand in his.

"Tomorrow I will bring you to our home, *zira*."

"But I thought this was your home."

"It is my family home." His thumb traced the soft skin of her small hand. "My home lies west of here—not too far, in the Towering Forests."

"Towering Forests, what's that, a place where trees grow as big as skyscrapers?" she said jokingly.

"I know not what a skyscraper is, but these trees do indeed grow big."

"Do you have a house there?"

He smiled mysteriously. "You will see."

"I hate it when you say that."

He laughed, sated and relaxed. "Why?"

"Because nine out of ten times it turns out to be something I don't like."

His eyes flicked to her. "You like everything I have shown you, Adeeann. You just need time to adjust to it."

She had a sinking suspicion he was right. Not that it didn't miff her just the same. "Think you have me figured out, do you?"

He chuckled. "By *Aiyah*, no. I have never claimed to be a healer."

"Very funny."

"How did Traed appear to you tonight?"

Deana thought a moment. "I think he felt very relieved to be back home amongst people who care about him."

"I thought the same. I hope he is strong enough to endure what faces him."

"You mean going against his father?"

Lorgin nodded. "That and more. It is good Yaniff is taking him under his guidance. Traed has always respected him."

"Who wouldn't respect Yaniff? Even your rebellious brother respects him."

"Except that Rejar always refers to him as 'the old man.' Do not tell Rejar, but I think it amuses Yaniff." Lorgin yawned. "I vow I will sleep well this night."

He turned to her, resting his face in his palm. "Adeeann?"

"Hmm?" Her eyes were already drifting shut.

"Mayhap next time you can be the one to 'snooker' me?"

Her answer was her pillow bouncing off his head.

Late in the night, Yaniff walked through the woods in the moonlight. In the distance he could barely discern the house of Krue through the trees. His penetrating gaze observed the stone walls and darkened windows as if he were seeing through the masonry into something else all together. He stroked the feathers of his winged companion absently, inhaling the fresh cool air of the Aviaran night.

"So, Bojo, all the players are assembled at last. Like pieces of a puzzle, they come together. Destiny, my friend, will be the thread that weaves the picture they make.''

His words were still echoing through the trees as he disappeared between the mist and the moonlight.

Chapter Sixteen

"It is so beautiful here, Lorgin."

They had been walking through the woods for about twenty minutes on their way to his home in the Towering Forests. Deana surmised that Lorgin lived about half an hour's walk from his parents' home.

She let the peace and solitude of the land flow through her, deeply inhaling the cool, spice-scented air of the Aviaran forest.

Lorgin watched her as she walked beside him, so obviously taken by his homeland. This pleased him greatly. She had donned one of the *krilli* caftans this morning, a predominantly gold one delicately embroidered with black threads. The dress complemented the colors of his ribbons in her woven hair. This also pleased him.

"It is you who are beautiful, *zira*."

She smiled shyly at the unexpected compliment.

Such a woman of contrasts, he thought. Uncommonly bold

one moment, unfathomably demure the next. Always incredibly responsive to him.

Lorgin smiled to himself. He'd had to weave her hair twice this day already, and they had yet to have their midday meal. He wondered if she had any idea exactly what weaving his woman's hair meant to an Aviaran male. True, the ribbons identified her as belonging to his house and to him, but over time, the custom amongst the men had taken on another meaning as well, as a record of their daily sexual activity. Aviaran men often counted how many times a day they wove their women's hair. It sometimes became a good-natured jest amongst the men as to how many times they had been called upon for the task.

And would not his Adeeann be furious if she knew how entwined male sexual prowess was with those interwoven ribbons in her hair?

He laughed out loud as he thought of how enraged her expression would be. She would probably refuse to wear his ribbons—a refusal he would never permit. Best for them both if she not discover this second meaning of the weaving.

"What's so funny?" Deana looked at him with an earnest expression he found totally delightful under the circumstances.

He leaned over, lightly brushing her lips with his. "Nothing, my little *gharta*."

As they walked along, it occurred to Deana that this was the perfect opportunity to find out where Yaniff lived. After all, if she hoped to see him, she needed to be able to find him first.

"Lorgin, does Yaniff live near your parents?"

If he hadn't been watching a young *zeena* hop through the underbrush, he probably would have wondered about the question. As it was, he absently replied, "As a matter of fact, this pathway coming up here on our right leads directly to his home.'' Lorgin smiled at her. ''Or not.''

She furrowed her brow. ''What do you mean?''

''If Yaniff is not of a mind for visitors, the pathway mysteriously curves back on itself and the would-be visitor finds himself back on this main road.''

''Clever of him. What a great way to get rid of uninvited visitors.'' She looked at him pointedly: the ultimate uninvited visitor. ''I'll have to ask him how to do that.''

Lorgin placed his hand over his heart. ''You wound me,'' he said teasingly.

''Impossible,'' she scoffed. He winked at her, taking her hand as they walked along.

Now that she knew how to find Yaniff, she wondered how much time she had to play with. As casually as she could, she asked, ''How long do you think we'll be here on Aviara?''

''Yaniff searches for Theardar's location on the Rim. I hope it will not be too much longer now that Yaniff knows who it is he seeks.''

''Does this process of . . . *searching* usually take a long time?'' She knew he referred to some kind of mental tracking system that the old mystic possessed. How it worked, she couldn't even speculate.

''Theardar has probably erected a shield. As a sixth-level mystic, he would have this ability. Yaniff seeks to penetrate this shield to locate his exact position. Look, Adeeann.'' He took her shoulders in his hands, standing her in front of him.

They had come to the edge of the woods. There was a glade in front of them and across the glade was the Towering Forest.

It literally took her breath away.

Trees. Enormous trees. Some reaching five hundred to a

thousand feet in the air. The diameter of the trunks had to be at least a hundred feet!

She leaned back against Lorgin as she gazed up, trying to see the tops of the mighty trees. Even from this distance she could feel a sense of the ancient and powerful supremacy of the forest. It was as if one could feel the serenity, the wisdom dominating those tranquil woods.

"It's—it's unbelievable!" Her voice was hushed with reverence. It somehow did not seem right to talk in normal tones in the presence of such natural majesty.

Lorgin's arms encircled her. "It is beautiful, is it not?" He leaned his chin against the top of her head. "There is a peace of being there that you will find nowhere else in the universe. Come, let us go home."

He took her hand again, leading her across the glade toward the trees.

They entered the forest.

Deana wondered at the powerful tree limbs reaching to the Aviaran sky. Each limb surely was over fifty feet wide. The huge broad leaves rustled in the breeze, a sound at once pacifying and invigorating. She noted that some of the leaves were turned sideways, and questioned Lorgin about it.

"They let in light to the forest below. See?" He pointed to the forest floor, which was dappled in sunlight.

This puzzled her. "For their roots, you mean?"

"No. For us."

Deana stopped short.

"What do you mean, for us?"

He admired the beauty before him, speaking in low tones. "These trees have a consciousness, Adeeann."

"They're alive?" Her voice had gone up an octave.

"Not in the way you are thinking. Not like you and I. It is hard to explain. Mystical."

"Try."

"The trees have a sense of *knowing*. They are sacred to this planet. We protect them always, for they are the source of all life on Aviara."

Deana examined the broad leaves. "The oxygen!"

"The air, yes. They produce most of the air we breathe. They are also the home of many creatures, but all who live here must live in harmony. On rare occasions these trees will open for one of us."

Her head whipped around to him, suddenly understanding. "You live within the tree, don't you?"

"Yes. The Alliance gifted me with their permission after I had performed a certain deed for them."

Deana thought Lorgin glossed over this "deed" pretty nonchalantly. She could just imagine what act of courage he had performed to achieve such a gift.

"Once their permission was granted, it then went before the Guild."

"The body of mystics you've mentioned?"

He nodded. "It was eventually approved, but even though I had finally achieved the sanction of the Guild, I still had to see if I could find a tree that would accept me. Others had gotten so far, only to be refused."

"You must have wanted to live here very much."

"All my life."

Lorgin came to a halt before one of the massive trees. She noted a platform at its base, connected to the tree by a series of limbs. He placed his palm gently against the bark.

"This tree accepted me."

He stepped onto the platform, motioning Deana to join him. She gingerly stepped on. At once the platform began to rise, seemingly lifted by the limbs! Deana closed her eyes, a little frightened.

"Will—will it mind my being here?"

"No." His arms came around her. "Do not be afraid of anything here. Once the tree accepted me, it accepted all that is my life. It became my home." Deana opened her eyes, hugging him tightly to her.

"I'm not really afraid, Lorgin. I think I'm just awestruck. I know you would never let anything harm me."

Her unconscious statement of her belief in him, so long in coming, shattered him. A strangled sound issued from his throat just before his lips swiftly descended on hers. His kissed her deeply, passionately, surprising her.

"What was that for?"

He pressed his lips against her forehead. "I do not believe I will tell you just yet. Perhaps it is for you to discover."

Deana mentally shrugged, chalking it up as another Aviaran oddity.

The platform came to rest about two-thirds of the way up the tree, adjacent to an immense flat branch, which in itself resembled a vast platform. Deana looked around in wonder.

This was somewhere over the rainbow.

A garden lay before her. Beautiful pastel-colored flowers were everywhere, swaying in the light wind. Crystal chimes hung from every conceivable branch, tinkling softly. The peaceful sounds were augmented by the joyous songs of the trilling creatures she had noticed before. The tree's broad leaves, now turned to a vertical position for maximum light, rustled softly in the wind.

Lorgin stepped off the platform onto the wide ledge. He held his hand out to her. Deana hardly was aware of taking it as she surveyed her surroundings. Instead of hard wood below her feet, as she expected, there was earth and grass. Grass growing on a tree limb!

The limbs seemed to intersect as they went in differing

directions, creating several "yards." Each flat-topped limb had to be at least fifty feet wide. A pathway led from the platform they were on toward the main trunk of the tree, where an opening existed for a doorway. She looked along the trunk, now noticing several smaller openings which she presumed were windows.

Lorgin didn't head to the doorway right away. Instead he took her on a tour of the outside. There were five "yards," each displaying a different garden. In one garden she noted strange vegetables and fruit growing. In another there were smaller trees, plants, and exotic flowers. In still another, she noted a large hammock swaying to the sound of chimes.

But the real surprise came at the rear of the trunk.

A clear stream flowed down the side of the tree, gathering into a small pool before it drained off the side, forming a waterfall one level down. Deana sank to her knees by the stream and ran her fingers through the clear water. When she looked up, there were tears in her eyes.

"This is the most beautiful place I've ever seen."

Lorgin bent down beside her on one knee. "And you are my most beautiful place." He lifted her cool, wet fingers to his lips. "I cannot wait to make love to you here with this tranquillity of spirit around us. I have dreamed of it."

She cupped his strong face. "What a beautiful thing to say."

Lorgin, realizing what he had just said out loud, turned slightly sheepish. "Sometimes the warrior gets too poetic."

She stroked his jaw. "I don't mind."

Not only did she not mind, but Lorgin suspected by her softening expression that she might even be partial to it. He kissed her palm. "If my words are pleasing to you, perhaps my actions will be more so." His tongue flicked the center of her hand in a ticklish motion. She giggled. He smiled against her palm at the girlish sound.

"Are you going to take me inside now?"

Lorgin regarded her through half-lidded eyes. "Should *I* not be asking *you* this?" he purred.

Deana's face flamed as it always did when he came out with one of his outrageous remarks. She pulled her hand out of his, pushing sharply at his shoulders to unbalance him. It worked. He toppled over, nearly into the pond. Only his excellent reflexes and coordination saved him from a dunking.

Deana stood above him with a righteous look on her face.

He grinned up at her from the ground, lying prone with his chin resting in the crook of his arm. "And here I thought you liked my poetic words."

"I'm a tough critic." She started to walk away, then turned back to him with an impish grin.

Lorgin seemed to be thinking over her statement as he got to his feet. He came abreast of her, throwing his arm around her shoulders. "Then I shall have to make *doubly* sure you are well pleased."

Deana had a breathless feeling she knew exactly what he was really saying. Lorgin was contemplating another *two* rounds. She couldn't believe it. He had taken her twice this morning already. And before breakfast, too. Did the man never tire? She peeked over at his vigorous profile. No, Lorgin never failed to rise to the occasion. The man was incredibly sexual.

Not that she was complaining.

His words alone had already made her wet for him. And wanting him. God, how she wanted him . . .

His touch, his caress, his embrace. She could taste him, smell him, *feel* him around her. *Within her.* Hadn't he told her, shown her, that he had placed himself within her always? *"Even now,"* he had said. Yes, even now.

The realization almost caused her to groan aloud as she entered the dwelling with him. Quickly, she broke free of his arm lest he discern the power he was acquiring over her. She used her interest in the interior to camouflage her raging desire. In her mind it was a weakness he must never be aware of. Because she knew, *knew* he would use her desire to manipulate her to his will. He had done it before.

As devastating as his mastery over her had been, she knew it would be even worse should he decide to repeat what he had done to her at Traed's keep. Worse now, because she acknowledged that sometimes, lately, a part of her *wanted* to surrender completely to him, to this power he had over her. And it frightened her.

"Well?"

Deana's head snapped up to see Lorgin standing across from her, arms crossed in expectation. She had been so wrapped up in her thoughts, she wasn't sure what he was asking her. "Well, what?"

Lorgin exhaled noisily. "What do you think of my home?"

"Oh."

He gave her a strange look.

She looked around the interior, now really seeing it. It was a large hollowed-out space in the core of the tree. In the center of the room was a huge dining table flanked by several chairs. Cabinets along the wall. A cooking area. Scattered jewel-toned woven rugs decorating dark wooden floors. Several low tables. A long high-backed bench with thick, richly patterned cushions facing a . . . *fireplace?* A fireplace in a tree? That didn't seem so smart.

Her gaze followed a curved stairway which seemed to have been carved into the side of the trunk. It circled upward to a loft. She could see a large platform bed, also wooden, with a broad, dense mattress on it. Mattresses had become a welcome sight since her experiences on Ryka Twelve.

She knew Lorgin was waiting expectantly for her opinion. She smiled widely at him as she scanned the room again. "I feel like I'm in Chip and Dale's house."

Lorgin looked confused. "Who is this Chipandale?"

He said it as if it were one word. Her hand came up to cover her mouth as she giggled. How do you explain the nuances of two house-proud chipmunks? "They have a very *nice* house." She grinned. "I like it, Lorgin." He seemed very pleased, almost relieved. She hadn't realized that her opinion about his home would mean so much to him.

"There is only one thing I'm confused about. How can you have a fireplace in here?"

"The trees of the Towering Forest do not burn."

That surprised her. She examined the wood more closely, running her hand along it. "But they are comprised of wood, aren't they?"

"Yes, of course. Remember when I told you that the Guild watches over them, protects them?"

"Yes, but—"

"The trees are spellbound, Adeeann. For thousands of years it has been thus."

She looked more closely at the table, now noticing that the curved legs seemed to be attached to the floor. *As if it had grown from the floor.* She rapidly surveyed all the other furniture, noting the same situation.

Lorgin confirmed her suspicions. "It is all part of the tree. Although formed to my design."

"I don't understand. Do you talk to the tree?" That sounded singularly stupid.

"No. I commune in pictures. The exchange is not"—he grasped for the right words to explain—"not a conversation. It is more a connection. The tree is not an individual, a being in the sense that we are. As I said, there is a 'knowing.' "

"So . . . you convey in some way what you want?"

He nodded. "I meditate what would please me. The tree will then grow to my desire, in order to seek harmony with me."

"It grows as you do? A perfect environment."

He curled his hand around a chair back, his gaze going up to the sole bedroom in the loft. "Yes. Our home can change as we change."

What did he mean by that? She looked at him askance.

"Perhaps you would like to *change* something now?" His light, sexy tone was decidedly teasing.

She was not in the least amused. Her look was quelling. "No, it's perfect the way it is." She walked over to a window and stared out at the panoramic view. "Tell me, Lorgin, what does the tree get out of all this?"

"The joy of life within, *zira*." She didn't realize he had come up behind her until his expressive hands caressed her shoulders.

"All caring beings seek such alliances." His velvet lips briefly found her throat before his breath fanned her ear. "Let me explain it to you," he whispered huskily as he picked her up in his arms, carrying her up the stairs.

Rejar sat in the square at a small cafe table, slowly sipping a warm glass of *mir*. He was feeling oddly restless.

The night before, as was his wont, he had gone out carousing. Strangely, it had not helped. In fact, if anything, the feeling had intensified.

His feral gaze drifted across the esplanade, momentarily stopping on the attractive woman at the next table. She had been trying to garner his attention since he had sat down, and she had not been very discreet about it.

He observed her in a rather clinical fashion. Nice hair. Pretty face. Lush mouth. Voluptuous figure. Passionate nature. Somewhat developed senses. Adequate drive. Aroused by him.

So why was he not already making his way across the short distance that separated them?

He did not understand it. Why was he hesitating?

He *loved* women.

In truth, he lived for women.

He reveled in their textures and their tastes; color of hair, skin tones, shape of features, expressions of personality. Their scent. Such pleasures were often so intense to him as to almost cause him to go into a trance.

He had been known to completely immerse himself in the exploration of the senses. it was a peculiar trait to male Familiars, the ability to totally lose oneself in the sensual.

And even amongst Familiars, Rejar had been exemplary.

Perhaps it was his mixed blood, or a trait singular to him, but it was well known in Familiar circles that Rejar ta'al Krue had been gifted with *more*.

So what was wrong with him?

For the first time since he had reached his maturity, he was unmoved. Why, he could not say. Perhaps he needed the company of a female at this moment for other reasons. Women could bring comfort in many ways; all male Familiars knew this. It was another reason women sought out his kind. Familiar's love for women went beyond the physical. They were dedicated to pleasure with the female in all its forms.

Still, there was this *restlessness* . . .

Perhaps he should visit with his brother's wife, Adeeann. She was a very intelligent woman, and he had developed a friendship with her apart from the blood tie. He would not soon forget how she had placed herself before the *xathu* beast to save his brother. It was a fearless act; she had the heart of the cat.

He liked her. She had a way of seeing things differently than his people did. She would be good to talk to.

His eyes lit on the display in the window of a shop across the plaza. He smiled decisively. *Perfect.* Getting to his feet, he headed to the shop, the disappointed young lady he had left in the square already forgotten.

Deana opened her eyes at the low sound of the chimes. Before he had left, Lorgin had told her that the large chime would sound when the platform was in use. Someone was coming. She knew it couldn't be Lorgin because he had left a few minutes ago to attend to some business with the Guild.

She supposed she had better get out of this hammock and see who it was. So much for a nap before dinner. Lorgin had been true to his word, making love to her passionately *twice* before leaving. She was exhausted.

Lorgin had admirably "explained" with his lips, fingers, tongue, and body. Controlling her pace with a master hand, he had guided their pleasure, wringing every drop of response she possessed. Tirelessly giving of himself in return.

Afterward, he had insisted on reweaving her hair, even though she told him he needn't bother as he'd probably only take it down again. He simply set about doing it while intermittently kissing her neck, shoulders, and hair, complaining good-naturedly about why she wished to take away his enjoyment. She responded that he had just had plenty of enjoyment.

The platform leveled out as she sat up. Rejar! And he was carrying a huge crystal statue of a unicorn. She smiled in delight. He had come to visit! She rushed over to him.

"Rejar! Lorgin just left a little while ago."

"Then I will visit with you." He smiled, handing her the statue.

"It's beautiful, thank you!" She carefully carried the figure into the house, placing it on the low table by the bench. Rejar sank to the floor in front of the table, snapping off the horn of the unicorn.

Deana was shocked. "Why did you break it?"

Rejar brought the horn to his mouth, sucking on the stick. "Mmmm . . . spun honey—delicious. I brought it to share with you, Adeeann."

Candy! So, he had missed her company. How sweet!

Deana smirked as she watched him lick the candy. She thought of legends she had heard about unicorn horns being ground for aphrodisiacs. "If I were you, Rejar, I'd take a different piece."

"Why?" he spoke around the horn in his mouth.

"Believe me, from what I've seen, you don't need that particular portion."

Rejar grinned, clenching the stick of candy between his strong white teeth. *{What was it you once said? One can never be too . . . rich.}*

She grinned. "You know?"

{Why do you think I took it?}

They laughed.

Deana joined him on the floor, breaking off the tail portion. The taste was heavenly. "Say, this is great!"

Rejar raised an eyebrow as if to say, "Would I recommend less?"

They talked as they ate the unicorn. Mostly about inconsequential things. Too inconsequential, she thought.

Rejar seemed strangely reticent, almost as if he were distracted. Although they hadn't known each other long, the extreme experiences they had undergone together had forged a certain bond. They had seen each other react to adversity; they had enjoyed each other's company.

Deana discovered that she genuinely liked Lorgin's unpredictable younger brother. He was the type of man she could develop a friendship with. He would never overstep the bounds of the friendship; he would be a supportive and trustworthy ally. She suspected he had actually sought out her company today. Something was bothering him.

"Is something wrong, Rejar?" she casually asked as she viewed the remains of the statue. They had already managed to down half the poor beast and were not inclined to stop. She snapped off an ear.

{No . . . Yes . . . Maybe . . . I do not know.}

"Ah, a definitive answer. I like those."

He smiled faintly, then spoke aloud again. "I have been restless of late. It disturbs me."

She looked perplexed. "Restless how?"

"I do not know. I cannot explain it."

"Restless as in—" she moved her hand back and forth— "female company restless?"

It took him a moment to figure out what she was saying. He grinned, revealing an engaging dimple. "No. It is something else, something different." He took another piece of candy.

"And you can't figure it out. Has it ever happened to you before?"

No. And the feeling seems to be increasing. Adeeann?}

"Yes?"

Rejar stared at the pattern of the carpet. "Sometimes a Familiar can sense his own death approaching. In this way he can prepare for it."

She gasped. "You don't think—"

He shook his head. "I do not know for certain, but I do not think it is this."

She leaned over, placing her hand on his arm. "Maybe you should talk to Lorgin about this?"

He shook his head again. *{No, I do not wish to alarm him, especially now. His quest calls him; he must not be sidetracked.}*

"I understand. Well, I know I'm probably not much help, but if you need to talk to someone, I'm here."

His eyes shimmered. "I am grateful."

"Here, have another piece of spun honey; candy always helps."

About an hour later, the low chimes sounded again, signaling Lorgin's return. He entered the house carrying a large covered tureen and wearing a big smile.

"Look what I have brought from Suleila for our evening meal. Your favorite *calan* stew, Rejar! I vow I am hungry and the—" He looked at two identically sticky faces; then his gaze fell to the table where only a small piece of hoof remained as evidence.

"Do not tell me the two of you have eaten an entire statue of spun crystal!"

Both of them clutched their stomachs and groaned.

Lorgin was astonished. "Why did you eat so much of it?"

"It was so good, we couldn't stop," Deana moaned.

"Well, if you think that was good, wait until you taste this." He lifted the cover off the tureen with a flourish. A small otterlike head poked up out of the liquid, blinking its eyes.

"Oh my God!" Deana covered her mouth and quickly ran toward the hidden alcove bathroom at the rear of the room.

In the same moment the little animal jumped out of the tureen, shaking stew everywhere, but mostly onto Lorgin.

"Sookah!" Rejar chastised his little pet.

321

The animal skittered and slid across the floor toward him, scampering up his leg and onto his chest. Sookah pecked him on the lips, giving him a quick kiss, then began licking Rejar's sticky face.

Rejar ran a finger gently over the little head, coming away with his favorite stew on it. "Mayhap I should be licking you." He licked the stew off his finger. "You should be more careful, Sookah, lest you become a meal for some hungry Charl." He looked over at Lorgin, laughing at his brother's florid complexion.

Lorgin was definitely furious. "Now it is ruined!" He tossed the stew out, tureen and all. Throwing his brother a disgusted look, he headed to the bathroom to see if Adeeann was all right.

She was not all right. She was vomiting her guts out. Deana clutched her stomach as another spasm rocked her. She wanted to die. Curl up and die. A strong arm came around her waist, supporting her as she leaned over the Aviaran version of a commode.

She was not happy for the help.

"Good grief, Lorgin, get out of here!" she managed between ragged breaths.

"Do not be foolish; you are ill."

"I am not—oh God!" He helped her lean over. "This is terribly embarrassing. Please leave!"

"I will not hear of it. Lean back against my arm. *Now,* Adeeann." Too drained to argue, she did as he said. "Here." He placed a cool cloth across her forehead. "Let me know if you need to go forward, and I will help you."

She nodded weakly. "I don't think there's anything left." Her stomach turned over again, causing the dry heaves.

Lorgin gently smoothed back her hair as he bent forward with her. "It will pass soon."

"Do you think it was the spun honey?" she asked him seriously.

The corners of his mouth lifted. "Well, you did eat an awful lot of it, did you not, *zira*?"

She looked at him, mortified as she saw his splattered clothes. "Did I do that? I'm sorry."

Lorgin looked down. "No, it was Sookah. She splattered me when she ran to Rejar. Are you feeling better now?"

She nodded gingerly.

"Good." He picked her up and carried her up a back stairway to the loft. "Rest for a while. I will return to the house with Rejar and bring back another dish for our meal."

"I'm not very hungry."

"No, I do not imagine you are. Still, you might be later. Tomorrow, if you feel better, you can go to the sacri with Suleila. She will help you purchase some supplies for us."

"I hate food shopping." What made him think she would do such a domestic thing? Perhaps he's going senile, she thought irritably.

He appraised her knowingly. Still the gharta. "Very well, I will do it." He went to a cabinet, retrieving some fresh clothes, changing as he spoke. "I will not be gone long."

Deana rose up on the bed, leaning on her elbows. "Lorgin?"

"Hmm?" He looked over at her as he laced up his shirt.

"Don't tell Rejar I . . . threw up. It was really nice of him to bring the candy and all. I don't want him to feel bad."

"Of course not. You have had an eventful day. I will tell him you are tired. It is the truth, is it not?" He winked at her.

She was asleep by the time the brothers left, her peaceful nap unknowingly aided by the tree which shielded her as she slept, its graceful leaves fanning out to protect her from a strong breeze.

Chapter Seventeen

Traed sat at Yaniff's scarred wooden table observing the old master's home. It was a place of unsettling simplicity.

Yaniff placed a cup of *mir* in front of Traed, seating himself across the table from him. Traed suspected he was about to hear some things of which, perhaps, he might prefer to remain in ignorance. He was not altogether convinced it had not been a mistake to return to Aviara.

Yaniff's fathomless eyes pierced the younger man. "Do you know why the Guild excommunicated your father?"

Traed crossed his booted feet. His fingers were tightly interlaced, resting on the table. He leaned back in his chair.

"I only know what Lorgin has told me."

"Which is?"

Traed scowled. "What is the point of this?"

"Which is?" Yaniff repeated calmly.

A muscle ticked in Traed's jaw. "He said that my father kidnapped my mother from the Tan-Shi, took her against her will, performing the Transference ceremony. There is the why, Yaniff. Satisfied?''

"Not quite. Perhaps you did not hear all of his words."

Traed's green eyes narrowed. "I heard them."

"Then perhaps you did not *listen* to them."

"Do not circle your words with me, Yaniff. If you wish to tell me something, then do so. I find I no longer possess the patience I once had."

Yaniff snorted. "You have the patience of honey rolling uphill when it suits you, Traed. I will say what I have to say to you in my own fashion. Whether it meets your approval or not."

Traed glanced away, shamed by his outburst to this most revered mystic. "Forgive me."

Yaniff inclined his head slightly. "Now, Traed, did Lorgin not tell you the true reason for the excommunication?''

"Lorgin told me the Guild was ... unhappy with my father's behavior in regards to his culpability. He implied that the reason they barred him was because of his treatment of the situation."

Yaniff peered at Traed unrelentingly. "Tell me; who circles his words now?"

Traed slammed the flat of his hand onto the table top. "What would you have me say? That my own father was thrown out of the Guild because of his cruel and irrational behavior toward his only son?"

Rather than seeming upset by the heated words, Yaniff seemed strangely pleased. "You have just said it."

Traed sank back into his chair, suddenly weary. "What would you have of me, Yaniff? Tell me and be done with it."

Yaniff picked up his cup of warm *mir* slowly sipping the relaxing brew. "Lorgin has been called upon by both the Alliance and the Guild."

Traed was not overly surprised. "He is on a quest for them?"

"Yes."

"Who set him upon this quest?"

"I did."

Traed raised an eyebrow. "And?"

"There were some inexplicable disturbances on the Rim. At first I believed them to be inconsequential—just slight flutters and twitches in the continuum. Nothing to be concerned about. However, these disturbances began to increase. The manifestations of these disturbances became quite alarming."

"So, having the Charl at your disposal, you sent Lorgin out to investigate for you. What did he find?"

"It is more complicated than that. You began your training years ago. You know there can be many facets to a seemingly simple stone."

"Do not speak to me of Charl training! I will not hear of it! Think you I would heed the teachings of such a body of righteous hypocrites after what they did to my bloodline?"

"You condemn all Charl for the actions of the Guild?"

"Do not ask me such questions; I will not answer."

"Has it ever occurred to you that the Guild has regretted its decision?"

Traed slashed his hand through the air. "It is of no interest to me!"

"Ah, but it is, Traed. They ask that you take your rightful place by joining them."

Traed laughed, a sarcastic sound devoid of humor. "How touching after all these years," he sneered.

"Your father is a sixth-level mystic, Traed. You have a destiny to follow."

"Perhaps. *But not with the Charl.*"

Yaniff nodded sagely. "You may be right in that."

"So, have you called me back to ask me to recant and join the Charl?"

"No. That is not why you are here. As I mentioned to you,

Lorgin set out to investigate the situation regarding the disturbances.''

"What did he find?"

"For one thing, he found Adeeann."

Traed was surprised. "His wife?"

"She wears the Shimalee."

"I know—I have seen it. It is connected in some way to these disturbances?"

"Yes. I had discovered that the disturbances on the Rim were causing rifts in time and space. Since all corridors of time and space are linked by the Shimalees, there definitely appears to be a connection."

Traed thought about the serious ramifications should the continuity of the continuum be compromised. He could not help but be concerned. "Continue, Yaniff."

"Lorgin knew of the prophecy regarding the first in the line of Krue and she who wears the Shimalee, but at the time, he did not know how interconnected it would become with this quest. He took Adeeann to wife, bringing her with him. Then he set about to track down a rumor I had heard—a rumor about a man, not a diviner, who had somehow found a phasing stone. One can only speculate that such a man would seek to unlock its mysteries. Eventually, Lorgin was able to discover his identity."

"*Someone is creating these rifts?* By *Aiyah*, why would anyone do such a thing?"

"Here is where we come full circle, Traed. As much as you dislike Charl analogy, you will forgive me my allusion: another facet of the stone is revealed."

"How so?"

"The action of the Guild comes back to haunt them, as I warned them it would."

Traed seemed confused. "I do not understand."

Yaniff leveled his compelling gaze directly onto Traed.

"It is Theardar who is causing the rifts. Theardar who found the phasing stone. Theardar who very well might destroy all existence with his tampering."

Traed slumped in his seat, deathly pale. "My father uses his powers in darkness?"

"It is so."

Traed closed his eyes, the enormity of what his father was doing overwhelming him. "What do you want from me?" he whispered brokenly.

"I seek Theardar on the Rim. Lorgin will go to face him. Will you stand with us?"

A moan of pain issued from Traed's throat. "Do not ask this of me, I beg you!"

"I do not ask it lightly, I assure you. It is a terrible thing to ask a son to stand against his father. Your life has not been an easy one, Traed. This will not be the only painful decision you will make in your life, but perhaps the most lasting."

Traed bolted out of his chair, turning away from Yaniff. He was silent for a long time. When he spoke, his voice was very quiet, very low. "How do you propose I make such a decision, mystic? Do not tell me there is no Charl platitude you can hand out just for this occasion?"

"I understand your bitterness."

He turned around to stare at the old man. "Do you?"

Yaniff's face held sorrow. "More than you know."

Traed was immediately contrite. He knelt down in front of the old mystic.

"Forgive me, Master." Unconsciously he used the Charl title a supplicant calls his teacher. A title he had not spoken in years. Not since Lorgin and he were boys, studying together for the Charl, deeply honored to have been chosen to study with Yaniff.

Yaniff placed a withered hand upon the bent head of Traed ta'al Theardar. So good a man, he lamented; so tormented a soul.

"Arise, Traed. There is more. Another facet of the stone approaches. Your loyalties are soon to be divided further."

"What do you mean?"

A light knock sounded at the door.

"Enter, Rejar."

The door to the cottage swung open and Rejar ta'al Krue entered, his Familiar eyes immediately adjusting from bright sunlight to the darkened interior.

"I wish to speak with you, old man." His eyes flew to Traed. "Alone."

"Sit, Rejar. What you have to say to me is best said in front of Traed as well."

Rejar hesitated, not at all sure he should be saying what he had come to say in front of Traed.

Yaniff got up and poured Rejar a warm cup of *mir*. Placing it in front of the Familiar, he said, "You must learn to trust me, my young friend. Speak what is in your heart."

Taking the *mir* in his hands, Rejar sipped slowly, thinking over his words. He would not enter Traed's mind with his thoughts and therefore was forced to speak aloud.

When he was ready, he looked directly across the table into Traed's green eyes. "He is my brother of the line. I have sensed it."

Shock flitted across Traed's face, followed by anger. "What lie does this Familiar speak?"

Rejar was incensed. "No lie, Traed! I have sensed Lodarres blood in you and the bloodline is strong!" He turned to Yaniff. "How can this be, Yaniff? Familiar senses do not deceive, yet I cannot accept what my insight tells me is true, for to do so dishonors my name!"

Traed got to his feet, furious. "How dare you impugn the name of Krue? A man of honor!" Traed whipped out his light saber in the blink of an eye, bringing it to bear on Rejar.

Yaniff looked from one to the other of them, well pleased that Traed rose to defend the name of Rejar's father. "Put away your light saber, Traed, and sit. What Rejar has said is the truth."

Retracting his blade, Traed staggered back to his chair, clearly startled by yet another unexpected revelation. *A brother of the line.* What Charl trickery was this?

It was impossible. He said as much.

"Since you are here, and you are indeed a Lodarres, Traed, it is not impossible, is it?"

"Explain yourself!"

Yaniff took a deep breath. "Your mother was the sister of Krue."

"No." Rejar was emphatic. "My father had no siblings."

"Yes, Rejar, he did. He had one younger sister, whom he loved dearly."

The potential of Yaniff's words was affecting both men. If it were true, Traed would be a son of the line to Krue. Since Traed was the only offspring of Krue's only sibling, the power of descent in him would be strong. By Aviaran law, and Charl mystic belief, Traed could be called son of Krue.

Rejar was shaken. "Why has this sister never been mentioned to us? Lorgin and I both were raised with the impression that my father had no other members in his line." •

"The Tan-Shi were outraged when Marilan was taken. Since Theardar was a Charl, they partitioned the Guild for equanimity. Marilan had already taken the Oath, so the Tan-Shi asked the Guild that all references to her familial ties be forever severed, her name never mentioned outside the context of the Tan-Shi. The Guild rendered judgment in their favor. From that day forward, Krue could not acknowledge her existence as his sister." Yaniff stared intently at Traed. "Nor claim you to his line, Traed. No matter how much he desired it."

"Why punish my father for Theardar's act?" Rejar revolted against this seemingly unfair ruling by the Guild.

"He was a Charl. It was not personal. The Tan-Shi was demanding all Charl to share in the responsibility of one of their kind. They felt, and probably rightly so, that the Charl should have foreseen the problem and been more attentive to their own."

"Foreseen the problem?" Traed hissed. "An interesting choice of words, Yaniff. Did either the Tan-Shi or the Guild ever consider my existence or what such a decree would mean to me? *I never even knew who my mother was."*

"As I said, Traed, the Guild regrets its decision in regards to you. They seek to mend the breach."

"How unfortunate for them!" he snapped.

The room went silent for several moments as Yaniff gave both men time for heated emotions to cool.

"I ask that neither of you, as yet, discuss what has been revealed here with Lorgin. As you know, as the eldest, he would be honor bound. It is imperative he not be sidetracked at this time; Lorgin must remain focused on his objective."

Both men knew what Yaniff was saying. The old mystic believed it was more than a possibility that Lorgin might well be moved to stand for Traed. Lorgin would confront Theardar not as an agent of the Alliance, but with revenge in his heart. As first in the line of Krue, he would seek to make Theardar answer to him for Theardar's conduct to the line of Lodarres. Such a confrontation could only bring grief at its conclusion..

Rejar gazed down at the table; Traed glanced away. Both men nodded curtly.

Traed rose, standing with his back to them, staring vacantly out the window. When he spoke, his low voice did not hide the conflict within him. "I will accompany you to the Rim. I *will not* stand against my father."

Yaniff inclined his head, relieved. "Very well, Traed." *It was enough,* he thought . . .

For a moment Yaniff's conscience panged him for his manipulation of the younger man. Resigned to it, the mystic nonetheless grieved in his heart. In truth, Traed would suffer greatly for what lay ahead. There was no help for it.

It was done.

He addressed both of them. "Go. Walk with each other as brothers. If you seek it, you will find that the two of you have much in common."

The men rose, awkward with each other in light of their new relationship. Traed hesitated at the door, an ironic expression crossing his intense features; he turned back to Yaniff.

"Lorgin said much the same to me on Zarrain. At the time, I thought his reasoning faulty."

Yaniff stroked Bojo's feathers contemplatively. "You will find, as I have, Traed, that the reasoning of Lorgin ta'al Krue is rarely faulty."

Deana made her way through the woods, hoping she was following the right path to Yaniff's house. Her pastel caftan shimmered in the daylight, sunlight picking up the gold threads in the dress and in her hair. She prayed Yaniff was feeling sociable today and she wouldn't find herself back on the main road.

The perfect opportunity had presented itself this morning; it would be a shame to waste it. Lorgin had told her he had further business with the Guild that day, suggesting she might like to visit with Suleila. Since she had suffered no lasting effects from her bout of overindulgence with the spun honey, she had seized upon the opening, telling Lorgin that, in all likelihood, she would.

"Always take the left fork going there through the woods, the right coming back. You will not get lost," he had said.

"If I can remember it the correct way," was her flip reply.

"Just remember how 'right' it is to come home, zira." She had stuck her tongue out at him then.

When she had expressed her concern about wild creatures, both two and multilegged, he tossed the words *enchanted, Guild, have no worry* over his shoulder as he headed to the platform.

Enchanted. She should have realized.

It was a lovely walk, though. Breathing deeply, it suddenly struck Deana how wonderful she felt. It had been a long time since she had walked in the woods by herself. It was something no sane Earth woman would do. But, here on Aviara, things were different. No city noises. No exhaust fumes. No crazed maniacs to worry about . . . well, maybe one crazed maniac. Theardar.

Aviara would be the perfect vacation spot for world-weary Earthlings, she mused. Too bad she couldn't work out a deal with a local travel agency. Of course, there would be scores of loud-mouthed tourists overrunning these beautiful woods, taking snapshots of people taking snapshots, carpeting the forest floor with wadded-up hamburger wrappers, turning the Towering Forest into a chic pied-a-terre. Hmm . . . Bad idea.

A small cottage came into view as she rounded a bend in the path.

Yaniff's home!

She approached the dwelling, somewhat surprised at the simplicity of the surroundings. Somehow she had pictured Yaniff living in a home similar to Lorgin's parents'. This small rustic cottage was the antithesis of their stately home.

She raised her hand to knock on the door.

Inside the house, Yaniff gazed up at Bojo who was nesting in his favorite spot in the rafters. Traed and Rejar had left a few moments ago. "A busy day for wizards, eh, Bojo? Come in, Adeeann."

Deana gingerly opened the door, peering inside. "How did you know it was me?"

"Come, sit down. I want you to try something." Yaniff bustled over to a sideboard, walking back with a small cup of hot, dark liquid in his hand. He placed it proudly before her, obviously waiting for her to taste it.

Sitting down at the ancient wooden table, she cautiously brought the cup to her lips. What ever it was, it was *horrible*.

Yaniff beamed at her. "Well, what do you think, Adeeann?"

That's when it hit her. *Coffee.* He had been trying to make coffee for her. The dear, kind, misguided man.

"It's . . . close, Yaniff." She discreetly placed the cup on the table.

The old wizard frowned. "I will keep working on it."

Deana was touched that he would try so hard to bring a portion of her world to her. "Thank you, Yaniff. It's very sweet of you." She could've sworn he blushed.

"So, what brings you to visit with me today, Adeeann? Somehow I do not think you have come just to see me, although I would not mind this," he hastily added.

Deana took a deep breath, knowing she would have to state her case and state it well. Logically. Dispassionately. The relationship between Lorgin and Yaniff was a close one. The only way Yaniff would help her, she knew, was if she could show him the mistake Lorgin had made. If he believed her to be right, regardless of Lorgin's wishes, she suspected that Yaniff would help her.

"It has to do with this." She held up her necklace.

"The Shimalee."

"Yes."

"What about it?"

"I'm the wrong woman!" she blurted out. So much for stating her case dispassionately.

Yaniff's lips twitched. "What do you mean?"

Her eyes filled with tears and the words poured out of her in a tumultuous rush. "Oh, Yaniff, I'm not the right woman. Lorgin has made a terrible mistake! He thinks he's married to me, and I just found this—this *thing* in a junk shop. *My God, a junk shop!* What will he do when he finds out the truth? What will happen to him? I don't know what to do! *I desire him all the time* and I don't really look like this—"

"Adeeann, calm down. Please, do not upset yourself so. Here, drink some of this *mir*; it will relax you." He pushed his cup into her hand. She took a large swallow. "Better?" She nodded dejectedly. "Now, let us sort this problem out. First of all, what do you mean you do not look thus?"

"It's true," she sniffed. "I don't know what happened, but as soon as I met Lorgin I looked better—I can't explain it. At first I thought he had cast some kind of spell on me—"

"Lorgin does not do spells."

"Yes, I know; he told me. So the only thing I can think of is this stupid necklace-" She looked up, belatedly realizing she probably had insulted one of their icons. "Oops. Sorry."

Yaniff waved it away. "Come to the mirror, Adeeann." She did as he bid, standing next to him in front of a small gilded wall mirror. " 'Remove the Shimalee."

"Lorgin told me not to."

Yaniff smiled down at her, her statement revealing much to him. "It is quite all right, here. I assure you."

She carefully removed the necklace and placed it on the table.

"Now look in the mirror and tell me what you see."

Deana did as he bid. "I look the same. I mean I look *different*, but the same."

"So we can assume it is safe to say it is not the necklace effecting this change in you. Tell me, what do you think is different in the way you look?"

Deana shrugged. "It's hard to define. I just sort of *look better*. Prettier."

Yaniff stroked his chin as if pondering the dilemma. "Perhaps you have always looked this way, *but never noticed it*?"

She screwed up her face as she gazed in the mirror. "I don't think so."

"To Lorgin you have always looked thus?"

She nodded. "Yes. That's why I suspected him right off."

"Hmm . . . I will have to think on this problem awhile." Yaniff hid his smile behind a cough. *She had never noticed her own beauty until Lorgin had shown it to her.*

"Perhaps we can put aside this problem for later, and try to sort out the rest now." He handed the Shimalee back to her, making sure she clasped it securely around her neck, then led her back to the table.

"About the Shimalee—you say that Lorgin has the wrong woman. This could be serious, indeed. You know he has taken you to wife under Aviaran and Charl law."

Her eyes widened. "I know. It's terrible! What is he going to do?"

Yaniff cleared his throat to stop the chuckle bubbling its way up his throat. Lorgin ta'al Krue would think of something, he was sure. "Let us go over, together, the circumstances of how you came to have the Shimalee. There may be some small . . . fact that was overlooked."

Deana leaned intently forward in her chair. "Good idea! Here's what happened: It was a terrible day; I got fired from my job, sat in pi—something wet, ruined my coat, got stuck in the parking lot due to an accident, went into a junk shop I had never seen before—"

He held up his hands. "Please, I am having trouble making sense out of this. What happened to you in the shop?"

"Well, this old guy came out wearing a Red Sox baseball cap, no less; he was the owner. I found this necklace—"

"How?"

"What?"

"How did you find the necklace?"

"Oh. It was under a bunch of boxes in the rear of the store. The guy with the baseball cap asked me if I really wanted to buy—"

"What made you look under the boxes?"

She shrugged. "I don't really know. I remember having a feeling there might be something good under there—"

"Aha!" Yaniff snapped his fingers.

"What aha?"

"There it is! The Shimalee sang to you."

"It did no such thing."

"Who is to say? You see the terrible series of events which happened to you that day as coincidences; I see them as interconnected events. The disruption of the continuity of your life was heralded by the Shimalee coming to you."

"Are you trying to tell me that all the rotten things that happened to me on that day happened because this Shimalee thing was preparing to make a presence in my life?"

"Just so. It was singing to you, disrupting your life line. Once you had the Shimalee in your possession, it plucked Lorgin out of the space/time continuum, depositing him in your vicinity. Remember, the Shimalee bends dimensions; the corridor of time and space opened between the two of you, bringing you together. You see? It is the Prophecy."

337

"What a crock!"

"You think so?" Yaniff asked innocently.

"Believe me, I know I'm not this woman! A man like Lorgin would never—Oh, Yaniff you must believe me!"

"I believe that *you believe* what you are saying."

Tears ran down her cheeks. "You have to believe me, Yaniff!"

She was very agitated. Yaniff took her hands in his. "Why is it so important that I believe you, child?"

"Be-because I want you to send me home!"

Yaniff raised his eyebrows. "I see." He gazed knowingly upon her bent head, watching the tears track down her cheeks. She needed his guidance, that much was obvious.

"Why did you not say so at once?" he admonished her gently. Deana's head snapped up.

"You'll help me?"

"Of course." His crafty eyes observed her. "I will send you now." He made to rise.

"Wait!"

Yaniff feigned surprise. "What is it? You said you wish to leave."

"Yes, but . . . *not now.*"

"Ah." The wizard sat down.

"I mean—I have to say goodbye to . . . to . . . *everyone*," she pleaded with him. "I—you will send me home later, won't you?"

"Whenever you are ready. But surely you will wish to *abandon* us soon?"

She fidgeted in her seat. "Well . . . now that I know I *can* go back, I suppose there's no harm in seeing the quest through."

Yaniff sipped his *mir*. "And what quest would that be?"

She blinked. "What do you mean?"

"There are many quests surrounding you, Adeeann. There

is Lorgin's quest for the Alliance, Traed's quest for his lost destiny, Rejar's quest, not yet begun, but soon, soon . . . And then, there is your quest."

"My quest?"

"Yes."

"I don't have a quest."

Yaniff did not respond.

Deana observed the mystic carefully. In the time she had known him, she had never heard Yaniff utter an idle statement. She peered at him sideways. "I do?"

He smiled slightly. "Yes, you do."

Damn! "So, like, what is it?"

"That, you will have to figure out for yourself. Although I will tell you this: best you figure it out soon, for it is almost at its end."

Yaniff's cryptic words followed her as she ran the entire distance back to the strength of Lorgin's arms.

She found him sprawled on the grass in the middle of the flower garden, wearing nothing but his black leather pants.

He was fast asleep.

His deep, even breaths told her he hadn't heard the low chimes signaling her return. Deana had never seen him so relaxed.

And why shouldn't he be? After all, this was his home.

Deana was startled to realize that even though they had been sharing a bed for quite some time, this was the first time she had actually seen him asleep. Always, in the past, he had awakened before she did, alert and controlled.

It was strange to see him looking so vulnerable, lying there in the tazmin flowers, his long golden hair spread out across the carpet of blossoms.

He seemed so at peace. His thick black lashes formed two perfect crescents against his cheekbones; his firm, sensitive mouth was slightly parted. It was an incredibly handsome face.

One richly muscled arm was thrown carelessly above his head, unknowingly displaying his perfectly delineated chest for her inspection. Here was raw strength at rest . . . He looked golden and powerful, like some great jungle cat napping in the sun after a successful hunt.

The laces near the waistband of his pants had loosened, causing his pants to gape intriguingly, further adding to her impression of sensual vulnerability.

Her gaze moved down.

No vulnerability here, she admitted, noting the bulge between his thighs. Even at rest, this part of him was impressive. Armed and dangerous. *Waiting to strike.*

He shifted in his sleep, bringing the arm he had tossed over his head back down to his side, his hand falling to curve lightly against his stomach.

He was such a beautiful man.

Not just his form, she realized, but him. His kindness and control. His sense of humor. His intelligence. His genuine concern for those he cared about. His joy in passion. And, yes, she hesitated to admit, even his arrogance.

She would miss him terribly when this was over.

Deana had never met a man who made her feel more *alive.*

Frankly, she wanted him desperately. Now. Inside of her. All of him.

In the countless times they had made love, Deana had never taken the initiative. She never had the chance.

That was about to change, she decided recklessly.

Now that Yaniff had given her the ability to *choose* when to return home, somehow their relationship felt different. Lorgin did not hold all the cards anymore, and she was about to point that out to him in her not-so-subtle way. *Surprise, Lorgin.*

Quietly, so as not to awaken him, she slipped her caftan over her head, draping it on a nearby bench. She shook the ribbons out of her hair, letting the long red tresses fall free around her.

Silently she knelt down beside him, sitting on her haunches among the fragrant flowers. Even though they were not touching, she could feel the warmth from his body next to her.

His clean sandalwood scent caressed her nostrils as she bent over him.

Ever so softly, she pressed her lips against the strong column of his throat, where his vital pulse beat rhythmically.

His eyelids fluttered.

Chapter Eighteen

"Mmm . . . Adeeann."

His voice was a lazy rasp of velvet.

Still in the aftergrip of sleep, he wrapped his arm casually around her waist, bringing her down to lie next to him. Holding her securely in his arms, he nuzzled his chin against the top of her head and promptly drifted back to sleep.

Oh, no, Lorgin. I have quite a time in store for you and napping isn't on the agenda.

Moving up in his arms, she let the tip of her tongue touch the little indentation under his beautifully sculpted lower lip.

He stirred beneath her.

She draped her leg over his thighs, fastening her open mouth against his throat.

His eyes opened a fraction.

Her lips leisurely traveled down to his collarbone, taking tiny sips of his skin.

His hands suddenly splayed powerfully against the bareness of her back.

She froze, looking up at him. After all, this was Lorgin. She wasn't quite sure how he was going to react to her aggression.

He silently regarded her for several moments through slitted eyes, which were starting to incandescently spark beneath his lowered lids. As if he had made a decision of some kind, he firmly lifted her chin with a bent finger, bringing her mouth down to his own.

The kiss was a controlled, guarded exchange. He made no move to deepen it, or intensify it. Deana read his message loud and clear; she could almost hear his bold voice in her mind: *If you wish this to go further, zira, you had better see to it.*

All right, so he was *allowing* her free reign.

Admittedly, it took some of the control, okay, a lot of the control away from her. Just a couple of months ago, she would have balked at the very notion of him "allowing" her to take the helm. She recognized the oxymoron, but somehow, with a man like Lorgin, it seemed . . . appropriate.

He was too strong, too arrogant, too *male*.

If she was honest with herself, comparing other males of her acquaintance to him was a lesson in futility. They were a different species entirely. She had never met anyone like him, and probably never would again.

One did not take liberties with such a man as Lorgin unless he permitted it first.

The only thing a girl could do under the circumstances was to see how *uncontrolled* she could make him.

That being the case, she really intended to tingle his navel.

When he released her mouth, their eyes met briefly—his contained and waiting, hers promising and mischievous.

Deana brushed his lips several times with her own—playful, fleeting movements—before trailing her tongue down the

343

slight cleft of his chin. She felt the corners of his mouth lift ever so slightly against her cheeks, rather like a triumphant expression of pleasure he didn't want her to know about.

Just wait, Mr. ta'al Krue. Just wait.

Her hands clasped his upper arms, kneading the rock-hard biceps, noting for a moment how tiny her hands looked against the broad columns of muscle. She rubbed her face against his sculpted chest, purposely letting her hair slide against the taut skin. He was magnificent, every solid muscle well defined. Golden satin over steel.

She flicked his flat brown nipple with her tongue, smiling as it instantly hardened. Her teeth grazed against the little nubbin, just to let him know she noticed. The steady thumping of his heartbeat increased.

Sliding down the flat plane of his stomach, she ran her mouth teasingly against the indentation delineating his torso in a languorous, meandering pathway. When she reached the waistband of his pants, she hesitated just the right amount of time to let him wonder, before reaching down to completely separate the gaping laces. Her scalding, pliable mouth pressed against the tender skin right below his bellybutton.

Lorgin audibly sucked in his breath.

Ah, she thought, a Lorgin hot button. She caught that vulnerable skin between her teeth, tugging gently. Then she blew on the wet spot, cooling it dry.

Something hard poked the underside of her chin.

She smiled against him, letting her chin roll back and forth over the bulbous crest of the rod peeking out from the top of the undone laces. His fingers suddenly entwined in her hair. For an instant, it seemed as though he had stopped breathing.

Her nimble fingers set about undoing the rest of his laces—slowly. By the time she was finished, his breathing was not gentle and deep as it had been when she had first come upon him in the garden. It was ragged and shallow.

The first touch of her tongue caused him to jerk.

"Adeeann . . ." The fingers in her hair clenched. His voice was low, sexy, breathless.

"Yes, Lorgin?" She murmured against him, remembering a similar scene by a pool when their roles had been reversed.

She ran her mouth down the length of him, inch by impressive inch. His skin here was like the softest of velvets. It felt like eiderdown against her heated lips. Eiderdown encasing stone. Working her way back up, she licked a tiny drop of liquid which had seeped out of the tip of his erection.

He shivered.

"Adeeann . . ."

His hands weren't clenched now, they were pressing her against him.

"That is my name," she replied in imitation of him. Sliding her hand down inside his gaping pants, she gently cupped him. Then took him full in her mouth.

He moaned aloud.

"Adeeann!"

Her name came from between clenched teeth.

She looked up at him, pausing to let him see himself in her mouth. His eyes were amethyst slits of fire as he regarded her beneath lids heavy with passion. He closed his eyes, groaning as he sought for control.

When the edge of her teeth scraped against him, his hands came under her arms, quickly raising her along the length of him to fasten his mouth onto hers. This kiss was not like the last one he had given her, controlled, even remote. *This kiss was fire.*

He plundered her mouth fiercely, his tongue invading her with exquisite command, his hands on the back of her head holding her locked to him. She kissed him back with equal ardor, unwilling to relinquish her aggressive role.

He immediately kicked off his pants.

When he started to roll over to place her beneath him, she pressed firmly against his shoulders, letting him know that this time she wanted to do it *her way*. He acquiesced, sliding beneath her again.

Deana lay on top of him, their bodies touching full length, reveling in the feel of his bare body beneath her. It was rather like harnessing a typhoon, she thought.

His dynamic arms completely encircled her, clasping her waist tightly to him. She covered his face with tiny, nibbling kisses, caught up in the moment, frantic almost.

Lorgin's tongue circled the perimeter of her ear. "What are you waiting for?" he gasped.

What was she waiting for? Good question.

The problem was she wanted them to try an unusual position she had in mind, but she wasn't exactly sure how to proceed. She had never done it before. Oh sure, she knew what went where—*but how?* How could she seduce him with a thrilling new style if she couldn't get the mechanics right?

She dropped her forehead against his chin.

Now this was utterly embarrassing!

The last thing she wanted to do was fumble around trying to figure out logistics. She gritted her teeth. There was no other choice.

"Will you help me?" she whispered.

"Help you?" he whispered back. "Help you do what?"

He was not making this easy. "You know . . ." She rolled her eyes meaningfully.

Lorgin grinned. Two large dimples popped into his cheeks. "You mean you want to see if I know how to do this?" He rubbed his nose teasingly against hers.

"Lorgin!"

She pushed against his chest, raising the top half of her body. "If you're going to be difficult—"

He smiled, reaching down to grab her under the knee; he brought her leg up and over to the side, letting the other fall between his thighs. Then he positioned himself, guiding her down on him with his other hand, deeply penetrating her while she was lying on top of him.

"Is this what you had in mind, my Little Fire?" His face still reflected his amusement as he surged into her. She gasped at the new sensation.

It was an incredibly tight fit.

"I can feel you so deep, Lorgin." She choked, overcome by the intense feeling.

That did it. His amusement fled, replaced by a searing, almost pagan hunger. Impossibly, he expanded even further inside her, embedding himself deeper in her sheath.

"How deep, Adeeann, how deep?" His voice was raw now, breathy, wild. Hands on her hips, he pulled her down even tighter against the base of his shaft.

"Oh my God!" she whimpered, the angle of her position combined with his deep penetration convincing her she was going to be torn asunder with ravishing pleasure.

His hand twisted in her hair, tugging her down forcefully to his mouth. This kiss was totally unrestrained, almost brutal in its intensity. As if the gates had opened, he flooded her with his power, sending wave after wave to her.

This was it—the high point of her adventure. She was going to die of pleasure.

"Move on me, *zira*."

His words slowly pierced her passion-drugged brain. *Move on him?* Was he kidding? He was in so tight, it felt as if they were locked together permanently.

When she hesitated, his capable hands guided her hips forward to him, sliding her a couple of inches up on his shaft, leaving a slick wet surface behind. He waited just a second, then guided her back down, showing her just what to do.

Would wonders never cease? She didn't think any movement was going to be possible. She experimented on her own with a little wiggling upward movement. By Lorgin's groan, she knew it worked. She slid down. In no time at all, she picked up a rhythm and went with it, Lorgin "helping" her now and then with a slight arching of his hips. A sizzle of current trailed in his wake.

She quickly discovered the joys of changing the pace, by alternately slowing down and speeding up. At these times, Lorgin clenched his teeth and bit out a few choice words in a foreign tongue. She did not think for one minute that he was telling her to have a nice day.

Soon she got too caught up in the action to be cognizant of what she was doing to him. Because she was doing it to herself as well. Mindless, ceaseless pleasure, building and building. Lorgin began throbbing inside of her; a part of her marveled that he was able to hold back his climax until she was willing to join him, seeing as how the man was, by this time, almost completely out of control.

On her next downward movement, he grabbed her hips forcefully, slamming her down against him in a grinding motion, sending them both over the top.

He poured into her, filling her in a never ending series of ejaculations, both of them yelling out their release.

She collapsed totally prostrate on him. Spent. Drained. Lorgin beneath her seemed half dead.

When his breath returned to a manageable level, he facetiously croaked in her ear, "Is this any way to treat your husband?"

She raised her head. It was an effort, but she managed.

Hair disheveled, cheeks still flushed with heat, she looked him in the eye and stuck her tongue out at him.

Lorgin raised a mischievous eyebrow, wrapped his arms around her, and rolled down the slight incline with her braced in his arms, Deana squealing all the while. Without stopping, he spun them right into the small pool at the base of the waterfall.

Sputtering and splashing, Deana surfaced. Throwing her hair out of her eyes, she grinned, saying, "Trying to cool me off?"

He laughed, his hair dripping ribbons of water down his chest. "On the contrary, zira." He took her in his wet arms, bringing her flat against him. "I am hoping this cool water is a stimulating contrast to this . . . *heat.*" He took her hand, placing it on his revived erection.

Deana was shocked. "Again?"

His mouth came down to hers. "Yes, again and again and again . . ."

Later, that night, they sat outside gazing up at the stars, Deana comfortably seated between his bent legs, leaning back against his chest.

"What are the chances . . ." she ruminated "I mean, it's hard to believe we actually met, considering the vastness of space."

Lorgin, who knew there had been no chance involved, simply replied, "I would cross a hundred universes to find you, Adccann."

The following morning, Lorgin showed Deana the vegetable garden, carefully pointing out the various fruits and vegetables growing there.

"What do you do when you leave to go on a mission for the Alliance? Does someone care for the garden?"

He shook his head. "No, these plants require little maintenance."

"Let me guess—they're enchanted."

Lorgin tried to hide his grin as he plucked a small round purple fruit from a vine. "Here, taste this." He popped it in her mouth before she could object. Her eyes widened in surprise.

"Ummm, it's good! Tastes something like a passion fruit."

"*A passion fruit?* I will have to get some of those," he teased.

Deana was about to respond that he didn't need any passion fruit, when she spotted a familiar winged creature alighting on a branch behind Lorgin's shoulder.

"Look, Lorgin." She pointed. "Isn't that Bojo?"

Lorgin turned, staring at the strange bird. Bojo, noticing he had captured Lorgin's attention, spread his wings and flew away.

Lorgin's expression was at once serious. "Yaniff is sending for me. He has found Theardar." He took her hand, leading her back indoors.

"I might be a while. You could visit with Suleila if you wish." He bent down to kiss her as he fastened his cloak.

"I will, Lorgin." Noting his mood, she was not going to dissent. Besides, if Lorgin was right and Yaniff had found Theardar, she would need to say her goodbyes to his parents in her own way.

Lorgin and Yaniff walked through the forest at the old mystic's suggestion.

"We might as well enjoy the Aviaran day whilst we can."

"Where did you find Theardar?" Lorgin wasted no time on preliminaries.

"On a small barren planet, far into the Rim. It is a bleak,

strange place—perfect for such dire experiments.''

''Is there an appropriate tunnel point?''

''Of course.''

''When do I leave?''

''As soon as possible. His tamperings are bordering on the cataclysmic. Already some outlying regions are experiencing ripple effect from his irresponsibility.''

''I will say goodbye to Adeeann and be ready to leave.''

Yaniff sighed. ''You know by now she must accompany you, Lorgin.''

''I do not wish it. I expect a dangerous mission. I knew as much when I agreed to take it on both for you and the Alliance. However, surely you cannot expect me to expose my wife to this danger?''

''Let me explain something to you. Adeeann is your wife, in a sense, because of this danger. By now, I know you realize that your quest and the prophecy are interrelated. As much as you desire it, *she cannot remain behind*. Her presence is essential.''

Lorgin's hand went unconsciously to his Cearix. ''Why? Why is her presence so essential?''

Yaniff shrugged. ''This I cannot say. I only know it is so.''

He narrowed his eyes. ''Cannot say or will not say?''

Yaniff would not respond.

They walked in silence then. For the first time in his life, Lorgin contemplated going against his old master.

Yaniff abruptly stopped, placing his hand on Lorgin's arm. ''You must not falter now, Lorgin.'' His ancient eyes pierced the younger man. ''I tell you it is imperative she be there. I would have your oath on it. Now.''

Lorgin felt as if his heart were stopping. Yaniff was demanding he prove his loyalty by swearing an oath. Every principle he had lived by came down to this moment. Should he obey his teacher and friend, or keep his woman safe, away from any danger? His expression reflected his indecision.

"Speak now—do not waste my time any longer!"

Lorgin knew Yaniff would not force his hand like this unless he believed it to be absolutely necessary. The ancient wizard was the most revered seer on the planet. A lifetime of Charl mystic training came to the fore. He would have to protect Adeeann while he faced Theardar.

"She will be there."

Yaniff relaxed instantly. "Good."

They walked on for a time, each with their own thoughts.

"Your wife came to see me yesterday," Yaniff casually said.

"Did she?"

Yaniff was silent.

Lorgin's curiosity overrode his sense of propriety. "Did she have a particular reason or was it a social visit?"

"She thought she had a reason. In reality, she did not."

Lorgin's glance skittered Yaniff's way. "I see."

They continued a few paces in silence.

"She carries your child."

Lorgin missed a step.

For a moment his face reflected boundless joy, then quickly darkened. "Has the woman no sense? Why did she not wait until the danger is past? I vow I will—"

"She does not know."

Lorgin's jaw dropped. "How could she not?"

Yaniff smiled slightly. "Things are . . . different in her world, Lorgin. She is not aware the Transference gave her the power to choose."

Yaniff gave Lorgin a few moments to digest this and all it implied.

Lorgin rubbed the back of his neck as he gazed off into

the woods. When he looked back at Yaniff, his eyes were alight with knowledge.

"You understand now."

"Yes." Even though his Adeeann had been ignorant of the ways of the Transference, she now carried his babe. Which could only mean *she had desired it.*

"Will you tell her?"

Lorgin thought a moment. "No. She will find out for herself soon enough.

Yaniff nodded. Lorgin ta'al Krue was wise for his years. Yes, a good student. Soon to be a good father.

Deana gathered her bundle of purchases, sitting in a comfortable chair which faced a window to the garden.

Earlier she had visited a delighted Suleila, who insisted they go shopping together. Dragging the younger girl with her, the impetuous Familiar female took her to some of the shops in the hamlet Deana had seen several days ago.

It had been a rather fun day.

Deana had discovered a lot to like in the mischievous woman who so reminded her of Rejar. Suleila, it seemed, was always up for a good time. Like a whirlwind, she had ushered her into shop after shop, examining items with many a humorous comment.

Suleila purchased loads of items. Dresses, scarves, handcrafted items, shawls—you name it, she bought it. After a couple of frenetic hours, Suleila realized that Deana wasn't purchasing anything.

She turned to her with a puzzled frown. "Why do you not buy anything, daughter? Do you not see at least one thing that you like? After all, we must keep our shop owners in business. We have a responsibility. I tell Krue this often."

Deana grinned. "I bet you do. What does he have to say about that bit of reasoning?"

Suleila smiled coquettishly, revealing an astonishing beauty not dimmed by her years. "Oh, he agrees. Especially when I point out to him how much he benefits by my purchases." She held up a filmy-looking night robe.

Deana laughed. "You know, Rejar is very much your son."

"He wears sheer night robes?" Suleila joked.

"No, I think he's more apt to take them off."

"His father's son, then." She winked. "But seriously, Adeeann, why do you not buy anything?"

Deana shrugged. "I don't have any money."

Suleila giggled behind a hand-painted screen, sticking her head out. "You are very funny, Adeeann. These merchants recognize Lorgin's ribbons in your hair. Lorgin will be pleased to pay for anything you wish."

Yes, he probably would. Lorgin was an extremely generous man. However, she was not about to start charging up bills to him as if he were her—Well, she was not going to get into any explanations with his vivacious nextmother. She rapidly thought up an excuse.

"Ummm, I haven't seen anything yet that catches my eye."

"Oh, well, perhaps the next shop." It appeared that Suleila was a shopping force to be reckoned with.

Deana did see something she liked in the next shop.

It was a weaver's shop where her eye had been caught by several skeins of the most gorgeous yarn she had ever seen. Silky, yet thick, the brilliantly colored yarns captured her imagination.

Suleila noticed her attention. "You like these?"

"Oh yes," she breathed.

"Then you must purchase some of the fabric. I know a talented seamstress—"

"No, you don't understand. I want the yarn itself."

Suleila's brow furrowed. "Whatever for?"

Deana turned an impassioned eye on the older woman. "Crocheting." Here was something to occupy her free time. Not that she had had much of it here on Aviara. And since she was to be here only a short time, she didn't want to get too involved in anything.

"Crocheting? What is this?"

Deana put her arm around the Familiar's shoulders. "Let me tell you all about the frustrating hobby of crocheting . . ."

Suleila had been enthused. They bought the yarn, rushing back to Suleila's house, where they talked Krue into fashioning a hook. When Deana demonstrated a few rows of double crochet, Suleila seemed disappointed.

"It is ugly," she said with blunt honesty.

"True, but for some unknown reason it soon takes over your life. Before you know it, your home is filled with items—little useless blankets, horrendous chair pads, uncomfortable slippers, even small covers for tea pots."

Suleila laughed.

Bidding Krue and Suleila a fond farewell (for they had no idea she was truly saying goodbye), she hastened back to Lorgin's tree.

This was not like the clay incident! Here was a hobby worthy of the name. By this evening she would be consumed in the addiction.

She began to crochet, the needle flying in her dexterous fingers.

She didn't know how much time had passed, but when she looked up Lorgin was standing in the doorway watching her with oblique intensity.

"What is this you do with the threads?"

She smiled at him. "It's called crocheting. I couldn't help but try it when I saw this beautiful yarn. I hope it wasn't too expensive," she said absently. "Krue helped me fashion a hook. Suleila was fascinated . . . sort of."

He looked at her work dubiously. "What do you do with it?"

"This is called a granny square. You make zillions of these, then sew them all together to make an afghan. I hate the sewing part. Once, I made one giant granny square so I wouldn't have to sew anything together. All my friends laughed at it, but I thought . . . What?" He was looking at her strangely.

"Know you not how much I love you?"

Deana sucked in her breath, dropping needle and crochet onto the floor. "I . . . *Lorgin.*"

He knelt before her, taking her hands in his. "I vow I would willingly give my life for yours. Know that if there were any way to leave you safe in our home and not take you with me on this quest, I would. Your presence is essential, so Yaniff tells me, although he will not elaborate. I fear for your safety, Adeeann, but we must see this through to the end—together.

She had never seen Lorgin so upset. She absently stroked his hair, her mind focusing on his admission. *He said he loved her.*

"I—I didn't know." Whether she was referring to his declaration of love or the importance of her presence to his quest was unclear even to her.

"When—when do we leave?"

"On the morrow—early." He gathered her around the waist, resting his head on her lap. *Against his child.* "I pray I have done the right thing."

"What do you mean?"

When he lifted his head his eyes were damp. Instead of directly answering her, he said, "I could not bear it if anything happened to you."

She looked down at him as if focusing from out of a fog. My God, how could she have not known how deeply he cared about her? The answer was there on his face. *He loved her.*

"When we get to the Rim, you must promise me to do exactly as I say, *zira*. Without hesitation. Promise me now." The hands at her waist squeezed, ensuring her cooperation.

"I—yes, I promise."

His head fell back to her lap, his hands clasping her tightly around her middle. "Then we stand a chance."

Why was he so concerned about facing Theardar? From what she had seen, Lorgin was a fearsome warrior, brave, intelligent, capable. The fencing exhibition on Zarrain displayed a brilliant skill. Rejar had told her he had been invincible in the past, their strongest warrior.

She teased him, trying desperately to lighten his mood. "Of course we do. After all, you're not just any old warrior. If I were Theardar I'd be running already."

"You do not understand. Theardar is a sixth-level mystic; I am but a four. It will be impossible for me to fight him on an equal ground. His powers far outweigh mine. This is not what concerns me, though. There is always a chink in an opponent's armor, if you but seek it. Our other skills may be equally matched. Know I do not hesitate to face him, regardless of the outcome. I am concerned about you."

"Me? Whatever for? I don't even know Theardar—why would he seek to harm me?"

Lorgin did not answer right away. He thought it best she not know of the Shimalee connection for fear it would influence her actions in some unforeseen negative way. So instead he replied, "He would seek to hurt me through you." That much was true, he lamented.

357

Suddenly she was frightened. So far all of this had been one great lark to her. Oh sure, she felt for these people, was concerned about Lorgin's quest, Traed's problems, and Rejar's worries, *but as an observer*. Since she never intended to stay, she never felt totally involved. After all, these weren't her worlds; this wasn't her fight. The whole episode took on the trappings of an adventure to her. One she would remember over the years as an amazing portion of her life. Now Lorgin was telling her she could be hurt, perhaps killed. She was involved in the deepest sense.

"I'm scared, Lorgin."

One hand cupped her face. "No. No, you must not be. I *will* protect you."

"At the cost of your own life?" she asked, horrified.

"If I must." He smiled poignantly then. "I once told you, long ago, when we first met, that I was Chi'in tse Leau. Nothing has changed to alter that. I will always walk beside you, protect you . . . *love you*."

Deana started crying. She couldn't help it.

Lorgin gently scooped her up in his arms, carrying her upstairs. He tenderly undressed her, laying her down on their bed as if she were the most precious thing in the universe to him.

And indeed she was.

That night he whispered wonderful things to her, pretty things—things to make her tears stop, things to make her clutch him to her, things to alleviate her fear.

But the most amazing revelation to him that night, the most incredible discovery he made, was that she had not known he loved her, loved her from almost the moment he had met her—the moment he had looked down into that sweetly engaging face of hers, which in turn looked up at him alight with mischievous wonder. She never said anything out loud to him about her shock at his declaration, but he had seen her face well when he had spoken the words.

An Aviaran man did not speak often of his love, did not think it necessary. His actions, he believed, spoke for him. When he took the Right and entered into the Oath, he was, in effect saying: *I forsake all others for you.* What could be plainer? Yet this woman knew not their ways. Knew not his heart.

So he told her of his love over and over, reenforcing his declaration with hushed kisses and tender caresses. He made love to her knowing it was very possibly the last time, for he did not expect to survive the upcoming confrontation.

And he was eternally grateful that on this eve, possibly their last, he had seen the need to put into words what was so obvious to him.

This time, when they reached the culmination of their tender, bittersweet lovemaking, Lorgin felt compelled to re-affirm his vows. His hushed words echoed in the silent room, a counterpart to his being.

"Be apart from me no more, forever, my beloved Adeeann."

Chapter Nineteen

They met at Yaniff's cottage early in the morning. Four people with turbulent, unresolved emotions and one very old wizard.

Lorgin was surprised to see his brother there. "Rejar joins us?"

"Yes; it is so," Yaniff replied.

Lorgin's brow furrowed. "Is this necessary?" The last thing he wanted was to put his brother in danger, as well.

"Most necessary," was all Yaniff would say on the matter. He signaled to Bojo to alight on his shoulder. "I, too, accompany you. Although, know you that my role is naught but observer. Too delicate are the balances of nature for me to use my powers in Theardar's presence. To the Hall of Tunnels."

So the five of them set out for the Rim, Yaniff alone knowing that three of the four lives accompanying him were about to be forever altered.

It was a bleak, desolate place.
Lifeless. White rocks and white sand.

It was night here. The glow of four moons illuminated the white sand, causing the ground to appear a sea of glittering snow. In a strange mood, Deana thought that Hollywood could not have provided a more perfect location for this final showdown. It was eerie as hell.

The group had been silent, desultory during the trip to the tunnels. Now they walked along purposefully, not wasting time on conversation, each wanting to get it over with at last.

They crested a rise and there below them was a semicircular formation of thirteen clear crystal columns. Like an ancient Druid ceremonial ground, it stood as a testimonial to some forgotten, long-gone race of beings. Silent and waiting. In the middle of the arc of columns stood three large white boulders, almost sacrificial in nature.

Standing beside the three boulders was Theardar.

He wore the long dark robes of a high-level mystic. Ribbons of his salt-and-pepper hair streamed out behind him as a small round object rotated in the air several feet above his hands. The phasing stone.

When he turned to look at them, Deana noted at once that the cloudy gray eyes were quite mad.

Theardar did not seem particularly surprised to see them. On the contrary. He spoke to Yaniff as if he had always been there, not just recently arrived.

"Yaniff!" He gestured the wizard to him. "Come see this. It is quite extraordinary." He peered at Lorgin. "And my good friend Krue has joined us this day."

Deana raised her eyebrows. It was obvious that Theardar had mistaken Lorgin for his father, or else he had lost track of any time sequence. At any rate, he seemed a jovial enough old fellow, even in his madness. Perhaps Lorgin had misjudged the situation. Maybe they really had nothing to fear from him. Could Yaniff quietly talk him into giving up the stone?

She knew she was completely wrong in her assessment by a small gesture Lorgin made: he took her hand protectively in his own, stepping slightly in front of her. He sensed danger.

Theardar had noted the action, looking more closely at Lorgin. "So—not Krue after all, but the whelp."

"What is this place?" Traed asked.

Theardar turned to Traed, noticing him for the first time. "Ah, what indeed." His eyes narrowed of a sudden as he gazed upon his son. "Come here, Traed."

Dutifully, Traed approached his father. "Yes, Father?"

"I want you to see something."

Theardar raised his hands, and an arc of light went from them to the revolving stone above him. The ground around them trembled as if they were experiencing an aftershock to an earthquake. The air seemed to vibrate with electricity. Deana swore she could feel the hair on the back of her neck stand on end. The stone started to pulse a white light. About fifteen feet in front of the three large boulders, the scenery shimmered. A rectangular band of light framed what appeared to be a . . . *doorway*.

Within the frame shapes began to coalesce. A walkway . . . trees . . . a large house—Lorgin's family home! The door to the house opened and a pretty girl skipped outside, joy on her young face. She had very dark mahogany hair, almost black and her eyes shone a brilliant pastel green.

Deana sucked in her breath. It was a doorway in time!

Lorgin stiffened beside her, his grip on her hand tightening. Eyes narrowed, he confronted Yaniff, his tone deadly low. "Why does she *come from my home*, Yaniff?" Lorgin did not expect an answer, nor did he wait for one. He thrust Deana to Rejar's protective arms, whipping out his lightblade.

Theardar did not seem particularly concerned. "Oh, did not Yaniff tell you?"

"Do not listen to him, Lorgin. He seeks to unfocus you."

Theardar grinned evilly, removing any thoughts Deana had of him being a nice but misguided man. "Yes, well, perhaps I do. Pay it no mind then, son of Krue," he taunted.

"What goes on here?" Lorgin demanded.

"Leave it!" Yaniff hissed.

Lorgin hesitated for a tension-fraught moment, then retracted his blade.

"Wise but disappointing, whelp. Now where was I before such a rude interruption?" Without warning, Theardar grabbed Traed roughly by the hair, causing the band which held it back to snap. The waist-long strands fell around the younger man's face as he was hauled to a crouching position next to his father. "Look, Traed!"

Deana would never forget Traed's expression in that moment.

It was his first sight of the woman who bore him, then died.

Marilan, his mother

His fixated gaze held a mixture of wonder at seeing the mother he had never known, so young and alive, combined with horror at what his father was doing. In the glow of the portal, with his hair streaming around him, Traed looked, Deana thought, younger and infinitely more vulnerable.

"You cannot do this, Father!" Traed's shaky voice was a broken whisper of sound.

"Fool!" Theardar hissed. "You never did have any sense! *I have done it.*"

Deana cringed at the thoughtlessly cruel words Theardar spat at his son. But Traed must have developed a thick hide over the years, for he turned to his father saying in a steely voice, "What do you hope to gain from this?"

"What do I hope to gain? Why, *everything,* boy. I intend to right the wrong that was done me all those years ago. I intend to bring my Marilan back to me by rewriting history.''

Traed did not understand what his father was implying. ''What are you talking about?''

''I intend, my ever wayward son, to reverse time. When I do, I will stop Marilan from taking the oath of the Tan-shi. And everything will be as it should have been.''

Traed could not believe what he was hearing. ''You are mad!''

Yaniff stepped next to Lorgin, speaking discreetly to him. ''You must stop him, Lorgin. He will disrupt the very fabric of time and destroy us all.''

''Mad, am I? Look again upon your sweet mother's face and tell me that I am mad. *Look, Traed.*'' Grabbing Traed's jaw in a crushing grip, he forced the younger man to gaze at the scene in front of him. Traed's eyes filled with tears as Theardar continued.

''She wanted nothing to do with you, do you know that? She hated every day you grew in her body. Every day that you drained her life away.''

Traed shut his eyes, moaning. It was the sound of a mortally wounded animal.

Yaniff stepped forward. ''He is confused, Traed. She wanted you more than life itself. Never forget—Marilan *chose* to have you. She once told me the only thing she regretted leaving was you.''

''You lie!'' Theardar whirled at him, enraged. ''Marilan loved me, do you hear?''

Yaniff tried to reason with him. ''Do not do this thing, Theardar. I vow—no good can come of it. Come, give your Cearix to your son as an act of faith in him. End this bitterness now.''

''My Cearix?'' Theardar seemed surprised for a moment. But only a moment. ''Think you I would give my Cearix to a son such as this? A son who murdered his own mother? This is what I do with my Cearix!'' Theardar grabbed the knife out of his waistband and flung it blade first into the ground where it swayed, hilt up in the night.

Rejar watched Traed with deep sorrow in his heart. Surely this brother of the line deserved to have a Lodarres stand for him. He now regretted the promise Yaniff had extracted from him.

"You wrong your son," Yaniff confronted Theardar.

"And you dare not interfere, old one, for well you know that our combined powers in opposition will be catastrophic.'' Theardar turned to Traed. "Tell me now, son, do you align yourself with my enemies?''

Traed's answer was quiet. "I align myself with no one, as you know, Father.'' Traed's glittering eyes focused on his sire. "But these are not your enemies. *You* are your enemy.''

Theardar was taken aback. "You dare speak to me thus? You who are of my blood? Your disrespect cannot go unanswered. *You are no longer my son!*''

Lorgin and Rejar sucked in their breath. For a father to disavow his son was unheard of. The man was not only mad, but cruel as well. He had taken Traed's bloodline from him. A man without a bloodline was less than nothing. Theardar had just stripped Traed of everything he was and all he could hope to be.

Traed was stunned.

Yaniff pointed his staff at the man he had once called student. "You will not do this, Theardar. I will not allow it.'' He placed his withered hand on Traed's shoulder. "By Aviaran law, I claim this Traed to be Traed ta'al Yaniff, *my son*.'' Traed looked at Yaniff, shocked. "Now he has a bloodline.''

And what a bloodline! The most revered on Aviara. Theardar faltered a minute, the enormity of what he had done sinking in. He had cast aside his only son.

"You cannot do this! The ancient law states there must be a blood tie."

Yaniff would only say, "It is done."

Theardar seemed surprised and so did Lorgin. Yaniff had all but admitted a blood tie to Traed. Rejar stared at the old mystic for an answer that he alone knew the question to.

Theardar shrugged. "It will be for naught, for when I overlap time, all will change." He sneered at Traed disgustedly. "My new son will be worthy of my name."

Traed instantly stiffened, erecting a barrier against his father's malice. Deana reached out to him, intending to offer him a gesture of comfort, but Lorgin held her back, shaking his head.

"Leave him his pride, Adeeann," he murmured in her ear.

Yaniff motioned to Bojo, who lifted off his shoulders to land on top of one of the crystal columns. Squaring his deceptively frail shoulders, he said, "You know I cannot allow this, Theardar."

"You cannot allow this? *You?* Come, Yaniff, do not make me laugh. How oft in in the past have you played your little games to suit your own purposes?" Theardar stared pointedly at Lorgin.

Only Yaniff knew what the other man was implying. "Well you know our role. Well you also know you breach mystic law by discussing this in front of others."

Theardar scratched his chin, ignoring Yaniff's admonition. "Tell me, Yaniff, how do you propose to stop me? Surely this"—he spread a disdainful arm out to encompass the group—"is not your arsenal? A Familiar, a woman, a fourth-level warrior, and my useless . . . son. I admit, the warrior might prove some amusement, but all in all, you disappoint me."

"Am I too obvious for you? A pity. I try so hard not to disappoint."

"You are a fool, Yaniff. An old fool."

"Have you looked closely at the woman, Theardar? No? Perhaps you should, as she wears the Shimalee."

Lorgin sucked in his breath, horrified that Yaniff was purposely placing Adeeann in Theardar's focus. "Yaniff! What are you doing?"

Yaniff ignored Lorgin's outburst. "Look close, Theardar. She is a diviner. What think you now? Still disappointed?"

Theardar whipped around, catching Deana in the grip of his fiery stare. "The Shimalee!"

Yaniff turned calmly to Deana. "Sing the stone from him, Adeeann. Use the Shimalee. You can do it."

"No!" Theardar screamed. He raised his arms, bringing the stone back to him, into his immediate possession. The image of Marilan disappeared. Then he turned his wrath on Deana. "Remove the Shimalee, or die with it around your neck."

Deana turned white, totally immobilized by the dire threat.

In the next instant Lorgin stepped forward, removing his lightsaber. "You must go through me first. You did say I would provide you with some amusement, did you not?"

"Your lightshield will not save you, whelp." Four bolts of ragged power came at Lorgin like lightning daggers.

Valiantly he parried them off, using his blade to break the energy flow.

Theardar narrowed his icy eyes. "You are amusing. But even amusements have their limit." He sent a rapid succession of fiery bolts at Lorgin, who dispersed them in an astonishing show of swordsmanship.

"Interesting. But I want that necklace." He ignored Lorgin, going directly toward Deana.

Lorgin threw a field of fire Deana's way, encompassing her

in a protective perimeter of flames. "As I said, you must go through me."

Theardar stopped, almost amazed at the young man's audacity. "I am trying to decide if you are inordinately courageous or unbelievably stupid. I think I will opt for stupid."

A cage of force surrounded Lorgin.

Bands of power arced around him, encasing him. Lorgin tried to break free, using not just his power, but physical strength as well. His muscles bulged as he pushed against the field, using his bare hands against the sizzling bars of light.

"He may break free of you, Theardar," Yaniff calmly said, as if watching a man battle for his life were a mundane thing.

"Impossible." But at that moment Lorgin did break through a barrier. "He is strong. But . . . not strong enough." Two snakes of lightning shot out of Theardar's hands to curl around Lorgin's wrists, stretching his arms out to his sides as if he were chained and hanging from an invisible wall.

The protective field of fire around Deana flicked and died as Lorgin used all his strength to fight against the manacles holding him.

"Sing to the stones, Adeeann," Yaniff called out.

She couldn't do this. Didn't believe she could do this. But for the sake of these people, she had to try. Lifting her hands to touch the stones around her neck, she closed her eyes.

She would never know if she could have done it.

At that moment, she heard Lorgin's groan of pain. Afraid for him, she opened her eyes, seeing an arc of lightning sear around him. Her attention was broken, and Theardar captured her like a viper does its prey. She could not look away from his crazed eyes no matter how hard she tried.

"Give me the necklace."

Yaniff spoke quickly to Rejar. "Try to break his hold!"

Rejar immediately approached Theardar from his left, seeking to bewilder him. If he could but shift Theardar's focus for one moment, his brother might break free and overpower him.

Theardar did not even glance his way. "Call your Familiar back, Yaniff, or he will be sorry."

{Perhaps we will be sorry together.}

Rejar's flip reply cost him dearly. He instantly fell to his knees, clutching his head, his acute senses flooded by powerful sensations. All of them agonizing.

"Rejar!"

Traed ran to him, unable to help the younger man with the pain he was in. *Pain.* It was what his father knew best how to inflict. Traed's thoughts turned bitter within him; wherever Theardar went, pain and destruction followed. His brother of the line, Rejar, lay on the ground writhing in agony; another brother fought for his life and his love. A beautiful love that Theardar would sooner see destroyed . . .

It must end! *It must.*

"Father, stop this!" Traed pleaded with him from the bottom of his heart.

Theardar completely ignored his son's impassioned entreaty.

"Wait, Theardar," Yaniff called out. "The necklace cannot be removed by anyone but her. I have seen to it. If you attempt it, you both die. Give this up now."

Theardar stopped and turned to stare down at the old mystic. "Now, that is really annoying of you, old one." He shrugged fatalistically. "A pity for her, for if she cannot sing to the stones, then they pose no threat to me."

Lorgin realized at once what was about to occur. He thrashed against the power bonds. *"Break his hold on me, Yaniff!"*

His shout echoed in the night.

"I cannot, Lorgin. The resultant forces would tear you apart."

"I care not!"

But Yaniff would not sacrifice one to save another. Theardar was going to kill her. Adeeann! *And his child* . . .

He struggled frantically against the invisible ropes, yelling, "Release me, Yaniff! Do you hear? Release me!"

She was going to die.

Deana looked to Lorgin, seeing the helpless expression of agony on his face. Their eyes met and held.

Then everything seemed to happen in slow motion to her.

Theardar throwing back his hands in preparation to deliver the killer bolt he intended to aim at her—

Traed's strong arm suddenly coming up, a look of final resolve crossing his face as he pushed her behind him to shield her with his body—

Lorgin's raw yell of "Tr-a-e-d!" carrying every drop of anguish and despair contained within him. And sure knowledge that a spiritual brother was about to die for protecting his wife—

The bolt arcing toward them—

And then suddenly Theardar's eyes clearing for a moment, seeing the bolt he had released hurling in a deadly arc toward his son.

His son.

He was about to kill his own son!

"Traed?" Theardar rasped, his eyes focused in horror. Without hesitation, he called the bolt back onto himself.

Such power once released could not be controlled.

Theardar was killed instantly.

Traed sank to his knees, consumed by emotions he had no name for. His father was dead. Vaporized. And in that last moment before he had called the bolt back to himself, Traed had seen love in his father's eyes. *Love for him.*

Had his very existence killed both his parents?

Traed bowed his head, his hair falling forward to obscure his face. "Destroyed by love, Father," he whispered.

He felt Yaniff's hand on his shoulder. "No, Traed. Theardar destroyed love, then was destroyed by it. It is natural law."

Yaniff bent over and pulled Theardar's Cearix from the ground where he had cast it. "I believe the Theardar I once knew would have wanted you to have this, Traed."

Traed shook his head. "You keep it, Yaniff. I cannot consider having it now."

"Very well. But a son needs a heritage; here—I give you mine. Should you decide someday to carry Theardar's, I will understand."

Traed took the blade, staring at the intricately carved handle of the ancient knife. "I am moved, Yaniff," he whispered. "Know that I will carry it with honor."

Yaniff patted his shoulder. "Of course you will."

Lorgin, released from his bonds, ran to Deana, clutching her to him in a crushing embrace.

"Are you all right? Are you all right?" he kept repeating, hugging her to him, kissing her all over her face, her hair, the top of her head.

"Yes, yes!" she sobbed against him, holding him just as tightly, shaking now that the danger was past.

Rejar shook his head, slowly rising. The pain that had invaded his senses was gone, but he had a horrible headache. He sank gratefully down on a boulder, his head in his hands.

"Are you all right, Rejar?"

He felt Lorgin's hand on his shoulder, shaking him slightly.

{Yes; I am fine. Do not concern yourself.}

Yaniff and Traed walked over to them.

"Traed and I will go on ahead," Yaniff said and turned to leave.

"Wait." Lorgin stopped Traed. There were questions he wanted answers to. "I think we need to talk."

"Later, Lorgin." Traed seemed drained.

"Very well. Know this, though; I will not forget that you stood for what was mine. Ever."

Traed contemplated Lorgin with absolutely no expression on his face.

Watching him, so contained and removed, Deana wondered if it had all been too much for him. Would he once again become the way he'd been when they had first found him at the keep—controlled and emotionless? She prayed not; he had saved her life, and she hoped with all her heart he could put this behind him and find some measure of happiness in his life.

Yaniff said to her in a very low tone, "He is fine, Adeeann. He needs time."

Lorgin, seeing Traed's condition, decided to say no more on the subject. Instead, he turned to Yaniff. "I would speak to you as well, Yaniff. I am not at all sure I can condone what you have done. I fear you have played us all like pieces in a board game. I do not know if I can forgive you for this manipulation. You placed all of my family in grave danger."

Yaniff nodded, as if in agreement with Lorgin's words. "I did not expect otherwise from you, Lorgin. But you will think on it and in time realize that what was done was a true course. When you are ready, I will still be your teacher. Nothing will change that, my friend."

Lorgin would not respond. Somewhere in the back of his mind, he suspected that Yaniff had the right of it, but he was not ready yet, his emotions being too raw, his potential loss still too fresh in his thoughts, to concede the point.

The old wizard turned to his promising Familiar. "When next I see you, Rejar, your life will be greatly altered."

Yaniff and Traed left them then, heading toward the tunnel point. Bojo, wings flapping, flew beside them.

As they crested the rise, the old wizard discreetly looked over his shoulder to make sure Adeeann was not watching him. He did not think the Earth woman would appreciate the intricacies of guiding reality.

Seeing that her attention was elsewhere, he reached into his robes, removing a blue cloth article from some hidden pocket. The strange object had a mysterious large red symbol sewn into the front of it.

"What is that?" Traed asked.

"Here, my young son; a gift." Yaniff plopped the object on Traed's head.

Traed's green gaze questioned him from under the brim. "What do you put on my head?"

"It is called a cap."

"But where does it come from?"

The tunnel opened up in front of them. Yaniff placed his arm around Traed's shoulders as he led him into the maw.

"Let me tell you, my son, of a wondrous game of sport played on a faraway planet. It is called baseball . . ."

Chapter Twenty

It was Rejar who noticed the discrepancy.

{Where is the phasing stone?}

Lorgin stopped caressing his wife's waist, turning with concern at Rejar's words. Releasing her, he began scouring the ground with his brother.

Deana was confused. "Wouldn't it have . . . disintegrated with Theardar?"

"No." Lorgin paced the area. "The stones are indestructible."

{Perhaps Yaniff took it?}

"I do not know, but it is not here; that much is obvious."

{What should we do?}

"There is nothing to do for now. Yaniff will have to be consulted, of course." Lorgin winced. Was this another clever ploy of the wizard's to embroil them yet again in one of his schemes?

Deana interrupted his unpleasant thoughts.

"Lorgin, do you think Traed will be all right? Despite what Yaniff said, the pain on his face when he . . ."

He sighed. "Time will tell, *zira*. He performed a completely selfless act—it took more than courage to do what he did. A man will sacrifice his life for a just cause, but Traed knew that in placing himself before you he was condemning his father." Lorgin hesitated. "I do not know if I could have done it. It was a terrible decision to be forced to make."

{I wonder what made Theardar call back the bolt . . . a moment of sheer insanity?}

"No," Lorgin responded. "A moment of sheer clarity." He turned back to Adeeann, his eyes falling to the Shimalee around her neck.

His heart sank.

He would have to get rid of it, that he knew for a certainty. It was too dangerous for everyone concerned to have the necklace accessible.

There was only one way he knew to be rid of it.

He would have to enter the tunnels with it, flinging it in any direction it would go. Such action was sure to cause violent upheaval within the matrix. Who knew if he would survive? And if he did, where would he end up? Far from home, with perhaps no internal guidance to return.

There was, unfortunately, no help for it.

Taking a deep breath, he asked Deana to remove the Shimalee from around her neck.

She readily complied, having no idea what he wanted with it, but happy to be rid of the damn thing just the same.

Rejar, however, knew.

{Give the Shimalee to me, Lorgin.}

Lorgin silently met his brother's eyes.

{I will enter the tunnels with it. I will make sure it is forever lost in the corridors of time.}

Lorgin was more than hesitant. As the eldest, he had an obligation to his brother, but, in truth, he did not want to leave his wife. He should not let his heart rule here. He had been trained to make decisions based on what was best for all concerned.

Nonetheless, when he asked his brother, "But what of you?" he knew that for the first time in his life, he *was* going to let his heart rule. Rejar wanted them to be together. His brother knew what he was doing.

{I always land on my feet.} Rejar gave Lorgin his famous feral grin.

Lorgin gave him the Shimalee and embraced him. "Thank you, brother."

"You'll be okay won't you, Rejar?"

The Familiar turned to Deana, giving her a swift hug. "Of course." He spoke low in her ear. "The restlessness—I think, mayhap, this is a part of it."

She nodded against him to let him know she understood.

Lorgin called the tunnel forth.

Rejar entered without looking back.

He took the necklace in his hand and, spinning around, hurled it into the miasma. And waited.

He did not have to wait long.

A rumble started from all directions as the matrix attempted to absorb the Shimalee.

Tremors escalated into vast light waves of churning disturbance.

Caught in the riotous cosmic storm, Rejar was flung down the corridors of space/time.

"Do you think he's all right?"

Deana turned a worried face to Lorgin. They had felt some

back rumbling of the disturbances after the tunnel had sealed.

"We can only hope. It was a noble deed."

"Yes. I just hope he doesn't suffer too much for it."

Lorgin smiled faintly. "Knowing my brother, suffering could be a relative term."

Deana also smiled, wishing Rejar well.

Lorgin regarded her through half-lowered lids. Suddenly he held out his hand to her. "Come, Adeeann, we go back to Aviara now—*back home.*"

He was waiting for her to take his hand.

He was waiting for a hell of a lot more.

It was over. The quest was over. Was she the diviner Yaniff claimed she was? She would never know for sure.

But did it matter?

She could leave Lorgin now. Once they got back to Aviara, Yaniff would send her back at her request. And she could go.

Leave Lorgin.

Say goodbye. Never see his smiling, handsome face again. Never laugh with him over things only the two of them knew. Never make sweet love with him again.

He was waiting for her to take his hand.

He knew.

Somehow she wasn't surprised. Lorgin had been one step ahead of her since she had met him. Always in control. Always devastating.

Leave Lorgin?

She could no more leave this man than stop breathing. But if she took his hand, she was saying farewell forever to her past life. Could she do that?

Deana had an unwanted revelation. She *was* the woman in the prophecy! It had to be her, for hadn't he told her how much he loved her? Just let some other woman show up to claim him!

Lorgin belonged to her. He had told her so just last night. Repeatedly.

Yes, she could say goodbye to everything she had known, because all that mattered to her was standing right here in front of her. Yaniff was right; *her quest* was at its end. She was complete.

Eyes filled with tears, she stepped forward, slowly, placing her hand softly in his. As his hand closed around hers, his amethyst eyes sparkled down at her.

"I love you," she said.

He brought her hand to his chest and placed it against his heart, covering it with his own.

"Of this, *Dee-ann-ah*, I had no doubt."

Then Lorgin ta'al Krue, knight of the Charl, holder of the fourth power, first in the line of Krue, brought his Adeeann home.

For a warrior was always true to his word.

SPECIAL SNEAK PREVIEW FOLLOWS!

Madeline Baker writing as Amanda Ashley

Cursed by the darkness, he searches through the ages for the redeeming light, the one woman who can save him. A creature of moonlight and fancy, she fears the handsome stranger whose eyes promise endless ecstasy even while his mouth whispers dark secrets. They are two people longing for fulfillment, yearning for a love like no other. Alone, they will face a desolate destiny. Together, they will share undying passion, defy eternity, and embrace the night.

He walked the streets for hours after he left the orphanage, his thoughts filled with Sara, her fragile beauty, her sweet innocence, her unwavering trust. She had accepted him into her life without question, and the knowledge cut him to the quick. He did not like deceiving her, hiding the dark secret of what he was, nor did he like to think about how badly she would be hurt when his nighttime visits ceased, as they surely must.

He had loved her from the moment he first saw her, but always from a distance, worshiping her as the moon might worship the sun, basking in her heat, her light, but wisely staying away lest he be burned.

And foolishly, he had strayed too close. He had soothed her tears, held her in his arms, and now he was paying the price. He was burning, like a moth drawn to a flame. Burning with need. With desire. With an unholy lust, not for her body, but for the very essence of her life.

It sickened him that he should want her that way, that he could even consider such a despicable thing. And yet he could think of little else. Ah, to hold her in his arms, to feel his body become one with hers as he drank of her sweetness. . . .

For a moment, he closed his eyes and let himself imagine it, and then he swore a long vile oath filled with pain and longing.

Hands clenched, he turned down a dark street, his self-anger turning to loathing, and the loathing to rage. He felt the need to kill, to strike out, to make someone else suffer as he was suffering.

Pity the poor mortal who next crossed his path, he thought. Then he gave himself over to the hunger pounding through him.

She woke covered with perspiration, Gabriel's name on her lips. Shivering, she drew the covers up to her chin.

It had only been a dream. Only a dream.

She spoke the words aloud, finding comfort in the sound of her own voice. A distant bell chimed the hour. Four o'clock.

Gradually, her breathing returned to normal. Only a dream, she said again, but it had been so real. She had felt the cold breath of the night, smelled the rank odor of fear rising from the body of the faceless man cowering in the shadows. She had sensed a deep anger, a wild uncontrollable evil personified by a being in a flowing black cloak. Even now, she could feel his anguish, his loneliness, the alienation that cut him off from the rest of humanity.

It had all been so clear in the dream, but now it made no sense. No sense at all.

With a slight shake of her head, she snuggled deeper under

the covers and closed her eyes.

It was just a dream, nothing more.

Sunk in the depths of despair, Gabriel prowled the deserted abbey. What had happened to his self-control? Not for centuries had he taken enough blood to kill, only enough to assuage the pain of the hunger, to ease his unholy thirst.

A low groan rose in his throat. Sara had happened. He wanted her and he couldn't have her. Somehow, his desire and his frustration had gotten tangled up with his lust for blood.

It couldn't happen again. It had taken him centuries to learn to control the hunger, to give himself the illusion that he was more man than monster.

Had he been able, he would have prayed for forgiveness, but he had forfeited the right to divine intervention long ago.

"Where will we go tonight?"

Gabriel stared at her. She'd been waiting for him again, clothed in her new dress, her eyes bright with anticipation. Her goodness drew him, soothed him, calmed his dark side even as her beauty, her innocence, teased his desire.

He stared at the pulse throbbing in her throat. "Go?"

Sara nodded.

With an effort, he lifted his gaze to her face. "Where would you like to go?"

"I don't suppose you have a horse?"

"A horse?"

"I've always wanted to ride."

He bowed from the waist. "Whatever you wish, milady," he said. "I'll not be gone long."

It was like having found a magic wand, Sara mused as she waited for him to return. She had only to voice her desire, and he produced it.

Twenty minutes later, she was seated before him on a prancing black stallion. It was a beautiful animal, tall and muscular, with a flowing mane and tail.

She leaned forward to stroke the stallion's neck. His coat felt like velvet beneath her hand. "What's his name?"

"Necromancer," Gabriel replied, pride and affection evident in his tone.

"Necromancer? What does it mean?"

"One who communicates with the spirits of the dead."

Sara glanced at him over her shoulder. "That seems an odd name for a horse."

"Odd, perhaps," Gabriel replied cryptically, "but fitting."

"Fitting? In what way?"

"Do you want to ride, Sara, or spend the night asking foolish questions?"

She pouted prettily for a moment and then grinned at him. "Ride!"

A word from Gabriel and they were cantering through the dark night, heading into the countryside.

"Faster," Sara urged.

"You're not afraid?"

"Not with you."

"You should be afraid, Sara Jayne," he muttered under his breath, "especially with me."

He squeezed the stallion's flanks with his knees and the horse shot forward, his powerful hooves skimming across the ground.

Sara shrieked with delight as they raced through the darkness. This was power, she thought, the surging body of the horse, the man's strong arm wrapped securely around her waist. The wind whipped through her hair, stinging her cheeks and making her eyes water, but she only threw back her head and laughed.

384

"Faster!" she cried, reveling in the sense of freedom that surged within her.

Hedges and trees and sleeping farmhouses passed by in a blur. Once, they jumped a four-foot hedge, and she felt as if she were flying. Sounds and scents blended together: the chirping of crickets, the bark of a dog, the smell of damp earth and lathered horseflesh, and over all the touch of Gabriel's breath upon her cheek, the steadying strength of his arm around her waist.

Gabriel let the horse run until the animal's sides were heaving and covered with foamy lather, and then he drew back on the reins, gently but firmly, and the stallion slowed, then stopped.

"That was wonderful!" Sara exclaimed.

She turned to face him, and in the bright light of the moon, he saw that her cheeks were flushed, her lips parted, her eyes shining like the sun.

How beautiful she was! His Sara, so full of life. What cruel fate had decreed that she should be bound to a wheelchair? She was a vivacious girl on the brink of womanhood. She should be clothed in silks and satins, surrounded by gallant young men.

Dismounting, he lifted her from the back of the horse. Carrying her across the damp grass, he sat down on a large boulder, settling her in his lap.

"Thank you, Gabriel," she murmured.

"It was my pleasure, milady."

"Hardly that," she replied with a saucy grin. "I'm sure ladies don't ride pell-mell through the dark astride a big black devil horse."

"No," he said, his gray eyes glinting with amusement, "they don't."

"Have you known many ladies?"

385

"A few." He stroked her cheek with his forefinger, his touch as light as thistledown.

"And were they accomplished and beautiful?"

Gabriel nodded. "But none so beautiful as you."

She basked in his words, in the silent affirmation she read in his eyes.

"Who are you, Gabriel?" she asked, her voice soft and dreamy. "Are you man or magician?"

"Neither."

"But still my angel?"

"Always, *cara.*"

With a sigh, she rested her head against his shoulder and closed her eyes. How wonderful, to sit here in the dark of night with his arms around her. She could almost forget that she was crippled. Almost.

She lost all track of time as she sat there, secure in his arms. She heard the chirp of crickets, the sighing of the wind through the trees, the pounding of Gabriel's heart beneath her cheek.

Her breath caught in her throat as she felt the touch of his hand in her hair and then the brush of his lips.

Abruptly, he stood up. Before she quite knew what was happening, she was on the horse's back and Gabriel was swinging up behind her. He moved with the lithe grace of a cat vaulting a fence.

She sensed a change in him, a tension she didn't understand. A moment later, his arm was locked around her waist and they were riding through the night.

She leaned back against him, braced against the solid wall of his chest. She felt his arm tighten around her, felt his breath on her cheek.

Pleasure surged through her at his touch and she placed her hand over his forearm, drawing his arm more securely around her, tacitly telling him that she enjoyed his nearness.

She thought she heard a gasp, as if he was in pain, but she shook the notion aside, telling herself it was probably just the wind crying through the trees.

Too soon, they were back at the orphanage.

"You'll come tomorrow?" she asked as he settled her in her bed, covering her as if she were a child.

"Tomorrow," he promised. "Sleep well, *cara*."

"Dream of me," she murmured.

With a nod, he turned away. Dream of her, he thought. If only he could!

"Where would you like to go tonight?" Gabriel asked the following evening.

"I don't care, so long as it's with you."

Moments later, he was carrying her along a pathway in the park across from the orphanage.

Sara marveled that he held her so effortlessly, that it felt so right to be carried in his arms. She rested her head on his shoulder, content. A faint breeze played hide and seek with the leaves of the trees. A lover's moon hung low in the sky. The air was fragrant with night blooming flowers, but it was Gabriel's scent that rose all around her—warm and musky, reminiscent of aged wine and expensive cologne.

He moved lightly along the pathway, his footsteps making hardly a sound. When they came to a stone bench near a quiet pool, he sat down, placing her on the bench beside him.

It was a lovely place, a fairy place. Elegant ferns, tall and lacy, grew in wild profusion near the pool. In the distance, she heard the questioning hoot of an owl.

"What did you do all day?" she asked, turning to look at him.

Gabriel shrugged. "Nothing to speak of. And you?"

"I read to the children. Sister Mary Josepha has been giving me more and more responsibility."

"And does that make you happy?"

"Yes. I've grown very fond of my little charges. They so need to be loved. To be touched. I had never realized how important it was, to be held, until—" A faint flush stained her cheeks. "Until you held me. There's such comfort in the touch of a human hand."

Gabriel grunted softly. Human, indeed, he thought bleakly.

Sara smiled. "They seem to like me, the children. I don't know why."

But he knew why. She had so much love to give, and no outlet for it.

"I hate to think of all the time I wasted wallowing in self-pity," Sara remarked. "I spent so much time sitting in my room, sulking because I couldn't walk, when I could have been helping the children, loving them." She glanced up at Gabriel. "They're so easy to love."

"So are you." He had not meant to speak the words aloud, but they slipped out. "I mean, it must be easy for the children to love you. You have so much to give."

She smiled, but it was a sad kind of smile. "Perhaps that's because no one else wants it."

"Sara—"

"It's all right. Maybe that's why I was put here, to comfort the little lost lambs that no one else wants."

I want you. The words thundered in his mind, in his heart, in his soul.

Abruptly, he stood up and moved away from the bench. He couldn't sit beside her, feel her warmth, hear the blood humming in her veins, sense the sadness dragging at her heart, and not touch her, take her.

He stared into the depths of the dark pool, the water as

black as the emptiness of his soul. He'd been alone for so long, yearning for someone who would share his life, needing someone to see him for what he was and love him anyway.

A low groan rose in his throat as the centuries of loneliness wrapped around him.

"Gabriel?" Her voice called out to him, soft, warm, caring.

With a cry, he whirled around and knelt at her feet. Hesitantly, he took her hands in his.

"Sara, can you pretend I'm one of the children? Can you hold me, and comfort me, just for tonight?"

"I don't understand."

"Don't ask questions, *cara*. Please just hold me. Touch me."

She gazed down at him, into the fathomless depths of his dark gray eyes, and the loneliness she saw there pierced her heart. Tears stung her eyes as she reached for him.

He buried his face in her lap, ashamed of the need that he could no longer deny. And then he felt her hand stroke his hair, light as a summer breeze. Ah, the touch of a human hand, warm, fragile, pulsing with life.

Time ceased to have meaning as he knelt there, his head cradled in her lap, her hand moving in his hair, caressing his nape, feathering across his cheek. No wonder the children loved her. There was tranquility in her touch, serenity in her hand. A sense of peace settled over him, stilling his hunger. He felt the tension drain out of him, to be replaced with a nearly forgotten sense of calm. It was a feeling as close to forgiveness as he would ever know.

After a time, he lifted his head. Slightly embarrassed, he gazed up at her, but there was no censure in her eyes, no disdain, only a wealth of understanding.

"Why are you so alone, my angel?" she asked quietly.

"I have always been alone," he replied, and even now,

when he was nearer to peace of spirit than he had been for centuries, he was aware of the vast gulf that separated him, not only from Sara, but from all of humanity as well.

Gently, she cupped his cheek with her hand. "Is there no one to love you then?"

"No one."

"I would love you, Gabriel."

"No!"

Stricken by the force of his denial, she let her hand fall into her lap. "Is the thought of my love so revolting?"

"No, don't ever think that." He sat back on his heels, wishing that he could sit at her feet forever, that he could spend the rest of his existence worshiping her beauty, the generosity of her spirit. "I'm not worthy of you, *cara*. I would not have you waste your love on me."

"Why, Gabriel? What have you done that you feel unworthy of love?"

Filled with the guilt of a thousand lifetimes, he closed his eyes and his mind filled with an image of blood. Rivers of blood. Oceans of death. Centuries of killing, of bloodletting. Damned. The Dark Gift had given him eternal life—and eternal damnation.

Thinking to frighten her away, he let her look deep into his eyes, knowing that what she saw within his soul would speak more eloquently than words.

He clenched his hands, waiting for the compassion in her eyes to turn to revulsion. But it didn't happen.

She gazed down at his upturned face for an endless moment, and then he felt the touch of her hand in his hair.

"My poor angel," she whispered. "Can't you tell me what it is that haunts you so?"

He shook his head, unable to speak past the lump in his throat.

"Gabriel." His name, nothing more, and then she leaned forward and kissed him.

It was no more than a feathering of her lips across his, but it exploded through him like concentrated sunlight. Hotter than a midsummer day, brighter than lightning, it burned through him and for a moment he felt whole again. Clean again.

Humbled to the core of his being, he bowed his head so she couldn't see his tears.

"I will love you, Gabriel," she said, still stroking his hair. "I can't help myself."

"Sara—"

"You don't have to love me back," she said quickly "I just wanted you to know that you're not alone anymore."

A long shuddering sigh coursed through him, and then he took her hands in his, holding them tightly, feeling the heat of her blood, the pulse of her heart. Gently, he kissed her fingertips, and then, gaining his feet, he swung her into his arms.

"It's late," he said, his voice thick with the tide of emotions roiling within him. "We should go before you catch a chill."

"You're not angry?"

"No, *cara*."

How could he be angry with her? She was light and life, hope and innocence. He was tempted to fall to his knees and beg her forgiveness for his whole miserable existence.

But he couldn't burden her with the knowledge of what he was. He couldn't tarnish her love with the truth.

It was near dawn when they reached the orphanage. Once he had her settled in bed, he knelt beside her. "Thank you, Sara."

She turned on her side, a slight smile lifting the corners of her mouth as she took his hand in hers. "For what?"

"For your sweetness. For your words of love. I'll treasure them always."

"Gabriel." The smile faded from her lips. "You're not trying to tell me good-bye, are you?"

He stared down at their joined hands: hers small and pale and fragile, pulsing with the energy of life; his large and cold, indelibly stained with blood and death.

If he had a shred of honor left, he would tell her good-bye, and never see her again.

But then, even when he had been a mortal man, he'd always had trouble doing the honorable thing when it conflicted with something he wanted. And he wanted—no, needed— Sara. Needed her as he'd never needed anything else in his accursed life. And perhaps, in a way, she needed him. And even if it wasn't so, it eased his conscience to think it true.

"Gabriel?"

"No, *cara*, I'm not planning to tell you good-bye. Not now. Not ever."

The sweet relief in her eyes stabbed him to the heart. And he, cold, selfish monster that he was, was glad of it. Right or wrong, he couldn't let her go.

"Till tomorrow then?" she said, smiling once more.

"Till tomorrow, *cara mia*," he murmured. And for all the tomorrows of your life.